RICHES OF THE EARTH

RICHES OF THE EARTH

Wendy Robertson

BCA

LONDON NEW YORK SYDNEY TORONTO

This edition published 1992
by BCA
by arrangement with Headline Books Ltd
First Reprint 1992

CN 6655

Printed and bound in Great Britain by
Mackays of Chatham PLC, Chatham, Kent

For Bryan

PART ONE

1895–1905

Chapter One

Susanah's head was wrenched to one side. Her shoulder hurt. Perspiration was running down her scalp and into her eyes. She fumed against them from her narrow niche under the slatted bench seat of the railway carriage.

Her mind went back to her parents' conversation half an hour before, on the station platform, when she had discovered she and her brother Tollie would have to travel this way on the train, crouched like cats under the seat. They had talked over her head, as though she were a stone.

'Four tickets is enough to buy, Ceiri.'

'But there's Susanah and Tollie,' her mother had protested. 'They surely travel with us, Caradoc?'

Susanah had made her fingers curl tightly inside her apron pockets so she could feel the comforting pain of eight nails, neat half-moons, digging into her palms. If that hurt enough, she was flesh not stone.

She had pondered the fact that she and Tollie wouldn't be going with the rest of them, her eyes ranging absently over the intricate ironwork which framed and decorated the high points of the platform. Her ears tuned themselves to the violent clangour of the voices in the echoing railway station.

So. They would be left here at the station on their own. But what about the boxes? She had seen her bed loaded on to a wagon, her blankets packed into the boxes. Could they go back to the little house in the street where she had been born? That couldn't be. She had seen its door locked with the big key, so rarely used. She had seen her brothers, Davey and Lew, haring back to the colliery-office to put the key into the hands of Mr Richards himself.

It was hot in the station. Sweat had built up under her thick plait and then started to trickle down her back. Her face, to her satisfaction, stayed smooth.

'Four tickets are enough to buy.' Her father's deep voice printed itself on the air again.

'Well, you're saying they must hide themselves near us on the train. Is that what you want?'

Susanah's fingers had unclenched.

Caradoc Laydon Jones' response was almost tender, delicious: sickly sweet as a toffee apple. He was looking at the slender figure of his wife Ceiri, who was well accustomed now to his finely honed ability to taunt with a sweet tongue. 'But isn't that stealing, Ceiri? Wouldn't you say that's stealing?'

Then he strode off, walking well ahead of the rest of them, his broad shape blocking out Susanah's view of the watery spring sun. Her world was filled with his tall figure, the heavy box hoist lightly on his shoulder, and the lumpy, almost human, shape of the sack clasped in one large hand.

The train had gurgled and hissed its way into the station and, drowning in the press of bodies, Tollie and Susanah were hustled into a carriage. Ceiri stowed them under the seat, on blankets she had pulled from one of the bags.

Caradoc had climbed on to the train at the very last minute. His view of the carriage was entirely legitimate; it would be the view of the guard, who'd come to check the occupants. Four people matched with four tickets.

Now, from her crouched position under the seat, Susanah could feel the train screeching and crunching its way along the track. The wheezing and grinding of the wheels on the track seemed very close to Susanah's ear: the floor beneath her cheek must be very close to the ground. She pressed her cheek hard against the wood, wishing she could push it clean through the floor. Then she'd see the shining steel rails and the stout wooden sleepers as they counted their way north.

Davey, sitting directly above Susanah, squirmed uneasily. She saw his feet move as he crossed his legs first one way then the other.

'They could come up, Da, our Susanah and Tollie? Come up from under there, see the countryside, couldn't they? I can watch next time for the guard . . .'

Listening to his voice with its characteristic tremble, Susanah closed her eyes and saw what he saw. She had been able to do this since she was very small, seeing through her brother's eyes what she could not see with her own. It was a gift which had frightened her at first, but which in time she came to take for granted. Now through her closed lids she could see the country racing away, streaming past in greens and browns; the rising grey of the far land.

'They could stretch their legs, Da. Get some air . . . '

She winced when she heard the ringing slap as Caradoc brought his hand across Davey's cheek. Ceiri looked up from the baby, half sang her protest, then swallowed it back. Lew grinned across at Davey's discomfort, examining his red-stained cheek with clinical interest.

Among the boxes on the floor, crouched on her blanket under the slatted seat, Susanah fumbled with the feeling – the possibility – that she too had done something wrong. Being here under the seat was the punishment. And Tollie must be another wrongdoer, even though, curled up wide-eyed here on his blanket, he looked as innocent as an angel. Above her, watching the greens and browns and the distant greys, Davey had just been slapped for defending her in her transgressions.

She sometimes wondered what her mother did to deserve *her* punishment, regularly meted out by their father. The first time Susanah had actually witnessed this punishment she had been halfway upstairs when she heard the familiar faint protest in her mother's voice. Creeping down, she had put her face to the crack on the wooden boards that separated the staircase from the kitchen.

4

Her mother had been standing behind the chair, her long narrow face looking up at him. His face was large and smooth, his beard soft and so clean.

His hand had come across and her body had spun across the room, falling soft and light as a leaf on to the rug which covered the square stones of the kitchen floor. (Mama had made the rug herself. Susanah had helped her, one stitch for ten of her mother's.) Then her father had been on to her, doing that extraordinary pressing that he did on her, her face turned away.

Susanah noticed then, and at other times, that these actions of punishment seemed to bring her father to balance, to give him some peace. In many ways they brought a temporary calm to the house, which sometimes lasted the whole of the next day.

On the train, Susanah lay quiet with Tollie, well nested among the tangle of boots and boxes, the smells of trouser and old grease, the pepper of new dust. From her space under the slatted seat she could hear her sister, Jenny, whimpering in her mother's arms. Then, with the familiar rustling of shawl and dress and the waft of that indefinable scent, half body, half milk, Susanah heard her mother settle in her seat to feed the baby.

Susanah loved Jenny, the baby, in a special way. She had been there when she had been born. Without her, the baby and her mother would be dead. The Woman had told her that.

At first, that day in the little Welsh house, she had tried to pretend she wasn't there in the bedroom, pushing herself hard into the narrow corner under the eaves, trying to make herself so small that she would be invisible as the rough drop of curtain or the distant wheel of the pit above its raggle of buildings.

Mama was on the bed, silent for this moment, after hours of painful moaning, of threshing left and right. The Woman was there, tall and hooknosed, almost man-faced. Her wide dress was snail sheen black. She was looking down at Mama, her old face as still as the stone of the mountains. Then she looked around; her grey eyes stopped on Susanah, frowning. 'What is it you doin' here, lamb?'

Her voice was soft. Susanah stared at her, back into those mountain eyes. Do not send me away. She willed it.

'All right. Stay if you want. But no shouting or crying! Just stay very still. Hear me, do you?' The Woman's glance moved to the younger woman standing on the other side of the bed, Susanah's Auntie Peg. She was trembling. Sweat was running down her face and she was clutching a piece of the sheet in her hand, pleating and re-pleating it with busy fingers. 'How many is it, kinder, you've had, then?' the Woman asked.

Auntie Peg shook her head, her mouth folded tight.

'No children?' The Woman sighed, a breath up from her heels. 'Well. Now then . . . Peggy, isn't it? Ceiri's set to go, right away from us, to whoever is out there, God or gods. D'you see that? She has no bit of strength left and no way to help herself. What you see now, what we do here, you must not tell. Hear me?'

Auntie Peg's eyes were bulging from her brow; her lips trembled as she stiffly moved her head to agree.

The Woman pulled a chair from the corner of the room and stood it beside the bed. Susanah took a little step forward to see better as she heaved Mama from the bed and sat her on the chair. Mama's head had rolled back, her eyes were half closed. The Woman made Auntie Peg hold her while she whipped the greyish sheet from the bed and laid it on the floor.

Then she pushed Peggy out of the way, put her arm around Mama and started to whisper, whisper in her ear.

Susanah leaned forward. She could hear the urging, the urgency, but they were not words she had ever heard before.

Mama started to sit up straight then, staring in front of her, black hair sticking in baby curls around her face. Her face was white. She seemed to be listening, listening to something that the rest of them could not hear. Then she jerked upwards, a yell escaping her mouth.

The Woman looked across at Auntie Peggy. 'Now, get hold of her other side, girl, like this.' She held Mama at the shoulder, under her arm. Susanah stared at the long uncut fingernails digging into flesh as Aunt Peggy stumbled across to take hold on her side. Between them they lifted Mama from the chair to the blanket on the floor so that she ended up half sitting, half squatting.

'Now, lovely, now, Ceiri! You can do this . . . gently now . . . gently . . . now!'

A shudder travelled through Ceiri. Susanah could see it from where she was standing, in her space under the eaves. The hoarse shout her mother made softened to a moan, a helpless moan. Auntie Peg crumpled into a faint. The Woman clicked her teeth and heaved Mama back into the chair. 'Now, stay still, sweetheart, stay still.'

Susanah could see the back of the Woman's dress and the triangle of sopping sweat that stained it from shoulder to hem. The Woman stooped to lift up Auntie Peg's ragdoll body and dumped her in a corner, muttering, 'No use, no use . . .'

Mama started up her moaning again. The Woman's gaze wandered round the room. Her eye lighted again on Susanah. 'Right, sweetheart! Do you want to do something really special for your ma?'

Susanah took a step forward, her head going with a nod.

'All I want is you hold her hand. Just stand against her that side. Like your Auntie Peg, but maybe with a bit more sense, hey?'

They took Mama from the chair and back to the blanket. Susanah stood there beside her, holding her hand and the top of her arm. Susanah's head, even though she was standing, was not much higher than her mother's, as she squatted there. Mama was heavy against her. Susanah's arms ached.

The Woman muttered on again: those strange words. Mama's body was lighter now, pulling up and away from Susanah. The surge, the ripple, was travelling through her, transmitting itself to her daughter. Her hand clutched Susanah's so tightly that she could not clutch hers back, even though she

wanted to show her mother she was there. She could feel the bruises growing on her hand.

'Ri-ight!' The Woman almost sang the word.

The shudders were moving now in a continuous rhythm. The Woman was
kneeling, one arm around Mama, the other down below. Susanah inhabited
a wild world of twitches and groans from her mother, of satisfied grunts,
soft crooning from the Woman. She stared hard into her mother's face. Her
brown eyes were wide open, but she was seeing nothing. She could only
see inside, inside her own body. Finally she expelled a high-pitched cry, as
controlled as a whistle, followed by a long sigh.

Susanah looked down. The baby was almost contained within the
Woman's large hand: a little girl with bulbous crack between her legs. She
was flushed red from top to toe, as red as Dada's face when he was angry.
Susanah thought the baby must be angry at the pain of getting here, into the
world.

The Woman had put Mama back in the chair now and freed the baby
somehow. It was crying. The Woman looked around at the rumpled bed,
then back to Mama, slumped in the chair. She rolled the baby in a cloth and
thrust it at Susanah. 'Here, lovely, here's your work. Hold not too tight, nor
too soft. I need to finish your ma off. A way to go yet.'

Susanah turned the small, bound body so she could see the round face
covered by dark oil and strands of trailing blood; black hair greased on to
a round head; eyes tight shut; one hand escaping the binding rag. The fingers were slender and curving, the nails perfect, and the light shone through
her skin. She put her nose to the baby, smelling her strange smell; the
baby's eyes opened briefly and then she began a high-pitched mewing like
a cat.

Now, crouched on the train chugging and clanking its way from Wales
up to County Durham, Susanah was aching with the wish that she were up
there on the seat, watching her mother feed Jenny. Being so responsible for
them both, she had always loved that ritual. Sometimes she would look at
the dots on her own chest and wonder how it could happen, that a woman
could feed a baby with herself.

She thought again how she had watched as the Woman whispered, whispered into her mother's ear, getting her to squat, crouching like some old
frog on the pad of blankets and the grey sheet. It was their secret now, only
theirs, the Woman had said. How it was done.

From where she crouched now, Susanah could see her mother's boots.
They were scuffed, worn down at the heel. Under the layer of railway dust,
though, she could still see the faint bloom of hard and patient rubbing. She
touched the hem of Ceiri's skirt and the grimy rim of petticoat as it lay
beside her, stroking one finger along the soft edge.

Part of the hem was caught by Caradoc's boot; this was brown, tied twice
round the ankle, the hairy cloth of his trousers clinging to bulging calves.

Then came Davey's legs, in unfamiliar black serge, overfull and droop-
ing too low on his ankle. She thought how quiet Davey had been, his square
face white and tense, as he helped their father to load the bags and boxes

7

at Newport.

Furthest away from Susanah were Lew's legs, bare and sturdy, the dirt ingrained behind the knee above the grey woollen socks.

The socks were new. The night before, going to bed in the stripped-bare house in Wales, Susanah remembered seeing the second sock on the kitchen table. It was half finished, stretched square on four needles. Ceiri must have completed it some time in the dark hours. It was easy to picture her, putting it with its pair on the table, stroking it smooth. Ready for Lew in the morning. Ready for this journey north.

Chapter Two

Jonty Clelland cut the hairy string and pulled the brown paper away from the sculptured surface beneath. He stroked the leather with his fingertips, his lips curving silently as he spelled out 'E-N-C-Y-C-L-O-P-A-E-D-I-A'.

'Happy birthday, Jonty.' Bea smiled down at his square, frowning face. Old-fashioned, they called him, already made old. Ten years old today, he looked out at the world with the weight of a person three times his age. 'Don't you like your present? Your dad sent away for it specially. From the newspaper.'

She wished John George were here to watch the slow wonder of their son as he savoured this experience with his usual thoroughness. Still, Corella was here smiling with her, sharing Jonty's obvious pleasure. Corella, as tall as her mother, though lumpish in her school uniform, had been a co-conspirator in the purchase of the book.

Jonty freed the leather volume entirely from the wrapping paper which he folded into a neat square. Then he started to flick the pages, stopping now and then at a picture, to run his fingers down the shiny page, to pull the book to him and smell the new paper.

He stared up at them, brown eyes shining, a slight smile on the serious face.

'You'll be able to look up anything, 'stead of asking all those endless questions,' said Corella.

'It should be useful, Mother, Corella, really useful. Can I take it to school?'

Bea shook her head. They would take it from him, taunt him, beat him for his pretension. 'I don't think so, Jonty. Keep it for tonight.'

Jonty floated through the day at school. The lessons were easy for him. He was reprimanded as usual by Mr Robertson, this time for gazing out of the window during an explanation of the evolution of plants. 'You haven't heard a thing I have said, Jonty Clelland, sitting there half asleep . . .'

'I did, sir. It was about chlorophyll . . .' He stood up. Then, adopting a slight Scottish accent, he repeated the teacher's explanation word for word. A ripple of laughter flittered across the class. He groaned inwardly.

'Here, boy! Stand out.'

Jonty stood at the front and put his hand out in resignation, only shuddering slightly as the cane whistled down.

'That's for insolence.' The teacher realigned the hand. 'And this is for being too clever by half.'

9

Jonty could never work out how being clever and knowing a lot devolved into insolence and ended up in so much stick. It happened in the playground as well as the classroom, where he was often challenged to a fist fight for uttering a long word. He added 'retribution' to the mental list of words he was compiling to look up in his encyclopaedia that night. The list, including 'Africa', 'Greece', 'evolution' and 'congress', now came to five. Sufficient for one night, he thought.

That night, he was only halfway through 'Africa' when his mother called him to stop for tea. Then, after saying the grace, his father reminded him about the men's meeting. At last, now he was ten years old, he was considered old enough to attend. He was torn between the treat of the book and the treat of the meeting. He could not talk about his dilemma as he knew his father did not see there was a choice. Naturally, the meeting was more important.

He was allowed to sit behind the semi-circle of men in their second-best jackets and caps. The bubble of chat and conversation faded as his father stood up, a tall thin figure in preacher black, his bright eyes gleaming over his spectacles. The men settled back to listen as John George bent his face to his paper. His strong voice began gently, pausing now and then to repeat a sentence a little louder for emphasis.

He told them about a book he had read about the family and the state and the way in which these two things were linked together inextricably. Of course, there were different kinds of families, in different kinds of relationship with the state. His voice rose, a tremor in it. '. . . and don't we know of families where the children go unshod, unschooled, unfed? And what of those folks who say, "Why! They deserve it." Ye'll say these families are full of drunkards and men who toss pennies in gambling games, the pastimes of the Devil. I've heard it said here.'

Jonty admired the way his father paused, then took off his glasses and polished them with his handkerchief before lowering his voice almost to a whisper.

'I say to you, my friends, that drunkenness and gambling are masks for the pains of poverty. For odd moments in wretched lives they feel they have some control over their fates. But we all know here that such men have no power, no influence. Don't we? No likelihood of it. Don't we know that?'

He paused again to let the ripple of response work its way around the room. 'The truth is that they are kept poor and desperate because that fits in with the patterns of state. The same as we are kept with a little trickle of the world's wealth to keep us sweet as long as we stand on the line they ordain. It is convenient. It is a useful pattern, to hold wages down, to make sure that no job is more secure than the whim of the owner, than is allowed by his demands for high profit.

'Now . . . here at the chapel we talk about salvation as though it were apart from these processes, outside of the realities of the world. Quite away from children in bare feet and mothers with bare tables. You will quote me, friends, on the need to render unto Caesar his own coin. But I say to you that people who are so poor and desperate cannot reach salvation. Don't you think, friends, that we who have the good fortune to work and to enjoy salvation should labour further to improve the position of such poor folks, work to help them get work, to get a roof over their heads, to get their children shoes and medicines? I say Our Lord would have us help them in their struggle for these rights. Then they will come to salvation, unhampered by poverty's leaden weight, unhindered by the oblivion offered by the opiates of sin.'

He sat down.

Jonty was hot with pleasure at his father's passion and the tense respect with which his words were greeted, the explosion of comment, the shouts of approval and objection.

Jade Smith, who was sitting directly in front of Jonty, leapt to his feet, grasping the back of the bench in front of him. 'With all respect to Mr Clelland, who I know is very clever, reading all his books and papers like he does, I say to him he is blinded by all this reading, to the truth as it shines out around him. You can see – anybody can see – that the poor are poor because they're lazy and slothful. They drink instead of thinking. Even what little they have they squander. They're dedicated to sinful waste instead of Christian thrift and husbandry. Coming to Christ, they'd know they should look out for themselves, they would abstain from the . . . er . . . excess that casts 'm down so far.'

John George stood up and looked down at Jade's burly figure, smiling faintly at the round eyes of his son as Jonty leaned sideways behind Jade to get a better view. 'We all applaud, Jade Smith, how you've got on in the world. We all see how hard you work in the pit . . .'

'Greedy, though!' The shout from the side was greeted with grunts of assent. Jade was known to be mean in the share-out of work on his shift.

'. . . Then there are your commercial ventures. The round with the draperies. The new shop. We know you make your contribution here at the chapel because you are kind enough to let us know. But consider the pharisees. Did Our Lord heap praise on them? I would say to you, beware the perils of pride and complacency.'

Jade Smith sat down, fleshy bottom lip out, arms folded across his chest. Jonty stood up. 'I agree with my father, we need to . . .'

The room stilled. Seats creaked as people turned round to see whose was the childish voice.

'Who said you could say owt?' Jade Smith turned and scowled at him. 'Hold your whisht.'

'Too big for his boots!' another voice growled.

'I only wanted . . .'

'Out! No place for you here.'

There were mutters of agreement. Jonty looked across the room at his father, whose head was on one side, eyebrows raised. He said nothing.

Three minutes later, from outside the oak door, Jonty heard the gust of discussion blow again and felt glum, though not resentful, at his exclusion.

Turning into the Front Street he bumped into the upholstered thigh of Miss Antrobus, his Sunday School teacher.

11

'Ah. Jonty Clelland! Just the one.' She smiled her perfunctory smile, her eyes blank as grey shale. 'Your piece. The piece for Sunday. Do you have it off? You didn't come to say it for me Monday night as I suggested.'

'Piece? Oh, yes.'

'Well, say it, then.'

'Here?'

'Yes.'

He sighed. He hadn't memorised it; he didn't need to. He closed his eyes and the page of the book was in front of him:

> 'See what a lovely shell,
> Small and pure as a pearl
> Lying close to my foot
> Frail but a work divine . . .'

He chanted it right to the end and she clapped her podgy hands. The fleshy sound reminded Jonty of the way the butcher slapped his hand on to a side of pork as he recommended its qualities to his mother. He twitched his nose. The cool evening air was made quite sticky by something Miss Antrobus wore that smelled of violets.

He was looking for an excuse to escape when around the corner came a little family procession, its members laden with bags and boxes. At the head of the line strode a big man carrying an enormous box and a bag. He had pit boots hanging around his neck on a string and carried his heavy burdens lightly, as though they were filled with air. Behind him came a woman, a baby tied to her by a wide shawl, leaving her hands free for two bags. Jonty felt a clean breath of spring air as she passed, wiping out for the moment the sickly violet aura of Miss Antrobus.

Straggling along behind the mother were two boys, both taller than Jonty. They kept their eyes to the ground, avoiding his glance. Last in line was a small child, a boy, being pulled along by a thin girl with a dirty face who must be the sister. She looked Jonty in the eye, staring at him until he was forced to drop his gaze altogether.

The man turned and bellowed to her in a language Jonty did not know. The girl started to run with a skittish step, dragging the child behind her and followed her father into Selby Street.

'Welsh,' said Miss Antrobus. 'They're getting down here now. Lots of Welsh families in Priorton.' She snorted, exhaling hot violets. 'An ungodly language.'

Jonty ran.

Once home, he told his mother what he had wanted to say earlier in the meeting. He started to bristle at the recollection at being put out.

Bea smiled at him, her eyes shadowed and deep. 'Don't worry, son. Your time will come. You'll get your say. As you say, selfishness and shame are two sides of the same coin.'

He hadn't said that, but she often talked to him in this way, somehow implanting half the dialogue in his mouth to make her own argument.

12

Continuing, she started to become angry and stabbed a fork into the table, upsetting Corella, who was just finishing her homework. 'Some of them never bother to look outside their own little lives, their own petty affairs. The world begins and ends with them and their back yards.'

She stomped about the house until she unearthed a book and made them sit while she read them some writing from Thomas Paine. On less angry nights it would have been a poet, probably Byron, whose poems were laid about the place – on the piano, on the windowsills, and even in the scullery beside the jam.

Towards bedtime she was still talking on about the French and their fight for equality a hundred years ago. Jonty sometimes thought his whole life was a history lesson. When he brought a friend from school back with him, he would grow red at this talking. The fact was that the visitors often sat there entranced and sometimes went home to cause trouble, even get a thrashing, for calling up the very phrases which his mother had delivered to them.

Listening to her, he remembered the time his father had come in on one of these discussions, black from the pit, no dinner on the table. John George had laughed, saying how she bred sedition in his own household. She'd have them in irons. The two of them roared together at this and he'd put his black and sooty arms around her, pulling her to him.

Jonty and Corella had been hustled to bed early that night, their father muttering something about being on early turn at the pit the next day.

This evening, John George came back from the meeting full of good spirits, saying it had been lively and there was a lot of interest in his paper, requests to read it, even. Three people had taken Bea's neat handwritten copies.

'I hear our Jonty got himself excluded.' She smiled up at him.

'So he did.' John George glanced across at his son, who was at the table with the encyclopaedia open at 'congress'. 'Your time'll come, Jonty. One day they'll listen.' His eye dropped to the book. 'And how did the present go down, then?'

'Excellent,' said Jonty. 'You can look up anything.'

His parents exchanged glances and smiled.

'Is it you who has him sounding like an old man, or me?' said John George.

Bea shrugged. 'He reads, we talk, you preach. Between the three of us he'll not end up talking like the little lads down the street.'

John George grinned. 'He'll end up a good fighter or a good talker or both.'

Jonty looked from one to the other.

'I got the cane today,' he announced.

'What for?' said Bea calmly. Jonty often got the cane.

'For insolence, Mr Robertson said.'

'He would have his point,' said John George.

Jonty sighed and closed his book. 'I saw another family arrive, Dad. Making for Selby Street.'

'Caradoc Laydon Jones,' said his father. 'Another one from South Wales, cousin to the Lewises. They were talking about him down the pit today. They say he's a formidable worker. And a big chapel man. Should be a useful man, at the pit and in Gibsley, too.'

Chapter Three

Caradoc Laydon Jones hammered a second time at the faded brown door. The rest of the family stood at a distance in the dirt road, their bags and packages tumbled around them.

A thin-faced woman opened the door a little way, then wider.

'Mrs Kenton, is it?'

She nodded.

'There was a letter from my cousin Davey Lewis, said you would have a key to number seventy-one. Next door.' He had to stiffen his mouth to frame it round the English. Neither his wife nor his children could understand a word he said.

She squinted up at him. 'I've got the key aal reet, hinney, but it winnet do you no good tonight. House is empty.'

'A wagon should have come.'

'Nee wagon, hinney. But I've lit the fire like Davey Lewis asked.'

Caradoc turned to Ceiri and scowled. 'The woman says no wagon has been. She has lit a fire, but there are no beds, no furniture.'

Ceiri, clutching Jenny closer, put a hand on Susanah.

The woman said, 'Hadaway in wi' yer. I winnet see the woman and the bairns without a bed. They can share with us. But then that's us bustin' at the seams with just one loft atween us. Mebbe you and the lads can stretch on the floor in number seventy-one. It's warm enough. Davey filled the coal so you'd have the fire. I've got broth here of a kind, warm you after the journey. Davey brought some pot stuff up from his garden.'

That night, after eating the broth, welcome despite the sticky bowls, Susanah and Tollie ended up sharing a ticking mattress in the bedroom under the eaves with Mrs Kenton's offspring, Joan and Vivian, while their mother and Jenny shared with Mrs Kenton. Shoved against the peeling wall, Susanah pulled Tollie close to her and closed her eyes to shut out the bold stares and mouths that asked questions in a strange tongue.

The next morning she was still clutching Tollie as she looked from the crop-haired Joan to curly-haired Vivian pulling on his stiff trousers. It was only then she realised that Joan was the girl. She tried to ask her about her shaved head. Joan shook her head, not understanding. Susanah took her own long locks and scissored them with her fingers, raising her eyebrows in enquiry. Joan gave a hearty, black-toothed laugh and her fingers made tiny crawling movements over her hair. Then she made cracking sounds, one fin-

15

gernail against another, shook her head and made scissor movements over her own hair.

Susanah laughed and shuddered at the same time.

After bread and tea they all crept next door to where Caradoc was striding about the echoing house, his heavy work boots striking sparks off the bare stone floor. After what seemed ages he set out for the pit to sort out his work.

Ceiri poked the fire and put on another shovel of coals. They all relaxed.

With their father safely out of the way, Susanah and Tollie made for the river, which they had noticed on their way from the station. Susanah had loved their river in Wales, a frothy grey flow lit from inside, which always seemed to be channelling its way back up to the mountain rather than flowing out of it. The river here in Gibsley was broad and slow-moving; no mountains here. Instead, the low rounded breast of hill, green woodland in the cleft; the scoring scree of the spoil heap; the evening gloss of the seepage pool, called White Pool.

'S'anah! S'anah! Come and see!' Tollie, who had run ahead, came back to pull her by the hand, racing her up a back lane, pushing her across stones, through bushes. 'Now see this!'

There must have been a hundred, two hundred frogs on the path by the pool, leaping away from her feet as she and Tollie walked through them. Tollie laughed and jumped about, the spring in his chubby legs as explosive as that of any frog. Susanah lifted one of the frogs up to her face and looked at the single eye visible from the side. It stared back at her, bulging and bland.

The two of them were still there, carrying the wandering leapers back towards the pool, when their brother Davey arrived panting, to tell them the wagon had arrived and they were to come for their dinner. Susanah raced back towards the house, wondering at this new place they'd come to, where it rained frogs like it did in the Bible.

Caradoc Laydon Jones had been assured by his cousin that there was work, well-paid work, in Gibsley, which, like many other County Durham villages, had grown up around a deep hole in the ground and a pit wheel. The narrow huddle of streets had been built in the sixties, thrown up with the minimum of expense and in the maximum of hurry to house the pitmen who were streaming in from all parts of Britain. Men brought in to win the coal from the dark earth, rich seams of coal which provided the spark for other great changes in people's work and lives.

The streets in Gibsley village lay on the hill leading up from the pit, small streets linking the Front Street and Back Street like the rungs of a ladder. The houses, most with single windows at the top and bottom, opened straight on to the dirt roads.

Caradoc passed St Andrew's church which, with its school alongside, dominated the Front Street. This building dwarfed the nearby Primitives chapel, set narrowly with minor dignity alongside the Reading Room. He noted with a downturned mouth some public houses, placed on corners and much flashed with fancy tiles, figured glass and painted signs.

The Wesleyan chapel crouched at the far end of the Front Street, nearly into the yard of White Pool Colliery. White Pool Colliery was the particular hole in the ground around which Gibsley had grown up, and was Caradoc's destination on his morning walk from Selby Street.

Set back a little behind the chapel was a large house with two trees at the gate, beside which stood a pony and trap. A lad in a cap was pulling at the pony's harness. As Caradoc watched, the door of the house opened and a small man whose silver hair flowed behind him in the wind came bustling down the path.

At the colliery, the overman, a heavy-eyed man called Bob Stephenson, took Caradoc outside the building to talk, away from the noisy coal screens. Bringing out his pipe, he spat into the black dust and cast his eye from Caradoc's bushy hair to his serviceable heavy boots.

'Davey Lewis your cousin, then?'

'That's right.'

'Good worker, Davey.'

'I trained him meself. I'm a better worker than him. Always was. Known for it.' Caradoc put his weight on to the other foot and met the overman's gaze.

'Why, you might just be lucky, Mr Laydon Jones. This raw chest epidemic's scything 'em down. I'm a canny few men short on this shift. Mebbe fifteen. Always a feast or a famine here with labour.'

'I can start now. Today.'

'Looks like you've come ready set up. You could work on bank right away.'

'I'm a hewer. I work underground.'

Stephenson cast his eye up at the wheel. 'Bin down a deep pit, have yer?'

'Once. Mostly drift.'

'Some o' the Welsh lads've never been down a deep shaft. See them shaking in the cage, first time.'

'A pit's a pit. The coal's there to get,' said Caradoc.

Stephenson turned at the sound of a pony and trap swerving through the mud in the main gateway. He went across and touched his cap at the silver-haired man whom Caradoc had seen sweeping out of the house earlier.

'Mornin', Mr Jackman.'

'Morning, Stephenson. Will you go to the office and tell Mr Carmedy that I'm to meet Lord Chase at the station? We've got a meeting over in Darlington at the bank. I'll be back by two.'

'Right, Mr Jackman.'

Mr Jackman's sharp eye lit on Caradoc, who returned him stare for stare. 'Who's the big feller?'

'Welshman come to be set on. Hewer. Thought I'd have him on the screens today, mebbe at the face early shift tomorrow. He can work marrers with Freddy Stapleton. Yer knaa, him's marrer went sick yesterday. He's workin' his stall hisself today so his count'll be down. Never good at the best of times, Freddy. Too busy whistlin' and playin' about.'

'Well, that'n looks big enough. Set him on. Ye can tell Carmedy I say so.' Jackman pulled his rein to the left and clicked with the corner of his mouth to make the pony turn. He had to drive around Caradoc, who continued to give him a hard stare. Then he set off for his weekly visit to Lord Chase, the owner of White Pool Pit. Lord Chase wouldn't be pleased that the tallies were down when the demand for coal was building up again.

Sourly, Bob Stephenson watched the dust rise behind the pony trap as it rattled along Front Street. He liked to do his own setting on. Now he'd have to go lick-spittling to Carmedy, the undermanager. Jackman would check up. He was like that.

At home Susanah was set to mind Jenny while her mother put the house to rights, drafting a willing Davey and an unwilling Lew in to help. At the end of the day the house had the hum and the smell of normality. Then their father came back from his shift, ate his meal and had his bath without comment as though this were his fortieth, rather than his first day in his new house.

When the table was cleared after the meal he lifted his great box on to the table. The care with which he had carried the box from Wales had not been wasted. Not a tool nor a part was out of place. He unwrapped the square of velvet and smoothed it out on to the wooden surface. Then he started to place in rows the screws and wheels, the magic pattern pieces of a hundred clocks.

'Here's Freddy Stapleton.' Bob Stephenson brought a small, sharp-faced man across to where Caradoc leaned on the door.

Freddy grinned up at him. 'A bit big for a pitman, isn' tha? Didn't Bob here tell yer the seams is no more than eighteen inches? Tha'll get stuck in the undercut.'

Caradoc looked at the little man with his sharp red nose and his pot belly and knew him for a drinker. He scowled at Stephenson, who had put him as partner to this man, and stood up straight. 'Well, there's work to do. Let's get on,' he said.

As they took the long walk from the bottom of the shaft to the face Caradoc answered Freddy's innocent questions with grunts, and as they worked in the early part of the shift he remained silent. This was too much for Freddy, who started to whistle and sing as he worked, filling the quiet space between them with his own sound.

The only noise that Caradoc made was to mutter imprecations as Freddy got in his way.

'What was that, marrer?'

'I said, can't you keep out of my way? You'll have my pick in your shoulder if you don't watch out.'

Freddy grinned. 'Well, marrer, if tha wants us out of the way tha'll have to tell us in me own tongue. Tha't in England now and English it is.'

As they sat down for their bread and cold tea halfway through the shift they were joined by a tall thin man who had to bend nearly double to make his way along the seam. 'What cheer, Freddy!'

'What cheer, John George! This is Caradoc Laydon Jones, me new marrer. Not a man for the words, but you should see him shift coal!' said Freddy cheerfully. 'Two ton to my one!'

John George wiped a hand on the back of his shorts and held it out. 'How do! John George Clelland. You'd be Davey Lewis's cousin, is it? He's a good lad, Davey.'

Caradoc looked at the hand and waited too long before he took it.

'You're a chapel man, they say?'

'Aye.'

'It's a canny chapel here. Plenty going on.'

'Tha should hear John George preach!' said Freddy, gargling the cold tea in his hot dry throat. 'Man, he can make a stone weep!'

'Do you speak, Mr Laydon Jones? In chapel?'

'Aye. Times.'

'We have this meetin' on a Sat'day, Mr Jones. Sat'day night. Talk and politics and affairs. Ye'd be welcome there.'

'Affairs?'

'Well, the talk now is of the party to represent Labour proper. Mostly Liberals they are, in the chapel, but that's a shopkeepers' party. Some of us . . .'

Caradoc stood up and hafted his pick from one hand to the other. 'Well, Mr Clelland, on Saturday nights I've other work to do. And I've work to do now.' He turned his back on them and first squatted, then lay sideways on his wooden board so he could continue his work on the undercut.

John George Clelland exchanged glances with Freddy Stapleton, who shrugged. 'Bloody Welshmen,' he murmured. 'Miserable lot. Who'd want a Welshman for a marrer?'

Susanah crouched on the stairs, watching Caradoc through the crack in the wooden wall as he sat with double candles on one side and a paraffin lamp on the other. His thick hair fell like a rope curtain, and his chin was almost level with his large hands, as deft as any woman's as they picked up tiny screws and handled pieces of wire as fine as spiders' webs.

There was a bang at the door and her mother glided across to open it. She recognised the man who came in, a tall thin man who had preached on Sunday night in the chapel. He placed a washed-out sack, lumpy with what it contained, beside her father on the table.

'Now, Mr Laydon Jones.'

'Now, Mr Clelland.'

The two men, one thin as a scarecrow, the other broad as a bull, looked at each other across the kitchen table. Her father did not stand up.

'Mark Dennis said you were a rare hand with timepieces, Mr Laydon Jones.'

'Aye.'

He pulled a mantel clock out of the sack. 'Will you have a look at this? The clock in here is from me mother. I have to say it has not gone for ten years. Jonty dropped it in a game of catch. My son, that is. Although it has a fine case there is sommat very much missin' in a clock, however bonny, which doesn't go.' Mr Clelland had eyes of pale bright blue, and his lips formed a delicate double curve, like the scratchy line of a bird in flight, high up against the clouds.

'Aye.' Her father grasped the clock and turned it to catch the light from the lamp.

Mr Clelland reached into the sack. 'And this watch, it stopped this Sunday mornin' as I was comin' back from Houghton. But I heard a fine preacher there. Jacob Smith, a fine preacher, even if he is a Baptist.'

'There'll be a charge.'

Mr Clelland raised an eyebrow. 'I'd no doubt there would be, Mr Laydon Jones. Our Lord says, doesn't he, that the labourer is worthy of his hire?'

Her father was silent and Mr Clelland's glance moved round the room, finally settling on the long bench, where her mother was sitting doing her crocheting, across the body of the sleeping Jenny.

'Your family have settled in the village, Mr Laydon Jones?'

'Well enough.'

He moved to the door and turned round. 'I'm just on my way to the Saturday meeting, Mr Laydon Jones. The speaker is talking about Ireland. Home Rule. You wouldn't . . . ?'

Caradoc did stand up then. His eyepiece dropped to the floor. His wife flinched, put down her crocheting and stared hard from him to Mr Clelland. 'I've no time,' he said. 'No time to waste jawing on about the things of the world, things that . . . talk . . . will never change.'

Mr Clelland smiled into Caradoc's eyes and shook his head slightly. Ceiri watched the door click behind him.

'What was that about?' she asked.

'The man's a fool,' he grunted, sitting down to peer more closely at the mantel clock. 'Too busy for his own good.'

Susanah's father's work with timepieces was good, and word of it spread quickly in the village and up to Priorton, the town three miles distant. Soon there was a steady trickle of callers at the house, carrying their packages. Caradoc dealt with all of them in his usual brusque fashion. This put no one off, as he was shrewd enough to keep his work, which was always perfectly executed, just a shade cheaper than anyone else.

The callers carrying clocks and watches in bags of various shapes and sizes ranged from Mr Jackman, the manager at the pit, who sent his watch with Mr Carmedy, to Mrs Simpson, whose husband had died in South African war and whose timepiece hadn't worked since the army sent it home. Another keen customer was Miss Antrobus, bustling through the door in her haze of violets. Her mantel clock caused Caradoc particular trouble as it always seemed to stop working once it got back on to her mantelpiece.

One Sunday in June she was practising her usual wingless hover beside the minister at the chapel door when she alighted on Caradoc. 'Mr Jones . . .' She cut in between the family, her hand on Caradoc's sleeve. Ceiri drew to one side, with the children, tired and hunched into their Sunday clothes. '. . . Would you believe it? The clock has stopped again.'

Caradoc shifted uneasily under her grasp. 'It was working well enough when I left it. Perfect, in fact.'

'I know. Just what I said to Mammy. Mr Jones did such a good job. A genius with mechanisms, I said. Then she said – would you believe it? – get him down here to look at the room. The room's at fault. Can you believe it? The room's at fault. That's what she said.'

'It's said that places have an effect on mechanisms . . .'

'So,' she gleamed up at him, 'I said to Mammy, the only thing for it is for Mr Laydon Jones to see the things here on the mantelpiece.'

The minister was looking warily from one bulky figure to the other. He eased the close collar from his neck, wondering why he felt so hot.

'We keep the Sabbath,' said Caradoc shortly. 'There is no question . . .'

She smiled. 'I would not dream, Mr Jones . . .'

'I'm on foreshift tomorrow. I'll be up there at three.'

Miss Antrobus lived in a cottage up the hill out of the village with her mother, the widow of a forest manager, who stayed on by the grace and favour of Lord Chase. Old Mrs Antrobus was a source of amusement to the village children. They sniggered, mimicking her high toneless voice as she sat there with the big ear-trumpet she brought into chapel. 'Eh? Eh? Speak up, speak up! A body cannot hear!'

Davey told Susanah that Miss Antrobus was a shield bug in disguise. He showed her the illustration in his insect book to prove it. 'See there? The greenish colour? The big breastplate? See? No mistakin' it, I'm tellin' yer.'

On Monday, having had his dinner and his bath, Caradoc changed into his best jacket and cap, then walked up the hill. The door to the little cottage flew open almost before he touched it. Miss Antrobus stood there in the green bombazine dress. Its tucked front, she knew, made the most of her generous bosom. Her hair, normally pulled back severely, was loosely plaited and pinned up such a way as to suggest it might loosen easily. Her finger was to her lips as she took his arm and led him through the kitchen. The old woman was asleep in a chair beside the fire, her arms folded tightly across her breast, her mouth open, lips sinking inwards over toothless gums.

Miss Antrobus led Caradoc through to the parlour where another fire was burning in an elaborate grate. The clock stood on a newspaper on a small round mahogany table. 'There, now, you can see it at home. Usually it's on the mantelpiece, there in the centre.'

Miss Antrobus's hand hovered over a carafe and glasses which stood on a tray beside the clock. 'I have this madeira wine, Mr Jones, sent for the health by my brother in Edinburgh. Will you have a glass with me, before you set to work on my poor old clock?'

Caradoc sat down heavily on the chair and nodded slowly, spreading his legs out before the bright fire. He watched as the shiny fabric pulled against her plump shoulder as she poured the red liquid. He put two hands up for

21

the tiny glass, enclosing her plump fingers in his.

She put a hand on his shoulder. 'There,' she said, 'I knew we could be friends.'

Susanah could see that her mother did not like the trouble Miss Antrobus caused her father. When he was away on these visits she was always restless, pacing the house until he returned. When he did return he was usually in quite a good mood, smelling of violets and a sweet smell which Susanah did not recognise as madeira wine. But her mother's face would be black and thundery. Susanah puzzled about this, as she knew Caradoc would charge Miss Antrobus for his work. It would be paid for, whatever he did. He had a rate for everything, in his head. He kept everything there. There were no books. He did not, could not write.

A number of the clocks, mended but not yet collected, went up on to the walls of the cottage, purring and ticking, clicking and chiming through the day and through the night. The scrubbed table and the daily washed stone floor made up a suitably plain framework for the fine woods, shining walnut inlays, gilded numerals and painted faces of the many clocks.

Susanah felt she must have known how to tell the time from the day she was born, forgetting that Davey had taught her it when she was three, as he had taught her so many things. At four years old her father had tested her on the clock, and she had got every question right. She had smiled her pleasure at his unsmiling face, conscious of her mother's narrow fluttering presence in the corner.

Now they were settled in the new house Susanah started teaching Tollie the clock. It seemed that for ages he could not even recognise or say the hours. She sweated at the thought of her father testing him. Then one day a miracle happened and Tollie could say the hours. Soon, soon, he would learn the rest. Day after day she would go over and over with him the intricacies of the minute hand. He always managed to look at her, blankly and reproachfully all in the same glance, as he stumbled into the wrong answer.

Caradoc defeated Susanah in this race with time. It was on the day when, after several visits, he finally got Miss Antrobus's clock to work and stay working. He had enjoyed sitting down on her padded chair, drinking in the fulsome praise, the earnest touch and the melting glances along with his two glasses of madeira. 'Ophelia? A strange name, that is,' he said.

'It is in *Hamlet*, Mr Jones, Shakespeare. I will read you some. Here: "I would give you some violets, but they withered all, when my father died." Do the words not roll right over you?'

'Fine words,' he said shortly. His hand reached out and he turned her broad shoulder towards him. 'Your mother, she's well asleep in there?'

She wriggled, then stood up. 'She's had two doses of her medicine, poor soul. She was so restless and it does help her. There's poppies in it.' Miss Antrobus looked at the hand on her shoulder. 'I have another clock, Mr Jones. A gift from Lord Chase when my father died. It is on the landing. Perhaps you would like to see it?'

He followed the stately body with its green bombazine casing up the narrow cottage stairs.

Caradoc seemed in good spirits when he got home later; his eyes were shining and his step was light. It was then that he set about testing Tollie on the time. Susanah watched as he underrated the miracle of Tollie telling the hours, moving in remorselessly on Tollie's uncertainty about the minutes.

Tollie's voice died to nothing and he stood, wide-eyed and silent, in front of Caradoc. The door clicked as Davey went out of the house, his face white, his eyes angry. Susanah stayed and watched as her father, strap in hand, beat Tollie, who gulped back sobs at every stroke. Her eyes stayed on the hand that was doing all this. It was neater and cleaner than any miner's hand she had ever seen. The hand that she had watched plumb the interiors of clocks and watches with delicate precision now grasped the strap which was battering away at Tollie.

She started forward but her mother grasped Susanah's arm and held her back, finally letting her go to follow the sobbing Tollie up the stairs. She would convince Tollie that it didn't matter. None of it mattered.

But as she stroked Tollie's thick hair and calmed his shaking body Susanah knew that every single thing her father did mattered. He had control over her life, all their lives. Even time stretched out for him. Perhaps it was something to do with the clocks that gave Caradoc some kind of Lordship over time; he stretched and stretched it to suit himself, yet he was never in a hurry. He did his shift at the pit. He mended the clocks in the continuous stream in which they came into the house. In the shed in the back yard he made the bait tins and tin bottles in which his workmates liked to take their food underground. He made cooking tins out of sheet metal for the wives. And the profit he made from this vanished into his tin box while her mother cut and contrived to keep their backs covered and the house running. He went to prayer meetings on weekday evenings, and he kept the Sabbath, never working on a Sunday.

And soon he was making time for a weekly visit to Miss Antrobus. Her mother told her the two of them read the Scriptures, as Caradoc liked to hear them now, in English.

Susanah knew that her father ordered life just as he chose. Even when it came to Mr Clelland.

Chapter Four

'John George, will you stop mithering on about this man Jones! On, on you go, gettin' my head spinning. So what if he won't come to your Saturday meeting? So what if he won't join us in the party? So what if he's driving poor Freddy mad, not talkin' to him like he does? So what if he does make a bigger pile of that black gold you dig than any man in White Pool Pit? Leave him to his peace, I'm tellin' you.'

Bea Clelland, like her son Jonty, was small, square and conspicuously brown-skinned, whatever the weather. She frequently told Jonty that their forefathers had come from Spain, by way of Ireland, having been washed up on its western shore when the Armada foundered. 'Then before that, pet,' she would sometimes say, mysteriously, 'Africa, who knows?'

John George Clelland smiled at his wife, stroking his hand down his narrow face. 'But I'm drawn to the man, Bea. I've this feeling that I want to get on to the inside of 'im. I've never had it so strongly. The feller seems to me like a good man wasted, Bea. There's something wrong there, Bea. Something wanting.'

Bea laughed. 'Now, J G! That one's saved! Haven't you seen his face in chapel? Haven't you heard him speak about the perils of the flesh? Mind, maybe there's something in what you say. Me, I think that the ones who go on about all that have it rather too much on their minds!'

Listening to them as he sat at the table, Jonty wrestled with this thought. It was the first time his mother had commented on his father's preoccupation with the Welshman. She had put her finger at the heart of things, somehow.

Ideas excited her, ideas sifted from her reading and refined and hammered out in the argumentative conversations she sometimes had with his father. But she liked people too, and would only hold with ideas that fitted with what she knew of the folk around her.

There were the Gibsley people whom she met every day, and those whom she met occasionally through the chapel life and the politics which, she said, were meat and drink to her.

She would pass the time of day with the gipsies and hawkers who wandered through the village, travelling north and south with the seasons. She would speak to the Catholic father in the street, when others in the village would cross over rather than be touched by the swish of his long papish cloak. She welcomed into her home men from London, Edinburgh, and

25

some from Ireland: men who visited the district to address meetings, to gain support for their ideas. For as long as he could remember, Jonty had frequently come down on a Sunday morning to find some tousled figure asleep under a blanket on the front room couch.

Another distinct group of people whom his mother drew to her were the women who came to the area speaking about votes for women. They would stay over on their own way north or south, migrating like the gipsies, although not equally tied by the seasons.

These discussions among the women were always open to Jonty. Although the topic of female suffrage was a hot one in his house, it was not judged to be so risky, so potentially treasonable for young ears as the discussions of the Irish men who argued darker measures in support of their cause.

Jonty relished the sight of his mother in full flow, hands on hips, standing before the fire, holding forth to these women, better dressed and better shod than herself and talking in accents so different from their own.

He loved her best when she was on the attack. Then she would rain questions at them, as Jonty watched hands tighten round bulky handbags and lips draw back in polite offence. 'You'll have woman servants, I think, Mrs Bennet-Smith? What do you pay them? What hours do they work? What holidays have they? Who washes your clothes? Who minds your children? . . .'

She did have her favourites, the most prominent of whom was Miss Marsden, a giant of a woman with huge hands and the gentlest of horsey faces. On Miss Marsden's visits, Bea would make a fuss about the food, which was not normal for her. Usually she called food just 'coke for the boiler' and laughed at women who could only talk recipes and appetites.

One week-end in November Miss Marsden extended her stay in the district so she could give a talk on the Suffragists in the Reading Room in Gibsley. On Saturday night the room was full; people had travelled miles through the rain and mist to hear her. Her audience were mostly women and girls, with a sprinkling of men, a full row of them at the back. Jonty sat in the second row from the front. Beside him sat his father, not watching Miss Marsden, but fixing Bea (who was chairing the meeting) with his intent gaze.

This night, the men in the back row took an active part. They hissed and gobbled like turkeys. But each time they started hissing, Miss Marsden would laugh heartily, then just stand and stare at them until they stopped.

Teachers from the elementary school were there, as were the Gibsley Sunday School teachers, including Miss Antrobus, who looked very fierce for half of the time, then went to sleep, sunk into a post-madeira haze. Bea told Jonty afterwards that the argument was quite beyond Miss Antrobus. At one point the only sounds to be heard in the room were turkey-gobbling from the back and Miss Antrobus snoring at the front.

From where he sat, Jonty's mind wandered back to a visit he had just made to the house in Selby Street with his grandmother's clock which had stopped again. Before the meeting his father had sent him to deliver the clock to Mr Laydon Jones.

To Jonty's relief the big man was not in the house. The wife opened the door and smiled at him, signing with her hands and speaking in her language. He watched her floating like some dainty skeletal leaf before him as she ushered him into the kitchen.

It was very neat and hot in there, the brass ornaments and fire irons glittering in the light of the fire. He examined the dozens of clocks on the walls with his usual careful eye. His father had talked about this business with the clocks when he went on about Mr Jones. What a brilliant man he must be, what skill. Jonty decided his mother was right: his father did watch Mr Jones with too close an eye. There were times in the chapel when the men were standing close, even when their backs were to each other, when the air seemed to crackle between them.

The Welsh woman said words Jonty did not understand and motioned him to the table, where he put down his paper parcel and sat on the chair she had pulled out. It was unusual to be invited to sit down; when Mr Jones was in he got no further than the threshwood.

Mrs Jones placed a cupful of blackcurrant cordial in front of him and he gulped it down gratefully. It tasted sweet and there was something in it which made his jaws ache.

The daughter, Susanah, was sitting on the long bench by the back wall playing cat's cradle with the child Jenny, who at two could walk and play quite well now. She watched the boy sitting red-faced at their table. He looked funny in his dark suit and his collar and tie which were tight and neat, though none-too-clean.

Jonty was as conscious of this girl as his father had been of her father. He had seen her in the girls' yard at school. She was always shining clean, very different from the travel-stained waif he had first spotted two years before in the Front Street. He liked her small sturdy frame, so different from the lumpish height of Corella, who had the misfortune of inheriting their father's height and their mother's broad frame. He liked Susanah's clear way of looking at another person. She was doing it now, gazing at him over the child's head as she finished the rhyme. He liked the way her voice lingered long over the vowels, like music.

Jonty wanted to talk to her, to mention the meeting in the Reading Room, and Miss Marsden, and tell her that other girls would be there. But the girl finished the game with the string and stood up, the baby still in her arms. Then she looked at him with long eyes that were so piercing, so full of unexploded laughter that he drank off the cordial too quickly and fled.

As he'd walked down the street, the winter sun had seemed very hot. He'd coughed with the choked cordial and his cheeks burnt with the alcohol by the time he finally reached the sanctuary of the meeting. Here was the safe familiarity of talk about democratic rights and representation, the warmth of feeling from his father by his side for his mother on the platform. This was simple compared with that house and its timid woman and its bold girl and the malevolent presence of its absent father.

Chapter Five

It was a bright spring day. The white light cast slanting shadows across the schoolyard as the children lined up. The infants stood in pairs, a boy and a girl holding hands; the older boys and girls stood in separate and parallel lines.

The Friday morning walk across to the service at St Andrew's was a weekly ritual. First, the children had to come out of the school gate then turn and walk the length of Front Street and back, their feet gradually marking step together as the teachers alongside like platoon sergeants. Then they had to walk up to the church, under the lych gate, along the path by the graves and up to the old porch.

St Andrew's was a large, echoing building, designed as an adjunct to a seminary now lost under the cobbles of Selby Street. The chapels, at either end of Front Street, were always packed to the doors on Sundays, whereas the church dwarfed its congregation to insignificance.

Reaching the church door at last, the marching children made their way under the weary eye of the vicar, Mr Stonham, who always broadcast the view that his assignment to the Gibsley parish was God's judgement on some forgotten crime in his youth.

In Susanah's first week at school, when she took part in this strange march-past, the vicar had stopped her. He had placed his black walking stick at her shoulder and, quite delicately, pushed her back in line. She had shaken her head as he spoke to her, not understanding anything he said.

The girl behind her, Betty Stapleton, had turned Susanah round to face her. Then she had lifted the side of her skirt and bobbed, pulling Susanah down with her. Susanah mimicked this gesture and the vicar had nodded a scowling satisfaction. Then he had pushed Susanah on, still using the black stick. She'd noticed that its silver knob was elaborately worked into the form of a large bird, fluffed nicely on her nest.

So Susanah had learnt that when you passed the vicar the girls curtseyed and the boys touched the point on their head where their cap might have been. This was only done around the school. If a child did this in the street, the gesture would evoke parental chastisement for undue respect towards the hated High Church.

Ceiri had warned Susanah about the practices in the established church, and what she must on no account do. She must not kneel at the sight of

29

the cross and she must not above all make the sign of the cross, as *they* did.

But in the church there was no real pressure from the vicar to do these strange things; three-quarters of the children, like Susanah, walked stolidly up the aisle to sit without any magical gestures in their seats at the front.

Today, as always, she stared hard at the few children who did go through the actions. She still wondered what it felt like, to kneel there, to make that sign. Did you see something then? Did God put his hand on you? Did the Devil spin howling away?

One day, in her second spring at Gibsley, she had tried this moving of the hands across her body. The only place that had the privacy for such a forbidden act was the brick privy across the back lane from the house in Selby Street.

Her mother, who was ironing, had told her go out into the fresh air and Susanah had made her way furtively to the privy across the back lane. First she'd checked the bolt carefully, pulling it backwards and forwards and finally snugly home in the locked position. Then she'd knelt down on the floor, which she had scrubbed clean and whitened with a block that morning before school. Then she closed her eyes, imagining the whitewashed wall to be the very end of the church with its lacey stone screen and the figure of Jesus bulging like a skinned rabbit, hanging from the cross. Then, very carefully, she made the sign of the cross.

Nothing had happened, except that the picture of the church faded away and was replaced by the streaming yellow-greens and rising greys she had seen once through Davey's eyes from under a slatted wooden seat. The countryside running past the train.

Something must be wrong, she'd thought. She must be doing the actions in the wrong order. She should do it again. She tried crossing herself in a different order. The land-streaming-by picture was replaced by a picture of their own kitchen wall, her father's clocks ticking away. Then even that faded.

It had been so hard to keep her eyes closed. Her nose had twitched, the fire ash, the disinfectant, the sickly over-sweet smell of the contents of the midden seeping into her. She could hear a fly buzzing. It must be very large. It was rattling. The door was rattling.

She realised her brother Lew had his eye to the diamond-shaped hole at the top of the door: he must have been clinging there like a monkey. 'S'anah! S'anah! What you doin' there on the floor? I wan' go!'

At teatime Lew had let on to their father about Susanah kneeling on the privy floor. He demanded to know what it was about and she'd blurted out about crossing herself. It was hard to deny, with Lew's smug story repeated yet again and the tell-tale whitewash at knee level on her skirt. This time her father had unbuckled his belt to beat her. The only thing that had surprised her was that her mother looked on in unusual, if anxious, approval.

At the Friday services the whole school sang in loud and hearty voices.

Today the sound poured forth just as loudly and heartily as when the children chanted their tables or spoke their poems in unison. However Susanah found that this rasping roar hurt her ears, so she concentrated on looking at the jewel colours of the windows, or the way the brasses shimmered in the dusty sunlight.

On the other hand she did love the sound of the singing in the chapel. She liked it especially at the Sunday evening service, the only one of the four which her mother attended. Ceiri would stand there, her face scrubbed so clean that the pale white of her skin took on a blue glow. She wore her hair pulled back under a little black bonnet, but a few hairs always managed to escape, frizzing back out into fine curls. She always stood to Caradoc's right, with her right hand on Jenny who would wriggle her way through the service. In her left hand would be her battered Bible, whose print was so small that she had to hold it close to her eyes to read the Gospel in Welsh as it assailed her ears in English. Caradoc, in his best jacket, his heavy hair smoothed back with water, would sing out in his powerful basso profundo voice which underscored the voices of the other chapel men in such harmonies that the joy prickled Susanah's skin. Ceiri's voice piped out like water over velvet, with a sure touch on the music, although it swam through the words with no understanding. Looking around, Susanah would watch the faces of men and women, faces she knew well. They were normally severe, forbidding or preoccupied. But on a Sunday, in the chapel, they were open and full of potent feeling, which was being directed quite safely towards the Lord. The music was their legitimate passion.

Four or five times in a year the Welsh families in the village would walk the three miles into the larger town of Priorton which, having a larger Welsh community, had a Welsh chapel. Here the whole of the service was in Welsh. At these services the music was at its most fine and Ceiri was at her most content. But as the years had passed, Caradoc allowed his family to make this journey to Priorton less and less. He judged it a waste of time when their own chapel was so near. And they all, except Ceiri, spoke the English well now.

And now, two years after her religious experiments in the privy, Susanah again stood in the line with the older children, feeling infinitely wiser than she'd felt on that first walk-past. This time it was Joan Kenton, who was walking just ahead of Susanah, the Reverend Stonham put his stick out to stop.

Joan had grown considerably since she had shared her bed with Susanah on that first night in Gibsley. She was still plain and heavy with the foot-planted tread of a hulking boy, and ever since the time of the infestation she had kept her hair cut short so that it stuck out all over her head.

'Hands!' Mr Stonham's voice squeaked out.

Joan put out her hands. They were rimmed with old sores and lined with old dirt. The nails were long and set in with black soil. Susanah had a flashing image of her father's hands: large and spotlessly clean from washing and scrubbing when he came in from the pit; soft from the sheepfleece he rubbed them on while working on his clocks.

31

Joan's hands were dirty from the hours and days of grubbing work she did on the slip of land her mother had retrieved from the edge of the wild green space that backed on to the streets. She grew vegetables in every season to help her mother, who had no income except that of an older brother who worked at the pit for a boy's wage.

'Over!' The Reverend Stonham delicately lifted one grubby hand, then another with his walking stick.

The palms were only slightly cleaner than their backs.

By now the parallel lines of children had curved into a long semi-circle of onlookers; smiles and grins were half-hidden on some faces. Miss Carmedy, Susanah's teacher, had come from her place at the head of the queue and was standing behind her. The boys' teacher, Mr Robertson, was beside the vicar.

The vicar's tone was high, pained. 'It must be remembered that even your own mentor Mr . . . er . . . John Wesley admitted that cleanliness is indeed next to Godliness. We may be poor but we must be clean. Here you are not dirty miners doing dirty work . . .'

His voice hit the word 'miners' like a knife grinding on stone. There were no smiles now. A murmuring ripple flashed along the queue; Susanah heard Miss Carmedy click her teeth. She knew the teacher's brother worked at the pit, but he was the undermanager. He would emerge from the Colliery Office without a speck on him. She had seen him riding down Front Street on his bicycle, his trousers clipped neatly round his ankles.

'. . . now what, children, do we do about dirt, about dirty hands?'

Most heads were down; Susanah's were not the only hands clenched into fists.

'Sir!' Tod Barraclough, a farmer's son, had his hand up. The vicar nodded his permission to speak. 'Sir. The pump. You get them washed at the pump.'

To the side of the lychgate was an old pump which was used for outside watering by Mr Hocking, the verger and school caretaker.

Joan Kenton was marched back down the church path towards the pump, Tod Barraclough by her side. The rest watched in silence as the water coughed and spluttered its way on to Joan's hands. She rubbed at them violently, the water spitting into a glistening spray in the clear air. Tod stopped pumping and Joan rubbed her hands hard together; then she wiped them, back, then front, on the seat of her thick skirt. The two of them marched back to the church door.

The vicar leaned over on his cane to peer at the cleaner hands. He snorted down his nose. 'It would take a week to get those clean, young woman. Your mother ought to be ashamed of herself. Should know better than send you to school like that. I have a good mind to speak to her . . .'

'Dinnet dee that, sir!' Joan's mouth was hard, the sides pulled down into an ugly line. It was a demand as much as an appeal.

'Well, Miss Carmedy.' The vicar looked over Susanah's head at the teacher. 'Perhaps this lesson needs some . . . er . . . reinforcement? Perhaps four strokes?'

Miss Carmedy moved around Susanah to pull Joan to her side. Her usually mild spoon-shaped face was grim and cold. She nodded briefly, but did not look up into Mr Stonham's face. Mr Robertson straightened up the line of boys, pushing one or two of them hard, with rough hands, ready for their walk-past.

When, hurried away from the church by Miss Carmedy, they got back to school after the service, the caning of Joan Kenton seemed to have slipped Miss Carmedy's mind altogether. No one reminded her of the vicar's suggestion. To Susanah's watchful delight, Joan Kenton went unpunished.

Chapter Six

'The Lord forbade him to put off his hat to any, high or low.' Jonty had whispered the words to himself as he watched the vicar's drama with Joan Kenton unfold in the churchyard.

His father had brought him Quaker texts back from one of his train and bicycle preaching trips. Since then the words of George Fox had been echoing and re-echoing in Jonty's head. And here as he'd stood by the church porch and witnessed one of the vicar's customary dramas, he'd understood why the words had stayed with him.

This time, the vicar had been making that odd mannish girl Joan Kenton his target. Her brother, Vivian was in Jonty's class at school and was turn about, womanish in another direction. His hair was long and Jonty had heard that he baked for his mother while she was out selling from her basket the vegetables that the sister grew. It was even said he wore skirts and shawls in the house. The plaguing which he got was cut back when Joan was around, as she would give a beating to anyone who called her brother names.

Now, Jonty thought idly that it was a pity she could not treat the vicar to one of her beatings. His ears had pricked up, though, when, in castigating Joan, the vicar had scathingly quoted their own John Wesley and denigrated miners in his vicious tones. He noted that even the teachers were moved to anger at this. Miss Carmedy, the dragon lady from the girls' classes, had been standing behind Susanah Laydon Jones and was especially red. Rather like a rust-coloured horse, he thought.

The service had lasted a ticking age. It had been hard to concentrate on the vicar's homily about the need for humility, obedience and gratitude that the Lord had granted them the gift of service and the privilege of work. His voice droned on about the power of prayer, to make supplication to the Lord, so that He might intercede for their many sins. The rustle of shuffling feet echoed through the nave.

At the end of the service the vicar waited as they all filed past, averting their gaze from his face. The girls echoed genuflection in their ugly bob, the boys touched their imaginary forelocks. Now, after the incident with Joan, Jonty had George Fox in his mind, his voice in his ears. I too will refuse to put off my hat to any man, he thought. Never again.

He walked straight past.

'Stop, boy!'

The vicar coughed and spluttered, his head swelling like a balloon-headed snake. Johnson stood stiffly before him. Mr Robertson ordered Jonty to pay the courtesy to the vicar. He stood firm. The vicar raised his black stick and struck Jonty diagonally across the shoulders, the stick whistling in front of his face. He reeled with the blow but stayed where he was.

The vicar turned to the schoolmaster. 'I look forward, Mr Robertson, to seeing just what you will do about this . . . incident. Good morning!'

He spat out the words and stalked off.

John George was concerned that Freddy Stapleton had lost his familiar whistle. The singing and the whistling that witnessed his presence in the pit had stopped altogether in the recent months. Freddy's work alongside Caradoc Laydon Jones was now carried out in a silence only punctuated by grunts and short instructions.

John George stood in the cage as it sank down through the strata. Beside him Freddy rocked on the balls of his feet, his eyes wild and red-veined.

'What cheer, J G,' he said glumly.

'Not much cheer with you, Freddy. Looks like you've lost a bob and found sixpence!'

'Me head aches and me legs ache, but apart from that I'm bliddy marvellous.' Freddy's hand, grasping the heavy leather belt, was shaking.

'All that time spent down the Steam Mill don't help any, Freddy.'

'I know it. But working down this hole is bad enough without . . .' He lifted his head. Caradoc Jones was leaning against the bars in the corner of the crowded cage, his eyes open but, as always, looking inward.

Feet shuffled uneasily around them. In this job, so much depended on this relationship of 'marrers', or work partners. John George knew the feeling between these two men was dangerous. There was talk now of bad luck for the whole shift.

Caradoc was respected as a hard worker and a clever man, but feared for his powerful personality and envied for his known wealth. Freddy was an idle bugger but the men enjoyed his light-hearted banter and appreciated his 'risky' songs. True, the two men were different but down here differences had to be worked out from both sides or the relationship would crack and that was dangerous for all. John George knew trouble was coming and there was nothing he could do about it.

At bait time the sudden sound of uproar drove John George along to the section where Freddy worked with Caradoc.

'Get up, get up, you guzzler, fool!' Caradoc was half kicking, half nudging the prone figure of his partner, curled up beside a heap of stone in the dim half-light of the lamps. John George put himself between the two of them and looked down at Freddy, who was lying there, his eyes tight shut.

He put his hand on Freddy's plump shoulder. 'What did you do, Mr Laydon Jones?' he asked quietly.

'I did nothing. The man's a fool. Here!' He pushed over the metal water can into John George's face. The scent of gin made his nose tickle. 'Boozin'

36

down here too! He'll have us all dead. I'm seein' Stephenson. Nay, Carmedy. No more am I workin' with that fool. No more is he workin' in a seam where I am.'

John George heard a sigh from the curled-up figure beneath his hand and looked down again. One eye opened and winked up at him before it closed again and the breathing deepened almost to the heavy snore of a drunk.

'If you'd treat him more like a marrer and less like a pariah he wouldn't turn to drink.'

Caradoc snorted. 'A man's in charge of his own soul, Mr Clelland. He looks after it himself. He faces the Lord on Judgement Day alone. I'm not my brother's keeper. If he can't work, that's his trouble, not mine.' He leaned down and pulled the slack figure of Freddy Stapleton out of his way to the edge of the stall, and hafted his pick.

Infuriated, John George lunged at him but Caradoc stood neatly to one side. 'Now, Mr Clelland, isn't that against all your pretty ideas, raising your hand against your brother?'

That night Bea endured the full tale more than once before she held up her hand. 'Enough, J G! The man had his point. It must be dangerous for a man to turn up down there half drunk and finish himself off with his tea bottle.'

'But the man'll lose his job, Bea. Caradoc Jones will see to that. And, as Freddy says, it's bad enough down that hole without being shoulder to shoulder with a sanctimonious bigot who is obsessed with profit.'

Bea leaned over and patted her husband's arm. 'Leave it, J G! It mightn't happen, and if it does you can do sommat about it.'

He sighed deeply, then sat back and closed his eyes, only to open them at a great rattle, unusually, on the front door. Seeing Mr Robertson the schoolmaster, he became conscious that he was without his collar, and that his waistcoat was unbuttoned.

'Mr Clelland.'

'Yes?'

'I need to talk to you about Jonty. About his attitude. His behaviour.'

John George raised his eyebrows, then smiled slightly. He led his visitor through to the front room and offered him the most comfortable chair. Then he excused himself while he put on his collar and jacket, calling Bea to join him from upstairs where she had been sorting old papers.

Mr Robertson looked uneasily at them, from the round shining black eyes of the woman to the bright pale eyes of the preacher. 'Perhaps I should just speak with you, Mr Clelland.'

'Our son has two parents.'

'Very well.' He stood up and looked at them again as they stood shoulder to shoulder. 'Jonty has become increasingly self-willed in the classroom. All kinds of things. And then this morning . . .'

'One minute, Mr Robertson,' said Bea. 'Seeing as we're talking about our Jonty I think he should be here.'

Jonty came through the middle door, where he had been listening, his ear pressed quite hard to the wooden panel.

'I was speaking to your parents, Jonty, about your disgraceful behaviour this morning with the Reverend Stonham . . .'

Bea turned to Jonty, her face severe. 'So what is it you've been doing, Jonty? What did you do that was so bad that Mr Robertson has trailed all the way down here from Priorton on a Friday night?'

Jonty told his parents what had happened to Joan Kenton, and how that made him think about things. And how, walking out of the church, the words of George Fox had come seeping back into his mind. Then he said how he knew that he would not take off his hat nor touch his forelock for anyone, even the Reverend Stonham. '"The Lord forbade him to take off his hat to anyone, high or low." Isn't that what he said?'

Bea stood very still, arms folded across her broad chest, as he said the words. His father coughed – it might even have been a laugh, but Jonty was not sure.

John George looked at Mr Robertson, and then he spoke. Given the beliefs in their family and in the wider world, which was changing fast, no one could gainsay the wisdom of the words, he informed the teacher. Mr Robertson coloured up at this, and John George repeated, 'No one!' in a loud preacher's voice.

There was a pause and then he set about one of his milk and cream speeches, spiked up, as he'd say, with the cinnamon of sweet reason. About strategies of invading the citadel and arming yourself with the weapons of the enemy. How they, the enemy, were gatekeepers preventing the inheritance of the ordinary people in their own country.

Mr Robertson, forced to listen to what amounted to a sermon, stood grim-faced, wriggling his shoulders and shaking his head at the words.

John George turned to Jonty. 'Yet . . . yet, Jonty, there're times when we're obliged to render unto Caesar his own coin. Mr Robertson, what will you do with this reprobate?'

'Mr Stonham insists on an appropriate punishment and a complete apology. Tonight.'

'You may do as you think right,' said Bea, moving to stand beside her son. 'But on the understanding that we disagree both with your principle and your practice.'

Walking to the vicarage, Mr Robertson placed himself three feet away from Jonty, as though the boy were some germ he did not wish to catch. It was a mutual feeling. Jonty had had the punishment: his hand was bruised to the point of bleeding from the nine strokes he had been given in the privacy of the deserted schoolroom. Six for the insult to the vicar. Three for not agreeing to apologise immediately. The beating had been administered with a venom distilled in the grilling Mr Robertson himself had had to endure from Bea and John George. Now was the time for the apology.

They strode along the dark driveway, past the rustle and muffled snorts of the horses in the stables, to the broad front door. They were shown into a chilly, smoky study by Tillie Jaques, who had been at Jonty's school last year and was only twelve herself.

The Reverend Stonham came into the room, his face glistening and red as port wine, his breath exhaling a fruity scent. He listened to Jonty's very short apology and stood there for several minutes, allowing a long silence to grow.

Then the words rolled out. 'I have it on your teacher's authority that you are very clever, young man. But intellectual power, even that such as yours, is as ash in the pit without the grace of humility. There is no certainty,' he said, his voice lowering, 'that it will not come to be the abode of the Devil.'

Jonty examined the white froth at the corner of Mr Stonham's mouth. He wondered if perhaps it was a large crumb of bread. He was suddenly very hungry. It must be nearly suppertime now.

The voice rolled on. 'I have been informed that you are to go up to the grammar school, that your ambition is to enter the teaching profession. That you wish to attend one of our teaching colleges. Such ambitions in this modern world are, I admit, being nurtured in the most unlikely places. However, it might be salutary for you to remember that such ambitions would require, to be sure, a reference from my good self. The colleges are church institutions. People without respect for these institutions can hardly expect to be deemed suitable for teaching. I trust that you are fully aware of this?'

The temperature of the room, already cold, seemed to drop to below zero. As Jonty left the room, he managed to 'touch his forelock' in such a way as to raise Mr Stonham's anger yet again. The glare that this evoked was very satisfying.

Jonty parted from the silent Mr Robertson at the corner of his street. As he walked along the road his feet seemed to skim the frosted surface. He felt certain that he and George Fox were right. Neither of them, he thought piously, could be turned from the way of right action by the mere extremity of pain.

Nevertheless, there was great comfort in the bowl of broth that his father had ready for him on his return and the soothing stroke of his mother's fingers as she rubbed zinc and castor oil into his sore palms.

Chapter Seven

The worst thing for Susanah about going to school was always that she had to part with her brothers at the school gates. The great stone doorway swallowed them, sucking in their heads, arms and legs like grit going down a plughole. The word BOYS was carved in stone above their entrance: the word GIRLS carved above the one which Susanah went through. In summer the bold letters threw sharp shadows in the slanting morning sun.

Separate people they might be, but up till then they had been connected by the unseen web of word and glances, games and tears, work and play. The first rip in this spider-filament had happened at the gate of the school when Davey pushed her through the Girls doorway and went on through his.

Fighting was the normal daily custom in the boys' schoolyard, and the boys themselves were frequently beaten by the masters in the classroom. Davey would often come home with a black eye one day, a cane-striped hand the next.

Lew, taller even than Davey by the time he reached ten, never seemed to suffer either kind of assault. Even at home he managed to escape Caradoc's bubbling wrath. Lew was sly. He knew when to be seen, and when to be invisible. Davey was more open, more angry. He watched out for people, spoke up too much, and put himself at risk.

There would be whole days, as they all lived alongside Caradoc, when their father seemed not to notice them at all. He was fully taken up with his work in the shed and with his clocks. Spare time and energy would be spent on Ceiri, talking away to her in very rapid Welsh, too quick for the children as the years went on.

Then things would change and on some days his children would be the target for this too-close attention. Davey, being beaten by the teacher for some misdeed, would then stand in grave danger of a second beating from Caradoc to reinforce the teacher's message.

One spring day, Susanah was sitting watching her brother as he ate at the tea table. The bright May light was streaming through the window and fingering the strands of Davey's fair hair as he fiddled with his fork. Looking across at him, Susanah thought that soon he would not even be with her to go to the school door. He had taken the test and passed with flying colours. Now he could leave school early and start work at the pit. Soon. Her father had seen Mr Carmedy. It was all arranged.

Davey was reaching out for the last piece of bread on the plate in the centre of the scrubbed wooden table when his father caught his hand, much smaller than his own, and turned it over. 'Is it punishment the teacher gives you? What needs that?'

'I asked this question, Da.' Davey knew better than to twist his hand away. 'Mr Robertson, he said that the Norman people overwhelmed the Saxons who had fought back the Celtish people. And these people and their descendants remain there to this day, on the outside edges: the ignorant backward people of these islands, in Wales and Ireland . . .' The teacher's dry Scots tones resounded and echoed in Davey's voice.

Caradoc snorted down his nose, his clean soft hand still holding hard on to Davey's smaller one.

'. . . So I said that I didn't know about Ireland but in Wales the people weren't backward and ignorant, because I had been there. And they weren't. And that I was Welsh and, but for one lad, am top of the class.'

'What says he?'

'The only thing he says, Da, is to get out to the front, where I get the cane for talking out of turn.'

The silence pinged off the walls and licked around the ticking of the clocks. Davey finally and with some courage started to wriggle against the tightness of his father's clasp. 'Jonty Clelland, though, he got the cane, too, Da. He said to Mr Robertson, what about the Scots? They must be Celtish people, too, pushed out against the fringe. And were they ignorant and backward as well? So Mr Robertson heaved him out and gave him a good belting. More 'n me.'

Davey's hand was released and they all breathed easier. Ceiri spread some bramble jelly on Jenny's slice of bread, stroking the gleaming red stuff right to its very corners.

Susanah stared, thinking about the time Tollie and she had collected brambles from the tangle of bushes around the water pool. Tollie's full lips had been stained bright red from the berries, with a thicker, brighter red in the creases at the corner of his mouth. She had had to wipe his mouth with her apron, dipped in the pool.

Davey's voice began to sing out now, with more ease to it. 'That Jonty, Da. In trouble today again. For somebody always top, he talks himself into loads of trouble. Talks like the Bible or a history book and many a time gets a beltin' for it.'

'He can't fight for toffee! Jonty Clelland!' Lew's voice, already deeper than Davey's, was full of scorn. 'Won't fight in the yard when fights're on. A yeller coward. Lies there and takes it.'

'Not that often. Never hits nobody, don't get hit neither, when you reckon up,' said Davey. 'Talks his way into trouble but can jaw hisself out as well. In any case, he can't be yeller. He got six zingers for this lot today. Coming in on my side.'

Ceiri looked at Caradoc, who was wiping his plate with the last of his bread, making its flat white surface shiny clean, wasting nothing. 'That will be the preacher's son, Caradoc. Perhaps the boy has his father's gift. Now he talks well from the pulpit, that Mr Clelland. A fine flow.'

Caradoc scowled at her. 'How would you know? It is English he speaks. Barely a word you have, even now.'

'I can hear it, Caradoc,' she insisted, 'I can hear it. I hear the shining in his voice.'

The English language remained such a burden for her. Susanah had to talk for her in the market, and she refused flatly to go to any women's meetings at the chapel. Increasingly she stayed close to the house, sending Susanah out to the shops and the market with a list of items dictated by her.

Caradoc grunted. 'Same in the pit, that preacher. Talks on and on. More talk than work. A fool to himself. Got that drunken sot Stapleton back into the pit and now it's him that'll have to work marerrs with him. No one else will. A fool to himself.'

Susanah had an image of her father working on and on, down there under the earth, his brow furrowed, his mouth folded against speech. He would win the best coal, make sure he and his marrer had the biggest share of the credit between them. There'd be no drunkards, no backsliders beside him. He would see to that.

Later that day Susanah was sitting at the table writing the shopping list in her immaculate hand. Ceiri peered over her shoulder, leaning sideways to balance the growing Jenny who was really too big to rest on her hip.

Her mother's breath smelled sweet on Susanah's cheek. 'You have a pretty hand at writing, Susanah.'

'You, too, Mama.'

'Not in this tongue, though.'

'You could learn it. See how Dada speaks it now. Even preaches from the pulpit in his turn.'

'Ah, he's quick, your father. Very clever.'

'But not at writing.'

Susanah had seen him mark his name with a cross, on a note to do with lending money to some other pitman, written out by Davey. There had been concentration on his face, the tongue showing at the corner of the mouth, the awkward handling of the pen as he made his mark.

'No. No writing. No schooling he had. Not at school at all, your father. There was a rule that he should not go to school.'

'A rule?'

Ceiri's finger moved over Susanah's shoulder bone, making her look up into her mother's face. Reflected there in the large black irises she could see the face of a young man, large and open, crouching over a table which was too low for his bulk, carving something in wood. Ceiri blinked and the image was gone. Then she started clucking over Jenny, who was dragging her hair down from her bun. Susanah pulled her mother's face back round towards her so she could see the image of the young man again. She wanted to ask about the 'rule', the anger that was in him now, but her mother had wandered away from her, absorbed once more in Jenny.

Pleasing her mother was Susanah's pleasure. Those first few seasons in

Gibsley she gathered baskets of rosehips and blackberries for her, just to make Ceiri's eyes sparkle. With the fruit she made pots of jelly which went with the batches of bread she baked on Tuesdays and Fridays. The sticky jam would pull the summer sweetness of the hedges back into Susanah's mouth in the early winter dark. As well as this, Ceiri made bottled cordials which were a good change from milkless tea. Being with her on Tuesdays and Fridays for the baking, Susanah knew also that she fermented the juice still further and stored the dark liquor in a narrow section of roof space. Another secret to keep.

Coming in from school one day, a step ahead of Davey, Susanah found her mother on her hands and knees on the kitchen floor. She smelt of steeped blackberries tinged with alcohol and she was muttering about a bracelet, a lost bracelet. Her eyes were looking inwards. Susanah was reminded of the way those eyes had looked when Jenny was being born. The child herself was crying in the corner now, her face red and angry.

'What bracelet, Mama? What bracelet is it?' asked Susanah.

'He gave it me, Caradoc. Took me on this walk down by the wood path. A bracelet in gold. You ask your father.' Her voice lifted.

Davey looked across at the middle door which separated the kitchen from the front room where Caradoc was sleeping the brief sleep he took at the end of early shift. Soon he would be back among them, busy with his clocks or the welding of tin in the wash-house.

'I'll see to the little'n,' Susanah whispered. So saying, she picked up the child and brought her up to her face, large nose to small one, and blew gently through pursed lips. She knew this would soothe her. At last the long cry smoothed to sobs and then the sobs stretched into gurgles.

'Here, Ma.' Davey pulled his mother into a chair and quietened her by fashioning a bracelet from a scrap of string that he had in his pocket. 'Now then! Here's your bracelet.' He repeated the words over and over again, and she fingered the string as it lay on her wrist. He put his arm around her shoulder and rocked her back and forth, just as Susanah rocked Jenny. Her mother still seemed preoccupied.

A clattering knock at the back door made both their heads turn, then swing back to the middle door which protected the sleeping Caradoc. Susanah moved across towards the back door, holding Jenny over her hip, relishing the comfort of her strong little legs over her stomach and down her back.

A large girl, broad-faced and with clear grey eyes, looked down at her. 'Laydon Jones?'

Susanah nodded.

'I am Corella Clelland. My father says I'm to collect his watch?'

Davey stood close to Susanah's shoulder. The girl could not see into the room where Ceiri was slumped in the chair.

'He is not here,' said Davey. 'My father is not here.'

That was true. He was in but not here in the kitchen.

'The watch. I came for the watch.'

The voice was unflurried. Patient. Susanah had heard it soaring right to the roof in the descant at the chapel in recent weeks when, they said, the girl had come home from working in a school in Penrith, in Cumberland. Jonty's sister was a tall girl for such a light voice. Susanah thought her tone was softer than most of those who spoke the English which even now sounded harsh and clucking in her ears.

'It is not finished. My da said that one wasn't finished,' said Davey flatly. Caradoc must have instructed Davey what to say about Clelland's work.

The girl looked down at Susanah, across at Davey and smiled slightly, showing ragged, uneven teeth. 'I'll come another time.'

Davey shut the door behind her and they both turned their backs and leaned on it.

Susanah was ten in that summer before Davey started work at the pit and Jonty Clelland started at the grammar school. On Davey's first day at work, Susanah got up early with him. She had heard him stir and watched the dark outline of his figure moving against the crack of light that lipped through the rooftiles in their bedroom.

Their mother was already in the kitchen, stoking the fire and adjusting a steaming kettle over its hot glow. She had a thick shawl over her head and shoulders, on top of her sleeping dress. Using her inside eye folded within her, Susanah could usually see the younger woman that Ceiri had once been. On this dark morning she saw the older woman to come. Her arms and shoulders felt cold, icy cold, and she shivered.

Davey sat down at the table in front of the tea and bread Ceiri had put out for him. Susanah hitched up on to the bench beside him. His long dark eyes with their heavy brows stared at her over the rim of the cup, then shifted over to the hearth where his boots stood. They were old ones of Caradoc's, polished black for him by his mother. They were too big, too thick and too strong for Davey but Caradoc had said there was no money for new boots.

In five minutes the boots were laced up and Davey had pulled on a thick jacket which had also once been his father's. The jacket buried him completely as Ceiri stood before him. She opened his coat on one side and tucked in the bottle of cold tea; then she opened it on the other side and inserted the tin of jam sandwiches.

They walked with Davey to the gate, then his mother gave his shoulder a little push. Susanah walked beside him to the end of Selby Street backs. Around them the lights of the other houses flickered in the half-dark and there was a feeling of bustle, in spite of the early hour.

Davey turned and looked at his sister.

'Ye'll have to stop here, S'anah. Yeh can't come no further.' He was speaking English, unusual between them so close to home.

'Remember everything about it, Davey,' Susanah instructed. 'Everything. So you can tell me. Everything.'

He laughed. 'The only way to satisfy you would be to let you go down instead of me. You always ask questions. The pit? Ye're welcome to it, I can tell you.'

'Don't be daft!' Laughing, she pushed him on his way, imitating the little push her mother had given him at the back gate.

Walking back along the lane she thought that perhaps she really did want to go down into the pit. Another level, another world. The clank and whine of the pit wheel had been a long chorus in their lives, here and in Wales.

She wondered how Davey would find the grinding noise of the cage as it swooped down into the dark earth. Closing her eyes she could see the pitch-black galleries; the lamps like dull stars against the black envelope of the earth. His breath would be taken from him. She could hear the creak of gear and the clatter of ponies on walkways, the echoing cries of the pitmen as they called to each other in the dark.

'Woah, lass! Who's dreaming, then?' Betty's father had her by the shoulders. He was wearing a thick jacket, close-fastened against the cold.

'Out early, Susanah Laydon Jones?' His blue eyes, sober, were more watery and less sparkling.

'Our Davey's started work today, Mr Stapleton.'

'Well, don't you worry, charver. I'll keep an eye on him. His da in back shift, is he?'

Nothing had been said, but Susanah knew Davey was relieved that he was working opposite shifts from Caradoc. Mr Carmedy had put Freddy on the opposite shift too, to keep him apart from Caradoc and Susanah was happy to think that someone, even Mr Stapleton, would be there to keep an eye on her brother.

When she got back to the house, her mother had newspaper on the table and was giving a final clean and polish to Caradoc's boots which she had cleared of mud and dirt the night before. Soon the boots were very clean, even shining here and there. Her eyes glittered with tears as she smiled across to Susanah.

'Don't I wish I had as many pennies as times I've done this, S'anah? Now there's Davey's, too.'

'Can I not do Davey's boots?'

Her mother ignored this, rubbing harder at a perfectly clean heel. 'Young he is to go down there. A child.'

'What about Dada? Wasn't he that young?' The more her fear of her father turned to dislike, the more curious she was about him and why her mother loved him.

'Younger, I think. Perhaps ten. A little trapper boy down there twelve hours opening and shutting the traps in the dark. Not a soul to talk to.' She rubbed away in silence, the clocks ticking round at five o'clock.

'Ten, he would be,' she repeated finally. 'Do you know he had even worked before then? Around places on the land. Farms and things and such even before then. He had no life. Called names, love-begot like he was . . .'

'Love-begot?' Susanah rolled the word round, liking it.

'It's having no father. No father that is named. The mother not married.'

'There is another word, Mama. Joan and Vivian Kenton, they call them b –'

'Don't say it, sweetheart. Love-begot is a soft word for a hard thing. They had a hard time, his sister Bel and him.'

'His sister?' The name picked about at the back of her memory. There had been a lot of shouting once in the house in Wales, when a letter came.

'Your auntie, as well. She was such a pretty little thing, like a butterfly but strong and hard as an oak tree. Stronger than him, I'd sometimes think . . . well, there you are, Auntie Bel and himself shunned, their mother shamed. No school, no letters for him to learn. There was a rule about that from their father. School for her, none for him. It was her I knew, at the school . . .' She took a soft rag to the boots and finished the perfect shine. 'Then, as I say, your da was in the pit at ten, opening and shutting doors for the wagons. A little lad! There in the dark. And the size of him! And how he managed to grow so big, spending all his life down there, I don't know.'

'Did he get stuck?' Susanah asked, agape, 'Did he ever get stuck?'

Ceiri laughed at the thought, and Susanah saw the young woman, the girl again. Long black curling hair. 'Times he did, S'anah! Times he did. You ask him.'

Ask him? She wouldn't dare! Susanah thought how preposterous the suggestion was and saw for the first time that because she loved him, her mother would never understand the growing loathing her daughter felt for Caradoc.

She watched as Ceiri put clean paper on the hearth and placed the boots, filled as they were with the shadow of her father's foot, exactly in the centre. She passed her arms across them, like some magician, a smile on her face. Susanah's eye caught the string bracelet made for her by Davey many months before. 'You've still got Davey's bracelet.'

Ceiri fingered it. 'He's a good boy. Like his father. He gave me a bracelet, too. Gold. They call it Welsh gold.'

'So where's that, then? That bracelet? You never wore it.'

'It went.'

'Where did it go?'

Ceiri's eye shifted to the fireplace where the kettle was jetting steam. 'Now look at that! We'll be scalded to death.' She pulled the sleeve of her dress over her hand and lifted the steaming kettle out on to the hob. 'Now we need to get on. There's the washing to sort. So much to do.'

That night, Davey came home and went to sleep over his tea, his hands folded over his face. After that first morning he would not let Susanah walk alongside him on the lane. He cleaned his own boots before he went to bed. She was not allowed to touch them.

Chapter Eight

For Susanah, school was a great feast. There was so much you could do. You sat on the hard wood seat copying with a dipped pen: fine line up, broad line down; neat patterns on a page. You could set up a whispering chant towards yourself, towards your heart: passages from the history book, passages from the story book 'learned off' by the same heart. Then you could say them out loud for everyone, that bit of your heart on public display. It was all so easy, such a joy.

Betty Stapleton, who had shown Susanah how to curtsey to the vicar, was often made to sit beside her. Susanah's job was to show Betty her letters, to make her recognise them. Betty's eyes, those round shining saucers of china-blue, did not see the letters properly, no matter how much Susanah showed her. When she drew them they were the wrong way round, upside down, and always in the wrong order.

Susanah had warmed towards Betty Stapleton. It was true that she smelled of boiled potatoes and washing soda and her hair was never combed, but Susanah loved to show her things, to explain.

One day, Susanah took Betty down to the water pool to show her the frogs. She kneeled down so they could see their faces in the glossy surface.

'Here, Betty.' She leaned over and wiped her face and hands with the corner of her own pinny, as though she were Tollie, or even Jenny. Betty's pink skin glowed out and the black tidemark at the outer edges of her face and neck receded to insignificance. Looking down again she could see her face glowing white in the water as the pink melted, being sucked away by the dark surface.

After that time at the water pool, Betty obviously did the same under the single tap at home, and turned up at school, pink skin, tidemark gone and all.

Betty's clothes were always worn and holed; intended for larger and older bodies, they had to be hitched up and tied on. On the way to school and in the yard before the first bell, she often had to endure the pummelling and name-calling that was other people's fun.

She rewarded this treatment with a small smile for everyone, showing her sharp white teeth. Lew said she was half daft. Susanah talked about her to her mother, who said that Betty showed them all up, turning the other cheek like she did.

Susanah called for Betty on the way to school, making her way round the heaps of scrap wood in the long yard behind the Stapleton house. Betty's two brothers spent a lot of time breaking the scrap wood into firewood, which they hawked around Gibsley and further afield.

The Stapleton house was warm enough. As Betty's father worked at the pit at least there was coal for a good fire. However the furniture, frequently pledged against money he borrowed in the town, came and went in a random fashion, so the rooms were often very bare. Betty's mother would sit by the roaring fire in the emptied room for hours at a time. The house was not clean, not as clean, even, as the privy in which Susanah had practised the sign of the cross.

One Thursday afternoon three weeks later Susanah was playing five-stones with Betty's brothers John and Armer on the flagged floor of the kitchen. Betty was at her left, her warm potato-smelling body leaning up against Susanah, watching as she beat the boys in double quick time. Mrs Stapleton was sitting on the single chair by the fire as usual, watching the flames.

'What then? What then? Beatin' my lads at fivestones?' Mr Stapleton roared into the room, bringing with him the smoke and the warmth of the public house. Everything in the room rattled and shook. He demanded to join the game. When Susanah defeated him too, he laughed, then hauled her and the others to their feet. He pulled his wife out of her chair, then set them all in a ring around him to play the roses game in the empty, echoing room. After that, he kept them in the circle while he sang a lilting song about a girl and her lover. Susanah had never heard such songs, such words of extravagant romance. As he sang Mr Stapleton turned from her to Betty, looking them both deeply in the eyes as though they were that girl in the song. They all laughed helplessly. Even Mrs Stapleton wore a faint smile.

Then the song stopped and they all stood still, watching him. His face was red, his eyes were gleaming. He was swaying on his feet.

'Enough now, Freddy.' Mrs Stapleton's voice was weary, but still soft, like Ceiri's when she spoke to Tollie when he was naughty.

'Enough, not enough! I have not shown this bairn the trick, the magic I can do!'

They all looked up at him. 'Did tha know I can make a frog's head vanish, pet?'

Susanah shook her head.

'This little Jones lass, this wizard at the game of fivestones, this daughter of the Welsh wizard Caradoc, who can make a man's job vanish like Scotch mist! Could tha believe it, she's never even seen Freddy's own vanishing trick?'

There was a murmur of resistance from Mrs Stapleton. Betty and the two boys stood motionless, suddenly very stiff. Then, out of one of his sagging pockets he pulled something and hid it from their sight with his other hand.

Slowly he revealed the bulbous head, then one round eye, then the other, of the frog. Finally, the other hand moved and they could see its twitching body. 'Now, Miss Jones, you see how I magic the head of the frog away?'

He flourished his arm up above his head, then brought the frog to his mouth. Suddenly he bit off the frog's head and spat it into a corner, blood on his lips. Betty and the boys started to cry and their mother wailed. Susanah ran right through the door and up the Back Street, where her vomit spouted on to the wall at the back of the privies. Then she stood there watching the sick spill down the red brick like sour milk.

Outside her own back door she heaved to get her breath back to normal, then walked into the kitchen quite calmly, telling no one what she had seen. Not even Davey, although she was sure he would be interested.

Her father looked up when she walked in. 'Where've you been?' he said sharply.

She glanced at her mother. 'Playing down the road. At Betty's.'

'You want to stay away from that house. Slatterns and drunkards.' Caradoc leaned to one side while his wife poured him tea from a huge pot. 'He's finished today at the pit, that Stapleton. Feller turns up still with drink on him. No strength on him. And more of the demon in his water bottle. Useless. Score went right down because of him. We were all losing money.'

'Did he get into trouble?'

'Carmedy finally fired him. There's mutterings, but he'll stay fired. That fool Clelland's talking about action. Means inaction. Strike. But they won't. The man's a danger. They know that.'

'The poor woman. That poor family, Caradoc. His wife, she seems so worn. Such a face, she seems so old too soon. And I only see her the odd time she gets to the chapel.'

'You'd never see him there, in any chapel. A godless man.'

Freddy Stapleton stayed sacked from the pit for being drunk on shift. Carmedy had found another partner for Caradoc, an abstemious Cornishman called Sargant, and together they went on to become the highest earners on their shift.

Freddy returned to the pit to work now and then, but never underground where he was deemed dangerous. The Stapleton house became more permanently bare. The scrap wood in the yard had to be used for the family's own fire when the coal ran out and the boys went with Mr Stapleton picking on the heap for small scraps of waste coal to keep the house warm at all. But, despite her father's warnings and her memories of the frog incident, Susanah would sneak back to spend time with Betty, who still laughed in the face of life's hardships.

Chapter Nine

John George Clelland was a humble man. Sometimes he was a funny man. When he loved, he loved with the energy of a Titan. He loved Corella and Jonty as though they held the secrets of the universe in their young hearts. He loved Bea with a passion which he often told her was equal to the love he had for Jesus. He could not conceive one without the other. He would only concede that it was different. As different, he would tell her, as a melody from a thousand flutes compared with a glorious chorus of birdsong.

Jonty was now almost engulfed by his new life as a grammar school boy, mocked as a snob in Gibsley and mimicked as a yokel at the city school. He was exhausted in the evenings as he alighted from the train at Priorton and set out for the long walk to Gibsley. He was fascinated by the knowledge, held like a fly in amber, in the heavy books he carried to and fro. He grew even closer to his mother as she helped him with his books and checked his homework.

But Jonty still liked to watch his father and admired the way he went about his days, at home, at work and particularly the way he approached the chapel.

A good deal of talk went on at the meetings about 'salvation'. There was much discussion about 'being saved', and Jonty had seen people coming forward, their eyes in what was known as Light. He had witnessed people affirming their conversion, declaring they saw the Light in this or that place.

He saw his father watching all this, accepting. Sometimes, though, in talking to Jonty, John George would agree that people 'pretended' the experience to make the drama. Even this was the Lord's working, though. Even thus, he would say, they come to the Lord.

Jonty knew all this drama meant little to his father. It meant much less to him than the books and pamphlets that he read and the embattled discussions he had on his travels around the district, when he talked to all kinds of people, got into all types of argument.

Despite this, he was a loyal member of their chapel, taking a full part in its life and he met his obligation to do town and village missions, where he preached in the open to people. Jonty liked to go with his father on these missions.

One winter Saturday they were in Priorton, walking in Southgate, a strange place which turned day into night and night into, it was said, hell on earth.

John George looked calmly about him as he walked, his hand on Jonty's shoulder. Jonty wondered whether he would ever reach his father's height. At school now he felt like a midget. Even the boys of his age were growing taller than him and leaving him behind.

The two of them were well wrapped against the freezing night. The air was so cold that the hot air from the public houses was crystallising and hanging like steam around their doors.

Some of the miners they met, still in their working clothes, knew John George from the pit and called across in a friendly enough way.

'Now, JG? Savin' souls today?' one of them grinned.

'Now, Bernard, is yours on offer?' his father threw back.

'Nah. The Old Man's got it. Give it him last time I was laid off, to get me job back. It worked. Got set on the following Monday.'

'Jesus can save even a soul pledged to the Devil.'

'Nah. Never.'

'True, I tell you.'

The man laughed and came across and shook John George by the hand, but seemed no nearer to being saved.

Walking with his son, John George talked of the things that were always in his mind. Looking around him he held forth on the scandal of poverty among so much wealth, the money that spewed out of the dark places of the earth, delivered by the sweat and toil of working men. He spoke of boiling-up of talent and product in the modern world where there should be no poverty on the bottom rung, no temptation to drunkenness to escape from brutal toil, no gambling to paint a gilded image of life at the pitch or toss of a penny, no looking at the feet or in the gutter for the coin of gold. His voice rolled on as they plodded the street.

Long accustomed to the litany, the words flowed over Jonty. But he was warmed by the sheer sound of his father's voice as they walked along Southgate. The narrow street was stinking and cold, despite the steam dripping down the windows of the public houses which lined it.

John George's hand tightened on his shoulder as they heard the noise of struggle in an alleyway. The inward hang of the houses made its entrance night-dark. John George pushed his son behind him and walked straight into the alley as though it were lit by seventy-seven torches. Jonty followed close behind.

Two men were rolling on the ground, fighting. The one on top was a muscular whipcord of a man with a heavy moustache. The man underneath was rounder, both in face and body. Two other men were looking on eagerly, their fists and arms shadowing and mimicking the plunging actions of the topmost fighter. His opponent lay there like a sack of potatoes, allowing himself to be punched and slugged, his hands flailing loosely.

Jonty gulped away the leaden feeling inside him. He didn't quite know whether he was afraid of fighting. He saw it many days in the yard at school; there were battles about the slightest offence. He himself had been pulled into fights for something he had said. But the fighting always made him feel sick in the heart and in the brain. He could see no point in it and it frightened him.

Now he watched petrified as his father became involved in a street fight. He watched him as he strode towards the tangle of legs and arms which was two men. Tall as he was, he seemed suddenly two feet taller. The two spectators were thrown to one side like chaff in the wind. Then he lifted the attacker by the shoulders and put him gently up against a wall as though he were a garden rake. Bending down, he hauled the portly man off the ground and cocked an eye at Jonty, who moved closer and lent a shoulder to the enterprise. With one arm round Jonty's shoulder and the other round John George's neck, the stout man was half walked, half dragged out of the alley into the lighter, greyer air of the street.

In the light they could see that it was Freddy Stapleton, reeling drunk.

The three mile walk home did little to sober him and when they arrived at the Stapleton house Jonty was embarrassed to find the girl, Susanah Laydon Jones, there. She was sitting on a low stool at the door, brushing the hair of the Stapleton girl with long graceful strokes, her wrist turning at the bottom to twist it to a curl.

She'd just finished the business of washing and towelling Betty's hair when the back gate clicked. She watched the long top hairs, dry now, floating in the breeze, before she looked up.

Betty's father was being half dragged, half carried through the gate by Mr Clelland the preacher on one side of him and that boy Jonty Clelland on the other. Freddy Stapleton was muttering away to himself, his face a pattern of red and black bruising.

Mr Clelland's eyes, bright as the sun reflected on winter water, asked, 'Is your mammy in, young woman?'

Jonty was surprised at the anger he felt when his father mistook Susanah for the daughter of the house. He could not see how he could make that error, not at all. 'Not that one, Dad. That's Susanah Laydon Jones. Her dad's the one you're always on about. It's the other one.'

'You, then! Is your mammy in?'

Betty jumped up out from Susanah's knees and nodded, pointing to the house behind her. Susanah moved the stool from the threshold and watched while they heaved Mr Stapleton through the narrow doorway. Susanah and Betty crept in after them to watch.

Mrs Stapleton was standing by the grate, a low spark the only sign of fire in the dingy room.

'Your man's the worse for drink, missis.'

Freddy slithered to the floor and placed his hands carefully on the greasy stone to stop him falling further. He frowned and looked closely at the back of his hands as though they were some strange animal.

'Me son and I were missionin' up in Priorton, missis. In Southgate, a devilish place if ever there was one. And here's Freddy up an alley getting the beltin' of his life. Something about a horse that won. Or lost. Not quite sure which. Half dead when we got there, the other man was such a big feller –

sprawled on'm, squeezin' the life out of 'm.' He smiled slightly, looking down at Freddy's preoccupied form. 'So we were moved to save him, weren' we, Jonty?'

The girls in the doorway snickered as Jonty's brown skin turned red.

John George dipped into an inside pocket and drew out a book. He stared hard at Freddy's wife until she raised her eyes and looked at him. 'I watched Freddy, there on the floor in that stinkin' hole, and I heard this song in my head. Do you know it?'

Then in the dark smoky kitchen he began to sing in a high voice, sweet for a man. Susanah had noticed that sweetness in the chapel.

> 'There is a brother
> Whom someone should save.
> Throw out the lifeline,
> Throw out the lifeline,
> Someone is sinking today.'

On the floor, Freddy twitched and started to sing the song about the lover and the girl.

'Will you pray with me?'

The preacher knelt down and they all came across to kneel beside him. Jonty was slightly in front of Susanah. His hands, folded together, were golden brown, his springy hair trembled on the air as he bowed his head.

John George's voice, unlike his everyday voice, intoned the prayer with the practice and full flow of the preacher. 'Dear Lord. We have here Thy poor servant who has strayed from Thy ways like the lost sheep for whom we should all care. He has been ground down by poverty and lack of common care from his brothers. We ask Thee for a second chance, not just for him, but for his brothers who have let him and his dear ones fall by the wayside. For his and all our salvations we earnestly entreat Thy strength and support.'

For Susanah, the preacherly words smelled too much of chapel in the little bare house. The voice was light no longer, but thick and rich like black treacle. The room felt too hot, despite the tiny fire. Behind her lids she could see again the lacey stone screen of St Andrew's and the bulging sinews of the figure on the cross, moulded in plaster. Her fingers itched to make that magic sign.

'Amen,' intoned John George.

Only Susanah didn't join in saying it. She raced for the door and down the Back Street to her own house, just as she had on the night of the headless frog.

She leaned against the kitchen door, her mouth watering at the spicy smell of teacakes.

Her mother greeted her with flour on her nose. 'That you, Susanah? Don't you know I need you here when I bake on a Saturday?'

'Sorry, Mama. I was playing with Betty.'

56

'Well, there's only the washing-up to do now and the scullery to clean. So you can get right down to it.'

Tackling the mountain of dishes was a relief for Susanah. She put on the black apron and set about the task with a will, trying to wipe the church image out of her head with every rub. Her head was ringing with music, not with the sound of the salvation song, but with the lilting song of sweethearts.

Her mother went to the door to watch Tollie and Jenny wrestling together in the back yard. Caradoc was absent. Most Saturdays now he and Miss Antrobus did their Bible reading. Susanah breathed easier, but she could still feel her mother leaning against the door jamb, waiting keenly for his return.

That night, John George Clelland was all a-fizz, bubbling over with the event of the mission. 'A good man, Bea. A good man, Freddy Stapleton. I suddenly knew! Stinking of drink and dirty, too, but a good man. I felt it in my bones. Here, Bea, here is a man I was called to save. I will bring him away from the drink and back into work. I will pave his way. I know it, Bea!'

Jonty watched his mother as she poured her husband's tea into his thick white pot. She was sturdy and strong, but all her movements had grace, even pouring tea from a heavy brown teapot. She watched John George, bright-eyed, as he came to sit close to her, his shoulder to hers on the long settle. Like this, Jonty felt, it was as though they were welded together. One person.

The passion between them, this welding together, had happened at other times: when John George had been to a particularly satisfying meeting; when he had finished writing a sermon where the words had clicked into place like magic; when he had buzzed up with some new idea from his reading and she had capped or challenged it, and they had come to some new joint view.

At these times, as though pushed from behind, Jonty felt impelled to leave them. Corella, too. They left them to their joined arms, their shared laughter.

At Jonty's grammar school, they thought nothing of girls and less of women. Many of the masters were bachelors and the boys mirrored their teachers' contempt for women in grosser ways. Jonty resisted all this. He was glad he had a sister, even if she did call him pompous and tease him for being a preacher before his time. He was glad his mother was there to bring laughter into the house. Sometimes he felt sour about the way his mother and father welded themselves together, separate from Corella and himself. When he was little he had cried about it, not understanding and getting churned up. Those times Corella would creep into bed with him and warm him from the chill that came from inside himself.

The next day he was usually glad that his parents were like that, that his mother was there to light his father's eyes when he came in black and weary from the pit. They were good together.

Sometimes John George came home in a preaching mood. 'The interesting thing about the parable of the talents is that word, talent,' he said one day to Jonty.

'Talent?' said Jonty.

'Yes. Known for a coin. A piece of gold. The feller who translated it all those years back need not have used that word, but in choosin' he brought in wealth o' meanin'.'

'But I thought it was gold, real gold. I learned that when I was little. In Sunday School.'

'Miss Antrobus? She was always good on earthly rewards for earthly virtue.' His father chuckled.

Bea looked over her book towards them, as they sat talking by the fire. 'By that count, Caradoc Jones must be ten times blessed of the Lord, in her eyes.' Her tone was dry.

'Caradoc Laydon Jones is a good case, Jonty. A man of many talents, many gifts. Each one o' those gifts he's used, developed through the years. Profiting like he does just comes alongside that. The profit is not in the gold, Jonty, it is in the heightening of skill, the building of the self.'

'Like me,' said Jonty eagerly. 'I'm multiplying the talent given me, by working so hard at my reading and studying, then I'll know more 'n more. Then I'll get on at the Grammar School. Developing my talents like this, I'll go on to college like Corella . . .'

John George put his hand on his son's shoulder, the smallest of smiles on his lips. 'Now, that's a worthy way to think of it, but 'ware the sin of pride.'

'Sometimes, if we didn't know you better I'd think you sound just the faintest bit . . .' Bea smiled, searching for a kind way to say it, '. . . lacking in humility.'

Jonty went red. 'I agree with you that humility in offering forth your developing talents is essential. I agree with that.'

Still his father smiled, meeting Bea's gaze.

Beneath the table Jonty's hand clenched into a fist. Then he thought of Mr Monroe, his new Latin teacher, whose house he visited on Wednesdays for extra lessons. To pay for the lessons his mother copied out papers for him.

A radical clergyman who attended some of their meetings, the Reverend Monroe was of entirely different temper to Mr Stonham.

'Mr Monroe says that "knowledge lifts the veil from the eyes of the poor and makes them see the reality of their situation in the brightness of the day. Only then will they take the helm of their own lives and steer the ship of their own fate."' Jonty chanted the words like a poem.

Bea sighed and smiled at him at the same time.

He drove on. 'He wrote in my autograph book: "I am the master of my fate, I am the captain of my soul." Jonty was angry now, offended at his parents' humour, their smiling understanding, their closeness. He stood up, threw on his coat and slammed out of the door, hearing and ignoring Bea's appeal to return.

He wandered on to the green behind what Bea called the 'brick outhouses', on a flat stretch beside the river where a game of football was in progress. The boys were mostly his age, or a bit younger. He recognised some of them from the Elementary School. That place seemed as far away from him now as the earth from the sun.

A young boy, not much more than eight, was playing somewhere near the centre. He was flying like the wind. It was as though the ball, a rough thing tied together with string, was attached to his toe by elastic, so he could pull it back towards himself at will. This lad made it look so easy. The other boys, all older and heavier than he was, were great carthorses in comparison. The ball landed at Jonty's feet and the boy ran across and picked it up. He just stood there, flicking the heavy ball from knee to knee, then on to his head and back again into the air in a brilliant display before he went off to join the game again.

'Now, Jonty.' Davey Laydon Jones had materialised beside him.

'Now, Davey.' Jonty nodded, keeping his eye on the game. The ways of the two boys had diverged in the recent years and he thanked God the pit was not his fate. He knew he had not that kind of courage. He thought that Davey had that courage, had it without being brawny or boastful. He had seen it at school, when Davey used to stand up to the lugubrious Mr Robertson.

The game had now dissolved into dispute. The players were jumping up and down in the cold, rubbing their upper arms with their hands and slapping their thighs, their breath solidifying and mingling on the air.

Jonty turned again to look at Davey. He thought the other boy had shrunk somehow, his face looked paler and more bony.

'Do you get to see much football?' Davey was asking, his tone friendly.

'I've seen Priorton play a few league matches this season.'

'The league's in a mess, seems like. Matches cancelled here and there. Need to get themselves organised.'

'Me and me dad turned up for that Crook Howden match that was cancelled. Got wet through for nothing.'

'Have you seen Middlesbrough play? Great players, they have.'

'Risky watching them this season, according to the papers. There's smallpox over there, isn't there?'

'Took our Tollie to see them play at Leadgate. We didn't catch smallpox, just a good drenchin' in the rain. Got soaked through. But that's what's got him going with all this.' He turned his head towards the pitch, where the match had restarted. 'So what d'you think of the centre forward?'

'The young flyer? Very talented. Plays the others off the field, big as they are. Is he from round here?'

Davey laughed. 'Ye canna see who it is, can ye? It's our Tollie, me young brother.'

Jonty remembered a younger brother, practically a baby the last time he had seen him, round-faced and curly-haired, trailing along somewhere behind Susanah. 'Well, he's talent, for sure. Don't you play?'

'I used to, but the pit leaves me buggered . . .'

They watched Tollie weave his way round the opposition as though they were skittles put there for his convenience.

'He needs to be in a proper team, sommat more organised. Doesn't bring him on, it always being so easy,' said Davey.

Jonty laughed. 'A team? How'd you organise a whole team of people just to show off your Tollie's talent? Even when you'd done that, you'd need another team to play against. Then you'd need to join the Wear Valley league to get the competition, I suppose.'

'Yes, there's that league. These lads are just back street players with lumps of stone for goalposts. Couldn't compete.'

They watched in silence for a moment, clapping when Tollie scored yet another goal. Jonty turned and put a hand on Davey's shoulder, then lifted it off quickly, embarrassed. 'Why can't the chapel look into it, getting the pitch and the lads into the league? A proper pitch? There's funds, and my dad says they're always wanting ways of pulling folks from sin. It'd keep the lads away from the public houses and the pitch and toss?'

'Too busy praying and praising, up at chapel,' said Davey sourly.

'No. Some of them . . . my dad is always talking about the obligation . . . to help the p- to help. He would put his oar in. And your dad . . .'

Davey gave Jonty a heavy-browed scowl at that.

Jonty thought of Mr Laydon Jones, that clever and inventive man, so talented. Apart from all the rest of the things he could do, he was a brilliant preacher, if your tastes were for images of hellfire and damnation and the sins of the world. He couldn't half make them squirm, folks like Miss Antrobus. He even made Bea shudder sometimes, and that took some doing. And he did have high respect in the chapel for paying his tithe, which amounted to more than any other member. 'What if I tell my dad to talk to your dad about it? Between them . . .'

'Suit yourself.' Davey shrugged and turned again to concentrate on the game. 'To my eye nobody can talk to 'm.'

Jonty felt a bubbling excitement as he watched young Tollie. Then he felt a twinge of envy. His ears buzzed with the mutter of appreciation from the onlookers as the boy zigzagged about and outmanoeuvred the other lads. He thought it must be very warming to have the approval of your own kind, to use your talents immediately for their pleasure.

Chapter Ten

Susanah had loved Miss Carmedy, her teacher for her last two years at Gibsley school. Miss Carmedy was never in the village, apart from the times she was actually in the school or at church; she was one of the Reverend Stonham's Church of England flock. She lived with her brother, who was undermanager at White Pool Pit, a mile away in Cranaham village and she arrived at school in her own pony cart.

Miss Carmedy was a tall woman, and very narrow. Her face was like a spoon, her tiny nose like a quirky surprise. But her skin was soft and pink like a baby's and she had delicate fingernails on narrow fingers.

She had taught Susanah to read very quickly, and to love books of every kind. She had taught her to write in the decent copperplate that her mother so admired. She had shown her how to draw by making her look and look at things like a single flower, an apple or a cabbage. 'Now, Susanah,' she would ask, 'is there more shadow or less shadow above the edge of the leaf? What happens when the light hits it where it swells? What do you see? What do you see? Draw just what you see!'

So Susanah would look and look until her eyes were sore and in the end her apple would look like an apple and her cabbage would be so cabbage-like it would look as if you could crunch it.

Susanah was not in the end unhappy about leaving school; she loved to be at home with her mother. But her leaving displeased Miss Carmedy.

Susanah tried to explain how essential it was for her to be at home. 'There's a lot to do, Miss Carmedy. My mother is not so strong.'

The teacher continued to scowl. 'You have so much to do, Susanah Laydon Jones, so much to do here.'

When Miss Carmedy called at the house it was fortunate that Caradoc was at work. Ceiri jumped up like a cat when she saw the schoolmarm's tall, neat figure through the kitchen curtains. She kept her standing in the narrow lobby that separated the kitchen from the scullery and, in a flutter, told Susanah to go in. Crouched behind the door, Susanah strained to make sense of their voice murmur; her mother sounding high and plaintive, Miss Carmedy low and urgent.

Then Ceiri opened the door and Susanah fell into the lobby. Miss Carmedy was pushing a pile of rather battered volumes and a brand new blue-covered book into Ceiri's hands.

'Tell your teacher that she is not to give you anything. That your father would not like it,' her mother instructed, tight-lipped.

Susanah translated the message.

'Your mother speaks no English, Susanah?' asked Miss Carmedy.

'No, miss.'

'But you've been here so long, how long?'

'Four years, miss.'

'But how does she manage?'

Ceiri grasped Susanah's hand. 'What is she saying? What is she saying?' she demanded.

'She says how do you manage without the English?'

'Tell her she is to mind her own affairs.'

'What was that, Susanah?' Miss Carmedy heard the tone, her cheeks reddening.

'She just says that I should not take them.' Susanah took the blue book from her and fanned the pages open. Its fine creamy pages seemed hungry for a pencil's mark. She turned to Ceiri, willing her with all her might to let her have the book.

'Tell her that it is a present, Susanah. I give all the children a present when they leave school. And the books are just old ones I've no use for now. For you to keep reading.'

'It is a present . . .' Susanah repeated the message.

Her mother looked from the blue book and back up to her face. 'Well . . .' She took it from her, holding it by the corner as if it might burn her fingers. Then she put it back into Susanah's hands. 'Well, the old books would just waste. And perhaps you could have this one too, but you must be quiet about it . . .'

Suddenly they were whirled to one side as Lew came bursting in from the Back Street. This flurry gingered Ceiri into action and all at once she was shooing Miss Carmedy down the yard as though she were some recalcitrant duckling. She needed no English for that.

That night Caradoc came in late from a chapel meeting where he had argued violently and unsuccessfully against the use of chapel funds to roll a football pitch on ground offered by Carmedy on behalf of the colliery. There was also a proposal to buy a new ball and goalposts. But John George Clelland had worked skilfully on the committee to make sure his proposal was carried and Caradoc had been frustrated.

Lew waited until his father had sat down before, his face all innocence, he pulled the blue book from its hiding place, under a pile of blue towels and told Caradoc about Miss Carmedy's visit. His father's face set hard. He glanced from Susanah to Ceiri, his gaze eventually settling on his wife. 'You want nothing letting teachers in my house, woman. Nothing!'

'It was only . . .'

'Only nothing. Once in, and they have your soul, teachers!'

Caradoc seemed about to say something else, but stood up too suddenly, taking the table with him so that all the food and the dishes fell towards Ceiri. If she had not moved quickly she would have been splattered and cut. As it was, the mess of broken dishes and splashing food fell on to her clean floor. Caradoc took up the blue book and threw it to the back of the fire. Ceiri looked up at him. He grunted at her and stormed out.

It took Susanah and Ceiri an hour to clear the mess; it took a further hour for Ceiri to make another meal, which she put in the side oven for Caradoc. Susanah was in bed when he finally arrived home, but she could hear the talk and the quiet pleading down below.

A week later, Ceiri bought a pencil from Jade Smith, who travelled with his pack after his shift at the pit. She put it into Susanah's hands, and with it the charred drawing book which she had rescued from the fireback. Susanah turned the pages; it was only charred at one edge and was still very usable. Some pages, smooth as a kitten's back, were unharmed.

To keep the pencil and the book clean, Ceiri gave Susanah a starched print bag she had made from a little dress that Jenny had outgrown. The bag had a drawstring made of cotton crocheted into a cable. Together they found a hiding place for it in the front room cupboard. Ceiri tucked the bag tightly beside a pile of letters. They pushed the little pile of story books underneath the cupboard, where they were well hidden by the deep shadow.

It was their secret, the drawing book and pencil. Like the secret they shared about the way that Jenny had been born. Like the secret of the blackcurrant cordial.

Watching her mother lock the cupboard door and put the key in its hiding place Susanah asked, 'Those letters, they have Dada's name on?'

'That's right.'

'But they're not open. No one's read them.'

'Well, not reading, he wouldn't read them, would he?'

'But if he doesn't open them he won't know who they're from.'

'He knows who they're from.'

Susanah stayed silent, staring at Ceiri.

The book stayed in its place for most of that year. Susanah told herself there was so much to do in the house. It was no wonder neither she nor her mother had time for their precious package in the cupboard. But, in a way, she knew they were both afraid of it.

And at home Susanah was as apt a pupil for her mother as she had been for Miss Carmedy. The share she took of the work in the house made the working day shorter, leaving her mother more time to sit with her beloved crochet. Ceiri's hands were always busy. Her most recent task was a new bedcover, the twin of the one on the bed she shared with Caradoc. This was to be Susanah's, 'When you go to your own house'.

In these odd quieter hours Susanah would play on the floor with Jenny. They played the finger games and sang the rhymes that she herself had learned from her mother. Jenny was a quick pupil, much quicker than Tollie. Sometimes Susanah drew pictures for her on bag paper that the sugar came in, of animals and fairy children. Sometimes she read to her, stories from one of the books which had been Miss Carmedy's gift, retrieved from their hiding place under the front room cupboard.

Ceiri would tell them stories from her young days in Wales; stories of the magic of Glyndower, the Welsh prince, set in ancient times when Wales was a true kingdom.

In the early days after he started work, Susanah was conscious of waiting all day to see Davey, for him to tell her about his time in the pit, about the world underground. Her anticipation was wasted. When he came in at the end of his shift he would still be absent from her, lying asleep with his head on his hands at the table, or up in the bed he shared with Lew and Tollie.

Likewise, she looked forward to seeing Lew and Tollie at the end of school. Tollie, who had learned the time from her, who used to help her with the berry gathering, seemed now like Davey, to be running away from her all the time. Nowadays, he just dashed in, gulped his tea and raced up to the green to play football. Much bigger lads would come to call for him, ball in hand.

With its newly rolled pitch and smart goalposts, Gibsley chapel team was now attracting opposition teams willing to play friendlies, many of them teams already in the Wear Valley league. Lads from the Baptist chapel, even some of the church lads, were keen now to join. As the team attracted good opposition, some even changed their allegiance to the chapel to enhance their chances of playing. For a while Tollie lost his place to bigger lads, then they drafted him back in again when they were a man short. Then, because he scored two goals in a crucial match, he kept his place on the team.

There was a flush of extra games now and then when a local pit went on short time or closed, or if a group of lads were laid off when the colliery was cutting numbers. The keen ones played regularly, every Saturday when they could.

Susanah became interested in the football in spite of herself. Soon she was taking Jenny down on Saturdays to watch Tollie play, leaving her mother at her crocheting by the fire and her father looming over a clock at the table, with his tools and screws lined up in order on the back cloth he spread while he worked.

Susanah and Jenny always stood by the long wall which divided the side of the chapel from the colliery land where the new pitch was rolled. They laughed and clapped as Tollie weaved and swerved with the ball and scored goal after goal, whizzing the ball past the stout figure of Wedger Martin, a surprisingly swift-footed goalkeeper.

Over the following season the team established a sound reputation and the desire to wreak vengeance for the previous week's defeat became an important part of this week's drama in the village. Tollie was the star, relishing the buzz of fame he had acquired in the schoolyard and in the street.

But in the November of their third season a real stranger joined the play. This boy, Mervin Sargant, was Tollie's equal, easily keeping up with his sharp, scattering play. Nephew to Caradoc's hardworking marrer, Gil Sargant, he had recently arrived in Gibsley with a whole family of cousins and uncles from Cornwall, coming to join their Uncle Gil at White Pool Pit where yet another seam had been opened.

Mervin Sargant was broad and well-built and, being nearly a year older than Tollie, was much taller. His hair, on the one day in a month it had been washed, was white as hill snow. His elder brothers were equally tall and bright-haired, were instantly popular with the girls in chapel in spite of their rolling way of speaking. The white hair and the strange speech caused many a bloody fight with the local boys in those first months. Lew loved to ginger up a fight with the 'Cornish Dollies', as he called them, by telling slanted tales to one side or the other.

Mervin went straight to the pit to work alongside his brothers and Tollie was still at school. In spite of this they were immediately fascinated by each other, each excited, if a little disturbed, to find a match for their talent. Within a month there were calls that Tollie Laydon Jones and Mervin Sargant should always play on opposite teams; anything else would be unfair. They grinned at this and went on playing shoulder to shoulder. And after an initial phase prowling round each other like suspicious tigers, the two boys became firm friends. Mervin would often turn up at the Jones house at five o'clock on a bright summer morning, balancing a ball in one hand as he threw stones up at the bedroom. Standing at the window, Susanah would see the early sun silvering Mervin's white hair and go to wake her brother. Caradoc, sleeping heavily in the front room, never heard the summons. Susanah, usually awake with a cough that had persisted since the winter, would shake Tollie to consciousness and Mervin, if he ever caught sight of her at the window, would tip her a cheeky wink. By ten past five the two boys would be kicking the dew off the grass, practising long skimming shots on the green.

In Tollie's fourth season, Gibsley chapel team was accepted into the Wear Valley league and just called themselves Gibsley. The green space beside the chapel acquired a perimeter fence and people started to pay to watch the game.

In time the team were doing so well that the White Pool men, with the collusion of Mr Carmedy the undermanager, made sure that Tollie, now working, and Mervin only ever had morning shifts on a Saturday so they could be there to play in the afternoons. Half-time scores on a Saturday afternoon were chalked on the tubs as the men went up to the coalface, to keep them informed of their team's progress.

This was the time when Susanah's friend Betty started to come with them to watch the team, her prime excuse being that her brother Amer was now playing left half. Staying on at school longer than Susanah, Betty had learned the value of her china-blue eyes when focusing them on the boys. Her particular focus was Len Sargant, who played on the team alongside his younger brother. Betty carried on her flirting to the football match, which annoyed Susanah who was embarrassed at the shouts and calls which filtered across the field in their direction.

Susanah's favourite games were the Saturdays Davey wasn't at work, when he came and stood with them, shouting for Tollie with wild enthusiasm. Her least favourite days were when Jonty Clelland started to come and stand about, watching, in that odd way of his, brown-faced and bright-eyed. Being at the grammar school now, he was an almost complete stranger. She kept her head down, unwilling to meet his glance.

Betty had more contact with Jonty, because she was never away from the chapel. She was there four times on Sunday: two services and two sessions of Sunday School. Chapel was the one thing Caradoc was easy on Susanah about, insisting only that she went to the evening service with her mother and Jenny. Then she sometimes found herself watching Jonty Clelland, staring at the back of his head as he stood in the front row, his mother on one side, his sister on the other. His father was frequently absent. 'Off preaching again,' Caradoc would say sourly.

Betty was very impressed with the grammar school boy. 'Should see him at the Sunday School, S'anah! Little'ns are usually so bad wriggling about all over. Not with him. He tells them stories. You know. Funny things about how he saw things, and the world. You should see those children! Glued to him, caught by those eyes of his! Eee, that smile. He gets wrong now and then off Mr Montage for straying, but he doesn't take no notice. Out of sight and he's on again about fairies and goblins and the winged messenger called Mercury.'

'I can't see it,' said Susanah. 'Always seems like a stuffed cabbage to me. Too much idea of himself.'

Betty ignored her. She was enjoying helping Miss Antrobus with the babies class. The Sunday School teacher, a stickler for the rules and orders emanating from Mr Montage, was getting quite fat now. As well as keeping up her Saturday readings with Caradoc Laydon Jones, Miss Antrobus was very friendly with Jack Simmons, the minister.

Every Sunday evening after chapel she would stand near him in the lobby and catch people as they came out. Caradoc, made genial by an hour's singing and hot words, always stopped to speak to her, his fingers moving over the hard rim of his hat as he bent towards her. Ceiri boiled with dumb anger at this, pushing Susanah and Jenny ahead of her, muttering away in Welsh. Sometimes they were left to walk home themselves while Caradoc walked Miss Antrobus back up to her cottage. Then Ceiri would go straight to the loft for a glass of her cordial to calm her down and make her sweet for when Caradoc finally came home to sit in silence over his tea.

At the football matches, Davey was getting into the habit of going across to talk to Jonty, and it made Susanah fume. During the week Davey was too tired to talk to her, to pay her any attention at all. Now, here he was, for once rested after a night's sleep, and he had to go wandering off. She forced herself to resist the inclination to cling to his sleeve, to pull him back to her side.

But she stayed in her corner against the wall with Jenny and Betty, her eyes alternately glued to Tollie's quicksilver form and fixed on Mervin Sargant's long runs which would culminate in brilliant turning shots at the goal. She liked Mervin: she liked his cheeky grin when he called for Tollie; she liked the way his heavy body hurtled through the air as though, like the messenger Mercury, he had wings on his heels. Like many in Gibsley she felt personal pride that their team was winning everything they played and that Tollie and Mervin were recognised as heroes right across the district.

Towards the end of the game, Davey would deign to come back to stand beside the girls. Only once did Susanah voice any real protest. 'Why d'you talk to that Jonty Clelland, Davey? Right above himself now he is, at that school . . .'

She had heard her father say this, in the middle of a tirade about Mr Clelland winning good quantities of coal with his partner Freddy Stapleton, despite having that ex-drunkard for a marrer. '. . . And that lad, he's above himself. Speaking out of turn, quoting from those school books at his elders and betters,' had been his words.

'Jonty's all right, Susanah,' said Davey. 'A good 'n. Him with his dad fighting them bullheads on the chapel committee – not least our own father – has got these lads this pitch. And the goalposts. And a ball that isn't pig's gut stuffed with rags.' Davey's tone was stony, almost sneering. It reeked of the hard hours underground with only men for company.

Looking at her brother hard, Susanah saw how peaky he looked, how he had shrunk away from being her friend. She turned blank-faced back to the game, tying her scarf around her neck to keep out the cold.

. Lew had never been interested in the football. At any pretext he would go wandering off into the patches of woodland that filled the cracks and crevices in the land around Gibsley to snare rabbits and an occasional hare as welcome additions to the family table.

One day Susanah watched as Caradoc turned the dead animal over on the broad pantry shelf. Ceiri looked on anxiously, Lew standing there with a smirk.

'Good weight.' A rare note of praise from her father. 'This should save some pennies this week, Ceiri.'

One side of Ceiri was pleased at the gift, the bounty brought by her elder son. But here was Caradoc managing to spoil even that pleasure, so in the end she would be glum at the sight of the furry form, which meant more work and less money for her to manage on over the next week, for Caradoc would keep the saved pennies for himself.

Lew also brought back birds' eggs which he kept in a numbered collection in a box under the boys' bed. The thought of that box made Susanah shudder. The baby birds should have been flying around instead of lying there ungrown in their shells, each wrapped carefully in a piece of rag.

Sometimes she would come across Lew as she wandered the woods herself. He mostly hung around there, sometimes head down in a crowd over a game of pitch and toss, sometimes just darting around in the distance. Once she saw him at the far end of what they called Nanny's Wood. This time he was on his own. He must have caught two birds in a snare. He had them tethered, fluttering, to a low branch while he targeted them with stones from his catapult.

'No! No!' She launched herself at Lew, but he held her off as though she were no more than a rabbit herself. Finally she stopped kicking and he flung her violently into some bushes. It was early spring. The ground was soft and there were no leaves to cushion the spiky twigs. When she had scrambled out of their prickles, he was gone. The birds on the tree were dead, their necks neatly wrung.

Lew was so large now, the scale and shape of Caradoc. But Susanah thought the likeness stayed on the outside. She had grown up fearing and sometimes hating Caradoc, but he had never given her, as Lew did, this feeling of death.

She herself had grown, too, though in different ways. Her own wandering in the woods was often to collect berries, carrying them in a cloth bag which she wore with the long band across her chest. She wore it this way so that it would not fall off as she clambered over walls and through the bushes. She realised how much she had grown when the strap started tracking an indentation between the two sides of her chest, as clearly as the woodland marked the indentation in the land. When she put her hand to her chest to ease her cough she let it lay there on the new softer surfaces, amazed that they seemed to be growing of their own volition and were soft and firm at the same time. She remembered the skipping song:

> Jelly on a plate!
> Jelly on a plate!
> Wibble wobble,
> Wibble wobble,
> Jelly on a plate.

She made up her mind to find a way to deal with them, to stop the shadow between them deepening, to stop the soreness she felt from time to time. She would have to do something about it.

Chapter Eleven

The day Susanah chose to do something about her growing chest was her favourite kind of day, when her father was clear of the house on early shift. On these days she would help her mother get the work out of the way, then they would sit and talk. Some days Ceiri would give Jenny a spoonful of the blackcurrant cordial and take an empty cup herself to raid her own secret store of distilled juice in the roof. Then she would lay Jenny on the little bed that she shared with Susanah at night and throw herself on to the boys' bed, cup in hand. In half an hour all would be silence except for an occasional snuffle from Jenny and Ceiri's own light rippling snore.

These were the times when Susanah liked to walk the house as though it were her own.

On this particular August day, she let herself as usual into the shadowy space of the front room. The smell of polish tickled her nose; around her was a slightly meaty smell which was harder to pin down. The bed in which her parents slept stood in the corner, blankets neatly pulled across, bolster on top. Folded halfway over it was the crocheted cover, the twin of the one Ceiri was crocheting for Susanah. The rest of the space was entirely taken up with a big dark wood dresser, shiny with mirrors and polished wood, busy with doors and drawers, carvings and keyholes.

She pulled out the key from the hiding place in the green jug and started to open all the cupboards, examining the jumble of boxes and cotton bags item by item. She sought out again a little package she had seen before. Unfolding the cloth, she pulled out the delicately carved wooden spoon with its flower and leaf shapes twining around each other with such life that the plain wood seemed to glow with vivid colour. Susanah could see in its opulent surfaces the mark of Caradoc's hands: those same hands which dealt so precisely with the fine mechanisms of clocks. She pulled it close to her face, peering at it, into every crevice, trying to plumb the secret of this thing, so distant in every way from everything she knew of its maker.

Among other things in the cupboard there was the soldier's hat from the African War and a box of stones imprinted with the frozen shapes of animals and flowers which her father brought for her mother from time to time from the pit. There was also the heavy old Bible. It was not Caradoc's; his was bent and curled to the shape of his large hand, more to hold than read as he intoned the passages he had off by heart.

She opened the Bible and read, not for the first time, the names on the parchment fly-leaf. Caradoc George Jones b. 1864. Isabella Fortunata Jones b. 1865. The writing was large and beautifully formed, the 'J' having a long curling tail. Then underneath in the striking black spiky writing, in an entirely different hand, the names were changed. Caradoc George Laydon Jones b. 1864. Isabella Fortunata Laydon Jones b. 1865. Written with a flourish.

She thought about it. Ceiri had talked about Auntie Bel, the one like a butterfly who was hard as oak. She thought about Auntie Peg, who had fainted when Jenny was born and was her mother's cousin. This Isabella was her father's sister, a real aunt.

And why were they named twice in that way? She couldn't work it out but she knew her favourite writing was the first entry.

She moved the little bag which held her drawing book, to get at the pile of letters addressed to Caradoc; they were still sealed and tied with white crochet cotton. The writing was graceful, but not in the same hand as that on the Bible. The letters were unread, the date stamps years old. Sometimes she placed them on the Bible above Isabella's name. Aunt Bel? Were the letters from her? Why keep the letters sealed? She knew that her mother boiled away over her father being friendly with Miss Antrobus. Perhaps the letters were from another woman, like Miss Antrobus, and Ceiri had made sure the letters did not get to her father but kept them there, a still and unspoken communication through the years. Susanah tried to think of a way to open them, in secret, but there was never time on these quick morning forays.

Today Susanah dug into a side cupboard and pulled out one of Ceiri's cloth bags, a blue striped one, made from the back of one of Caradoc's old shirts. Inside were snowy white strips of cotton, some long, some short. They were unhemmed, even frayed here and there, but beautifully white. It was only since she had been home alone with Ceiri that Susanah had seen these strips, drying around the fire on Monday and being ironed on Tuesday. It didn't seem to happen every week. Just now and then. She'd once asked what they were for but her mother had told her they were nothing to concern her.

Susanah now laid two of the white strips carefully on the bed, then put all the things back in their original place. She closed and locked up all the cupboards and put the key back into its hiding place. Then, very quietly, she made her way into the little pantry off the scullery and closed the door. It was a long narrow space, smelling of fruit and bread, the tiny window at the end close-covered with a muslin curtain.

Listening hard for any sound, she took off her thick blouse and her thinner camisole, then looked at her chest with its unevenly swelling mounds. Those dots, which once seemed an improbable source of baby's milk, were changing now. She took one of the cotton strips and wound it round and round her chest, then tucked it in neatly under her left arm. Then she did the same with the other strip, this time tucking it in under her right arm. Then she put on her camisole and the blouse, which now fell down gracefully straight from her shoulders. No embarrassing humps.

Then she lifted her shoulder sack down from its hook. It still had the pink stain from her last blackberry-picking. She pulled it on crosswise as usual and it fell smoothly on her newly flat self. A sigh broke into a smile on her lips.

The back door clashed and she jumped, then stood stock still. There was rustling and puffing in the entrance, then padding footsteps in the kitchen. She stood a moment, then came out of the pantry.

Caradoc was standing in his thick pit socks just in the doorway to the kitchen. 'Where's your ma?' he scowled.

'Upstairs with Jenny. Having a . . . lie down.'

She expected him to shout, to yell for her mother, but he didn't do that.

'What were you doing in there?'

'Nothing.'

A hard hand came across her face. It stung and made her eyes water. 'Stealing, is it? Eating out of turn?'

'No. No.' She gulped as she stood there. 'My petticoat. It sagged down. I had to hitch it up.' It was easier to lie to him.

He looked at her, then down at her skirt. 'Well, girl, seeing your ma's having her lie-down, you can get the bath tin in.'

Caradoc only left a narrow space in the doorway for Susanah to squeeze through. As she squeezed, he leaned in further towards her and she could smell the gritty carbon smell of newly cut coal and feel him hard and lumpy against her. Then he stepped back and let her go, and started to pull off his top clothes, hanging them on their special hooks in the lobby.

The bath, nearly as big as Susanah, was hard to get off the hook in the yard. She heaved it in front of the fire and started to fill it with a lading-can from the boiler. Her eyes were on her father taking off the last layer of clothes, leaving only his pit shorts which he rolled up above his thigh. His face and the muscles of his upper body were streaked with coal dust. His eyes looked extra light by contrast, with white creases reaching like sun-rays on to his black cheeks. His lips and gums were too red against the night-black of his cheeks.

He kneeled down by the bath tin, working the lather from white to streaky grey, soaping his face, his shoulders, his hair. He splashed and blew as he cupped his hands with water to rinse off the grey scum. His face was clean now, his hair black and spiky. 'Here, girl. You do my back.'

Susanah caught the soap and flannel that he had thrown at her and set to work, rubbing away at the muscular shoulders, the hard back. She had seen Ceiri do it many times.

'Harder. Rub harder, girl. There's a shift of sweat and dust there.'

She rubbed harder, making grey circles where there had been black, then white circles where there had been grey. Davey had told her once that some men never washed their backs, that it was supposed to weaken them, but it hadn't seemed to weaken her father.

'Lean in, girl. Put your weight on it. Rub harder,' he ordered.

She was sweating now, frightened of the urgency in his voice. Then there was more noise. Jenny was standing in the doorway, the sand of sleep

71

still in her eyes, bawling her head off. Her mother's voice was shouting, 'Susanah!'

Ceiri thumped downstairs and snatched the cloth from her daughter, thrusting her through the door to where Jenny had subsided into sobs on the bottom step of the stairs. The door clicked behind Susanah. She recognised the rare tone of real protest in Ceiri's voice and, incredibly, she heard Caradoc laugh.

She picked up Jenny, carrying her into the yard towards the gate. 'Sssh, Jenny,' she whispered as the little girl wailed for her mother.

'No! No, look, I have my bag here. We'll go and find some blackberries.' Susanah pulled Jenny's legs around her and made her way down the street away from it all.

A few minutes later Susanah planted the protesting Jenny on the ground and, taking her hand, raced away from the house where her mother was finishing the work of cleaning her father's back. She made for a place where she knew the bushes were heavy with blackberries: a spot behind some brick sheds at the edge of White Pool Colliery land.

Jenny hung back at first and moaned about wanting to go home. After a while, though, she helped enthusiastically with the picking, her hands and face growing rosy red and then purple with the juice. She chattered away as they gathered. 'Here's lots, S'anah. Come here! . . . Here, S'anah, see this little nest a birdie's left.'

Between them they soon had the cotton bag filled and Susanah was looking around for something else to do.

She could not go straight home to face Caradoc and Ceiri, so she wandered along the Front Street and then down the pathway leading to St Andrew's graveyard. She read some of the inscriptions on the stones: Safe with Jesus; Called to God; Early to Sleep in the Bosom of the Lord; John James Lewis Our Last Son, killed by accident at White Pool Colliery; Sara Jane Hutchinson, a dutiful daughter. The dates were cut so sweetly into the grey stones: Died 1871; Died 1883; Died 1880; Died 1873; Died 1864. She looked more carefully at this last one. That was the year written in the big Bible, the year that her father was born. A year before Isabella. She must be his sister. She thought again that she should ask her mother about Isabella. What was she like? Big and tall, like Caradoc? Clever and hard as steel, just as he was?

The flies were buzzing and she felt hot. The binding round her chest was sticky with sweat. The heavy wooden church door stood open; the interior looked cool, like the dark space between the tall trees in the wood.

Taking Jenny by the hand, she crept in. The old stones gave out their relieving coolness, drenched them with the smell of dust and wax. Jenny's hand wriggled from Susanah's and she pattered back towards the big stone font.

Susanah edged forwards until she was halfway down the aisle, then stood still. The high window behind the altar was dark; the day outside was muggy and dull. Some light was trickling through the dust on the side windows and gleaming on to the stretched muscles of Jesus as they resisted the pull of the nails. The pink flesh seemed grey, even black, the deep lines round the eyes radiating in the pearly light. She looked around for Jenny and saw her muttering contentedly to herself on the step beneath the font.

The light from outside was brightening now. The sun was breaking free of the clouds. Susanah watched with close attention as the pink light, streaming through the red glass, brought a bloom to the rubbed gold of the cross. She moved her arm, disturbing fine-lit specks of dust and filling the air with the scent of bruised blackberries, very sweet.

Closing her eyes, she could see Ceiri leaning over Caradoc, rubbing, rubbing his back. Her face was wet, but she was not sure whether it was with tears or sweat.

Susanah's arms moved outwards and upwards of their own volition, to echo the pose of that figure on the cross, her hands dropping away at the same angle from the nails. Then, slow as a snail, her right hand came up to make the first part of that sign, the magic sign.

Suddenly she was grabbed under the arms without gentleness and her body was wrenched back. Even in fear she was pleased about the binding; such a grab would have made her newly tender chest sore. She was enveloped in a black robe, buttons cutting into her back. A voice was whispering close to her ear. 'So, child. What is happening here? Blasphemy!'

Under the hoarse tone, she recognised Vicar Stonham's precise voice. She let her arms drop but he still held her tight to him, a set of fingers where each breast would have been were she not in the safety of the binding.

After a long minute's silence, he loosened his grip. Still holding on to one shoulder, he turned Susanah round, pushing her away so he could look into her face. When he spoke, his voice was still soft and whispering. 'What do you seek here, child?'

'I just came to look, vicar.'

'Why?'

'Because it's . . . nice.'

'But that thing you were doing, child, it was blasphemy. An offence to the church.'

She lowered her head and stood still.

'That means that you should seek forgiveness. Forgiveness for this grave offence. Is that not so, child?'

'Yes, vicar.'

'Yes. Now. Come!'

Pulling her shoulder round, he thrust her before him and marched her up the aisle to the choir stalls. He wrenched her to a stop at a tall seat whose carved back was shaped like a church steeple, with fruit and faces cut into its sides.

The Reverend Stonham sat down in the seat and arranged the faded black skirts of his coat. Susanah could smell old food and pipe smoke among the dust. And other more meaty smells. The seat was narrow; his knees jutted out.

'Now, you will kneel before me and we will ask forgiveness for our sins, for we are all sinners, we each transgress, from the most lofty, yea, even to the most humble. Kneel!'

She was pushed down so that her shoulders touched his outjutting knees, like two sentinels in their black enveloping cloth.

'Hands together. Eyes closed.'

She obeyed the bidding, familiar from school. Behind her closed eyes she worried about Jenny. There was no sound, no sign of her in the silent church. She must be hiding like a little mouse.

'. . . Forgive this thy child and all others who sin, those who give way to weak desires and vague curiosity, for we are weak vessels . . .'

Susanah opened her eyes and a hand came on her shoulder, gripping it painfully, the other hand invisible inside the voluminous black cloth. His voice rumbled on, his hand alternately gripping and shaking her shoulder. Stay where you are, Jenny. Stay where you are, she willed.

Susanah started to wriggle. Mr Stonham stood up and pressed her face into the black cloth. She choked, feeling the bile rise to her mouth at the smell, which was worse than anything her father or Davey ever brought back from the pit. The man's hands were trembling now. With an effort she pulled herself free and ran, shouting, 'Jenny! Jenny!' and her sister cried out from her hiding place in the last pew and she scooped her up and ran out through the great wooden door.

As they came into the back yard Susanah could hear the ring of Caradoc's tinning hammer in the shed. To her surprise, Ceiri welcomed her, smilingly with open arms, making her sit down and have a cup of tea and a scone out of the tin. 'And all these blackberries! Aren't you clever helping our Susanah to get them!' she cooed over Susanah.

That night, when Caradoc and Davey were at a men's meeting at the chapel and Lew had gone across to the football field to watch Tollie play in a friendly, Ceiri looked hard at Susanah over her crochet.

'There's something . . . wrong with you, S'anah. Not quite right?'

Susanah wondered how all that had happened could show. How could her mother know about the church? Susanah had said nothing and Jenny seemed to have forgotten all about it.

'How's that, Mama?'

'Your shape, you've lost your shape.'

That was a relief, in a way. 'Well, I kind of wrapped myself . . . I found some cloths . . .'

'Show me.'

She removed her blouse and camisole to show her neatly bound chest. Ceiri smiled faintly. 'Where d'you get that binding?'

'In the cupboard in the front room. I saw you once, gettin' the key from the green jug.'

'But that's not what they're . . . Never mind. Soon enough. Why d'you do it, bind yourself like that?'

'They're lop-sided and, well, I'm sort of sore. They made my clothes look funny.'

'Yes, I suppose you would feel like that. For now you might just as well go on. Not a bad thing anyway, with that cough of yours . . . What's that?'

Ceiri's smile had vanished and she was on her feet. She turned Susanah's shoulder towards the lamp. She had seen the bruises reflecting the shape of Vicar Stonham's hand. It wasn't the first time Susanah had been bruised, but marks inflicted by Caradoc usually showed on her face or her legs.

'It was in the church. I went into the church. The vicar . . . And I had to kneel down and ask forgiveness. I had to kneel in front of him. He kept gripping my shoulder and shaking.'

Her mother's breath raked inwards. 'S'anah. Never go there. Never. He cannot be a good man.'

In guilty haste, Susanah pulled on her blouse. Then Ceiri buttoned it up for her just as she did for Jenny, pulling the collar over with a careful, soft hand. 'Promise me you will not go there. Into that church. Near that man. Ever.'

'I promise.'

Ceiri put a light hand on Susanah's sore shoulder. 'And the cloths, Susanah. Now you know where they are, you can use them. It is just as well that you do. Put them in the blue bag in the corner of the pantry and I'll see to the washing.' She paused and Susanah pulled away a little, evading her hard concentration. 'Susanah . . . Is there anything else?'

'Anything else?'

'Anything else happening to you?'

She was puzzled. 'No. Nothing else happening.'

'Well, if there is, if something did happen, you'd be sure to come and tell me.'

'Yes, Mama.'

Another six months went by before Susanah had something to tell her mother, before she found out what the clean white cloths were really for and how they were to be perpetually and secretly used. Every month, each month. Betty called menstruation the Curse but Ceiri always called it her Friend. I have got my Friend, she would say, sharing the secret now with Susanah and dragging around with greater difficulty than usual. Or if Susanah was bad-tempered and snappy she would ask her if her Friend was due. Another secret. A Friend this time.

Chapter Twelve

The journey by train, with the long walk to and from his house, had become part of the routine of Jonty's school day. Getting up to be out at seven was no bother in the Clelland household; his father had been in the pit working for an hour on early shift by that time. Corella, if she was home, was up by then, too. His mother stayed in bed, often tired from the late night's reading, writing letters or transcribing her husband's speeches and sermons. His father usually left the kettle on the boil and the breakfast ready on the table.

Watching his family, Jonty wondered where they got the energy from to keep going on and on. He once asked his mother if she did not want to let up, have a break from all the reading, the writing and the meetings.

'A break? Not now, love. There's so much to do. We're a party now, not just societies and unionists, self-serving talk shops. A party! On our way at last. We'll have our own members in parliament before long. A break? Not now, son, not now.'

On the Wednesdays Jonty stayed in town and went to the Reverend Monroe on Great Fell Terrace for extra Latin he usually caught the six thirty train back to Priorton. He had liked Dr Monroe from the first, taking in his stride the tutor's strange habit of pinching his pupil's knee to reinforce some teaching point.

One Wednesday, Jonty had settled into an empty carriage to return home when a woman climbed in and made a great business of throwing a bag and a satchel up on to the rack and sitting down opposite him. The woman's skin was very white and her hair glinted in the sun like a new penny. She was small, even smaller than Jonty, who still felt worryingly small. Her neck was fat and rich-looking, allowing her head to move with loose grace over her tight-pulled body. It was hard to tell how old she was. She might have been just older than Corella; she might have been just younger than his mother. She smelled sweet. He wrinkled his nose, trying to place the scent.

He had settled to read *Sesame and Lilies* by John Ruskin, which had been the topic of a conversation that day with the Reverend Monroe. Jonty had waxed enthusiastic about the way Ruskin got to the core of things like the importance of language and the meaning of beauty. He was particularly concerned about Ruskin's assertion of the importance of the Greek language. 'Could I learn Greek, Dr Monroe?' he'd asked. 'At least the Greek alphabet?'

Mr Monroe had smiled his yellow-teethed smile. 'Quite easy, dear boy, for you. But it'd take at least another hour every week . . .'

Jonty knew his teacher's polite hesitation was about money. 'Well then, will you teach me?' he said airily. 'My mother'll find a way.' It would mean eating more things made of oats, but he knew she would say yes. She always did.

In the carriage the woman leaned towards him; he could place the scent now. Lily of the valley, the waxy flower that sprung in clumps under the bushes beyond the water pool, defying the dark grit of the slag.

'Are you enjoying the Ruskin, then?' Her voice was soft and full of smiles. It had a familiar lilt which tugged something at the back of his mind.

'Yes.' Jonty's lips felt thick. His head was hot. He felt an uncomfortable stirring down below the book on his lap.

'What are you reading about?'

'He talks about the writer Milton, and how words come from all languages.'

'Have you got to the "Lilies" part yet? The Queen's Gardens, he calls it.'

Susanah Jones and her mother came unbidden into his mind. Now he knew where he recognised the tone. The woman's voice had the same singing quality. He coughed. 'No. I'm just on the first half of the book.'

'Well, you'll be noting his point that in Shakespeare there are no heroes, only heroines. But as for the rest, beware unlikely pedestals for women, won't you? Pedestals are prisons of a higher order.'

The woman leaned even nearer and turned one of the pages, looking at the book upside down. The waxy scent of lily of the valley was mixed now with the smell of her brown hair and the faint musty after-smell of perspiration.

By this time Jonty was as red as a chapel hassock and feeling grateful that the book was resting on his school bag which, in turn, was resting on his knee. What the Bible referred to as his loins seemed poised to jump right out of his pants.

The train slowed down and the woman stood up to reach for a small case which was swinging in the net rack above Jonty's head. The space inches from his face was bisected by her undulated body line reaching from her dimpled inner elbow to her knee, the soft fabric of the green dress making a tender flutter against the air.

'Oh, dear. In the corner, isn't it? Could you get it for me? So tall!' Her voice seemed to flute at him through space.

Jonty clambered up on to the seat and had to stretch to reach the bag, a complicated affair with many straps. Dumbly, he proffered the bag and she disengaged it from his clammy hand. Then, slowly, she took his palm and kissed it with soft lips. The shape of them burned hard into him. Its pain brought to his mind that six of the best delivered on that same hand by Mr Robertson many times, years ago, and he shuddered, astonished, as he watched her leave the carriage.

At the station the woman was met by a man in uniform and another woman, in a large green hat, who kissed her. The man took the cases from the porter and set off down the platform towards a glossy trap which was drawn up at a privileged position right opposite the big gate. The woman in the green hat led the way towards it like a ship in full sail, the little party cutting a swathe through the crowd of passengers setting out to walk home from the station after a hard day's work.

When Jonty got outside, the trap was throwing up dust on the road which led up the hill away from Gibsley. He looked down at his hand and could almost see the shape of her lips. He put his mouth to it and could feel the heat. In the next three weeks he would put his lips to it again and again and revisit that whole experience on the train. In all parts of his body. But as time went on, to his disappointment, the effect wore off.

The train incident made Jonty become ever more conscious of his sister Corella. The following night, she was teasing him about his desire to learn Greek.

'Now then, Jonty, are two languages not good enough for you? I'd have thought English and Latin would be good enough for anybody, even a sucking sponge brainbox Lord Almighty like you.'

She was lying back on his father's chair, her legs stretched out in front of the fire whose flicker outlined the sombre edge of her navy dress, emphasising her generous outline.

He looked sourly across at her, picked up his lamp and his books and stomped upstairs, making sure he clashed the door behind him.

Later, though, from behind the red curtain which divided their shared space, he listened to her preparing for bed, reckoning by the rustling sounds just where she was in her preparations for sleeping. He thought of her without clothes just before she drew her large nightdress over her head. With Corella there was no kneeling to pray stage, because from the age of two she had insisted on saying her prayers in bed as she did not wish to kneel. Unlike George Fox, she would not bow her head even to the Lord.

As for Jonty, he still knelt down to say his prayers, which, besides the Lord's Prayer, continually devolved into a conversation with an unseen listener. That night they talked about the strengthening of the fibre being brought about by trial and temptation. He did mention the forty days and forty nights, but that seemed a universe away from the scent of lily of the valley mingled with the sooty steam of a railway engine. And the thought of Corella's naked arms raised to receive her white cotton nightdress.

The following two Wednesdays Jonty watched for the woman, but failed to catch sight of her. After that, she was pocketed at the back of his mind, to be brought out when he came across a piece of more daring and passionate prose in his reading. Just occasionally he could use the mix of the two to create an erection which was for him a source of interest, pride and shame. The relief he afforded himself afterwards seemed in one way to put him more in touch with God and His exploding creativity, and yet in another to drive Jonty further away from their nightly conversational contact.

Corella also laughed at his going to the football matches regularly. His mother, though, encouraged him. 'It'll blow away all those murky cobwebs I see gathering sometimes round that serious old head of yours,' she'd say briskly. And Jonty felt a possessive pride in the Gibsley football team, revelling in its rise in the local league. He appreciated the fact that Davey stood beside him on the touchline on his Saturdays off when most of the others, boys who had gone to the Elementary School with him, kept their distance.

'What say about that Mervin Sargant, Jonty?' asked Davey one Saturday. 'Coming on, isn't he? Outstripping even our Tollie these days, I'd say.'

'I wouldn't say that, not at all.' Jonty defended Davey's brother.

'No, to be fair. Our Tollie's a class ahead of most others but young Sargant's a class ahead of him. Plays with his head and his feet. Could play in the bigger leagues, even now. Priorton's approached him, they say. Young as he is.'

'He's an interesting lad, Davey. He's got a head on him. He comes down chapel on with their Len, if he's on the right shift. Those Sargants've got some sound ideas. The Union . . . Socialism.'

'I can see your da'd be pleased at that,' commented Davey drily.

'You should come to the Tuesday meetings, Davey. You could out-argue them all, when you were at school.'

The Tuesday group had grown out of a Bible class and now met every week to discuss social and political topics.

'I'm workin' now. No time to natter on in some talk-shop about politics or philosophy. There's nee point.' Davey turned sourly back to the game. Then a smile cracked his grim face. 'There he goes!'

Jonty turned to catch sight of the long shot, set at an impossible angle, which beat the goalkeeper and slid tightly to the back of the net. He watched as the blond Sargant boy smiled his delight at the other players, then cantered back to the centre with an almost equine grace.

Pleasure at this graceful action flared through Jonty's body. Turning to follow the movement of the game, he caught sight of Susanah Laydon Jones who was often there with her little sister. He wanted to call over to her, to share his delight at the beauty he had just witnessed. She was muffled up, but her dark hair gleamed in the winter sun. She glowered back at him, a dark look which was the opposite of those bestowed on him by the woman on the train. It was strange, though, that he was drenched with the feeling he had had then: hot hands and face and a resentful stirring down below. Blood and life.

Chapter Thirteen

When Jonty was seventeen the Reverend Monroe wrote to John George suggesting he called at the house at Great Fell Terrace to discuss the boy's future. The time he suggested coincided with backshift so Bea Clelland went instead.

She sat on the battered leather couch and gazed enviously at the shelves laden with books to double depth and the tables covered with dusty papers.

'He's a clever young man, Mrs Clelland! Needs further scope for that brain.' Mr Monroe put a hand on each knee and leaned forward towards her. 'He wants stretching!'

'I . . . we know that.'

'He will pass his examinations with flying colours.'

'I know that too.'

'Oxbridge is the thing. I have an old friend at Oxford who . . . He'll need another year in school, and we'll work together on things to broaden him out . . .'

She held up her hand. 'Dr Monroe, what you're suggesting would give me great, even the greatest pleasure! But it's not possible. He'll have to work. His sister's still at college. That and Jonty coming here to you has taken everything. Now my husband, he's running into trouble at the pit, talking justice and equality and that. We've no certainty of money. Jonty'll have to work.'

The clergyman sighed and sat back in the chair, dislodging a cat who was perched on the back. 'So much waste,' he said. Then he sat up again. 'But if he works and prepares, perhaps in a year things will change?'

'What work could he . . .'

'In the school in your own village. Gibsley isn't it? I know the Reverend Stonham there. A man of uncertain mood and too much appetite, perhaps, but not so hard to persuade. And Jonty can come here to me on Saturdays and broaden his mind!'

'Come here? That's what I'm telling you. We can't pay any more.'

'No question, madam, of payment. It's a question of tidying away. I cannot bear to see a job unfinished. He shall be a teacher! I shall see to it!'

So on leaving the grammar school, Jonty was taken on as a pupil-teacher at Gibsley School.

He had not thought teaching would be so hard. The easy part was the knowledge, those neat parcels of thought, and the heavy baggage of skills.

The hard part was the physical presence of fifty nine-year-olds, sitting there in rows, filling the air with a warm and faintly rotten smell.

As the days went on, he was reminded of himself at nine, sitting eagerly at that desk at the front, on the right. The class had been smaller then. Now the village was growing quickly into a small town, with the new coalseams opening, new streets being thrown up and people coming to Gibsley to work from all over Britain.

Every working day Jonty had fifty bodies, fifty mouths, a hundred hands and a hundred eyes to deal with. From every exercise there were fifty pieces of work to view and judge quickly, much of it on slate, to be cleared for the next lesson.

The classroom glittered with fragile tension. It seemed he and the children were pulling at opposite ends of a long wire. He knew that if he let go, they would descend into tumbling chaos; they in their turn, with their superior combined strength, could pull and swing him in all sorts of directions quite against his will. This same will being pitted against such odds all day long, he soon found himself resorting to the very tools of sarcasm and humiliation that he had vowed to avoid. It was a relief that the children actually seemed prepared to work. Mr Robertson, who now saw himself as Jonty's mentor, kept urging him that the only answer was the stick. 'Keep 'm down right from the start, Mr Clelland. It's the only way.'

Jonty remembered very well how he himself had been kept down in that way. What a bumptious child he must have seemed; he became more sympathetic to the little Scots teacher. Even so, he did not resort to Mr Robertson's famous stick. It still struck him as barbarous.

On his second day as teacher the door to his classroom had been flung open and its glass partition rattled. Two top class boys were flung into the room followed by the bustling figure of Mr Robertson.

He recognised the heavy bulk of Tot Martin, son of Wedger, and the blond head of the youngest of the Sargants. The class sat in stunned, thrilled silence as Mr Robertson turned them to face the class. 'These two boys, Class One, are here to show you what happens to those who persecute the weak and who transgress God's laws.'

He lined up their hands, which Jonty saw were already fiery with bruises, and gave them four strokes each. Jonty flinched with each stroke. Then the boys were bustled through the partition to the next classroom where the performance was repeated.

Jonty had stood facing the blackboard for a full minute before he reached up and started to write: 'Blessed are the meek, for they shall inherit the earth.' 'Clean your sums off your slates and write that,' he said.

Mr Robertson came to his room after school. 'I saw the look on your face when I brought those lads in, Mr Clelland,' he stated, neutral.

'I thought it was barbarous.'

'Well said. It's a primitive job we have here. The taming of lions.'

'Barbarity doesn't solve barbarism.'

Mr Robertson smoothed back his thinning rusty hair. 'Do you know what they did? They got hold of that queer inversion of a feller Viv Kenton.

You know him? Brother to the formidable Joan?'

Jonty nodded. Joan was turning up at the house now, getting help from his mother with her reading.

'Well, they got hold of him and rolled him in the water pool. Then they took him and locked him in some old crees where they sank the first White Pool shaft. Kept him there three days. Did . . . unspeakable things. Now he's home with pneumonia and is raving like a lunatic.'

'What about the police?'

'Joan won't have it. Doesn't care for the police. But she was up here demanding satisfaction. She'd already given Wedger Martin a black eye. Mervin Sargant was with her, saying he'd go along with any punishment on his brother.'

Jonty was taken aback but stuck to his guns. 'Do you think that what you have been doing this morning would give her . . . satisfaction?'

'It's what we can do.' Robertson had shrugged.

In that first month he had come home from school and slept, his head on his hands over the table till nine o'clock, when his mother pushed him off to bed. At this time he even had difficulty in going to the weekly meetings at chapel.

After that, to his relief, he seemed to move on to another plateau of physical tolerance and mental energy. Even though he was still exhausted, things became easier. He could get through some preparation at night, attend political meetings in both Priorton and Gibsley. On Saturday mornings he would race up to the city for his session with Dr Monroe and race back in the afternoons to see the football match.

He was on the programme committee now for the Tuesday meeting, and to this meeting he would drag himself, even in the depths of exhaustion. He was proud that they had managed to get people prominent in local and sometimes national life to come to speak: an Irishman to talk about the way the Conservatives were blighting the just route towards Home Rule; Arthur Henderson, a Wesleyan preacher like his father, who had just become the third Labour member of parliament, representing Barnard Castle only eight miles from where they sat; and Miss Marsden again, fresh from barracking a Liberal politician in Newcastle, who came to talk about the Women's Social and Political Union, formed earlier in the year in Manchester.

Despite his tiredness, Jonty enjoyed them all. But his favourite speakers were men like his father: local people who had made a special study of somebody's writings on literature or politics and used the Tuesday platform to infect others with their enthusiasm. The Gibsley meetings got a reputation and people rode and walked good distances to attend.

Jonty's genuine interest in the football was repaid in the attendance at Tuesday meetings. People would talk to him on the touchline and turn up to hear the man or woman he had described with such enthusiasm at half-time the previous Saturday. Two who came, and continued to come, were Len Sargant and young Mervin. Mervin had long since outclassed Tollie Laydon Jones on the football field and was now universally sought after, playing regularly for Priorton and a prime weapon in their current good run in the cup. In the Tuesday meetings he would be very attentive and quiet, only now and then asking a very sharp question.

Miss Carmedy who had been the one to organise Jonty's pupil-teacher place after John George had approached her brother, at the pit, usually attended the meetings when there was a nationally known speaker. She would accost Jonty in the school corridor. 'And who is it next week, Mr Clelland?'

'A Quaker called Ledworth, Miss Carmedy. Ex-professional soldier who talks against war.'

'Ah. Nice meaty broth as always, Mr Clelland.' She would put her head on one side and smile at him. 'I'll be there. You can be sure I'll be there!'

Miss Carmedy never treated Jonty with anything less than grave professional respect and quietly encouraged him to try to make his way to teaching college. No doubt this work in school was good experience but really he should, she said, taste the sweets of college life.

It was strange for Jonty to think of her as his colleague now, having seen her first as a doughty lady teacher of the girls at school, the dragon teacher. He had watched her since then in his own front room, crossing swords with his mother, arguing about women's suffrage and world socialism. Now he had to think of her as a person who, like him, stood in front of fifty children, acting out a combination of lion-tamer and magician, prophet and scourge. He thought now that he liked her, and could see just why she had had to develop her dragonish characteristics.

Tonight Jonty rubbed his hands at the thought of the meeting, knowing there would be a stir among all those people, many of whom sang about peace on earth in chapel but with whom he had had numerous arguments about the futility of settling things with fists. With a bit of luck it would be a good and stormy meeting.

84

Chapter Fourteen

The Reading Room on Front Street was full to the doors. There were people standing at the back and in the side aisles; some younger men were squatting on their haunches in front of the first row, much to the discomfort of Mr and Mrs Jade Smith, Mrs Simpson (whose husband had been killed in the South African War), Mr Jackman, the manager at White Pool Pit, and Mr Carmedy. Miss Carmedy sat straight-backed by her brother.

Jonty looked round the crowded benches for a face that wasn't there, then went to sit on a low windowsill halfway back, squeezed in between Davey Laydon Jones and Mervin Sargant. At the end of the row nearest to them were Corella and Bea Clelland. Unlike the other women, who were in Sunday clothes, Bea was wearing her old thick black coat which had seen better days. Beside her was Joan Kenton who wore a scarf at her neck like a gipsy and boots under her canvas skirt. Joan was working for a farmer now. Through Bea teaching her to read on Sundays, the two had become firm friends, producing a thrilled disgust on the part of the chapel community: a combination of criticism for the breaking of the Sabbath and disbelief at the unlikely pairing.

The massive figures of Caradoc, Lew and Tollie Laydon Jones seemed to fill half the back row, the other half being crammed with Mervin's elder brothers, Len and Gregory. Jonty scanned the room again in vain for any female members of the Jones family. Betty Stapleton was there, with a flurry of girls from the Sunday School. Miss Antrobus, in front, was twisting her bulk around and hissing at them for quiet.

'Your da not coming, then, Jonty? I'd have thought it was just his ticket.' Davey had to shout above the buzz.

'My dad's chairing the meeting. He was to meet this Jonah Ledworth at the station. He'll be staying at our house tonight, the speaker. In my bed, I'd think. Too much a bigwig for the front room couch.'

Mervin Sargant smiled, showing his big white even teeth. 'You'd make a fortune, Jonty, if you charged rent. Always bigwigs at your place these days.'

The blond boy had grown more and more enthusiastic about the people who came to speak in the village. He often sat in on the discussions at the Clellands', which went on into the early hours. He listened assiduously, but did not speak. Of all the people that Jonty had plagued and persuaded to take part in the debates, Mervin Sargant was his great success. Davey came now and then, but Jonty's pleasure at this was clogged up by Davey's truculent rejection of all the new ideas being bandied around.

A draught hit the room from the back as the autumn wind blew in, followed by a thin neat man of military bearing wearing a checked jacket and cap and the tall spidery figure of John George Clelland. The boys pulled their legs back to the wall to let them pass. John George smiled and nodded at them.

There was a buzz as the two men settled on the platform, but when John George Clelland looked up and around the room, the noise drained into silence. He smiled broadly. 'It's good to see such interest tonight. Normally our debating society is well attended, but this crowded room demonstrates the particular interest in this topic in Gibsley. Can I introduce Jonah Ledworth, a veteran of the South African War. I'll start off by tellin' you what he will not tell you himself. In that war he was decorated for bravery no less than three times.'

The neat man scowled at this and scribbled on the pad he had in front of him.

'Mr Jonah Ledworth.'

After the applause, the man stood up and looked quietly, row for row, at the people crushed into the room.

'Courage,' he said in a low clear voice, 'takes many forms. I who have never been called on to do it marvel at the courage of men who day after day go down into the bowels of the earth – at great risk to life and limb – to win the coal which fuels our industry and keeps the family hearth warm and welcoming.'

He paused at the ripple of appreciation which greeted this.

'I, who was not made to endure it, applaud the courage of women who suffer sometimes also unto death so that we may have our sons and daughters, that our blood will survive.'

Bea Clelland and Joan Kenton clapped at this, and people turned round, straining to see who had applauded. Jonty's face burned.

'Courage on the field of war is quite another thing. It is sown in the field of nationalism, nurtured by the juice of obedience, and flowers in the heat of madness.'

A rumble erupted in the centre of the room. 'No!' 'No!' 'Rubbish!'

People turned to each other shaking their heads.

'He's wrong there!' 'That's not right!' The room echoed with the noise.

John George Clelland clattered his gavel on to the table and glared round. 'Let the man have his say!'

The room subsided into silence.

Jonah Ledworth looked around soberly. 'Fifteen years ago I would have been down there with you shouting that this was wrong. A load of poppycock.' He paused. 'Let me tell you what happened to me that changed my mind. This tale has to be restrained by the presence of women and young people at your meeting. Because of this, you will need to increase the horror twofold to get the true impression of how it affected me.'

He went on to talk about his training, about his growing pride in the regiment, about the comforts of his submission to the rule of blind obedience without resort to rational thinking. His voice remained steady, almost steely.

'Do you see, then,' he went on, 'that in such circumstances blind obedience led me to what were seen as "brave acts", to "acts of courage"? That loyalty to my regiment made me so crazy when my brother officer was injured I risked all to save him? The same madness that would come over me when my comrades were killed, a thirst for instant vengeance so great that I would feel that I had the strength of ten, the protection of an invincible armour?'

Ledworth was red-faced now, bright-eyed. The room rustled as people shared with him the insane glamour of what he described.

'For such acts, as your chairman has told you, I was honoured. It was – is – no honour, ladies and gentlemen, to dream those actions night after night, year after year. To see again the bayonet pierce human flesh, to see the last living light in a man's eyes, then the blind stare of death. To see a man's arm or face disintegrate at the impact of your bullet . . . '

He pulled a blue scarf from his pocket and mopped his face. 'In these dreams I was – am – no hero. On waking from these dreams I'm haunted by a small voice which says to me, "If you do it unto the least of my brothers, ye do it unto me." That Boer, that kaffir, that . . . German – is that where our thoughts are turning now? Are they not the brothers of Jesus?'

He left a quiet moment for this to sink in.

'But all this, ladies and gentlemen, was in the heat of battle and, if I can't forgive myself, priests and clerics will give me God's forgiveness for such acts carried out on the front line of battle.

'But that is not all I have to be forgiven for, ladies and gentlemen. There is another side to it. In the African War, there was another side. There were the orders to drive people from their homes. Homes like those you have left on this cold night to come here to listen to me. Homes with treasured objects. A crystal jug, I remember, a harmonium, smashed to pieces. A home with beloved people. An old grandmother. A new-born child. Driven out. The fabric burned to the ground. The cattle and the crops destroyed. There was no question of not obeying the order. Instant obedience was burned into our soul . . .'

He raised his voice to a shout. 'And there is worse! The people herded like cattle into compounds. Runaways shot. No food. Starvation. Children dying; cruelty; savage assaults . . .'

He was drained, almost incoherent, exhausted now, as he looked slowly round the room. With a visible effort he spoke again, his voice softening to a whisper. 'Is this courage? Is this honour? No, ladies and gentlemen. This is why we should not put one step on that road; why we should enthrone at the centre of our heart the words of Jesus: "If ye do it unto the least of my brothers, ye do it unto me."'

Mr Ledworth collapsed into his chair. There was a minute of dead silence. Then Mervin Sargant jumped down from the windowsill and started to clap.

Jonty followed and others in the room stood to applaud. There were boos and grumbles from some parts of the room. Davey sat in silence on the windowsill.

John George Clelland called the meeting to order. 'I'll remind you that this is a debating society, not a boxing match. You have a question, Mr Jackman?'

Mr Jackman stood up and, holding tight to his lapel, turned sideways so that he could talk to the hall as well as the platform. 'I know such . . . gentlemen . . . as Mr Lloyd George have shown themselves against that war. Even so, I've to say to you, Mr Ledworth, that what you've been saying amounts to treason. I am surprised that Mr Clelland has the . . . brass to bring those views into our midst. Just suppose everyone took up those fancy views of yours? Who'd be there to defend us in our hour of need? Who'd maintain our place in the world? We'd lose everything. Be overrun. Treason I say.' He sat down, glaring not at Ledworth but at John George Clelland.

Clelland cocked an eye at Mr Ledworth, who stood up.

'Our place in the world, as you recall it, was wrested from people by our overrunning them and taking by force of arms, sometimes by political cunning, what in right belonged to others. Land, gold, sovereignty.'

Mr Jackman scowled and Miss Carmedy smiled faintly at her brother, who was staring down at his hands. There was another roar at Jackman's words and John George had to work hard to regain order. 'I tell you what, I'll let everyone have their say. And perhaps Mr Ledworth'll try to make a summary point in response, otherwise we'll be going till midnight.'

A hot dispute arose, about patriotism and the diminishing of heroes, and about soldiers, men from this district who'd died to defend their country, who some said were being dishonoured by all this talk.

Eventually Mervin Sargant put up his hand. There was an extra hum of interest in the room. 'I'd like to say sommat if I can. Well, marrers, we all like to win. When I play football –'

There was a mutter of appreciation at this – 'I only want to win. I'd do almost anything to win. And if some feller hurt one of me brothers I'd fight them. Aye, and mebbe hand out a black eye or two at that . . .'

There was a cheer at this.

'. . . But listening here to this feller and thinking about things I've heard here in this room this past year, I know now what I'd not do. I'd not join an army whose job was to keep the money and lands of our exploiters safe. I'd not take up arms against me own. And when I say me own I don't mean Durham or Cornish men, I mean working lads, working folks. Those working farmers in Africa. Miners, whatever language they talk, who dig down there in the blackness like me; people who work in factories and like us dinnet know if they have a job from week to week. What's me quarrel with them? Why should I train mesel' to kill and shoot so I can kill some German pitman or farmer? And who here'd make war on old men and children, women and girls? Those camps. Just hearing about them made me sick.'

Silence descended on the room like a felt cloak as Mervin leaned back on to the windowsill red-faced. Jonty shouted his approval, clapping loudly and Len Sargant rumbled his from the back of the room.

Furious, Jade Smith leapt to his feet and roared, 'Lads like that should keep their counsel, speak when they're spoken to! It's all just a pack of lies. Lies from a pack of socialists. What you lot need is a good hiding. Teach you a lesson.'

There was a rumble of agreement at this and suddenly the room was in chaos. A big miner called Charlesworth leapt over a chair to get at Mervin Sargant. As he started to set about him scuffles broke out all around the room. Jonty tried to pull the man off Mervin and someone started to punch him. When Davey tried to help Jonty, another man started on him. Tollie and Lew and the Sargant brothers came across to lend a hand and were in turn set upon.

Caradoc stood up grimly and made his way to the door and Bea and Corella moved from their seats to stand by the wall, watching the proceedings with clinical interest.

With a stony face, John George Clelland tried to maintain order but gave up when people climbed on to the platform to get into closer argument with Jonah Ledworth. He finally had to pull his speaker through the crowd and out into the cold night, leaving the noise and the clatter of the fight behind them. They stood side by side in the road, watching the retreating back of Caradoc Laydon Jones alternately lit and lost by the street lamps.

John George turned to the other man. 'I'm sorry about that, Mr Ledworth,' he began helplessly.

Ledworth gave him a wry smile. 'It often happens. Perhaps it's the first awakening for some. What does happen is that those who take to the idea often become much stronger in it by having to defend it, by whatever means.'

'But that violence there, isn't that against your creed?'

'It is now, now I've had chance to work it out in the cool light of day. But at their age I would have been in there defending what I had to say with my fists.' He laughed. 'They'll learn.'

Bea squeezed out of the narrow doorway, hair awry and George introduced her to the speaker. 'You've had quite an effect in there, Mr Ledworth,' she smiled.

'I hope so, Mrs Clelland. I hope so.'

'Mervin Sargant picked up the point very well in your argument, the way he linked it with socialist principle.'

'Ah, Mrs Clelland, you'll remember, though, that I am not a socialist. Never was, and never will be. I am a Quaker. My preference, if anything, is Liberal.'

John George watched her blush at this. 'Well, Mr Ledworth, I'm pleased that your Quaker principles at least coincided with my socialist principles on this. But my view is that a Labour vote'd bring about what you want in the end.'

Mr Ledworth smiled thinly and nodded, then turned to John George. 'Now, can you get me to Priorton? Is there a train?'

'You could stay over if you like.'

89

He smiled again. 'Thank you, but I've friends in Priorton who I know expect me.'

After they'd waved him off John George and Bea walked back from the station together, arm in arm. He looked at his wife's firm profile. 'Spiked your guns there, I think?' he said, teasingly.

'Jonah Ledworth?' she said scornfully. 'How can a man have those ideas and *not* be Labour?'

'Mmm.'

'You know what, John George?'

'What?'

'I thought he was a cold fish.'

'You're just frustrated, dear Bea. If he had only deigned to stay the night you might have had yet another convert.'

They didn't comment on Jonty's bruised cheek and black eye when he finally arrived home and plonked himself on the brass fender in front of the fire.

'I see your friends took the speaker's words to heart,' John George said, eyebrows raised in amusement at his son's battlescars.

Jonty scowled. 'Not Davey Laydon Jones. He might have fought like a tiger on our side there, but it wasn't because he agreed with Mervin. We just walked back together. Can you believe what he said? "Well," he said, "after all, Ledworth did talk some good sense, didn't he? That thing he said about a soldier's job being no worse than being in the pit. That there are braver men in the pit? So why not join the army? At least you're in daylight. That makes sense." How could he?'

'Jonah Ledworth didn't say that.'

'I know. But Davey thinks he did. Says he thinks the army's worth a try.'

'Must be an idiot,' said Corella from where she sat at the table.

'He's no idiot. Never was. And what would you know about it?' Jonty banged the brass rods of the fender angrily until his hand was stinging.

Ten minutes later he jumped up to answer a rattle on the door. Davey was standing there, one hand on the jamb. 'I just want to say, Jonty, that I'd fight and die for the country, like those other blokes did in Africa. It's a man's duty, right enough. But that thing about the way they went on with the families. That's not right.'

Jonty continued the argument from his side of the door. 'But a soldier can't choose between one and the other. Don't you see?'

'Who is it, Jonty?' called Bea. 'Bring them in. There's a draught.'

Davey shook his head and refused to come in, vanishing into the night too quickly for Jonty to do anything about it.

Chapter Fifteen

There had been some objection at the management meeting to the idea of the Quaker Ledworth but that was nothing to the objection to the proposal the following year for a second annual young people's camp in Livesay Woods, ten miles up the valley.

Jack Simmons the minister was chairing the meeting. 'There are risks in such an enterprise. I'd me doubts last year. Then, visiting there midweek, what did I find? Ungodly music. Races. Revelry.' The last word carried with it into the air the burning smell of hell's flames.

Herbert Montage, sitting beside Jonty, stirred in his seat and looked at the faces round the table, some grave, some composed into neutrality. 'I had no criticism last year of the camp. It was me led it and it went well.' He kept his eyes on his hands, kept soft by his clerk's job in the pit offices. 'The music was folk songs. Who here has never sung "Scarborough Fair" in his youth? And there were foot races up through the woods, but no money prizes, no gambling.'

'"Scarborough Fair" is a nice little song,' put in Freddy Stapleton, who was doodling on a piece of paper in front of him. His nails were black and there was coal dust ingrained in the cuts, callouses across his palm.

'And,' said Jonty Clelland, 'the revelry you talk of, Mr Simmons, that was high spirits. Youth and energy, it was just bursting out . . .' Jack Simmons gave a visible shudder at this. 'But that's what we were there for, Herbert and Miss Durant, Len and me. To guide that, er, explosion . . . into righteous channels.'

'Aye, dealing with the young you need channels for it.'

Jonty looked in surprise at the support from dour Mr Robertson. The hands that had wielded the cane on hundreds of children lay small and surprisingly fragile on the scored surface of the table.

'They should keep to their school and to their work,' growled Caradoc Laydon Jones. 'The Devil has his use for idle hands.'

'But Our Lord ordained the seventh day for rest, isn't that true, friends?' put in John George Clelland.

Caradoc bristled. 'Sunday's one day in seven, Mr Clelland.' He laid hate in the speaking of the name. 'Proposal here before us is five days in seven.'

'How can we deny our young 'ns this chance to get out of the grime and the pit dirt?' said John George, laying one hand fist up on the table. 'River's clean up there. You've got the trees. Not a pit nor a colliery wheel in sight. Fresh air'll put them on the right road, in their bodies and their souls. God's good fresh air. They'll come back bristling for work at school and in the pit.'

'Lucky we are to have you here in Gibsley, Mr Clelland. Gifted as y'are at the saving of sinners,' said Caradoc, glancing at the slumped figure of Freddy Stapleton, 'and knowing as y'do plenty about the ways football preserves the souls of the young from sin so's we here needs pay for the pitch to be rolled and posts to be bought. And now these lads are tempted out to Priorton to play . . .'

'Good players,' interrupted Freddy. 'They say Newcastle's after young Sargant for next season. Why, winnin' the cup and league like that, fancy a Gibsley lad playing . . .'

Caradoc slashed a large hand as though he were cutting off Freddy's voice with the physical action. 'Y'even know, Mr Clelland, how cowardice and treason can be turned towards praise of the Lord so's we can pay some lunatic his train fare to come and rave his fill at us. And now here y'are telling us to spend chapel money putting all our young folk together and leave them out in the woods somewhere to sing songs and talk politics.' He folded his arms and met John George's eye.

John George stood then, rearing up over the table like a delicate spider, and leant across it towards Caradoc. 'I'd say to Mr Laydon Jones that making progress in the Lord means givin' people choices, sayin' as life is more 'n spending six hours a day on your knees hewing coal, it's more 'n spending twelve hours on the screens or at the traps. it's more 'n spending six days a week at a shop counter or a wash tub. We all need to lift our eyes to the horizon, to drag them away from the dirt we work in and the piles of gold we make for ourselves and others. "I lift mine eyes unto the hills, from whence cometh my help." It's there in the Book, Mr Laydon Jones.'

The room settled into an awkward silence. Mr Simmons shuffled the pile of papers in front of him.

'It'll take them from their school and from their work,' said Jade Smith, pursing his lips under his newly grown luxuriant moustache.

'There's a school holiday that week,' said Mr Robertson. 'That's why that week was proposed.'

Mr Carmedy coughed. He rarely spoke at the meetings, although he attended every one. 'I informed Mr Jackman of the scheme after it was mooted at the last meeting. He has said that those in the pit under seventeen can have the week as holiday.' He paused. 'They will have to miss their pay, of course, but that's their decision. And he has seen Lord Chase, who has made available fifteen pounds towards the costs of such a camp.' He gave a dry smile. 'His lordship was at the pit head two weeks ago and saw some young lads coming out of the cage. One was coughing his throat up.'

John George shook his head at this.

The silence was finally broken by Jade Smith. 'Well,' he said, 'if his lordship supports the camp . . .'

John George laughed. 'And you capitalists should stick together, eh,

Jade?' (Jade had now left the pit and had opened another shop in Priorton.)

'My objections to this enterprise are minuted. I can do no more,' said Jack Simmons. 'We do need assurances about the supervision of these young people. Apart from that, I suppose . . .'

'There will be me and Miss Durant,' said Mr Montage. 'And there will be Mr Jonty Clelland and Mr Len Sargant, who supervised last year.'

In the end Mr Simmons abstained and the only person to vote against was Caradoc, who cast his vote with grim satisfaction.

Mr Carmedy caught John George on the way out and walked along with him. He was a small man and had to scamper to keep up. 'I need a word, John George.'

'Aye, Mr Carmedy.' He had an inkling of what was coming.

'You know that I have great respect for you and your views. Always have. I can see there are changes and people like you and your good wife are part of them.' He laughed. 'My sister is always telling me your wife should be in parliament. She's a canny woman.'

'Aye.'

'Well, it's this, John George. Mr Jackman has been on at me about you. His lordship has read some of your letters to the paper. There is your . . . er . . . work with the union. Comes down to this, John George, his lordship is worried about someone like you at White Pool.'

'If Jackman tries to sack me he'll have a fight on his hands. He can't fault my work.'

'He knows that. It's not the sack.'

'He . . . and Lord Chase are telling me to pipe down, then?'

Carmedy nodded feverishly. 'That's it.'

'I can't do that.'

The undermanager nodded again, this time sadly. 'I can see that, John George. But I had to tell you.'

'Thanks for that, Mr Carmedy.' He paused. 'Did I tell you our next big speaker is an Irishman? Republican.' They paused, ready to part company on the corner. 'He'll set a few rabbits away. Mebbe you'd like to tell your sister, Mr Carmedy? She likes a good rousing speaker, does Miss Carmedy.'

Jonty hoped that Susanah would be at the camp. He had looked for her last time, but she wasn't there. All this year he had watched for her in chapel and felt good at seeing her, even though she always seemed to turn her head away when he looked in her direction.

She had been missing from chapel on four consecutive Sundays. He overheard talk of her illness and finally asked Davey about her.

'Just a bad chest at first. She has a canny dose of 'm most winters. This 'n's going on and on.' Davey laughed. 'Me da even let Ma get a doctor. Anyway, she's picking up a bit now. Talk of TB for a while, though.'

Jonty shivered. He was flooded with relief the following Sunday when Susanah was back in chapel, though she looked gaunt, with eyes as big as dinner plates. He managed to meet those eyes and nod and she gave a brief smile before she looked away.

He asked Betty Stapleton if her friend was coming to camp. 'It'd do her good, a bit of fresh air after she's been bad like that,' he said in as neutral a voice as he could manage.

Betty laughed at this. 'Her da barely lets her out of the house at all, never mind on what my dad calls a gallyvant. Anyway, you can't be allowed to mention her being poorly to Susanah. She throws sympathy off like spittin' out a bad taste.' She paused, meeting the intense glare of the young teacher. 'Mebbe you're right, though. It'd do her good to get out of that house . . . I'll have a go at 'ticing her.'

'How about getting Davey to help?'

Betty frowned at him, looking suddenly thoughtful. He could feel the red creeping up round his ears.

'I don't know,' she said. 'As far as his da is concerned the best thing Davey can do is say nowt. But mebbe . . . Do you know, that Davey, he watches her like a hawk. You should have seen him when she was really bad. Like a man off!'

'Get Davey on to it!' said Jonty. 'He'll manage. You watch!'

This time it had to happen. This time it had to come out into the open. This time he had managed to face Betty's openly speculative look. This time he had willed it as hard as a prayer.

'Susanah. You've got to come. I can't see why you stand aside from enjoyin' yerself. And it's chapel. I can't see it.'

Betty grasped both her friend's hands and squeezed tight. Susanah laughed and struggled free.

It was the summer they were both sixteen. Betty was totally involved now in chapel affairs. Freddy, her father, had moved on from being a simple conversion-witness to becoming a grudgingly respected member of the circuit committee. Chapel was at the centre of his life, one intoxication exchanged for another. He was still coming forward, one week in three, with the tale of his salvation, to encourage others to sign the pledge, to forswear the demon drink.

Betty's brothers, like Lew and Tollie, had graduated from school to the pit. Amer was with Lew at New Row Pit, John with Tollie at White Pool, alongside Davey and Tollie's friend Mervin Sargant. Betty herself was helping Jade Smith's wife in his little shop on the corner of Middle Street, while Jade himself bustled up to Priorton on the seven o'clock train from the Gibsley station to supervise his larger emporium.

Mrs Stapleton was much rounder and more content now; her house, with its smart furniture bought judiciously from advertisements in the newspaper, shone from front door to back. She even had a treadle sewing machine, obtained for her by Jade Smith and paid for at two shillings a week. Within a year, the machine had paid for itself with the sewing she did for the wives of the pit officials. On one chapel anniversary Betty had pointed out to Susanah ten little girls saying their 'pieces' in dresses made with her mother's machine.

Ceiri made all Susanah's clothes and the boys' shirts by hand. Susanah noted the flicker in her eyes when she told her mother how Mrs Stapleton's machine did the long seams good and strong in a few minutes.

Susanah had broached the value of a sewing machine to her father and was treated to a sour look. Where did she think the money was coming from? 'Mrs Stapleton got her machine by paying weekly,' she'd said. 'If I had a job like Betty, I could pay for a machine for Mama.'

Caradoc had smiled thinly at this. 'Paying by the week? Getting things through debt?' he'd sniffed. 'Freddy Stapleton might be wearing the coat of virtue, but underneath he still sports the shirt of self-indulgence. There's plenty to do here in this house, girl, never mind a job. Plenty to do here.'

It was true that she had plenty to do. In addition to helping Ceiri, she was now doing all the apprentice work on the clocks as Caradoc's idea of taking Lew out of New Row Pit to work full time on the clocks had had to be aborted. Lew had proved clumsy with the fine metal and unwilling to put in the hours.

Most days now, Susanah sat beside Caradoc as he showed her how to dismember the clocks, how to clean the parts, and how to reassemble them. He never did show her how to make the new parts, how to solve the finest technical problems, or how to achieve a fine finish. This final work was always done by him; on every job it was done by him. He kept charge of all the discussion of work with customers when they came to deliver or collect the clocks. No word was spoken about Susanah's role in the process; it was never mentioned outside the house. Susanah never saw any of the money earned by her endeavours. Susanah sighed. Enjoying herself didn't seem to enter into anyone's calculations, least of all her own.

Betty was an assistant Sunday School teacher now and attended every service, as well as meetings in the week. Like Caradoc, she was skilled at covering her inability to read, learning the texts and hymns by heart once her mother or Susanah had read them to her. She was very quick with this learning by heart, quicker than Susanah in the end.

Betty brought her abruptly back to the point. 'Are you listening, Susanah? Dreaming again. Always dreaming. I can't think where you get to in that head of yours. I'm telling you, you should come to the camp!'

Mr Simmons did not approve of the youth summer camp, said Betty. He thought such activities were fraught with moral danger. 'But I can't see why. It's all hymns, prayers and Bible class, and things like walking and climbing.'

Susanah laughed. 'You don't think my father would let us go near any camp, do you? He wouldn't let us out of his sight. What about all the work, all them clocks and watches? There's still a backlog of work from Christmas, when I couldn't get down to it for being poorly. And see how thick he is with Jack Simmons. You don't think he thinks any different?'

'But why shouldn't you go? And it's lovely out there, out in the open, no pit in sight.' Betty pulled Susanah out of the door and down to the yard gate. From this vantage point they could see the lifting gear and the wheels of three pits: New Row down the valley; White Pool and the ramshackle

Blinna wheel in the opposite direction. 'And if you get higher up the hill you can see more of them! Another three at least. I thought about you last time I walked up there, Susanah. The water, the flowers. Even the talks about poets and things. I kept thinking of you. Just your cup of tea. Not mine, but you . . .'

Betty had always laughed at Susanah for having her nose in a book, reading and re-reading Miss Carmedy's presents. Susanah still thought of Miss Carmedy with a whispering ache in her heart. She rarely saw her now.

Finally Betty prevailed over her friend. Susanah would go to the camp. Or at least she agreed she'd like to. Now only Caradoc needed to be persuaded.

That evening Caradoc and Susanah worked either side of the table as usual. She was dismantling a watch belonging to Josiah Sargant, father of Mervin, who said it was made of Cornish silver and mined by his own father whilst Caradoc was putting the final touches to a mantel clock belonging to the manager of Priorton Co-operative Society.

Suddenly Susanah could feel Davey behind her, his hand on the back of her chair. She could feel his breath. 'You should let her go, Da. She still has the cough. A bit of fresh air could clear it.'

Caradoc looked at her, his eye distorted by the watchmaker's glass. Susanah held her breath, waiting for the tirade. He took out the glass and rubbed his eye. The metal eyepiece had forced a tear into it and all at once she could see the very old man lying in wait inside him. Looking into his eyes was like looking into the cores of time. His hand, made young and soft by lanolin, held time in its palm.

'She's thinner, Caradoc. Eyes out like doorstops.' Ceiri's light voice came from the fireside.

They were talking over her as if she were a stone jug. Before the spring, and the visions of the church screen which were brought on in the depths of her fevers, she would have leapt up and taken her own part. But she was still very weak.

Caradoc sniffed and screwed in his eyepiece again. 'May as well get some benefit in this family from the money the chapel wastes on such trifles.'

'Mebbe Tollie should go,' said Davey. 'Keep an eye out for our Susanah.'

'Aye, mebbe so,' said Caradoc. 'He can mek up his week's wages in the next month. Still needs pay his way, though.'

Susanah felt Davey pressing her shoulders and saw Ceiri smiling up from her crochet. She sat in agony waiting for Caradoc to finish his work and fold over his cloth so that she could finish, too, and fly straight to Betty's house.

'You can go?' Betty caught Susanah's hands and swung her round and round until they banged up against the new rocking chair. Freddy Stapleton came in from the front room and smiled across at his wife. 'Somebody here's havin' a canny time.'

Suddenly Susanah had a vision of him again, this genial man, flourishing the frog which was about to lose its head. She shuddered and spurting coughs started to mix with her laughter.

'Woah! Woah! Calm down now, missis!' Mr Stapleton put his arm round both of the girls and steered them across to the table where he made them sit down. 'How about me makin' us all a cup of tea to celebrate the victory of right over might?'

So, coughing, smiling and occasionally hiccupping, Susanah enjoyed the unique experience of watching a man making tea in his own house, with his wife looking on placidly from a comfortable seat by the fire.

Now she had the camp to look forward to. It was a new experience, looking forward in this way.

Chapter Sixteen

Susanah ignored the excited chatter as she kept her nose to the window of the train and watched the land racing backwards as the train forged forwards. First a swim of grey and black, hills competing with pit heaps and grey stone streets, houses clustered round the little railway stations like piglets on a sow; then they were flying over a great viaduct, the ground so far down below, with people no bigger than beetles or woodlice; then the land became greener and they could see broad stretches of fast water. Then they were at Livesay where there were no grey heaps, no colliery wheels to be seen; the greys and blacks here were coloured by nature, not dyed by coal dust.

Livesay station was small, no bigger than a house itself. The party tumbled off the train and set off to walk, leaving Mr Simmons behind to fuss over the brake with its load of equipment and supplies.

Herbert Montage and Miss Durant led the way. The rest of them followed in crowds and clusters.

Susanah walked along in the middle of the crowd, clinging on to Betty's arm. Distancing herself from the hubbub around her, she watched the fine fall of new tweed against her leg as she picked her way carefully round the grassy clumps in her new box-calf boots.

Ceiri, by some miracle, had prised a guinea out of Caradoc and sent Susanah into Priorton to buy herself a new coat. Davey had stopped her on her way out of the house, pushing three half-crowns into her hand. 'Get some new boots, S'anah. You canna wear those with any new coat.'

Brother and sister had looked down at the boots she was wearing and laughed. The old boots were clean enough, but Davey had mended them a dozen times on his last, finally having to resort to patches. The patches succeeded in keeping the rain out, but the boots looked a thousand years old.

Jenny had loved Susanah in her new coat, and insisted on trailing round the kitchen with it draped over her own shoulders. 'Don't I look grand in it, too, S'anah? Why can't I come with you to the camp? I want to come.'

As they waved goodbye to Susanah, Ceiri had to hold tight on to Jenny to stop her following.

Now Tollie and Mervin Sargant were up in the front of the crowd, as was Jonty Clelland and Mervin's brother Len. Betty had a large fancy for Len, who like Jonty was a Sunday school teacher. This fancy showed too much for Susanah's comfort. She liked Betty as her own friend, not half-turned away, trying to catch some boy's eye.

Just ahead of Susanah and Betty were Corella Clelland and her friend Bessie. These two had brought a whole group of younger girls right from Penrith where Bessie ran her own little school and Corella now helped her. At one Friday meeting there had been an uproar led by Jade Smith about these outsiders being allowed to come, but Susanah could see no harm in it.

Her legs were aching and she was short of breath by the time Herbert Montage pulled them to a stop. It was a space where the broad river bisected a stretch of green meadow. The rush of water narrowed into the distance, where the banks were clasped together by an old stone bridge.

They all shouted and cheered their pleasure and some dumped their bags and parcels and went racing down to the river's edge. Betty and Susanah put their bags on the grass and sat on them.

'Whew!' said Betty. 'A'nt used to walking like that, laden down.'

'So this is it, Bet?'

'Yes. Don't you like it?'

Susanah looked at the broad river whose clear water ran over smooth grey stones; the clumps of broad-leaved horsechestnut trees and fragile birch trees with their silver peeling bark; the sky, mostly blue, with rags of cloud here and there; the clumps of brown-green grass underwoven with purple vetch and buttercups.

'No,' she said, smiling broadly.

A commotion on the road heralded the arrival of the brake as it turned, rumbling and creaking, on to the grass. It was driven by Mac Tillson, injured at the pit, who did jobs around the chapel. Beside him sat the minister, stiffly upright.

Betty and Susanah stood up and followed the others, who were crowding towards the brake. Mr Simmons motioned for silence. Then he stood on the steps of the brake and, with much coughing and squelching, blew his nose. He talked a fidgety long time, going on about the temptations of the Devil who took delight in strewing lewd enticements in the way of the young, 'like perfumed sewage'. There was, he said, a real need to spend the time here at the camp in quiet contemplation, to renew and revivify one's faith. And so on.

Susanah watched as a bead of sweat swelled to life on the minister's temple and furrowed its way down the deep line on his cheek towards the corner of his mouth. He paused a second, then licked his lips, taking in the bead of sweat. 'Beware! Beware the sin within thyself!' he said. 'Now, let us pray.'

She stared at her feet, not listening to the prayer, but seeing again the bright red light stream through jewelled windows of St Andrew's church, her body heating up with fear. Shaking the image of the Rev Stonham from her head, she wished the minister ill for spoiling this lovely place.

After the crackle of his voice faded, the bags and boxes were unloaded in a deflated silence. Then everyone watched as the brake, with its holy load, rumbled away under the expert hand of Mac Tillson. They could still see the minister waving his hands as he talked to Mr Montage and Miss Durant, who were trotting alongside the brake as it pulled through the trees.

The rest of them were standing silent, almost despondent, loosely grouped around the tea chests and packing cases, when Jonty Clelland leapt up on to a huge packing case which held the cooking pots. He stood there for a moment, looking around; it seemed he looked at each of them in turn, his brown face glowing. Susanah could feel the air being scoured of the taint of Mr Simmons's words.

'Friends,' he said, 'one thing you can be sure of. Be sure that we're here to breathe clean air, to share together the wonders of God's universe, to smell the flowers and trees, to listen to the song of His birds, to swim in His clear waters. Won't our very actions here praise His name? Won't He look upon us in delight? In this place we can recognise in ourselves gifts, talents which God gave us, celebrating the daylight and dignity in our own lives.'

To which there was a roar and clapping and shouts of Amen. Mr Montage and Miss Durant hurried back down the path towards them.

Corella Clelland leapt on to the box beside her brother. 'We have the chance here to share our ideas, to learn from each other . . .'

The words flowed on, the lighter voice counterpointing the belling resonance of the lower one, the ideas sometimes being repeated, the phrases blending into poetry. Finally, Corella looked round. 'So we're here, aren't we, to enjoy the blessing of the company of our comrades?'

'And to do that, marrers,' said Len Sargant, leaping on to the box as Jonty leapt down, 'we need shelter and food, so instead of yammerin' and gawpin' away, why don't we put up the tents and set up the fires and the cookin'?' He turned and grinned at the senior teachers, now standing on the edge of the crowd. They exchanged glances and nodded, smiling.

Susanah thought about the minister sitting stiffly upright in the brake as it trundled its way back to the station. She could feel the bruising bump as it hit a heavy sod. Serve him right, she thought. The people here were set on a good time, minister or no minister. Serve him right.

Chapter Seventeen

The rain and drizzle on the first day at camp disappointed Jonty, damping down and swamping out the joy of their arrival. There were a few moans, and much longing for the bright coal fires of home. In desperation, the leaders gathered everybody into the big meeting tent and held an impromptu concert around an illegal fire set in the earth in the centre.

Mr Montage, who had brought his squeezebox, accompanied Miss Durant in a song from *HMS Pinafore*. Corella recited 'Ode to a Grecian Urn' and others remembered their anniversary pieces. Betty Stapleton gave her rendition of a long poem about a lead miner in search of a golden donkey. This, being funny and done with the raising of brows and the occasional comic grimace, caused a good deal of laughter and was voted the best turn so far.

Then Len and his brother Mervin embarked on a two-handed poem about King George: 'In steps King George . . .' bellowed Len, leaping into the central space beside the fire and making Susanah jump.

Mervin sprang up to join him. 'King George is my name! With sword and pistol by my side I hope to win the game!'

'The game, sir?'

'The game, sir!'

'Take your sword and try, sir!'

At first they mimed a sword fight, then they settled for wrestling on the floor until Mervin was sitting on top of Len, whose head had dropped back, his eyes closed.

Then Mervin leapt to his feet and looked mournfully around the watching crowd. 'Oh dear, oh dear, what have I done? Killed my father's only son!'

Betty shouted, 'Send for the five-pound doctor!'

'There is no five-pound doctor!'

'Send for the ten-pound doctor!' Many more joined in.

Herbert Montage strode into the centre and knelt by Len's still figure.

Betty chanted, 'Here comes good old Doctor Brown, the best old doctor in the town.'

Mervin put a hand on Herbert's shoulder. 'What can you cure?'

'A dead man, to be sure!'

Herbert lifted Len's head and mimed the pouring in of medicine. Len shuddered, then leapt to his feet and danced about shaking hands vigorously with Herbert then Mervin.

Then, arms around each other's shoulder, they sang together:

> 'Oh, my brother's come alive again,
> We'll never fight no more!
> We'll be the bravest brothers that ever were before.
> With a pocket full of money and a barrel full of beer,
> We wish you Merry Christmas and a Happy New Year!'

There were cheers at this, the image of the sweating face of the minister resting uneasily on more than one mind.

When the cheers had faded, Betty tried to get Susanah to sing, without success. Jonty wished she had succeeded; he had been looking forward to the chance to watch the Jones girl other than from the corner of his eye.

The weather cleared on the second afternoon, heralding a lick of fine weather to signal the end of the day. At this point they had built into the day a free hour where people could walk and talk together. Most boys and some girls were playing ball games - the boys football, the girls handball over a high rope. Joan Kenton joined in with the boys. She had left the still fragile Vivian in the capable hands of Bea, who had persuaded her to go to camp and had insisted to Mr Montage that a place must be found for her.

Corella's girls from Penrith giggled at Joan at first, only to be silenced by a glowering look from the big girl. 'What's think tha't staring at, charver? Either join in or tek leave, will yer?'

Betty and Susanah watched the game for a while, Susanah glancing up from time to time from the blue book in which she was trying to draw a clump of grass.

'Not much to choose between those Sargant lads,' said Betty. 'Great big, they are. And that blond hair makes them stand out, don't it?'

'Mm.' Susanah watched with appreciation as Mervin abandoned playing down to the company and gave a virtuoso display of ball control: on to his head, then on to his neck and on to his head, then back on to his knees. The girls joined in the patter of applause as he finished. 'He has such a lot of life, has Mervin. Fizzes from him.'

'Mm. Len fizzes, too, but it's a . . . quieter fizz. Mebbe more like a plop!'

They were laughing at this as a sweating Mervin galloped up to them. 'He's sommat, isn't he?' said Betty.

Susanah nodded as he bowled on. 'Do you know what?' Betty went on. 'This feller from Middlesbrough's been down. Miracle-boy player, they're calling him. Offered him a job in a foundry if he signs for one of the 'Boro teams. Gunna be champions next season, that lot. Play N'castle off the parks, they say.'

'He'll have to live across there.'

'Looks like it. Worth it, though, for the football. And anything's better than the pit.'

Susanah nodded, thinking of Davey.

Over the last couple of days, Jonty had noticed that Susanah didn't join in anything much, but busied herself with a drawing book or a piece of crochet in pale yellow wool. Today he had positioned himself with a book of his own to read, whilst keeping half an eye on the match, at right angles to Susanah, a short distance away.

She was peering almost shortsightedly into a glass jar at a butterfly which was lying passively inside, wings spread. Occasionally she would add a line or two on the page, the tip of her tongue edging from the corner of her mouth.

At half time Mervin Sargant came up and flopped down beside her, breathing hard from his running. He bent his head towards the jar. She placed the book to one side while she picked it up to show him something about the butterfly. Now Jonty could see the page quite clearly. The butterfly was there on the page, viewed from all angles, Susanah's drawings like cobwebs on the cream surface. At the bottom of the page was a detailed study in the full range of shades which a mere pencil can produce. Curiously, it seemed to pulse with colour.

Where did she get that confidence, that still observation, that sure touch? As Susanah set to work again, her hair, quite dark, drifted forward to veil her face, which still looked pale and unhealthy. She must have felt his gaze because her head started to turn. However, by the time she looked round, Jonty was staring safely back at his text.

'You're a canny drawer,' Mervin was saying appreciatively.

'Yes, I know. You're a canny footballer.'

'I know that, too.' He pulled up a beefy leg and leaned his chin on it. 'Did your Tollie tell you I've had an offer from the Middlesbrough set-up?'

'Yes. He said something.'

'Fellers from Newcastle came as well.'

'So you are a canny footballer.'

'Feller from Middlesborough offered us a job in a foundry. Time off for games.' He pulled some grass and started to chew it.

'Sounds like a good thing.'

'Aye, but,' he went on, 'this feller. It's his foundry. "No politics, no agitation." That's what he said.'

'Will that bother you?'

'I dinnet kna. I'm well into the union now, with our Len. A member of the Labour party. Meks yer think. But I like me football an' it'll get us right on there. Lord Chase is cuttin' us off here one by one. We're in for a downturn again. Jonty's da's bein' threatened by Chase. But . . . goin' there'll mek us a boss's man all right. That sticks in me craw.'

Susanah picked up her pencil. 'Will you go?'

Mervin jumped to his feet. 'They're all at us to go. Our Len, your Tollie. Aye. I reckon so. But dinnet worry, I'll be back to plague yer!'

She took a stab at him with her pencil and he leapt off to rejoin his friends.

The evening discussions had been going well, sometimes very well. A small group of people, always including the Sargants, stayed up to thrash things out further, sitting around a lamp into the early hours, breaking the rules which Jonty himself had helped to formulate.

The discussion soon strayed from religion to theology and politics. This suited Len and Mervin Sargant, who got down to cases of just where they were putting up Labour men against the Liberals and Tories, and just where they thought they would get in. Len had it listed. Corella and Bessie joined the group, taking turns to babysit 'their girls'.

Jonty savoured it all. He would be in College in October and wondered if it would be like this. The place at Oxford had proved impossible to take up even with Mr Monroe's sponsorship. And with John George under threat of blacklisting from Lord Chase's collieries, even teaching college would prove difficult. However, Jonty had saved during his teaching and as well as this Bea had come up trumps, showing him a box of florins she had been saving for just this purpose since he had been born, and later by obtaining a job for herself as a clerkess in a warehouse in Priorton.

He could look forward to college now, with relish.

On the third evening of the camp, after wandering round for an hour, Jonty finally 'found' Susanah at the bridge, drawing away with her pencil as usual. Her face was small and slightly squared off: her eyes, as he watched her, became invisible as she narrowed them to take in the view. The pink tip of that busy tongue showed again as she concentrated on drawing a miniature version of the scene before them.

'Your tongue. Do you always draw with your tongue sticking out?' His brown, blunt-fingered hand placed itself on the bridge beside her book.

She could feel his glance travel over her shoulder and on to the page where she had just recreated, stroke by stroke, line by line, a tree on the opposite bank. The tree's roots plunged into the river; its long branches, heavy with leaves, arched over to dip their fingers into the clear water. Just downstream there was the clump of quaking grass that was her next task. Tiny fish jumped like silver pencils to celebrate the feast of flies which hovered over the water. All this her greedy pencil wanted to catch.

She closed her lips over her tongue. 'I don't stick my tongue out.'

'You do. I was watching you last night, just before dusk, drawing some butterfly in a jar.'

'Well then, it must be that I must stick my tongue out, if Jonty Clelland saw me do it twice.' She put her hand over her pad and turned to see that he was quite red from her remark.

There was a silence and he tried again. 'Are you enjoying it, Susanah? The camp?'

'Yes.'

'What do you like most about it?'

'The river and the trees. And the grass. And the birds.'

'Not the meeting last night? And the singing? And all the talking?'

'It's all right. But I like to look, not talk. And the same people talk every time.'

'You mean me?'

'Sometimes.'

'Do you think I'm . . . boring? Pompous?'

'I didn't say that.'

They watched the swifts gliding their snappy flight low over the water.

'What do you dislike most about this, then? The camp?'

'Having to be together with so many people all the time. Never time to be on your own.'

Now he was red again, half turning away. 'I'm sorry, then.'

'No. No,' she said quickly, 'I didn't mean you. Now. Here. It's just the crowd of people, all the time. It's funny. You live in a house full of people, but there is more space to be on your own at home.'

Jonty turned and leaned on the bridge beside her. 'You're good at drawing.'

'Yes, I know. Miss Carmedy taught me.'

'Miss Carmedy. She's a nice woman. A good teacher. We used to call her the dragon teacher.'

That made her laugh. 'I can see what you mean. A good name for a good woman. It must be satisfying, working at the school with her and the others?'

'It is. Hard work, though.'

She clenched her fist on the drawing. 'Hard? Hard? You should ask our Davey and our Tollie about hard. Even Lew.'

Jonty looked down at the flowing water.

'I know! I know! Nothing like the pit.'

'Sorry. Not really fair, that.'

'No. Say what you think. If you think anything, you should say it. Otherwise, how can people really talk? You have a nice voice. Did you know?'

It was her turn to go red. 'Don't be daft.'

'I'm not. It kind of sings.'

There was a pause, then he coughed. 'Did you know there are kingfishers further up the river? There were last year, anyway. You should see them now you've finally got here. Would you walk there to see them? After the meeting tomorrow night? About this time?'

'I can't do that.'

'Yes, you can. I'll get Corella to come, and Len Sargant. You can get Betty Stapleton. She's your friend, isn't she? Come on. You'll be getting away from the crowd. That's what you like, isn't it?'

She was silent, staring across the water. She could feel the heat of his face close to hers, smell the stuff he wore to tame his curly hair. Then she felt soft lips hard on her hot cheek and, trembling, remembered that she'd never before seen kingfishers. Tomorrow she would see them.

Before going back to his sleeping tent, Jonty sought out Corella. Ever efficient, she rarely moved without her carpet bag which contained everything she might need '. . . just in case'. Corella was a fair, if somewhat mechanical water-colourist. He thought she might have brought her paints . . . just in case.

'Yes. They're here somewhere. I thought there might be time, and brought them just in case. But what with the girls, the games, the talks . . .' She rummaged around in her bag.

'Can I have them?'

'Are you wanting to paint?'

He could appreciate the disbelieving tone in her voice. He was no artist. 'No, I want to give them to someone who can . . . should paint. She is an amazing hand at drawing. She should paint.'

'Who is this, then?' Corella asked, with that raising of the brows which was so characteristically hers.

Jonty told her about Susanah. 'The Jones family?' She started to laugh. 'And her father Caradoc Laydon Jones who Dad had the battle about Freddy with. You know they've never really made it up. Wouldn't put it past him to have had a hand in this blacklisting scheme. Nasty man. Did you know the girl does a good deal of work on the clocks? No credit, of course. Many women . . .'

'Yes, yes, Corella, but can I have the paints? For Susanah?'

'You mean you want to give them to her?'

'It'd be no good otherwise. You can't get to be a painter in two days.'

'But Jonty . . .'

'Look, I'll get you some more next time I'm paid. And you don't need them, anyway. You hardly do any painting these days.'

Corella grinned conspiratorially at him and rifling through her bag, finally handed them over. The paint-tin fitted into the palm of Jonty's hand and was thankfully invisible as he made his way through an uproarious game of rounders, illuminated by the bonfire. Tollie Laydon Jones politely waited for him to get out of shot before he bowled to Joan Kenton. Mervin Sargant had just clubbed the ball into the trees. Any team with those two on was bound to win. Jonty wondered how they could still see the ball in the half gloom when it escaped the range of the firelight.

He kneeled down at the side of the river and let the water run over the tin, inside and out, using the tiny brush to loosen the dun-coloured scum from the paint tablets. The water caught the colours and they flared into brightness before merging with the water, then fading into neutrality. Finally the colours in the tin showed bright and true. He dabbed the tin dry with his hankie, which meant he then had to wash that in the river.

Putting the wet hankie in one pocket and the shining nearly new tin in the other, he whistled as he made his way back through the rounders game, turning down a friendly offer from Joan, that he should have a go with her bat.

Jonty watched them all with benevolence. 'Tomorrow!' he thought. 'Tomorrow will be a good day. I know it.

108

Chapter Eighteen

'Kingfishers?' said Betty that night as she and Susanah prepared for bed. 'I'm not that interested in kingfishers, Susanah. Anyway, Len and Corella and them will be on making up the quiz for tomorrow, it being the last day. And Len, he says after he'll show me how to play draughts.'

Betty's face was ruddy with the sun and the fresh air. The life glowed from her; Susanah felt like hugging her herself. No wonder Len was following her around like a dog. Following her around, laughter only slightly out of earshot, full of half-jesting challenges: such happiness seemed to be the order of the day right through the camp.

Mervin Sargant had even winked at Susanah and said that he would show her a nice place to swim further down the river. She had laughed and told him to go away and play with the other children.

'Fair enough, Auntie Su. All I can say is you don't know what you're missing.' Then he ducked out of the way of her flying pencil.

She thought of the 'perfumed sewage' of the minister's warnings. But these were not ugly, the glances and secret touching, the laughter and the comradeship.

'But I said you'd come, Bet!' It was a weak try.

'Susanah, I really am sorry. I could . . .' She paused. She really didn't want to come. Like her father, Betty focussed always on whatever she herself wanted, although this seemed to make her no less lovable. Susanah thought of the intense love that his family poured on Freddy, despite his imperfections, his apparent search only for his own gratification, even in the process of salvation.

She gave Betty a hug and said that other folks'd be there anyway, so don't worry. Only later, lying on her camp bed, making out shapes and shadows through the canvas, did she recall that those 'others' would be busy with Betty constructing that quiz. Somehow that did not trouble her. She twisted and turned, feeling that it was not quite right to be this happy, to be this confident. She crossed her fingers and knew she would see the kingfishers.

Her thoughts became dreams. A man was walking beside her in a warm place. He was walking along swishing branches out of the way. They started to pull fat juicy blackberries off spiky brambles. Heat from the fruit throbbed into their hands. Then they were in a different place. He was sitting down in a crowded room, a place beside him. He pointed to the place and Susanah sat there with confidence, no hesitation, showing him her drawing book and warming to his praise. Then they were lying shoulder to shoulder, the sun in their eyes. She felt the length of his arm and the length of his leg burn into her side. Now they were walking together calmly through long grass, down long streets, then along the road towards White Pool Pit. She was happy because at long last she would see down there. She would know the world which Davey enclosed in his silences and sleep. Then there was the sound of crying, a roaring which made her whole body tremble like the train, she had felt long ago, coming up from Wales. He was crying. He was crying. Here! Here! She couldn't think of a name. Look at me! What is it? Then she fell back. It was her father's face, deep-furrowed and twisted, wet with tears.

'Susanah. Stop it!'

She sat up. 'Stop what?'

'Screaming and crying. You were screaming and crying.'

Susanah slumped back on to the bed. 'Sorry, Bet.'

Betty muttered as she stretched her legs back down under her blanket. Susanah closed her eyes and slept on without dreams.

Jonty was sitting on the bridge when she arrived, swinging his legs and kicking his heels off the stone.

She looked around. 'Where are they? The others?'

'Couldn't come. Something about a quiz.'

'Oh,' she said, innocently.

'What about Bet? I thought she'd come.'

'Couldn't come. Something about a quiz.'

They both laughed at that. He seemed so young now. For the first time he seemed young to her. He had always seemed so old, much older even than Davey, who was the same age and who had been in the same class at school.

'What do we do, then?' he said.

'You said you'd show me kingfishers.'

'Will . . . Should we . . .' He was smiling.

'I've brought my drawing book. I thought I'd draw them.'

'Very hard to see, kingfishers. One minute they're there, next minute, whoosh, they're gone.'

'Lightning sketch,' said Susanah and they laughed again.

They walked through trees, up inclines, Jonty slightly ahead along the narrow way. She started to breathe heavily, then to cough. He turned and frowned and she smiled at him through her splutters.

'Just let me get my breath back.'

'Is this too much? I forgot . . .'

'No. No. Just stop a minute.'

There was nowhere to sit. She leaned against the trunk of one tree; he leaned against another opposite.

He smiled faintly at her, dark eyes gleaming. 'I've a surprise for you, when we get there. A present.'

'Can I see?'

'No, wait till we get there.'

It was twenty minutes before they found the place. Here the river was narrower; the surface moved with subtle energy but no turbulence.

'Now!' He pulled her into slight shade to a spot where they had full sight of the river but were invisible from it. A log had been dragged across and loaded with the soft ends of leafy branches to make a comfortable seat.

'Someone's been here,' she said.

'Me. Raced up before breakfast to check it out, to get it ready. Had to give the kingfisher his orders, you know! Wanted him on parade or we'd've wasted a journey.'

'It's nice,' she said quietly.

She settled herself on the log and waited for him to tell her about the surprise. He sat beside her. As she turned to speak he put his finger to his lips and pointed.

The bird was sitting on a branch about twenty feet away: not much bigger than a sparrow, but chunkier, his long beak making him more top heavy. The late sun caught his blue feathers.

'There's the nest,' Jonty whispered, pointing towards the muddy rise of the riverbank. She shook her head. All she could see was a clay bank. He moved closer, one hand on her shoulder, the other pointing close past her cheek. 'Look, there, underneath that bit of root that's sticking out.'

It was just a dark hole. She had been looking for a nest of twigs like those in the bushes round the water pool. 'Yes, I see it.'

The hand on her shoulder gripped harder. 'Now!'

A flash of iridescent blue, the shining lift of fish. She gasped. Jonty relaxed. 'A good sight, isn't he?'

'He's lovely. So bright.'

'Did you see him properly? Could you draw him?'

'Well, I could draw him, but what's the point? Those colours. That's the whole thing about him. Without colour, it would be nothing.'

'Well . . .' He took something from his pocket and held it out with a wide flourish.

'What's this?'

'Your present.' He dropped a small black tin into her hand. She looked at the water colours in their tiny travelling pack. Miss Carmedy had a similar one which she always carried in her leather bag.

'You can paint the kingfisher with these.'

'Whose are they?'

'They're yours. I just gave them to you.'

She thought about that. 'Thank you,' she said. 'I'll have to keep them a secret, though.'

He understood. 'We all have secrets,' he said.

For thirty minutes she concentrated on the kingfisher. She filled three pages with sketches, trying with delicate touches of paint to get the bubble-bright colour of his back and wings.

Suddenly the kingfisher had stopped diving and the light was down. She laid her open book on the log to dry the last page.

She looked at Jonty. 'Thank you for both things, the kingfisher and the paints.'

He smiled. Her earlier idea of him as pompous and opinionated was in splinters. The smile drew her right into him. For a second she could see every part of him.

He shrugged. 'They're very easy gifts.'

There was an awkward pause which went on too long. He looked around. 'A lovely place like this can only be a gift from God . . .'

She stirred uncomfortably, pulling her book over and touching it with her finger to see if it was dry.

'. . . I'm sorry, am I preaching?'

She sighed tetchily. 'Just when I think that you're . . . well . . . not boring at all, there you go . . . Why does it have to be a gift from God? Why can't it just be itself? The bank, the river, the trees dipping in . . . The kingfisher.'

'The pagans would have given each part its own god.'

'Doesn't that make just as much sense?'

'What do you believe in, then?'

'I believe in what I can see.'

'That's too concrete. There must be more.'

'A concrete thing is a cross with a tortured figure stretched across it. What I see is not concrete. When I was little I used to see things all the time. Less now. I see images that come from my mother's mind. I used to see images from Davey before the pit got him. I saw inside you just now . . .'

He leaned across the drying book and kissed her hard on the lips. 'Pagan!'

She pulled back. 'I knew a woman. I was very little. She said, "God or gods." I remember that. I think she was a pagan. She saved my mother and Jenny.' A cold breeze whipped around the tree and she shuddered.

He kissed her for a second time and this time she reacted. The first kiss had passed almost without noticing. No one, apart from Jenny and Tollie when they were very small, had ever kissed her on the lips. She had never even seen a kiss between Ceiri and Caradoc, though she had witnessed more violent intimacy.

Then his lips moved against hers, his mouth opening very slightly; a shot of fire within him connected with a core somewhere inside her, like a string drawing the neck of a bag. For a single second that core, her own fire, rose to him, was there for him on her lips. Her stomach churned and she parted her thighs to give it some ease. Then she pulled away.

He stood up and looked down at her. 'I'm sorry. I shouldn't have . . .'

Standing up beside him, she gathered up her book, closing it carefully over the damp page. 'No. I chose to. I suppose it's like you said about the speaking. If you feel it you should do it. Or how will anyone know?'

He laughed at that. 'Did you know that I have watched you? Years I have watched you.'

She shuddered at the thought of this. This watching. He took her free hand. She could feel his thick, round-tipped fingers, the slight roughness on the back of his hand. She turned away and led him down the narrow path.

112

They talked and laughed without stopping. She thought about herself and Davey, in those short years before he went into the pit. There was talking and laughter then. This same sort of intimacy.

When they reached the last turning, Jonty pulled her to a stop. 'Do you know, I remember that time I saw you brushing Betty's hair. All those years ago! Do you know that?'

'I think I do.' She didn't, but it did seem right as he said it. When had he seen her brush Betty's hair?

He waited for her to say something to him about this now. She didn't speak. All she could have said was that he touched something inside her. No one could say that, out loud. So she stayed silent.

Voices floated up to them from below. They stood apart and resumed a more decorous downward path.

'Oh, good! We thought you must have started down.' It was Corella, muffled in a large cape against the evening chill, glancing nervously from Jonty to Susanah and back again. Betty was beside her, looking even more large-eyed than usual. She continued, 'Did you see the kingfishers?'

'What's the matter? Is something the matter?' Susanah asked, staring at Betty.

Corella put her arm through Susanah's. 'The minister's down there, Susanah. Down at the camp. He came up on the train. He said your . . . sister and your mother have . . . had an accident.'

Susanah knew she should have felt uneasy about all these good things. Here was the punishment.

Jonty's lower lip jutted out and his stomach clenched as he watched Corella wrap her in her cloak. Susanah now stood white-faced, peering out at Betty who was hovering at a distance, supplanted by Corella's massive presence.

'It was Jenny, Susanah. In the water pool. Your mother tried to save her,' Betty spluttered, stumbling in to embrace her friend.

Jonty cursed Betty's unstopped mouth, watching sullenly as Susanah finally put her face, soaking wet with unchecked tears, on her friend's shoulder. Then she started to cough her raking cough. Jonty blinked hard at the wide blind look in her eyes, as though his blink would bring them back to normal, her back to seeing him. Failing in this, he dragged his eyes from her and turned away. When he turned back again, all he could see were the backs of the three women as they scrambled the last hundred yards to the bridge.

He picked up a loose branch that lay at his feet and went to the tree whose image was now so neatly locked in Susanah's drawing book. He stood there and thrashed the tree hard. He flailed away until the assaulted branch was frayed, but he failed to produce a satisfactory thwack. He threw it down in disgust.

Bea was up and alone when he finally arrived home early the next morning. She was sitting writing at the table.

'Where's Corella?' he demanded.

She smiled faintly at him. 'It was one this morning when Mac Tillson got them back here in that old brake of his. And Corella was up before the crack of dawn to get back up to Livesay. She and Bessie're taking their girls straight over to Penrith.'

He looked round. 'Where's Dad?"

'Your father's gone off with Freddy. Turned up the worse for drink. Something about Caradoc. Poor Caradoc. Poor Freddy.' She screwed the top on her ink bottle. 'Sad news,' she said quietly.

Jonty flung himself into the fireside chair. 'Yes.' The tears were falling from his eyes, wetting his cheek, soaking his collar.

'The poor child. An innocent. And they say the mother . . .' Bea's chair scraped on the stone floor as she stood up. She came to stand behind him, her hands on his shoulders, her hard cheek on his hair. He could feel her warmth and physical power flowing into him. He knew again why his father constantly sought her touch. 'It's true, Jonty, what's said. Each loss diminishes all of us. Your sorrow does you credit.'

He put up a hand to cling to hers. 'I'm a bumbling idiot,' he sobbed, 'a bumbling idiot. I was no help. We were all so despairing. But it was for me I was despairing. I'd lost. I had no pity for the dead child and the woman. And I couldn't help Susanah. I left Corella to sweep her up, that way she has. I left Betty Stapleton to cry with her. We had been so close, you know? Susanah and me. A minute before? We were laughing together. Minutes before . . . Then this news came . . .'

Bea turned him to her, put her cheek on his. 'You'll have to bear this, son.'

'No!' he said. 'I can't bear it. I have waited for her. For so long I've waited.'

Chapter Nineteen

When Susanah and Tollie, shepherded by Corella and Betty, arrived in the small hours of the morning at Selby Street; Lew was sitting on a low stool beside the back door, his long legs sprawling across to form a very effective barrier. He had set up a chunk of wood as a target on the opposite wall and was skimming his whittling knife at the rag he had fixed at its centre.

He looked at Susanah with eyes blank as slates. She could read nothing. 'Back from holiday are we?' He stood up, towering over them all, even Corella.

'Stoppit, Lew,' Betty said.

Susanah sat heavily on the stool.

'Stop buggering about,' said Tollie grimly, putting out a hand to push him to one side.

Casually, Lew caught the hand, held on to it and looked across at Susanah 'She fell . . . Ma, that is. Into the water. Our Jenny was down there. Wanderin' round. Been moanin' around about you goin' off. Me da, he cracked her one and she ran off. He made Ma stay here. Jenny not bein' back by the afternoon, and him working in the shed, Ma went off searching for her.'

He let go of Tollie's hand and pulled at the knife which was deeply embedded in the wood. After silent minutes, he managed to wrench it out. 'Davey walked the lanes. Me, I went up in the woods, thought that was a likely place. You spent plenty time up there with our Jenny, didn't you, S'anah? I got down to the water pool just in time to see Ma go under. I got her, but Jenny had gone minutes before. She was floating, head down, hair spreading out in the water. Ma had seen her from the opposite side and just walked into the water.' His hand came down and the knife whirred viciously through the air again, thumping its way into the softened wood. 'Maybe it was the cordial made her think she could walk on water, like.'

Tollie hit him then, putting him only slightly off balance. Lew smiled bitterly into Corella Clelland's eyes. 'Our mother, Miss Clelland, has her own way of turning water into wine. She don't have to wait for no marriage at Cana.'

'Lew!'

Susanah wondered blankly why Betty kept protesting to Lew in that chapel voice. She stood up, swaying. 'She's inside?'

Corella's arm came round her on one side, Tollie's on the other.

'They both are,' said Lew.

In the kitchen, Davey was kneeling beside Ceiri who was half sitting, half lying on the pillow-heaped wooden settle. Her face, silvery grey in colour, looked surprisingly smooth and young. Her eyes were moving about under closed lids but she was fast asleep.

Davey looked at her for several seconds. 'She's very poorly, S'anah. Only here by a thread. Doctor said it was near the end . . . before *he* threw him out. She's waited for you.' Unshed tears were standing in his eyes.

'She should be in bed, Davey,' Susanah whispered.

He shook his head. 'She can't . . . Jenny. She's in there, Susanah. In the front room. On their bed.'

'Where's Da?'

Davey looked up at Lew.

A faint smile sketched itself on Lew's face. 'Freddy Stapleton came and took him down the garden. He's like a wild man, cursing the Almighty. Threw out the minister and the preachers, the doctor and the old women. Threw the lot out.' He clicked his whittling knife into its folded position and tucked it into his belt.

Tollie stood away from Susanah. 'I'll get after him,' he said.

Corella's arm tightened on Susanah's shoulder. Betty stared at her with eyes still red from crying.

Susanah frowned. Why were they staying, these two? She pulled away from Corella. Tollie was right. They'd look after their own. 'You can go now,' she said firmly.

Corella ran her hand down her sleeve. 'You're sure?'

'You too, Bet.'

Relief rippled across Betty's face. 'You're sure? I can stay . . .'

'No. Davey's here. Lew as well.' Her head was aching and she just wanted the two girls away. She watched as they stumbled awkwardly out of the house, then put her hand on the knob of the middle door.

Davey stood up. His eyes seemed far out of their sockets and had reddish grey shadows underneath. 'No, Davey. I'll see her myself.'

In the curtained gloom she could see that the bed had been covered by a white sheet. Slipping down to the floor beneath she could make out the shadowy pattern of Ceiri's lovely crocheted counterpane. Jenny lay on the sheet, covered neatly to the neck with another white sheet. Her face, rather heavy-browed like Caradoc's and Davey's, was closed and still. Her cheeks glowed pearly white through her fine lashes.

Susanah put her lips to her sister's icy brow. In that kiss trembled echoes of all the touching they had ever shared, from the very first touch in the Welsh cottage. The skin had been greased then with birth blood, not white like polished stone.

'Sorry, lamb. I am so sorry.' She put her face beside the cold one on the pillow. Rough hands pulled her off the bed and held her away. She turned her face, crying and sobbing, against the coarse shirt, the arms warm about her. Finally she got the right words out. 'I shouldn't have gone. It wouldn't have happened. I should have stayed.'

'Don't talk bloody rubbish.'

Her tears stopped as she looked up in surprise. It was Lew who'd said that. She was certain it had been Davey who'd pulled her away.

'Ma. She wants you. She needs you.'

'They would both be all right if I hadn't . . .'

'Bloody rubbish, I tell yer. Warrabout the years they had? Didn't yer give'm that? You and that old witch in Wales. Young Jenny had her ten years when it might've been nowt . . .' He looked down at her, his face still surly.

'How d'you know? It was a – '

'Secret? Secrets are just them things people agree not to talk about. They still know'm. Now, come on. Get your face dried and get in there. She wants you.'

Ceiri opened her eyes and smiled at Susanah: a face as young as the still face in the next room. 'Loveiy! Was it nice in the woods?' Her voice was like a single thread, the fragile residue of a strong cord.

Susanah hesitated. 'It was like heaven, Mama. I saw a kingfisher. I painted it. See?' She scrambled feverishly with her bag and brought out the book. 'And the weeping willow over the water. See?'

Ceiri peered and smiled. 'A lovely place. The riches of the earth. You see them, Susanah? Good.' Her voice was down to the tiniest of whispers. She put her small hand over Susanah's, where it lay on the book. 'Now will you get something for me, lovely?'

'Anything, Mama.'

'In the press. In one of the bags. A blue one, with white spots. Last of my wedding dress. There's a spoon there, a carved spoon.'

She knew where it was, lying there beside the package of letters. She got the spoon from the press without once looking at the figure on the bed. She knew Jenny was no longer there for her.

Ceiri stroked the spoon then held it up. 'There're birds on here. See?' She insisted that they all look, even Lew, who was sitting at the table pushing a cup around in patterned squares. 'Not kingfishers. What are they?'

Davey said the birds were partridges. Lew said scornfully they were pigeons. Anyone could see that.

'Do you know what it is, this?' Ceiri shook it wildly under Davey's nose. He smiled. 'It's a wooden spoon, Ma.'

Her eyes drooped. 'No, it isn't,' she whispered. 'A love song, it's a love song. He's got no words, so he carved me the song. He always has to show me. Can't tell me. Now it's the money. But that's not as pretty as the spoon. Not half so pretty, do you see?'

Then she went to sleep, the spoon clutched in her hand. Susanah went into the scullery to fill the kettle. When she had done this she transferred the purloined package of letters to her bag.

Now she stood there, her hands shaking, one hand over the other on the kettle handle. She started to pray. 'Our Father, which art . . .' It was no good. How did it go on? She tried in Welsh. That was no good. There was no Welsh in her head at all. Where had it gone? She wouldn't be able to talk to her mother now. God, let Ma stay, she pleaded. Don't let her leave me. I want her here. You've got Jenny now. Leave me Ma.

Then, in front of her, shimmering on the white-washed scullery wall, they were there, the two of them. Jenny, much younger and still fat-legged, was sitting on Ceiri's knee. Ceiri was nuzzling away at Jenny's cheek in that way she had. Susanah knew now that He wanted them. He was greedy and would take them both. The gods in the tree and the river and the little body of the kingfisher would not extract such vengeance for just a little bit of pleasure, such a tiny scrap of joy, would they? Would they?

It was three o'clock in the morning before Caradoc came home, half carried into the house by Tollie and John George Clelland, who hauled him into a chair and knelt down to pull off his boots. 'Freddy Stapleton came for me,' he said. 'Near out of his wits . . .'

'Da had him on drinking beer with whisky chasers down at the Steam Mill,' said Tollie. 'He had a pocket full of money and was buying the bar. On at Freddy for being a coward and not daring to drink. Then Freddy started on with him. Said he had to keep him company.'

Lew whistled. 'Never thought I'd see it.'

'So're the mighty fallen,' said Mr Clelland, sadly. 'A great oak crashes and takes with it weaker trees. Strange that yer father should turn to the man he despised to find some comfort in his despair.'

'I stood guard while Freddy went for Mr Clelland,' said Tollie, keeping his eyes away from the settle where his mother lay. 'I offered to go, but Freddy was too scared to stay. Da was fightin' drunk by then. Freddy could hardly walk himself.'

John George coughed and glanced at the still small figure on the settle. 'Would you like a prayer? You're all so hard pressed tonight. Caradoc, too.'

They looked uneasily at each other.

'No,' said Susanah.

The others shook their heads in agreement, seeing the rightness of it.

John George looked from one to another, lips thinning, colour rising.

'No thank you,' said Susanah more firmly.

'Well, it's time I got mesel' home.' He made to go, then turned back. 'I'll say me own prayer, for him and you, at home with our Bea.' Then he went, followed by Davey, who locked the door behind him.

Caradoc stood up from his chair, swaying. Then they all watched as he walked heavily across to his wife, staring down at her. He put one finger on the hand which still grasped the spoon. Then he swept her up, blankets and all, and sat down with her in his arms, rocking and whispering away in a Welsh which they could barely understand. It was the last time Welsh was used in the house on Selby Street.

With no spoken agreement, the four of them moved to the front room. Tollie went to stare out of a crack in the curtain. Davey very gingerly drew the thin white cloth over the face of the absent Jenny. Lew pulled four chairs from the corners of the room and set them in a little circle by the window.

They were sitting there, still silent, an hour later when Caradoc brought in Ceiri's body and laid it gently beside Jenny on the bed. He looked at them. 'Your mother has gone. I will not say to a better place as, if there were a God he would not take her from me in this . . . trivial way.'

Then he walked out into the dawn and they were left to comfort each other.

Chapter Twenty

Caradoc snored, then turned awkwardly in his twisted upright position on the settle. The blanket slipped away to show creased clothes and hands not so clean as usual. Susanah stood poised by the hearth, then continued to place pieces of coal one by one on the night-dead fire. She thrust the poker into the centre to draw the heat and went upstairs to dress.

Lew was snoring, also, but the other two were quiet. The bed she had shared with Jenny for ten years was neat, only ruffled at the edge where she herself had lain on top, unsleeping.

She ducked under the top cover, her head tenting it up, while she changed from night to day clothes. She thought of the many times she had played games with Jenny in this same tent, away from the boys' curious gaze. She stood up, straightened the cover, then dragged her hair back into an uncombed plait without looking at it. Davey's head reared up the heap of blankets at his end of the boys' bed.

'Da. He's awake?'

'He's stirring just now. He can't really have rested on that settle. I'm just going to get the breakfast on . . .'

'He'll have a sore head. Are you all right, S'anah?'

Lew snuffled and sat straight up out of sleep, in that way he had. Tollie had to roll over to accommodate this action. His head fell back to show the dried white tracks of the previous night's tears on his sleeping face.

' 'Course. Are you all right, Davey? How about you?'

'I'm all right.'

'I'm all right, too, if you're asking me,' said Lew, leaning his head against the wall and closing his eyes.

She left a tussle over blankets behind her and made her way down the steep stairs.

By this time her father was up and wearing his work clothes, pushing a kettle on to the now-bright fire. He put his face towards her, keeping his eyes down, hidden by his heavy brow.

'See your brothers get their breakfast and get themselves on to work. I have things to see to this morning and will be fully occupied. Then straight to the pit. A good thing I am on back shift.' He looked into the flames. 'The old women'll come first thing to see her right. The minister'll come, too. Tell him Saturday at eleven o'clock. And the doctor. There'll be another certificate. He did one already for your sister. Others'll come, poking around.

For your mother, you'll make them welcome. They'll make much of me being at work but rather there than sitting here listening to their mumbles.'

He went across and checked his pocket watch against the grandfather clock that had stood in the corner for three weeks. Opening the ornate glass door he made a fine adjustment to the minute hand. His pit boots struck sparks from the stone as he clumped from the kitchen.

Susanah went to the middle door and opened it a crack. In the vertical space she could see the shrouded figures on the bed, one small, one larger.

She shut the door with a click and brought a stool right up to the fire, her face to the flames, to take the freeze out of her bones.

Her mind turned to the day she watched her mother scrambling on the floor muttering about a bracelet. On the bed in the next room, lying beside Jenny, she was still wearing the string bracelet Davey had fashioned for her.

Susanah closed her eyes and put her mind to them, Ceiri and Caradoc. In her mind's eye she could see them, walking together down a muddy track, a high hedge on one side and a fast river on the other. They looked so much younger, Caradoc tall and heavy, with thick streaming hair and a rocking gait, Ceiri narrow, finely made, her hair black and curly. At first they kept a distance from each other, but gradually they walked ever closer. They were shoulder to shoulder when they reached a tree and turned to face each other, smiling. He reached deep into his pocket and with a flourish produced a wooden object. The spoon. Susanah recognised the spoon. She could feel the young Ceiri's happiness ripple through her. Ceiri stroked the surface of the spoon and brought it up to her nose to see the detail, to smell its woody smell. He laughed at her pleasure, then brought a finger to her lips to stop her tumble of words. His hand went in the other pocket and he pulled out an object that glittered in the sun. He took her hand and clasped it on to her wrist. She pulled up her wrist and stroked it against her cheek. Their happiness was like a song in the air and it reached out to Susanah. She put her hand towards it and her hand burnt with its heat.

'Go careful, you'll burn your hand.' Lew pulled her away from the fire. 'Isn't it time you got some breakfast on?'

She looked up into the closed face of her brother. 'He must've loved her, Lew.'

'Funny bloody way o' showin' it,' growled Davey, coming into the kitchen.

Soon, Davey and Lew had filled the whole room with their big frames and the gritty smell of the pit which emanated from their clothes.

'Are you going to work, then?'

'What'd the old man say if we didn't?'

She nodded. 'He did seem to expect . . .'

'Where is he?'

'He went off. No breakfast. Said he'd go straight to work when he'd done.'

'So what's he doing till two o'clock?' asked Davey.

'Back on the drink, you can bet on it,' said Lew. 'By, that was a sight for sore eyes last night. Never thought I'd see that. Ma'd've appreciated it.'

'You . . .' rasped Davey.

Susanah placed herself between them before the fight could start. 'Stop that. Give us a hand with this pan. You'll be late for work at this rate. You're not the ones on back shift.'

The day plodded on in a grey gauze fashion for Susanah as she opened the door time and time again to people coming to pay their respects. Betty came early and stayed with her, pottering around helpfully, occasionally darting worried glances at Susanah's hard, still face, her dry eyes.

Betty made the visitors cups of tea and offered round Ceiri's ginger biscuits still fresh in the tin. Susanah sat unspeaking as Mr Carmedy came, worried about the danger of the colliery pool, and conveyed his sister's regards. Then came the Smiths, Jade wearing a black tie and his wife wearing a black bonnet she had bought for the memorial service for the old Queen years before. Josiah Sargant came with his large blond nephews. Despite the occasion, Betty managed to exchange some mournful but meaningful looks with Len.

Again and again mouths rehearsed words of comfort which sounded to Susanah as though they were talking more of their own death, their own mortality. Some of them tiptoed into the front room. She left them to it, not wanting to know what they thought or did in there.

The only person whose way she barred was Miss Antrobus, also sporting her 'Queen's mourning'. 'No,' Susanah said firmly. 'Not yet. Tomorrow. You mustn't go in.'

The woman pulled up her fat shoulders so that she appeared to have no neck under her fluffy black collar. She reminded Susanah of a defensive pullet confronted with strangers on Davey's allotment. Susanah started to laugh.

Betty came to stand between her and Miss Antrobus. 'Mr Laydon Jones said no one was to go through, Miss Antrobus. And Susanah is very upset, Miss Antrobus. Very upset.'

'Well, if Caradoc . . .' She pulled her coat together and peered around Betty at Susanah, who was now covering her face with both hands. 'It's a hard time for you, dear, but you may rely on my help at all times. I know your father would want it.'

She swept out, leaving them wreathed in the scent of violets and sweat dried on wool. Betty went over and bolted the door behind her, then turned round to see Susanah now convulsed with laughter, tears running down her face. 'Did you see her, Bet, fluffing out her feathers. Did you see her?'

Now she was crying in earnest, and Betty put her arms around her, her face against hers, rocking from side to side.

Tollie, who had stayed upstairs all morning, refused any dinner. Like Caradoc, he was on afternoon shift. He was stone-faced as she hustled him out of the door, his bait box tucked into his pocket.

The afternoon stumbled on its way.

Their final callers were Vivian and Joan Kenton. Joan's face was clean, her hair combed back. Vivian wore a red and white striped scarf inside the neck of his rough shirt. He was clutching a bunch of dog roses and forget-me-nots. The bunch was tightly arranged, so that the massed forget-me-nots made a misty ring around the yellow and icing pink of the dog roses. He pushed it towards her. 'The dog roses is for pleasure and pain, the forget-me-nots is for not forgetting.'

'He picked'm and put'm together hisse'n,' said Joan.

They refused to come in and Susanah was left with the flowers at the back door. She put them as they were into a baking bowl full of water and placed them on the table under the window. They half floated, drifting into their own watery pattern.

'They're lovely,' said Betty.

'Mama would have liked them,' said Susanah.

She fed Lew and Davey when they came in from work and then she and Betty went upstairs while the lads bathed the pit dirt from their bodies. Then the four of them sat in silence, listening to the ticking of the clocks. At five, two of the case clocks made their jangling strike and there was a great rattle on the front door.

Mac Tillson stood there in a rusty black jacket. Beside him was a tall thin man whose face pointed towards the front like a mouse. He was all in black, clutching a stained black hat to his chest. 'Laydon Jones?'

She nodded.

He stood back to let her see the hearse with its single horse and fancy gold lettering. 'Castle and Son. Undertakers. Priorton. I'm Joe Castle. Told your da we'd get here before nightfall. We need to be gettin' started?'

She nodded again.

They watched as the two men lifted a single coffin from the hearse and carried it across the grass, puffing and blowing. It was a huge thing. She wondered briefly about Mat Tillson not being able to work at the pit if he was strong enough to lift this great box.

'There are two of them, you know,' said Lew, who was standing behind her. 'You need two.'

'This is for both,' puffed Joe Castle. 'Your da knocked us up before the crack of dawn, nay, before even that, and stood over us all morning. Special end panels, special bottom. specially adapted top. Only wax finish. Stood over us. I tell yer, he's a fearsome man.'

'He'd pay yer!' growled Davey.

One round mouse eye surveyed him. 'Oh, he put all right. Here, give us a hand through this door, will you?'

Susanah watched as they started to tip the coffin on its side to get it through the narrow door. 'You can't get it out like that. Not with them in it!'

He cocked a bright eye round the room. 'Window,' he said. 'Easy enough to tek the sash out.'

They were all whisked out of the front room while Joe Castle got on with his work. For a few minutes they sat listening to the thumps and mutterings that came at them through the middle door. Susanah thought about other times, other thumps and mutterings. Then Davey put on his cap and scarf and went out. Lew went to get a lump of wood from the shed and started to whittle away at it, coiling the white shavings into the hearth. Susanah thought that her mother would have stopped him doing that.

He caught her glance. 'What about taking our S'anah down to see your ma, Bet? A bit of fresh air. I'll stay to see to this feller.'

Bea Clelland looked up in amazement at the big man, then opened the door wider. 'Come in, Mr Laydon Jones.'

She followed him through. 'A sad day for you. It's Mr Laydon Jones, JG.'

Her husband was standing up. He started to put a hand out to shake that of the Welshman, but withdrew it before it could be rebuffed. 'Sit yerself down . . .'

'No, Mr Clelland, I'll not sit down.' He looked around at the warm, cluttered room. There was a pause which made Bea fidget, but very patiently John George waited.

'I wish to thank you for rescuing me from that den of iniquity last night. I made your friend Freddy Stapleton take me. Like him, I needed you.'

Another heavy pause.

'There's the problem as to who'll speak for Ceiri at the service. T'were up to me there'd be none. No God would do this . . .'

'No! No! Don't think that,' urged John George. Bea was crying.

'I don't want that fool Simmons speaking. You are a . . . kinder man. I'd be a kinder man if I could . . . Ceiri liked the sound of your voice. She said that.'

John George's hand went out and this time it was grasped. 'Honoured, old lad,' he said.

On Saturday the chapel was packed for the funeral: it seemed as if the whole village were there. Many of the people had never even spoken to Ceiri, who seemed to them a shadowy indistinct person. However, Caradoc was a leading member of the chapel and respects had to be paid. Young people, friends of Tollie, Lew and Davey, went to show their sympathy. There were those who went because they were stirred by the sadness of any mother and child lost in this way. There were those who went out of curiosity to see the famous double coffin. The numbers were swelled further by people from the Welsh chapel in Priorton, whose voices added greater glory to the hymns which were sung for Ceiri and Jenny.

The coffin was carried into the church by Caradoc and his sons, helped by Mervin Sargant and Len, with Freddy Stapleton and Jonty Clelland at the lighter end. The choice of Jonty had caused a fistfight between Davey and Lew, but Davey, who lost the fight, still insisted that Jonty helped to carry the coffin.

Minister Simmons conducted the funeral with the heavy dignity of custom. According to Lew, who was kicked by Davey for his opinion, the choice of Clelland to speak was a reward for rescuing Caradoc from the Steam Mill so discreetly on the night that Ceiri died.

John George used the text 'Suffer little children', weaving the innocence

123

of the mother and child together, using the shared coffin as an analogy for their eternal bonding. He spoke softly, his eyes moving along the rows from one person to the next. Each stirred and felt his own mortality; each grasped some seed of comfort from the soft words.

Susanah felt the weight, the press of people there. There were so many people. So many souls. So hard to breathe. It must be hard for those two in there, she thought, those two inside the waxed wood. She could smell it. It got into her nose, her throat, it made her want to cough.

The punishment was bound to be hard. She looked accusingly at the crucifix, set to one side. But how can it be right she demanded, that You punish me by punishing them? They didn't do it. They didn't walk up the river to see the kingfishers. They were innocent, gentle souls. The man is saying it here. Why not make me fall in the river, head down, not them? Not those two.

She watched Caradoc's fists clench and clench again as he listened with an impassive face, his head down. She remembered then that Ceiri had spoken of the magic in John George Clelland's voice and knew that that was why he had been chosen.

Tollie sat on the other side of her. He had his hand on Davey's shoulder. Davey had said nothing to anyone for days and, sitting there in the wooden pew, seemed hunched to half his size. Lew was sitting, impassive as ever, at the end of the row, tapping his fingers softly on the armrest. Coming out of the chapel, she tried to walk closer to Caradoc, but he kept two feet of space between them.

The crowds pressed on to the cemetery and there was silence in the sunny space as they listened to Minister Simmons's last words and watched the wide coffin being lowered into the dark space beneath. The earth receives its riches. Susanah cried now, with Davey on one side, and Tollie on the other, holding tight to her arms.

For two minutes she endured the dry hollow silence that followed the ceremony, then she turned and walked quickly through the cemetery, through the broad gates and on to the road back to Selby Street.

Jonty, at the end of the crowd, stood back to let her by. Then, seeing that neither her brothers nor her father hurried after her, he ran to catch her up.

She strode on, not acknowledging his presence. She did not look up.

'Your Davey says he's going away. The army, he says . . .'

This stopped her. 'What?'

'That's what he said. When he asked me to . . .'

She put her head down and walked on.

'Susanah, I am sorry about all this.' Hopeless words.

'Yes.' Her voice was a dull, flat voice.

'I need to know . . .'

'No. There is nothing. He, if there is a He, took them because I . . . we . . .'

'What?' Jonty gaped at her. 'That's nonsense. Rubbish. It was something that happened, a tragedy. Caused by nothing. No one.'

'Everything is caused, everything is connected.' She picked up her pace.

'Can I do something for you?' he begged. 'Anything?'

She slowed down and turned again to face him. Her hand went to the pocket of the coat, the coat that Ceiri had persuaded Caradoc to buy for her to go to camp. She brought out an envelope. 'If you like, you can post this. Up in Priorton, not down in the village with everybody knowing.'

He took the letter from her. 'I can easily do that. And . . .'

'And nothing. And after that, Jonty Clelland, you just get back to your school and off to your college . . .' There were no tears in her eyes and her voice was dry as autumn leaves.

She turned and ran on, vanishing round the corner of Front Street. Jonty smoothed the crumpled letter with his fingers. It was addressed in a large looping graceful hand to an address in Bath. The name took up the whole width of the envelope. Isabella Fortunata Laydon Jones. What kind of a person had a name like that?

PART TWO

1906–1914

Chapter Twenty-One

Clusters of people were climbing on and off the train which had just steamed into Priorton station. Two other trains were gurgling up their own steam, straining to get away. Heavy carts and delivery wagons jockeyed for position around the tall iron gateway. Their drivers were busy about their own particular business, with only partial interest in the plump woman who had just alighted, her green hat sporting its blue feather, her worn leather luggage and a complicated strapped satchel dumped around her feet.

The bustle at the station had been a surprise for Isabella the first time she had come to Priorton.

'It must be near the end of the world, my dear, and just as barren,' she told Tom Mulblaine after her first visit to Lady Chase, who, always too keen on touching, had kissed and hugged her soundly.

That time she had been led with some ceremony to the polished trap at the end of the platform. This time she was being treated to some openly curious looks, but no offers of help. None of the vehicles resembled a commercial coach or cab, so she approached a cart elaborately marked with the insignia of the Priorton Co-operative Society. A stout man was sitting in the driver's seat, smoking a pipe, while a young lad was loading bulky parcels into the back.

She heaved her satchel on to the step. 'I need a cab, something to get me to Gibsley village.'

The man looked around the station yard, twisting his neck from left to right to examine the street. 'Don't see no cab, missis.'

'That's why I'm asking. I can see that there is no cab.'

He removed the pipe. His bottom underlip showed red. 'Not from round here, are yeh? From London, are yeh?'

'No. I came from Bath. To York yesterday.'

'Could tell ye're not from round here. That voice. A canny posh voice you've got, pet.'

'Do I have to sing to you to get you to tell me about a cab?' Her pale eyes bored into his.

He grinned broadly and stuck the pipe back between his teeth. 'Climb up then, hinney. I'll drop you off at Clem Sorenson's. He hires. Here, Viv, tek the lady's bags and give her a leg up. Give the lady a leg up.'

The bags were whisked into the back and a gentle hand helped her into the front of the van. As the boy settled beside her she took a closer look at

129

him. The man snapped the leather reins and the cart lurched forwards.

'Ye're thinkin' he's a bonny lad, aren't ye?' The driver was smiling sideways at her, showing wide-gapped teeth.

The boy was quite beautiful. He was wearing the brown grey drab jacket of an errand boy, but his hair was long under his cap and slightly curled. His skin was soft and white, pink on its high points. Isabella, who had made a lifetime's study of such things, could sense little that was masculine about him. She had met men like this. In London and in Bath; that one time she had gone to Paris. Nice people. Intricate. But, unlike this boy, they usually had money, their own or other people's, to soften their lives.

She smiled. 'So he is.'

The driver looked hard at her. 'Not that he isn't a canny worker, mind. Old Clelland, who put in a word for him, promised he would work, and by God he did. Isn't that right, bonny lad?'

'Yes, Mr Ormerod.' The boy was sitting, quite composed, his hands folded in his lap; they were slender, well-shaped hands, the half-moons and rims of his nails showing quite white and clean.

'Mind you, I'd have had his sister like a shot if they'd let me. Strong as a hoss, your Joan. Could lift this wagon, never mind drive it. Couldn't she, Viv?'

The boy's still face broke into a wide smile. 'So she could, Mr Ormerod.'

'Not that Viv here isn't all right. Mebbe not as strong as a hoss, but'll work like one.' Mr Ormerod clicked his tongue and his teeth through his pipe, making a kind of kiss. The heavy horse strode out.

Isabella leaned forward to get a better view of the whole straight street along which they rode. It was lined with all kinds of shops: gown shops, milliners, furriers, provisioners, cafés and eating houses. The palatial frontage of the Priorton Co-operative Society, with all its departments, dominated one side of the High Street. She sat back comfortably in between Mr Ormerod and the sweet boy called Viv.

Half an hour later her confidence flagged when she found herself standing with her bags about her among the dust and the occasional cobble of Selby Street. A gas lamp flickered, floating in the air like an underpowered glow-worm in the far distance. The houses appeared to be in darkness – strange for such an early evening hour.

She knocked on number seventy-one. She could hear stirrings inside, but no answer. She pushed her bags up against the door and set out to find the back entrance. Passing fifteen doors, she finally found an entry to the backs. Once on the back lane there was light, blooming out from kitchen windows. She counted fifteen gates before she let herself into the sixteenth back yard. Here the light came from the little pantry window and a red glow from the kitchen in front of her.

She took a breath. Then, removing her glove, she gave the kitchen door a good hard rattle. There was a long pause before it was opened. A square sharp face peered at her into the darkness. An angular girl.

'Susanah? Is it Susanah?'

Pure fright on the face. The girl looked quickly behind her, then nodded.

'Well. I am Isabella Fortunata Laydon Jones. Your aunt, I'd imagine.' She smiled, showing her teeth, with only one or two missing. A green hat with a sweeping feather of iridescent blue caught the light from the kitchen. 'You look tired. I see my mother in you.' Susanah was grasped and hugged, her own body unyielding.

'You'd better come in. I don't know what he'll say. My father.'

'Doesn't he know?'

'No. I didn't know whether you'd come. No point.'

There was a strangled call from inside and the girl stood back. Isabella swept past her and was stuck in the tiny lobby before she found her way to the kitchen.

Caradoc, still himself but looking worn and old, sat there at the table with a broken-down clock in front of him. He stood up so his face was beyond the reach of the lamp. A young man, tall and heavy, favouring the younger Caradoc, was whittling wood by the fire. Another, smaller and sharp-faced like the girl, was turning the pages of a book by a lamp in the corner. He was head to head with two younger men, perhaps sixteen or seventeen. One of them had a head of startling blond hair. A fat woman with unlikely curls softening her scraped-back hair was sitting tatting in the only soft chair in the room.

'Da.' The girl's voice was trembling. 'This is . . .'

'I know who it is.' He sat down again, picked up his grinding tool and went on with his work.

The boys on the floor stood up. The younger ones were a head taller than the older.

'Davey, Tollie, and Tollie's friend Mervin Sargant. This is Isabella Fortunata Laydon Jones. Our father's sister . . . Lew!'

Lew stopped his whittling, looked at his aunt from head to toe, and whistled under his breath. Davey wiped his hand on his shirt, then put it out to shake hers. The others followed suit.

She smiled up into the handsome open face. 'Tollie?' she said.

'I know!' He grinned at her. 'It's really Oliver Ransom . . .'

'Ceiri's father!' She nodded.

'And this is me mate Mervin Sargant. He lives in Middlesbrough and is on a visit. He's a footballer there. Getting famous. The Boy Wonder they call him.'

Isabella's hand was engulfed in the hand of the footballer. She smiled up into his shining handsome face.

'And this is Miss Antrobus . . .'

The woman nodded. Her hands stayed tight with her tatting, continually twisting and turning it over as she worked, her narrow eyes focussing three inches to the left of Isabella's ear.

Susanah responded to her raised eyebrows. 'Miss Antrobus is a teacher at the Sunday School. She has . . . kindly . . . kept us company a bit, since . . .'

Isabella turned to Caradoc, who was sitting hard as flint at the table. 'I was sorry, sorry to hear about Ceiri . . .'

131

'Who? Who was it told you?' But already he was up and reaching for Susanah, swinging her round, shaking her, his hand raised.

Isabella came between them, pushing him back to the wall. 'That's enough, Caradoc. This is a little girl. Are you no better than *him*? No better than that man?' Her voice was angry, insistent.

His hands came down to his sides, his shoulders sagged. He sat down again.

She plumped herself in the seat opposite, moving her face into the ring of his lamplight. 'I was sorry to hear about Ceiri, Caradoc. So sorry. I loved Ceiri. I was glad the girl wrote. Your Susanah.' She nodded in her direction.

'She had no business.'

'It was a very affecting letter. I loved Ceiri,' she repeated. 'You know that.'

Standing behind the woman, Susanah could see her father's eyes flash.

'Harlot,' he said quietly, without emphasis.

Miss Antrobus gasped. Lew picked up his wood and started to cut away at it again. The others stood rigid. Isabella stared at Caradoc, keeping her eyes steady on his. He dropped his gaze to his hands and started to put the clock parts into some kind of order on the table. 'There's no room for you here.'

'True,' Miss Antrobus's reedy voice put in. 'As Caradoc says, there is no room. This house is very full.'

The year before there had been room for two more. Susanah's head ached. She could see Ceiri yet again in her chair, her hands busy with her crochet hook and the new counterpane, Jenny leaning against her knees.

'No space at all,' repeated Miss Antrobus, sitting now on Ceiri's chair.

Isabella looked from one to the other of them, a slight smile on her face.

'Two days' travelling and what a fine welcome I get.'

'D'you come a long way?' asked Tollie, embarrassed.

'From Bath. The other end of the country. Hundreds of miles.'

'That where you live?'

'Well, I did. I've left there now.'

Another long pause.

'Would you like some tea?' asked Susanah.

'That would be nice, dear.'

Standing in the pantry watching the water ping into the kettle, Susanah wondered where the woman would go that night. There was room in her bed, where Jenny had laid.

The sneck rattled. She opened the back door to Jonty Clelland and stood back as he walked in. Miss Antrobus was holding forth as they made their way into the kitchen. 'I would not advise, Miss Jones, interference between parent and child . . .'

Isabella stood up, ducked her face towards the other woman and hissed, 'You mind your own business, you old . . .'

Lew grinned and the others looked at the floor. Caradoc started across towards his sister.

Susanah pulled Jonty right into the room with an enthusiasm that made him gasp; his visits were accepted but he was usually treated with the wooden politeness Susanah reserved for Miss Antrobus. Miss Antrobus, his mother said, was moving in on Caradoc like a homing pigeon. Jonty said, more like a homing spider.

'This is my aunt, Jonty. My father's sister. Miss Isabella Fortunata Laydon Jones. Jonty Clelland.'

Caradoc withdrew to the fire, turning his back on the whole room, and leaned on the mantelshelf. Jonty crossed to the table to shake the woman's proffered hand. She dimpled a smile up at him and he felt the heat sheet through him.

'Clelland? I've just heard that name. I had a lift from the carrier. He had this curious apprentice, recommended him by a Mr Clelland.'

Jonty nodded.

'My father. And that'd be Vivian Kenton.'

'Pansyboy! Half girl,' growled Lew.

Miss Antrobus clicked her teeth.

Jonty, the heat receding, looked placidly down at the Sunday School teacher. 'Mr Ormerod says he does a good job, Miss Antrobus.'

Susanah looked at him. 'Jonty, my . . . aunt needs somewhere to stay. She can't stay here. Do you know somewhere?'

'Yes. You are just in time, Mr Clelland. I wonder if you know where a poor benighted woman might stay? It seems my brother's house is too full for guests.'

'There are no hotels, nor even rooming houses in Gibsley.' He took out his watch. 'There's the Queen's Hotel in Priorton, but it's late.'

'Oh dear, and I have just come from there.' Isabella was not worried. She observed the way Susanah looked at the dark boy, willing some response behind Caradoc's stiff back. He would respond.

'We could get you there tomorrow, Miss – er – Jones. Tonight you could stay at ours. Our Corella – my sister – is over in Penrith.' The young man was blushing, looking hard at Susanah. He tried to put his watch back into his pocket, dropped his cap and had to scramble on the floor for it.

Susanah watched him, thinking how strange it was to see him put out. He was normally so self possessed. She turned again to her aunt; this woman's vibrant energy and the violence like silver strings streaming towards her from Caradoc made the room shine and the air suddenly so very heavy, filled again with the cloying scent of blackberries. Now the silver was mixing with the green and the dark red of the blackberries, washing over her in successive tides. Then blackness. Cotton velvet blackness.

Tollie lunged to sweep Susanah up before she crashed on to the stone floor. There was noise and chaos in the room. Jonty looked on helplessly as Miss Antrobus took charge. A small strong hand pulled him away and in seconds he was outside the door with the unwelcome aunt.

For the last year, on every college vacation, Jonty had been calling assiduously at the house in Selby Street. His father, John George who had finally, inevitably, been dismissed from the pit, looked on in approval. 'We should show our brothers support in their hard times. I'd do it meself, if Caradoc'd let me close. I don't think he sees me as enemy any longer especially now I'm not at White Pool, but there's no chance of, well, him lettin' me near. Always impossible between us right from the first. At least there was a state of truce over Ceiri's funeral.'

Caradoc simply ignored Jonty when he was in the house. Mervin Sargant was often there on his day off, too. He, Davey and Tollie welcomed Jonty with his talk of neutral outside things like whether Middlesbrough would win the league. Then there was always socialism and the talk of war in Europe.

Davey was really set now on joining the army.

'I'll get mesel' away. Nothin' for us here,' he'd said last time the subject had been raised.

'You can't do that, Davey. You'd be killing people. That's not like you.'

'India. The regiment is in India.'

'They kill people there.'

'The pit kills people, doesn't it?'

'Not yet, then, Davey. Don't join yet. What about your sister? At least let your Susanah get properly better.'

'Aw, leave it, Jonty. Can't you leave it?' Then Davey had turned the conversation away. Davey always wanted the conversation away from himself.

Lew often plunged into the talk with cynical remarks designed to give offence, but he would never stay if they got on to a proper discussion. He preferred to return to his carving, or to slope off to the woods. Sometimes, as Jonty knew, he would visit the Steam Mill, a place liberated to him by his father's aberration.

In all this time it seemed that Susanah did not wish to see Jonty Clelland at all; it was as though the kingfishers had never been. She returned the art books he lent her unread, saying her eyes were sore since the illness that struck her down after the funeral.

So here he was, on the dim-lit back street with this woman, this stranger, Susanah's aunt, who was Caradoc's sister.

'Come on, then, Mr Clelland. Show me the way.'

Halfway down the lane, footsteps pattered after them. It was a breathless Susanah. 'You won't go right away? You'll come back and see us?' she panted, gazing anxiously at her aunt.

Isabella laughed and kissed the girl on her cold cheek, near her lips. 'I'm here. And I'll stay as long as you want me. It has taken me this long to come . . . Ceiri, how was she? How . . . ?'

'She missed Wales – home. Never learned the English. Not ever . . .' Susanah's voice was drained.

'Was he good to her? Kind?'

Susanah paused. 'He's a hard man, my da'. I think she was sometimes frightened. But he was her life, and I think he . . .'

Isabella sighed. 'There was nothing like the thing between them when they were young. You could have warmed your hands on it.'

'I know,' said Susanah. 'There was a spoon he must have carved for her then. Such carving. A lovely thing and she loved it. There must have been such love in the carving. She wanted it right at the end. And you should have seen him. He loved her all right.' Her eyes filled with unbidden tears. 'But he was – is – so hard. He was hard on her. Cruel.'

Isabella opened her arms and Susanah clung to her a moment before turning to trudge home up the dark back street.

Jonty had walked on with the bags and Isabella was forced to run to catch up with him. As they walked along Front Street, past the Reading Room, he fingered the satchel's straps. His cheeks burned in the growing dark. He knew now that his original hot reaction to Isabella had been one of recognition. He remembered the smell, lily of the valley. She was the woman. The woman from the train. How long ago had that been?

Bea, as he had anticipated, made the woman welcome. The price of the welcome, as always, was close sharp questioning, plumbing the depths of the other person's life and their ideas. But this was no burden to Isabella, who talked about herself with the ease of someone whose own life was her favourite story.

'An artist?' said Bea, intrigued.

'Well, a craftswoman, you might say. It was the third family where I was placed, as a girl. In service.'

'A maid?'

'I did pictures when I was there. Right from the start. Cut papers. Made models. My mother'd shown me. She was very good. This woman, Mrs Mendlesham, saw some of my scribbles and took an interest. More than that. She took it over.'

'She encouraged you?'

'She was one of these modern types. You know. All for women voting? She paid for some lessons and training. Took me up to London particularly for one teacher who specialised in architectural drawings. Buildings. Houses.'

'You'd have to admit that that was good of her,' said Bea grudgingly.

'Well, you might better say it was fair exchange. I was always an accurate copyist. In no time I was painting pictures of them all. I painted all the members of her family. I painted their buildings. Their pets. I was put to making copies for them, of famous paintings. Some out of books. Some out of galleries. Here in England and in other places. I was in Paris once. And St Petersburg. Doing pictures.'

Bea's indrawn breath came from pure envy. Jonty smiled at the way his mother's face was suddenly that of a greedy child.

There was a pause, and Isabella's face hardened. 'They "lent" me to their friends, to do similar pieces of work. One woman lived up here. I came here once to do Wendon Hall. Do you know it? That Lady Chase had taken a fancy to me in London. A fancy to me, or my work. I'm not sure which. Couldn't wait to get me up here.'

'You sold them your pictures?' said Bea, trying to fathom it all out.

Isabella laughed a pealing laugh. A shiver rippled right down to Jonty's little toes. 'No. No. Not at all. While I was working for them, for Mrs

Mendlesham, for her wages, she just assumed she owned what I did. In between paintings and special tasks, I was back to being her lady's maid. Writing her letters, seeing to her clothes.'

Bea drew in an angry breath, her envy gone.

The woman laughed again, showing the gaps in her teeth. 'Yes. You're right. A kind of bondage. That's all it was. But I was well off. I had a better wage than people around me, remember. And I travelled around, met some special people. Then she'd drag me back to be the lady's maid. She'd shake my halter, to make a point.'

'Slavery,' said Bea, her tone bitter.

'As bad as the pit,' said John George, who had been sitting quietly in the corner.

'Not quite, I think, Mr Clelland. In the end, though, we had this dispute over a watercolour. A great big row. The picture was a particular favourite of mine which I kept in my room. I'd done it from memory. A little house I'd known in Wales. By water, a running stream. They sent it to their niece in America. Without so much as a by your leave.'

'I can't think how you stood that all those years.'

'No better than the pit,' repeated John George.

'Well, I stood it up to then. It was comfortable. Then I lit off back to Bath, where I'd first had a place. I looked after this old lady and started to paint for myself. Sold everything I painted. I should have done it years before. Then the old dear went and died and left me a hundred pounds and I bought my own little gallery. Scenes of the town, antiquities, things like that. Visitors are quite keen on them.'

'And now?'

'Well, there was the letter from young Susanah. Such a sad letter. Such beautiful writing. So I gave the gallery to a friend of mine, a young painter. He'll be something one day. He's got himself this new little wife, which was a bit of a shock . . . The shop'll support them till they're on their feet.'

Jonty watched as his mother and father listened with an eager interest to the woman. He loved the lightness, the ease with which she described her life. It was like an entirely new taste in his mouth. He wanted to roll it around his tongue, react to all the fine differences, relish them.

That night he lay on his side of the red curtain with the wooden rings and listened to the rustling sounds imagining just what she was doing as the woman prepared for bed. He stayed awake for a long time, his head a jumble of Susanah and the kingfishers, Isabella on the train, Isabella travelling from grand house to grand house with her painting pack and her green hat with its trembling, shimmering feather. Eventually, his thoughts turned to dreams and the dreams to deep sleep.

He did not know what time it was when he woke up with a start to feel an unclothed body slip into bed beside him.

'Corella?'

'Not Corella, you naughty boy.' Her finger was on his lips.

Her lips were itchingly close to his ear. 'Not Corella . . .'

Chapter Twenty-Two

Susanah had been ill for a long time after her mother's and sister's deaths, the weakness in her chest exacerbated by shock and pain. Her sickness had brought Miss Antrobus creeping into the house on Selby Street, a presence disliked by everyone but Caradoc. He greeted her unctuous attentions with an uncharacteristic relief in the first place and an embarrassed tolerance as time went on.

During Susanah's illness, Miss Antrobus had assumed the role of Angel of Mercy with a juvenile enthusiasm, working harder physically than she had ever done in her whole life. She was there from dawn till dusk, cleaning, dusting, sweeping, ordering. To do this she had to leave her mother each day in the care of an ancient cousin whom she had enticed down from Edinburgh, with tales of poor motherless children and the compulsion of her own Christian duty.

Susanah had to admit that she kept the house efficiently, though not with Ceiri's tender sparkle. Ceiri was much missed. It was one thing to miss the person, Susanah thought, another to miss continually the traces they had imposed on your daily life without you noticing. The routine of smells and noise which had been the background harmony to their lives was gone. Things sounded and smelled out of order. The boys withdrew to the corners of the room, avoiding the hearth. Without Ceiri's looks and quiet presence, the hearth was a foreign place.

To Miss Antrobus's relief, Susanah finally struggled to her feet, insisting that she was better. Then, bit by bit, uttering wordy protestations, the older woman handed the brunt of the work over to Susanah. 'It will be good for you, child. Something to focus on. Remember the Devil and idle hands.'

She still came every day, 'To provide some guidance', arriving before eleven in the morning and leaving just before sunset. If Caradoc was on early shift, he would walk with her to her cottage and share two glasses of medicinal madeira brought down from Edinburgh by the cousin.

When chapel people dropped hints about the friendship she would say she felt called to it, poor Mr Laydon Jones being so affected by the loss of his wife that he avoided the chapel and tussled with God. 'And I'm blessed, blessed that I'm there to back up Our Lord and bring this poor sheep back to the fold.'

The Saturday after Isabella came to Gibsley, Miss Antrobus had Caradoc's house to herself. She had eaten Susanah's shepherd's pie, hustled the boys out to the football and sent Susanah off to the Saturday market. Now she stoked up the fire under the steaming kettle and settled in the chair with her tatting to wait for Caradoc. There was a rattle at the back door; she touched her side curls and set her face into its welcoming smile. The door rattled again. She got up to peer through the lace. Clicking her teeth, she went to the door and opened it a foot.

'Yes?'

'I wish to see my brother.'

Miss Antrobus drew herself up stiffly. 'He's not here. He is at work.'

'Then I'll see my niece. Or my nephews.'

'They're not here.'

Isabella had been put off by this tactic twice before. This time, though, she heaved the door back, making it creak, and flung the other woman aside. Marching past her, she strode through the kitchen to the front room. Then she went up the stairs and through the bedrooms before she came back to stand with her arms folded in front of the spluttering Miss Antrobus.

'You are no lady, I'll tell yer,' puffed Miss Antrobus.

'No more I am. But at least I know it. There are those around who think themselves "it" and are shit.' The vulgarity rolled strangely from her mouth and spat its way towards the other woman.

Miss Antrobus gasped. 'You have no right here. No right. Bleating on about Mrs Laydon Jones. Took you more than a year to get here. Some sister.'

'Susanah's letter travelled all round the country before it reached me. And then there were things to sort out.' Discovering that Tom Mulblaine had married a little wife had tipped the scales for her coming north. She knew that if things had been swimming along between them it might just have been a letter to her niece. 'And what right have you here, anyway?'

'I was invited.'

'So was I. Where is my niece?'

'None of your business.'

Isabella caught hold of the flesh on the upper part of Miss Antrobus's arms, and twisted it, making her squeal. 'She is at the market. In Priorton. The Saturday market.'

Isabella smiled sweetly. 'Thank you. You may tell my brother I'll call again. Probably tomorrow.'

Susanah ended up that Saturday on the old bridge at Priorton with Betty, talking to Mervin Sargant. She shouldn't have been there at the bridge. Her pathways, the ways she normally walked, were clearly marked for her.

On this Saturday, like all the others recently, she had set out carrying Miss Antrobus's elaborately scrawled list for the market. She clutched her two old baskets – baskets which had originally come in the cart from Wales, packed with cups and plates wrapped in dishcloths and pillowcases.

Caradoc had muttered away to Miss Antrobus. 'I can't see why the girl needs go up to the town. Waste of time. She's needed here.'

'But you know, Caradoc,' the reedy voice floated out into the kitchen, 'that she hasn't been well. Doesn't she need the fresh air and the exercise? And the fish and the vegetables – aren't they cheaper there than anywhere in the district? You know, too, we have to buy cheapest wherever it might be. Aren't you always telling me that care should be a signal of our lives, reflecting the bounty of the loaves and the fishes?'

'Well then, you need go yourself. There is enough for the girl to do here in the house. There is temptation in the town. You need go yourself.'

She bridled then. 'Don't I do enough, Caradoc, coming here, morning till night? Helping you and your poor motherless family?'

He growled but said nothing further.

It was a labour, toiling up the hill towards Priorton from the village. Halfway there Susanah always stood to get her breath back, looking back down towards Gibsley, at the houses which clung like ants on treacle around the standing tangle of the pit head.

Her head dwelt for a moment on thoughts of the walk back, her baskets full of fish and vegetables, flour and twine. It would be heavy-going right enough. Downhill, though, and that was always easier.

As she finally toiled up Gib Chare, the long steep lane into Priorton, she could see Betty ahead of her, on the same errand. The grey stone outlined her friend's long-skirted figure, with two shawls wrapped round her, one for her head, one for her shoulders, against the cold wind. A smile itched its way on to Susanah's face.

In a second, their boots were crunching companions on the cobbles; their skirts were swirling together in the tense wind of January. Betty tucked her surprisingly warm free hand into Susanah's elbow.

'Now, Susanah? Market day again?'

'Yes, don't it come round fast?'

Betty looked at her, a slight frown on her smooth round brow. 'How you manage to hump two baskets of the stuff back down there I can't think. And being poorly all last year. It takes me all my time to take the one basket. And that's changing hands all the time.'

Susanah laughed out loud at the indignant tone. 'You get used to it. All muscles, the Laydon Jones, aren't we?' She thought of Lew and Tollie, both more than six foot tall now, and broad as brick toilets. And Davey, shorter and more sinewy with muscles fired to hard iron with hewing coal in the pit.

'Anyway, Bet, it's a treat to get out of the house. That Antrobus woman is never away, ordering you about. She's there from dawn to dusk, now. And when Da's in he can have me spinning like a wooden top. If sommat doesn't suit, it's his boots you feel.' She was angry for a second, even angry at Betty for standing there, smooth and round and happy. Her smile became stiff on her face. 'Here's proof if you want it.'

She put down her baskets and grabbed Betty's arm to stop her brisk forward trot. She had stopped by a disused stone horse trough let into the long wall. Susanah tugged up her skirt. Bet peered at the bruises on both her shins.

'In from the pit and something doesn't suit and don't he put his boots in? He's got worse in the last year, since Ma died.'

'Susanah!' Betty's face had crumpled; tears glittered in her round eyes. She had her father's pale eyes. Susanah thought of Freddy's eyes lit bright, singing of the lover and his lass. Then screwed tight shut as he bit off the frog's head. Then she thought of them shimmering with the light of under-lit water, as they did nowadays, ever since the time that Jesus had saved him. He had had his lapse, supporting Caradoc when Ceiri died, but this was mentioned by no one.

She was angry at Betty and at herself for showing the bruises. It was a secret of the house, like all the other secrets. This one a secret even from the boys, who were always out when Caradoc got carried away in this par-ticular fashion. If they had known, there would be more trouble. Then they would be out of the house in an instant and lost to her.

It was stupid to tell Betty. It might drive her away, too. But Susanah had felt so good seeing her friend toiling up the hill; telling her had seemed called for, then.

She pushed her skirt down hard and laughed, shaking her head. She picked up the baskets. 'Never mind, girl. But coming up here on a market day, it's good to get away.'

The tears still stood in Betty's eyes. To cheer her up, Susanah started to talk about the arrival of her aunt.

Betty's face brightened. 'I did hear about it. They told my mother at the women's meeting. About her coming.' She lowered her voice. 'They say she wears face powder. And her skirt is a good three inches above her ankles.'

'Do they now?'

'And she's staying with the Clellands?'

'My father wouldn't have her in the house.'

'Why not?'

'Called her a harlot.'

Betty's shocked squeal in response to this was drowned as they turned a corner. They were thrust into the Saturday crowd, who were pressing shoul-der to shoulder the length of the High Street and into the market place. The square resounded with the clatter of carts and the shouts of market traders.

They walked along in silence, which made Betty restless. 'Are you day-dreaming again, S'anah?'

Susanah shook her head hard. Still sorry that she had led Betty to cry, she bounced her baskets to the ground again and turned to her. 'We don't need do the market right away, do we, Bet? We'll walk to the river. I never been to the river this far up. Never. Our Lew and Tollie, they've been up here. Fishing and that. But I've never been.'

'Come on, then, Susanah! Come on!'

Betty, cheerful now, was dragging her round the square into the Southgate, a street narrow as a pathway between tall trees, the sky a ribbon of winter light over the high buildings. Dark as it was, it was still noisy and cheery, with people buzzing like bees from shop to shop.

Halfway along, the street opened out a little; the light seeped further in. Here were houses clinging to the side of the hill at a tumbling angle. Further on, the windows of the inns and public houses were steaming and the fires inside were flaring. Narrow alleyways funnelled people and noise on to the busy thoroughfare.

Betty pulled her basket right up to her chest. She cast her eyes to the ground, her pace quickening. Susanah knew this was where Betty's father had been 'saved'. Caradoc talked of it as the very residence of the Devil.

It was cold. She could smell the must of clothes put on for Saturday, out of the pawnshop. She could smell the hot scents of cooked food. The steam was coming from the mouths of the men as they leaned against the walls, talking and arguing, thick wrists bulging from too short sleeves. Their voices were loud and raucous; they were moving their arms and hands with abandon, conducting their affairs like brass band leaders. The faces, some unclean, were tense and bright with the feeling of the place. They looked ordinary, though, with no touch of evil about them. The red glow which lit the edges of these faces was not the fire of Hell; she could see it coming from the cheerful hearths in the public houses.

There was less a smell of evil here than when Mr Simmons let fly like sour rain against the summer camps. She clawed back further in her mind. There was less evil here than when she was trapped in St Andrew's church, being made to pray against the vicar's knees for forgiveness. Forgive us our trespasses. Suffer little children to come to me.

Turning another corner, they were faced with a fight. Betty pulled Susanah to a stop. A heavy farmer's lad with a thick, ill-fitting jacket and a round hat was pushing again and again at a tall figure with white blond hair. Mervin Sargant.

'Bliddy footballers. Think yer God's gift. Think yer rool the bliddy roost. Worse than bliddy miners, I tell yer.' He emphasised every point with a punch. Mervin was exacerbating everything by laughing into his face and not responding. One final push from the farmer's lad caught him off balance and he was sprawling at Susanah's feet.

She fell over him, her skirt ballooning and her baskets flying in all directions.

'Sorry, miss . . . Sorry . . .' There was a comical apology on his face and his hands reached out, his body shaped to reflect his apologetic words. 'Oh, it's Susanah!'

'And sorry you should be, Mervin Sargant.' She shuddered then as her father's words came into her mouth, the words spitting out. 'These places are the residence of the Devil. You end up fighting and rowing like the worst of people. Why aren't you at the football? Our Tollie and Davey are down there!'

He pulled himself to his feet and peered down at her, his brow raised and wrinkled. He smelled of beer and looked much older than his seventeen years. 'No, no, you're wrong there, Susanah, I'm nay brawler. I'm just havin' a walk round. Had me fill of matches. This is me holiday. A bit of money, and I've gone missin'!' Then he laughed out loud and leaned over to pull her to her feet. 'Come on, missy, you look like an angry hedgehog. Nothing spoilt, is there?'

141

He handed Susanah her baskets and touched his cap, still smiling. She thought about the changes the years away from Gibsley had wrought. The charm was still there but it was too well practised, too used to response and adulation from both men and women.

'What's up here, Mervin? Are you all right, Susanah?'

Susanah turned and scowled when she saw Jonty Clelland marching up through the crowd with that bouncy stride of his.

'I'm fine.' She brushed down her skirt. 'What are you doing here?'

'Just walking through, on me way to a Labour meeting in the Baptist chapel in Viaduct Street.' He paused, looking from Betty, who was standing at a safe distance, to Mervin, who was looking around him and whistling under his breath.

'My aunt,' she said, by way of conversation. 'She's well?'

Susanah couldn't think why he should blush at this.

'She's very well. She came to your house twice to find you but was shown the door by the Antrobus.'

'The Antrobus?'

'As in the Antrobus spider.'

She had to laugh at this.

'So I told her that I would call on you myself, to tell you to come to our house to see her, Susanah. You'll save me a jawing if you come. She can be very pressing, your aunt.'

'Yes. I'll do that.'

'It seems she knows someone round here. Lady Chase. There might be a cottage on the Wendon estate.'

'She's staying, then?'

'She seems fully fixed on it.' Jonty cast his eye up and down the alleyway and wrinkled his nose. 'Can I . . . take you to where you're going?' His schoolmaster's tone suddenly rasped Susanah's nerve like a nutmeg grater.

'No. I . . . we'll take ourselves.'

Betty was talking, with worry in her voice, to Mervin. Susanah could sense the solid nature of her uncertainty as she came and took her elbow. 'Susanah, we should go back. This is a bad place.'

Susanah's mind felt its way from the schoolteacher tones of Jonty Clelland to Betty's prim chapel face. It was a familiar face, condemning, worried and guilty, all at the same time.

Susanah smiled. Jonty's censorious advice made her angry but Betty's made her laugh. The laugh lodged itself somewhere inside her and then exploded upwards. She shouted, grinning and poking Betty with her basket to push her ahead, past Mervin's quizzical gaze. 'No, lovely. Don't you see, we're just about there. Another corner and we'll see the river.'

Jonty watched them go, then turned to Mervin: 'You should get yourself down to the meeting. Your Len'll be there. Come and help us celebrate. There's fifty-eight of our lads in parliament. Who'd'a thought it. Something to work for now. Your Len's like a dog with two tails.'

'Nah. Me politickin' days're over. I'm the bosses' man, now, hadn't you

142

heard? Jump to their tune so's you can get on the team. There's to be no activities. No Labour party. Anyway, ye get out of the way of it, playin' football, don't yer?'

Jonty shook his head. 'I don't know about that, Mervin. I've never played football meself.'

Later, at the chapel in Viaduct Street, Jonty asked Len about Mervin.

'I think he was mebbe too young to go away, Jonty,' his brother replied sadly. 'A canny chance for him, but. Anyway, there's money around and the work's dead easy. They've shown him how to drink and gamble down there.' Len tightened his mouth. 'Yer might say they've given him a bit of an education.'

'But here on holiday and not even watching Tollie Jones play? Down Southgate instead of on the football field! Couldn't believe my eyes.'

'People change, Jonty.'

'Not everybody. You've not changed. Still the same old Len. Trust to your principles, whatever the cost. Same as me da.'

'Get away with yer. No need to say such things. No need at all.'

Susanah hustled Betty along until they were on to the bridge. They leaned over the old stone parapet, looking first one way and then the other, their eyes skimming the sparse winter banks of the fast-moving river. In one direction the river rushed towards them, swelled by late autumn rains. In the other, the wide arches of the viaduct framed the town and the country-side beyond.

There were narrow steps, slippery with moss and surface-damp, leading down to the riverside. They made their way down with difficulty, Betty clinging to the rusted iron handrail, Susanah, hampered by her baskets, nearly falling on top of her. The wind started to gust and they stood there rocking together, until the eddy lost its power.

Laughing with relief, they finally got to the bottom of the steps, stowed their baskets beside them and set off to walk more freely along the mead-owland that flanked the river.

They stopped to peer, crick-necked, upwards at the rearing mass of the viaduct as a train moved along, with stately speed, northwards.

'See this?' Susanah said to Betty, leaning back to take in the whole height of the arch under which they stood. 'See this, Bet? Better than any chapel, any church. My train came over this viaduct when I was little. When I first come up here.'

'What was it like, Susanah? In that train all those hours, coming right the way across the country? I only ever went on that little train up to Livesay Woods . . . Oh!' Her hand went to her mouth.

The memory hit Susanah like a mell hammer. Corella's arm around her shoulders. Betty's own stricken gaze. A small picture of a kingfisher, white paper glowing through translucent turquoise to show the sheen on his wings. Her mother clutching a carved wooden spoon.

The images, all of them, she put to one side. 'I only remember being crammed down there, under the seat, Bet. Our da wouldn't let Tollie nor me out from underneath the whole journey. There was all this grinding of the wheels, see? Going on and on. Sometimes when I think what it must be like in the pit, I think of that. Frightened and shut in. I know that's what our Davey feels. I have dreams, even now. One of them is that I've been swallowed by this dragon and I don't know whether, when I wake up, it was a dragon or a train, see? Mebbe it's the pit.'

They walked on, arm in arm, leaving the viaduct behind. Betty was more relaxed now, away from the uproarious human sounds of Southgate. She talked eagerly about the anniversary services at chapel, about the pieces being prepared by her 'little ones'.

Her words nibbled away at the edges of Susanah's mind. Deep inside, another bubble was building up. Suddenly this place did feel more like Livesay Woods than anything else. The same feeling of freedom, clean as the air around them, clear as the river running by them, a warm feeling on a cold day. The narrow pit house, the heavy demands of the men, the carping, slack presence of Miss Antrobus, these were fading away. Only the river existed, only these broad stretches of whitened winter grass.

'Hello-o!'

Reluctantly, they turned back and retraced their steps. Mervin was sitting on the steps beside their baskets. Susanah thought about the damp steps, the seeping moss. He would be cold.

'D'yer enjoy the river, then?' His voice had deepened. He grinned up at them, baring his brilliant teeth, even but for a gap on one side where he had been kicked in an early season game against Darlington.

Betty put her head on one side. 'And what is it to you, then, Mervin Sargant?'

Susanah sighed. Betty was away again, her face pink with the delicate aggression of the flirt. Walking out with Mervin's brother Len made no difference at all.

Mervin stood up, his face merry. 'Why, like, I was thinkin' what a waste it was that a pretty girl like you was walkin' out with a stick like our Len, next worst thing to a preacher. And then meeting up with you two with such a clash up there on Southgate was quite a thing, wasn't it? Like Snow White and Rose Red there in the dens of iniquity. So I thought to mesel' that I'd come down here and see you again.'

Susanah shook her head at this and they all laughed.

'Come on, now. Tek pity on a poor feller with nothing to do and nowhere to go. Lerrus walk along with yer!'

Betty went all a-twitter over him and was soon chattering away unstoppably as they walked back up into the town together. Mervin hovered alongside Betty as she did her shopping.

Susanah let them get ahead of her among the stalls and carts. She felt dull and lumpen as she plodded around the market and haggled for the goods on Miss Antrobus's list. Her legs were heavy and she was very tired. Her bubble had burst, with a splash. But as they walked back down towards Gibsley, Mervin between them carrying the baskets, she could sense that

Betty's bubble was just inflating. It made her feel even heavier, as dull as a pewter plate.

When Susanah arrived home, Miss Antrobus was sitting beside the bright fire on Ceiri's chair. She did not get up when Susanah heaved the baskets on to the table.

'Your father's late.'

'Yes. Was my aunt here?'

'Your aunt?'

'She's been here two or three times, I was told.'

'Yes. But I thought you shouldn't see her. Your father thought . . .'

'I'll see her. Never fear.' She laid her purchases out on the table. 'Miss Antrobus, your mother needs you.'

The woman stood up hurriedly. 'Is there a message?'

'No. But I'm sure your mother needs you . . .'

The fat shoulders rose, the face puffed out.

'. . . and I think people should go where they are needed and not stay where they are not needed.' Susanah went to the front room and returned with Miss Antrobus's coat and bag. She held them out.

'There is no need to be rude . . .'

'Thank you for all your help. The boys and me can manage now. My mother would not want us to impose on you any longer.'

An hour later, Caradoc glanced at Miss Antrobus's empty chair when he came in, but said nothing. He bathed, changed his clothes and ate his tea without a word. Susanah broke the silence with difficulty.

'I met Betty Stapleton in Priorton, Da.'

He grunted.

'I showed her the marks.'

'Marks?'

'On my legs.'

'You want nothing doing that.'

'There'll be no more marks or I'll show them all round. To the boys. In the chapel.' She paused. 'To your sister. There'll be no more marks. I am not my mother.'

He grunted again.

'And I told Miss Antrobus she was not needed here. She is not my mother either.'

He shot a look at her, but said nothing. After finishing his tea in his usual slow, methodical fashion, he put on his cap and walked up the hill to the cottage on his own.

Neither he nor Miss Antrobus mentioned her banishment from his house as they sat in the little front room and drank their two glasses of medicinal madeira, after which he followed her upstairs, past her snoring mother. There they performed their friendly ritual amid the smell of old sweat and the scent of violets: a remarkable achievement as it did not involve the total removal of any item of clothing.

Chapter Twenty-Three

'I've decided to stop preaching,' said Jonty finally, sitting up in his narrow bed.

'I like to think of you preaching.' Isabella sat up beside him as she tucked her arm in his to stop herself falling out. 'Standing there with that special light in your eyes.'

'It seems such a vanity, a hypocrisy. I do it less and less, now.'

'Now?'

He coloured. In the time she had been in Gibsley, they had never talked about their nightly contact, the passion that had to implode for want of outlet in the small house. It was getting so that the whole of his day was filled with the thought of these hours together.

He drove on, ignoring her small smile, her knowing eyes. 'There's vanity in it, in the feeling of power that fills you, as you stand there and sense the ripple of response from a hundred, two hundred people.' He took her hand off his inner thigh. 'Isabella, it's sometimes too easy to move them. They are vessels emptied to the last drop by hard lives. They've had a hard week: the men in the pit, the women toiling to raise family life to order and warmth. These folks are dry and hollow, waiting to be filled with grace and meaning. They know there has to be more to things than the pit and the cold scullery. It's almost too easy. One time I thought that hunger could be sated by the Gospel, by the search for salvation, by surrendering finally to the graces of God.'

Isabella smiled. 'Such preaching! I feel the power already. This must be the first time you've preached naked. Do you know you are so brown. So brown all over?' She ran her hand across his bare chest. He was still resisting her, looking hard at the wall opposite. She sighed. 'So that was before. What about now?'

'Now I am thinking that all that is just too easy. Len Sargant's been on at me for years about the preachers schooling people to be happy in their misery, how that has more to do with keeping the bad things going than with eternal salvation. And he is the best Christian I know, in the real sense. The meetings? Well, it's me who used to be the leading speaker. Now it's Len and his Labour party friends who have the platform. Now, it seems, man must be his own saviour and the means of it is him joining together with his comrades to gain a voice in state affairs.'

Isabella laughed and kissed his ear, making him wriggle. 'Well, Jonty, you'll find one thing to be serious about if you don't have the other. Will you miss it? The preaching?'

'I do little enough now. Just when I'm home on vacation. I do go to chapel, mostly travelling about with Dad to hear him preach, and then joining in the Sunday night discussions, but that's mostly politics. He doesn't discourage it, my father. Sees it all as part of the same parcel. The crowd going on these trips all round the country gets larger and larger. Len's always there. He's steady as a rock, is Len. Their Mervin – you know, the footballer, you saw him in Su– the Joneses' house. Well, he was keen, but he's a lost cause now, not interested at all. But our Tollie's often there. Sometimes we even miss chapel and go straight to the meeting. My contribution is often just be the prayer at the end, to bless our endeavours.'

'It all sounds like preaching to me. Every bit of it. Politics and all. I'd think you'd be a bit of dull Joe if you didn't have other quite remarkable assets.' She fitted a small hand again into the inside of his upper thigh.

He closed his eyes and breathed in deeply. 'Don't you ever go to a chapel, or a church?'

'I only ever went when I was forced. Then, sitting in family prayers in a house where the person leading the prayers had abused you in one way or another . . . Well, you start not believing it's a useful activity, then you end up believing in nothing.'

'It's odd. You being like that. And your . . . Mr Laydon Jones being so devout. Well, 'til his wife . . .'

'I had my passion. *Have* my passion. He has his. He has always had so much passion. Too much for any woman, so a lot of it spilled on to his Lord. Messy, in a way.'

'You have lots of passion.'

'Do I, now? Well, mine spills on to people, as you might have seen.' She leaned over and pulled a long shawl around her shoulders. 'Tell me about my niece.'

Jonty shrugged, trying not to look embarrassed. 'I saw her this afternoon. I was on my way to a house under the viaduct. I came on her in this . . . sleazy street. I was surprised to see her there. Mervin had tripped her when he was fouled in a fight. There are always fights there. What Mervin Sargant was doing there . . .' He paused, pushing his back against the wall. 'Anyway, I mentioned that the Antrobus wouldn't let you near. She says she'll come here.'

Isabella nodded. 'I think I sorted that woman out today, by the way. Gave her a good pinch on the arm. There's plenty to grab, there. Tell me something about Susanah. What's she like?'

Jonty signed, resigned to the interrogation. 'Her mother and sister dying just knocked all the stuffing out of her. She was so . . . whole . . . before, a kind of centre inside that family. Do you know she could draw like an angel?'

'Like her Auntie Bel, you mean?'

'She hasn't drawn since all that business. She was ill. She must have lost a stone in weight; just seems so shadowy now.'

'Is that a torch?'

'A torch?'

'A torch I see you carrying?'

He turned his shoulder against her and she pulled him back round. 'Now, come here to your Auntie Bel and don't sulk. Your parents will be home soon and we'll have to be down there reading our books again and having our bright conversation as though none of this has happened.'

It was the first time they had really talked here. The need for silence had confined them to touch so far. It was a rich exchange, Jonty knew. Isabella had so much to give and received his clumsy offerings so gracefully. Every night was another highly charged lesson. He had not thought it would be like this. He now viewed his parents' delight in each other with more insight and with not a little embarrassment. Even so, their cuddlings did not compare with this. He was sorry for Corella in her single state.

'Do you know, Isabella, this doesn't feel wrong,' he said as, giving way again to the racing urgency that was rippling through him, he pulled her on top of him by the long fringe of her shawl.

'Trust your feeling,' said Isabella, sinking gently on to him. 'Trust your feeling. Give no heed to those barbarians who tell you that your body lies. You have a beautiful body. Look at this. And this! Such a lovely body couldn't lie. Trust your feeling!'

Susanah had walked around the block three times before she could pluck up the courage to knock on the Clellands' door. She had lurked behind the privies and watched Jonty being swept along toward the school by a crowd of children. At least he would be out of the house.

Now, sitting opposite Isabella by the Clellands' hearth, she looked around her. The house failed to sparkle with that harsh cleanliness and shine which the best of Gibsley women wielded, like a glittering weapon, against the fates that had landed them in this place where dust and work-grit were an hourly menace. There was a musty smell about the house which always came, her mother used to say, when a room had not been often enough 'bottomed'. Still, Bea Clelland did keep a clean enough house. You could say that. And it was warm despite the fact that John George, banned now, had to pay for all his coal as well as rent. The fact that he was still in the house at all was due to the lenience and persuasiveness of Mr Carmedy, and the fact that he and Bea were paying the rent out of their savings. It must have been hard for Jonty to forsake that place at Oxford, she thought. But after what had happened to his father he'd been proved right.

Despite the leaping fire Susanah noticed the brasses at the hearth were let to go dull. The small cloth that Bea put on the table for their cup of tea was not shining white, which only came from two bleachings. The cups themselves, though, were a pretty china with a cornflower design.

Books and papers lay in piles on tables, on the two little windowsills and along the mantelpiece. The place was barren of the ornaments and brass knick-knacks which many Gibsley women acquired and hoarded, giving intricate interest to those dark interiors.

In this house, too, there were none of the religious tracts which were so popular. In her own home there were quite a few. The one over Caradoc and Ceiri's bed, in flaming red and gold, said, 'Be ye angry and sin not: let not the sun go down on your wrath'. Susanah had translated it for her mother the day Caradoc had put it up as a surprise. He must have wanted to please her, but would not tell her the words. When Susanah translated the words later, her mother had given one of her rare pealing laughs.

In the Clellands' house there was a framed sheet made out by hand in careful lettering. '*Tempus edax rerum.*' She recognised Jonty's slightly crooked youthful hand and wondered what it meant. For it was as foreign to her as English had been to Ceiri.

The walls in the house were decorated with paintings of lakeland scenes signed with a flourish by Corella Clelland. They were heavy studies, with the buildings and walls like boxes, the paint laid too heavy, for all that water and sky, that cloud and light.

Bea Clelland was wearing a thick garment, a combination of coat and cloak, which had a certain style. She talked a little as she poured tea, urging Isabella and her to eat the shop cakes and biscuits which she had set in order on the blue-patterned plate.

'Are you managing now, at home, Susanah? It must be hard there, you being the only girl.'

'Yes. I manage.' She bit into the biscuit, which was too sweet.

'They say Miss Antrobus, she gets round there. Gives a hand.'

She looked carefully into Bea's shrewd eyes. 'Yes, they say that,' she said.

Bea pulled a grease-spattered cosy on to the teapot and smiled across at Isabella. In their mutual smile Susanah could feel the heat like the dry heat of ironing: of friendship between them.

'You'll have to be hostess, Bel,' said Bea. 'I'm up to Priorton for a women's meeting. Be some sparks there.'

The door clicked behind her and Susanah was left with her aunt.

She watched the tea as it swirled beneath her narrow silver spoon. She wanted to say something interesting, even clever, to this stranger with her elaborate dress, her long heavy-lidded eyes and her powdered face. But her mind was blank, like a grey wall.

'Do you know, you are so like our mother, Susanah? Thinner and craggier, but Bea tells me you have been ill. Or was it Jonty? Anyway, given that, you might be her, sitting there.'

Susanah looked up from the tea and straight at her aunt. There were rings on her plump fingers; the colour of her hair was red at the edges, too red, like the biscuit in her hand was too sweet. She thought of the night when, flushed with despair at the loss of her mother and Jenny, she had written 'Come, come!' to this woman, convinced that her mother, in sending her for the carved spoon, had meant her to see the letters again and write to the unknown sender.

'Mama. Our mother,' the woman was saying. 'She was about your height and had the very hair, the very eyes. Looked not much more than twenty when she died. And she'd be all of forty-eight.'

The silence stretched, like a sheet wet and twisted to rope.

Susanah's own words finally spewed forth like her vomit on the night the head came off the frog. 'There is a Bible in the house, with your name . . . Caradoc's.'

Her aunt's grin was wide, like Tollie's when he was talking her through a brilliant goal, the most brilliant goal which only he could have scored. 'It's at your house, then? He kept that Bible? No. It would be Ceiri. I must see it.'

'There are two writings. Two hands.'

'Yes. First we got her name; she wrote that. Then his; he wrote that. The man who was our father, he put the Laydon in. He acknowledged us at a price.' She dropped her gaze, picked at her green crêpe sleeve. 'You knew we were bastards?'

Susanah flinched. 'Love-begot. My mother says . . . she used to say . . . love-begot.'

'Always one for the tender word, Ceiri. Always a tender girl. But bastard works. It is an efficient word.' She chuckled. 'Like harlot.'

'Is it . . . Are you that? A harlot?' It was the first time she had said that word.

'Not now I'm not. But once one of those, always one, they say. At first I was taken into the Laydon households, then . . . used like that. Caradoc nearly killed me when he found out that I was going. One of my ribs was broken.' Her eyes were opened wide, her face blank. 'He loved me, you see. That passion of his. There's nothing like the love between a sister and a brother.'

'You? He hurt *you*. It wasn't your fault.'

'At fourteen? And told it was an honour? I'm certain it wasn't my fault. Better anyway than scullerying. But the men, they all blame you. Your own men for disgracing them and the others for tempting them. Poor things. They're quite beyond control, men, and they use even that weakness as a strength. Caradoc probably beat me because he couldn't beat our father. Or the other men.'

Her voice was easy. Susanah could hear no note of shame. She stared at the glowing face, the bright eyes. 'How long . . . how long did it go on?'

'That? I was perhaps twenty when I stopped being passed around from family to friend like some dainty parcel. Decided "enough", squeezed good references out of a Laydon aunt with a conscience, went to Bath as a lady's maid where I was adopted as a kind of pet. Then onwards to a place where I was kept as a different kind of pet, in spite of my foul temper. A life above reproach, you will be delighted to hear. But beyond the pale of my holy vengeful brother. I wrote . . .'

'The letters are there,' Susanah interrupted. 'Not opened. I opened one to write.'

Now there was a shadow on Isabella's face and her full lips drooped. Susanah had to go on, say something. 'Ceiri said there was a condition about Caradoc. No school. He could not . . . cannot read.'

'More likely "will not", by now. He was always so clever, Caradoc. Too clever. The deal my mother did with him, the man who fathered us – I'll not say our father – was for the Laydon name, however partial. So, unlike some women in her position, she got a kind of acknowledgement and a hovel of a house; a bit of money. She could play him so far. In return, she had to endure a monthly visit from this dolt and there was to be no school for Caradoc. Schooling would make him more of a threat, see? Me, I was no threat. Girls, you see, you can use. No threat. So school was all right for me, see? But Caradoc, he took some living with. He would walk out all night when old Laydon was in the house, poor old love.' Her voice was beginning to swing now into Welsh rhythms, away from the tight schoolteacher tones. She had drawn closer and closer to Susanah as she spoke; her face in the end only inches away. Then she sat back.

'Enough of me. Enough of old Caradoc. What about you? What is it you are doing? Looking at you it's time you had a rest. They say it's really ill you've been. Bea said it, no, it would be that Jonty. Jonty. What a boy that is . . . So what will you do? Will you stay in that house with that old crow of a Sunday School teacher that has her beady eye on Caradoc's gold? Or will you come to stay with your poor old aunt in her cottage in the wood where she will sit like some old witch waiting for children to bite her gingerbread?'

Susanah laughed, clearing her head, clearing her blood. In the laughter, she finally felt sorry for Caradoc and began to understand her mother that little bit more. How strong she must have been, Ceiri.

Isabella continued. 'I think I might be rid of the old crow. But I don't mind a bit of gingerbread now and then. What's about a cottage? Well, I have an old crow of my own, name of Virginia Chase, well, Lady Chase. Has a cottage up there on the estate empty. Just right for a poor old auntie.'

Isabella's laughter pealed out and Susanah joined her, marvelling at the thought of her aunt and Lady Chase and all the possibilities this strange, lovely woman was bringing into their lives.

The laughter was still creaming up inside Susanah as she made her way back to the house in Selby Street. She turned a corner and bumped into Davey walking back from the pit. He was hunched forward; his face grey white under the black grit.

'Now, Susanah!'

'Now, Davey.' She moved as close as she could to him without touching. Their shadows joined on the road before them.

'Where you been, then? It's Monday.'

'I know it's neither market day nor milk day, but I've been out. It's a sin now, is it?'

'No sin. But where would you go?'

She stepped outwards so their shadows parted. 'I went down Clellands. To see our father's sister. Isabella Fortunata.'

Davey gawped. 'Is that her name? How come you know that name?'

'It's in the Bible in the press. With the bags Ceiri keeps . . . kept all those things in.'

'What bags?'

She thought again how they had all grown up in the same space but in different worlds. 'Oh, nothing.'

They trudged on. Davey's shoulders dropped still lower and even Susanah was outpacing him. She took a breath. 'How's the pit, then? Is it all right at the pit?'

He stopped and she turned to wait for him. He grabbed her and pulled her so close that she thought she would stop breathing. When they parted she knew her clean skirt must be covered with pit dirt, her face must be black. They both looked guiltily round the deserted street. Then he stared at her.

'The pit, hinney? Well, it's all down there, forty fathoms. Some of them men like the earth, the seams. They know its law, speak of it with respect, like it was a person. The stones, the movement, the passageways, the air. It's poetry for them. For me it's poison, every second I spend down there. The two-foot seams, the eighteen-inch seams. You know I hate the earth pressing down on me, the sour air. I hate the pit, didn't you know?'

They walked on and it was as though he had said nothing of importance. Susanah knew better than to respond. Her mind was burrowing away at the word 'harlot' and wondering whether Davey's despair could outstrip that of the young Isabella, let out, if not sold, to slavery. Isabella had constructed her own escape. But what could Davey do? Where could he go that was a better place?

She stopped at Jade Smith's shop. 'I need to go in for some more blue.'

'I'll get on then.'

She stood and watched him as he trudged on his way, then pushed open the door. There were three women in the shop and she watched Betty serve them before her turn came. Betty had never looked prettier. Her black hair was shining and her cheeks were flushed. She looked more rounded, more shapely in her print apron. She smiled her delight at her friend. 'Susanah! Not very often I see you here.'

'Jade Smith's too dear for me. And I don't need the tick, just a couple of dolly blues.' She fished in her purse. 'Anyway, what have you been up to? You weren't in chapel yesterday. Nor last Sunday.'

Betty was bright red, right to her hairline. She looked around the empty shop. 'I was in Middlesbrough,' she said. 'Went up on the train.'

'Middlesbrough?' Susanah frowned.

'To see Mervin! He wrote and asked!'

'Mervin? But he's only a . . .'

'He's only a year younger than us, S'anah. And he's no boy. Man enough _'

'What?'

'We went to a café for our dinner,' Betty hurried on. 'You should have seen it! And he doesn't half know how to go on . . .'

'What about Len, Betty? I thought you and he . . .'

'Len? He's an old sobersides. Hardly ever around. Meetings. His beloved union.'

'Does he know – Len?'

'Didn't seem to notice that I'd told him, even.'

'Oh, Betty, you are a bad girl!' Susanah was shocked but somehow excited by her friend's wickedness.

'Aren't I just? Now, are you goin' to pay me for those dolly blues, or just steal them from Jade Smith?'

Jonty raced home from school and was hot with delight when he found Isabella alone. For the first time she was off hand, even surly with him, putting his hand away like a naughty kitten.

'What is it, Bel? What's wrong?'

Isabella eyed him sourly when she told him of Susanah's visit. She frowned. 'The child is not well. So worn.'

'I told you,' he said. 'She's still mourning her mother and sister, even after a year. More than a year. She was really close to her mother. Did everything for her. Mrs Laydon Jones couldn't even speak English, not after ten years here.'

The frown stayed on Isabella's plump face. 'There is something else . . . Anyway, I need to get up to Wendon Hall. Your mother thinks I could get a cottage. Somewhere to live.'

He shifted uneasily in his chair, wondering if his mother, despite their caution, realised what was happening. It was hard to tell.

Isabella did not come through the red curtain that night, nor any other night that week. He had to lie there hearing her sounds, stifling his agony, his desire for her warm hands and the relieving universe of her body.

Bea went up to Wendon Hall with Isabella. Lady Chase, who had told the maid with some pleasure to bring Miss Jones up to her sitting-room, was taken aback by her companion, this broad woman with wild hair in somewhat eccentric clothes.

'Mrs Clelland, are you from the locality?' she said, agreeably enough.

Glancing at Isabella, Bea nodded, resisting the mischievous desire to say that her husband was blacklisted from Lord Chase's pits.

'I would like to stay for a while in the locality, Virginia.'

Lady Chase had insisted on this intimacy last time Isabella had visited the hall: a visit which had involved much kissing and stroking and languorous evenings beside the mountainous fire. Though she hadn't known it then, the same coal could just as well have been dug from the earth beneath their feet by her own brother. She smiled at the thought. 'I have family business in the area and I thought I would do some watercolours here.'

Lady Chase signed for the maid to hand round cakes. As she took her cake, the light from the fire glinted on a great ring on her right hand. 'Watercolours? You're not going to paint dirty pits and dirty miners, I hope.'

Bea put down her cup and restlessly shuffled her feet.

Isabella, glancing at her, said smoothly, 'I noticed the folly here in the grounds last time. And the rhododendron walk leading to the pool.' She looked around the room, heavy with draperies and prickling with pictures. 'And I thought perhaps you might like some interiors, perhaps some copies . . . Then perhaps his lordship would like a record of his farm buildings, the estate workers. The real problem is I need a . . . studio. A place to live and a place to work.'

'That is easy, my dear. Here! Here is where you can come. There is so much room . . .'

'Impossible, Virginia,' said Isabella decisively. She knew Lady Chase liked to be bossed. 'My family would be uncomfortable at that. My brother is one of those . . . dirty miners in Lord Chase's pit.'

Bea held her breath. That was it. There would be no cottage now.

Isabella was smiling into Lady Chase's eyes. 'A little cottage where I could work and have a little cat? And you could come to tea. I know, you could come and have your portrait painted. The very thing! Aphrodite! Could you get the costume?'

'I'm sure I . . . there is a cottage on the way up from Gibsley. Lord Chase's old nurse lived there, she died in December.'

Isabella jumped up, all draperies and lily of the valley, and leaned to put her cheek against that of the older woman. 'Lovely! Lovely! We'll have such fun, my dear Virginia.'

Bea held her peace until they were away from the hall and trudging down to the estate office with the letter from Lady Chase. Then she exploded. 'Well, Isabella, I've never, never seen such an exhibition of . . . of . . .'

Isabella linked her arm and cuddled in close. 'Harlotry?' She laughed and they walked on. When she spoke again, her tone was more sober. 'I can see it's against all you do and say, Bea. But it's the way I've learned to survive, see? Turn their weakness against themselves. It works with the women as well as the men. Brought up with a silver spoon but they've this real hunger for a bit of tenderness kindly given. It's not a matter of selling the tenderness, Bea. More a matter of fair exchange. I've managed a fair exchange ever since the first man. And he wreaked far more than he paid for.'

'It's undignified . . .' mumbled Bea, for once at a loss for words.

'Don't think of it. Don't you think if I'd had a ma or a sister like you I'd have worked out a different path? But I'm an old cat, Bea, and you can't teach an old cat new tricks. Just think! I've got my cottage and we'll be friends and maybe you can entertain me with some of those Bolshevik ideas. Or maybe we'll just laugh together. Not enough of that round here in my view!'

Jonty was clumsy with misery as he loaded the strappy painting satchel on to Clem Sorenson's trap.

Isabella reached down from her seat and tipped his chin up as though he were a two year old. 'Will you visit me in my new home, then?'

155

'Do you invite me?' His head went towards her.

'I do so emphatically.' She caught his hand and kissed it, palm up, just as she had on the train all those years ago. His hair stood erect at this. As she rode away, he raced into the scullery for a long drink of water to impose some calm on all his systems. His mother followed him back into the house. She was sitting reading a paper when he got back into the kitchen. Looking up at him through her glasses, she smiled and said nothing.

I am right in my decision not to preach, he thought. How could a person in this state dare to preach to others?

Chapter Twenty-Four

'I've someone here for you, Jonty.'

He looked up sheepishly as his father came into the kitchen in his chapel black. He still felt guilty about not going to chapel, although John George reproached him with neither look nor word. He raised his eyebrows at the sight of Davey Laydon Jones.

'You two could go into the front room. Just put a match to that fire, will you? Your mother's due back any minute and she'll more than fill the kitchen one way or another.'

Jonty set the silent Davey on the chair. He had just finished lighting and fussing over the fire when John George came in with two mugs of tea, planted them on the mantelpiece and left them to themselves.

'Something in particular, Davey?'

'I was talking to this feller down the football yesterday. On leave from the army. He said he'd take me back down to Wrexham with him and join me. They're off to India, he said.'

'Serious, are you? You're going in the army? Leave here?'

'Here has nothing for me. Just the pit. And my father who doesn't give a light for me, nor anybody else.'

'What about Susanah?'

There was a pause. Davey ignored Jonty's question but said, urgently, 'Go on, tell us what do you think about the idea, Jonty?'

'You know my views on that, Davey. You know them!'

'Tell us again.'

Jonty sighed. 'Kings and emperors, prime ministers and potentates use bodies of men like pawns in a game of chess that will reap benefit only to them.' He chanted the litany. 'And what king are you to fight for? Feller in love with pleasure, looking to his own interest. Never away from the races or the gambling tables or the company of women.'

'But there has to be an army. Every country has an army to defend itself.'

'In India?'

'It's our empire. We've got to defend it.'

'It's the King's empire and it's a dangerous place. Men are treated like so many cattle whether you're one of us or one of them. You could get killed or hurt, die of some disease even if you don't get into a battle.'

Davey stood up in front of the fire, which was roaring nicely now. 'Do

157

you know what it's like down the pit?'

'I think I do.'

Davey snorted like a horse. 'Well, schoolteacher, how about when your heart beats the cage to the bottom as it sinks like a stone? The beginning of the shift when you feel it'll be an age before the shift'll end and you'll have grown into an old man. How about when it's so bliddy hot the dust is solid in the air and you feel like you can bite it off in chunks? How about the corners where all you can smell is your own piss and the sour gas that *probably* isn't poisonous? The heat and the dirty sweat, the stink. How about working on your knees, hewing hour after hour? The sore eyes. The long walk inbye at the end of a bliddy tiring shift. How about getting home too tired to eat?'

Jonty waited a moment. 'My father seemed to stand it . . . He misses it now.'

'Yeah. My da can stand it. And comes home fit for other things. Some folk can do that, hold themselves off, hold themselves outside the destruction. Me, it sucks me up. Every shift's like that first one. Just as hard. Just as full of hell. The army – even a full battle'd be no worse than that, I tell yer.'

'But what about the comradeship? The clever men my father goes on about? The pride in the craft and the lore for which the pitmen are so famous?'

The look Davey gave then, a strange mixture of contempt and despair, drilled Jonty to the marrow. 'You can keep all that rubbish.' He said it slowly and carefully. 'Keep it and . . . It's not enough, Jonty, it's not enough.' He threw himself back into the chair.

Jonty changed tack. 'What about some other job? Work in a shop? Or some clerical work somewhere? You were always a good scholar . . .' He stopped as he was treated to another searing look.

'It's a Welsh regiment this feller belongs to,' said Davey. 'That tickled me. Said it was hard. But, like I said to him, it couldn't be as hard as the pit.'

No. Jonty saw it. For Davey Laydon Jones, there couldn't be an easy option, like a shop, or an office. 'You didn't really come here to listen to anything I'd say, did you?'

Davey shook his head, the corner of his mouth twisting to a smile. 'I knew what you'd say. I've heard some version of it often enough. But I thought I'd let you have your say, to show you how set I am on it. And to take my leave. And I wanted to ask you to do sommat for us.'

'Anything, Davey.'

'Watch out for our Susanah. Caradoc's calmed down a bit now, and that Sunday School teacher's not hanging around as much. But our Lew's as predictable as a weathercock, and all our Tollie can think of is the bliddy football.'

'You know I'll do that. But I'm at college now. I'm away half the time.'

Davey nodded knowingly. 'You're out of this pit well enough, aren't you, then?'

'You might say that. It's good being away. But I'll watch for Susanah when I'm home. Meanwhile, there's your aunt . . .'

Davey cocked an eye, smiling again. 'Aye. They say you're thick with her.'

Jonty went red. 'As I say, Isabella takes a strong interest in Susanah. I can't see Susanah takin' much notice o' me. But you can be sure, if she lets me, I'll watch out for her. No. I'll watch out for her anyway.'

They shook hands and Jonty wished Davey luck. He felt honoured at the confidence, while his heart despaired at the choice he had been forced to endorse. He took Davey through the house and watched him stride down the street, shoulders back, for all the world as though he was already marching under the sun.

Bea and George were standing together by the fire when he came back into the kitchen.

'What was that about, Jonty?' asked Bea.

'He's off to join the army. Not happy with the pit.'

'The Devil and the deep blue sea,' said John George.

'A waste. What a terrible waste,' said Bea. 'Where are you going?'

Jonty was pulling on his coat. 'For a walk. I need some fresh air.'

His parents exchanged a glance.

'Yes. You're right,' said Bea. 'Isabella needs to know. That family needs watching for, with no mother.'

The light was on in Isabella's and he walked straight in. She was there in the window painting at her easel. Susanah was beside her with a drawing pad on her knee.

'Jonty, is it! How very nice! No, sit down! Susanah, you have the apples to finish. Jonty, just scald that tea and get another cup. You can serve yourself and you can serve us while we work.' She smiled across at him innocently. Susanah put her head back down over her work. As he poured hot water from the small copper kettle he saw with satisfaction the little set of watercolours she was using, dipping into them with the tiniest of brushes.

'Isn't this nice,' Isabella beamed. 'Jonty visiting and Susanah here instead of at chapel, back to her drawing. She has talent, this child.'

He handed them their cups and sat down at the little round table, watching them uneasily.

'What is it, Jonty?' Isabella's voice was sharp. 'You're like a cat on hot rocks.'

'It was Davey. Davey came to see me.' He blurted it out. Susanah's head came up. 'About the army. He's joining, he says.'

The lid of the little paint tin clipped shut. Susanah had her coat on and was out of the door before either of them could say a word.

Isabella sighed and washed her paintbrush in the clean jar of water laid ready. She came over and put her hands on his shoulders. 'Dear boy, what a clumsy you are.' Her hands were dirty. She smelt of paint as well as lily of the valley.

'I said I would tell you. I told Davey that we would keep an eye open for

Susanah, me and you.'

She turned round. 'Now then, could you just undo this smock for me. I can't think what made me get one which fastened at the back.'

Her plump shoulders emerged from the shift which was all she had on underneath. He let the paint smock fall. She turned round. He looked dumbly at the deep cleft of her breasts, then up to her face and her long eyes which looked so coolly at him.

He raised his hands and dropped them helplessly. 'They make me feel so helpless, that family.'

'Do we now?' She smiled suddenly. 'Well, Jonty, now you've chased my little niece away and criticised my family, I think I'm in the mood for your special brand of preaching.'

She pulled his head to her, backed to a soft chair and sat on it so that he was on his knees in front of her. 'Now!' she said. 'You may say sorry first. And then you may start to preach!'

Chapter Twenty-Five

Betty grabbed Susanah's hand at the corner of Selby Street. 'There you are! I've been looking all over for you.' She put one hand on her chest, breathing heavily. 'I went to call for you but there was such a racket down there and Miss Antrobus squawking like a parrot down your yard . . .'

They ran hand in hand down the yard, past the figure of Miss Antrobus, who was now sitting sobbing, with her broad backside on the windowsill.

In the kitchen the table was up on its side and the chairs were upside down, their legs up in the air like dead animals. Lew was leaning flat against the window looking on but not participating in the fight before him.

Caradoc, wild-haired, was flinging himself around the room trying to rid himself of Davey who was clinging to his father's left shoulder and arm like a ferret at a great dog. Blood was running from Davey's mouth and his eye. Caradoc had a reddened cheek but there was no blood. He was grunting with rage.

'Lew!' Susanah shouted over the din. 'Stop them! Stop this!'

He grunted uneasily. 'Sooner said than done.'

She caught his arm and pushed him towards the struggling pair. 'Pull Davey off!' she instructed.

'What? The old feller'll murder him if he gets to turn round on him. Murder him! Our Davey's doing well, considering.'

'Pull Davey off! I'm tellin' you. I'll see to Caradoc.'

'You?'

'Pull him off.'

Lew strolled across, put one arm under Davey's, threaded it back behind his neck and pulled him off as though he were peeling a potato.

Released of his burden, Caradoc staggered back. Susanah stood in front of him, Davey and Lew behind her. Betty's hand slipped into hers and she realised her friend was at her shoulder. 'Now Dada . . .' How long was it since she had used that childish name? 'Leave Davey, just leave him!'

He put a hand forward to push her out of the way, then dropped it. His eyes, hot as molten metal a moment ago, cooled down.

'Our Davey's a good boy, Dada. Always been a good boy.' She gripped Betty's hand tight.

'A good boy, you're telling me. Hear what he said! This is no home. Canna wait to get away from it. He said . . .' Caradoc paused, pulling a hand

161

backwards across his mouth, ' . . . the pit was for beasts crawling under the earth.'

Another surge of energy forced him towards Davey again. Susanah grabbed his wrist and he pulled her close to him. She could feel the wiry muscles of his forearm and the thrust down below; she could smell the clean Sunday smell of him overlaid by blood and sweat. She looked into the long eyes, some detached part of her seeing Isabella's eyes too.

Caradoc dropped back, his hands to his sides. He put his fingers through his hair, smoothing it a little, then pulled his hands down the front of his black waistcoat and trousers to rid them of sweat.

She relaxed. 'Mama – Ceiri wouldn't want any of this, Dada.'

Caradoc leaned down and picked up his jacket from the floor, where it was tangled with an upturned chair. Putting it on, he kept his eyes on his sons and his daughter and on Betty Stapleton who stood behind Susanah now, her china-blue eyes full of tears.

'I'll walk Miss Antrobus home,' he said. 'She'll be outside.'

He moved heavily past the girls, looked hard at Davey, then stumped across out of the room. As he passed Lew, he seemed shorter than his son. Susanah thought that Lew who had always been shorter than Caradoc, must be getting taller.

Susanah was the only one to see Davey to the station. He had a black eye and a sore lip, but apart from that he was very clean, his footsteps light and springy.

They sat side by side on a long bench, ignoring the September drizzle which was gradually drenching his cap and setting watery beads on her woollen shawl.

'You'll tek good care o' yourself, S'anah? Mind, looking at you last night, I'm not sure you need it!'

'Take care of myself? I heard you had other people primed for that job. Aunt Bel. And, according to her, that Jonty Clelland.'

'He's all right, Jonty. Told you for years. Heart's in the right place under that stuffed shirt.'

'Anyway, he's away already, been that college in Durham a year. Now I'm rid of you both in one swoop.'

The train was making its royal progress into the station, coughing and spitting and belching steam. Davey climbed on board with his bag and leaned out of the window. 'You're a great girl, S'anah. I wish you could leave all this too.'

'You mean join the army?'

'Wish you could, S'anah. You and me in the army together. If they'd seen you facing up to Caradoc yesterday, they'd put you in the front line on the frontier.'

'I'd'a come down the pit with you if I could when I was little!'

His open face hardened again. 'If you had, love, you'd have had the guts to get out years ago.'

'Well, anyway, Davey. You take care of yourself.'

'You watch yourself, Smiler.'

She laughed at the childish nickname and he leaned down from the train and just trailed his hand over the front of her hair. 'If I ever meet a girl like you, I'll grab her and never stop running till I drop.'

'Oh, Davey,' she gulped back her tears.

But he had turned and was battling his way down the train. She caught a glimpse of him through the compartment window and he was gone.

Later that day as she fought her way through the washing and put her own version of Ceiri's wash-day broth on the range, her dull heart kept telling her that Davey wouldn't be coming home off foreshift or back shift or any other shift, today or any other day. All that was at an end.

It was four months before she had a letter from him. She carried it round in her apron pocket for weeks. In those four months Lew was mostly out of the house about his devious affairs on the edge of the gambling and drinking world of Gibsley. Tollie was out too, training midweek for Gibsley's Saturday game. Sometimes, to her concern, he went off with Lew, and there was beer on both their breaths when they returned.

Caradoc settled down again to his grim routine of work at the pit, welding and watchmending, with only occasional lapses into involuntary cordiality. Tollie, flashing in and out, eating gargantuan meals and occasionally bringing the Sargants for supper when his father was out, was the only spark of light and energy in Susanah's week.

She made time while Caradoc was at work to walk up the lane to Isabella's house. Sometimes they painted together, but often Susanah was too tired to do anything more than sit and drink tea from the yellow cups.

One day, coming back from Isabella's she tripped over Bea Clelland's feet. They were sticking out from where she sat on the step in the gateway of the Kenton house next door. Joan Kenton was in the yard, crouched down on her haunches with her back to the wall. Her hands were dirty and she was still wearing her farm boots which were crusted with mud.

Bea smiled up at Susanah, squeezing her eyes against the late afternoon sunshine. 'Hello, Susanah. Are you well?'

'Not bad. Though I have this cough. Nothing to complain about.'

'And Caradoc? I see he's going to chapel again.'

'I think he missed it. The singing mostly. He likes to sing. Miss Antrobus got him to go to hear the singing.'

Joan leaned forwards, peering up at Susanah. 'How about Davey? Does the army suit?'

Susanah pulled the letter from her pocket. 'I'd a letter the other week. Nothing for four months, then this.'

Bea looked at the envelope. 'Nice to get letters. I get letters from both of ours now.' She sighed. 'But the house seems so empty without'm. Letters don't fill a house.'

She had thought that even if he wasn't working John George would fill his time with reading and writing, meeting people and speaking. However, within a month of finishing work he had stopped preaching, within six weeks he had stopped going to meetings. When she asked him about it he was evasive, but finally said that being at the pit had made him what he was and without that he was nothing. She raged at him, laughed at him, cried with him, but nothing would move him. Now he spent his time sitting around doing very little. The stuffing was gently leaking out of him. The pile of books, obtained by Bea to fill the hours, remained unopened.

Susanah looked up and down the deserted back street and pushed the letter towards Bea. 'Read it. Caradoc's not interested, and Lew pretends he isn't. And our Tollie is so busy on what Betty used to call the gally vant that he can't slow down long enough to be properly concerned.'

Bea took the letter out of the envelope and smoothed it on to her knee. Joan peered over her shoulder. 'Read it for me, Bea. I can manage the book stuff now, thanks to you, but I canna read that scribble.'

Bea coughed and began to read in her clear voice. It was funny to hear Davey's words cut the air with Bea's voice.

Wrexham
10 December 1906

'Dear Susanah,
Sorry to light off like that, without much warning. Seemed the only way or I would have been persuaded to stay, by your looks if not by Caradoc's blows. It has been really hard here in Wrexham, the train-ing. The marching and everything. They are sticklers. You should hear the sergeant go on. I was lucky to get into such a good regiment. Quite a few ex-pitmen here, so we can share some stories. Interesting to hear Welsh spoken now and then. A bit of a surprise how much I can understand. At least I can see the sun here up on the surface, when it's out. I will see a lot of sun soon as they are sending us overseas pretty soon. I will write to you from there. Take care of yourself. I am sorry I have not come up to scratch for you.

Your loving brother,
Davey

A silence licked its way around the back street. A lurcher dog slunk out of the house and Joan bent to fondle his ears. Over the dog's head she looked up at Susanah. 'Don't half sound like a good set-up to me, S'anah. He's well out of here, I can tell you.'

'A nice letter. You'll be pleased to hear from him,' said Bea.

'Yes. He's a big miss.'

'Yes. So's our Jonty. It's so quiet in the house now, even with John George at home all day. He's a big miss, our Jonty,' she sighed.

'Is he still liking college?'

'Loving it as far as I can tell from his letters. And when he gets home he's full of it. Drowning in books and talk. Mind, they made him change his talk almost right away. They called it a clumsy accent, he said.'

'Always thought he talked proper anyway, meself,' put in Joan.

'It must be like heaven there for Jonty,' said Susanah. 'All those books.'

'Aye. It'd've been heaven for me at that age, or even now.' Bea's laugh was both rueful and jolly as she heaved herself to her feet. 'Well, I need to get back. John George'll be looking for me and I have a broth to make or a book to read. I can't remember which.'

Susanah and Joan watched her make her stately way down the street. 'It's a canny woman, that,' said Joan.

'Yes,' said Susanah. 'It's a canny woman.'

After that, Joan Kenton seemed to haunt her, always asking if there had been a letter from Davey. Susanah was puzzled by this. She hadn't noticed any interest before and could imagine Davey's hoot of disbelief at such a notion.

The next letter, two months later, came from India. Of all the people around her, it seemed that Joan now was the one most interested in Davey's life. She and Joan pored over the India letter many times.

Karachi
February 1906

Dear Susanah,

This is really a strange place. The heat goes right to your bones and comes through the other side. You pour with sweat all the time. Some places are crowded and poor like we haven't seen at home and there are colours and smells like you wouldn't even know in your dreams. They keep you on the hop here with duties, plenty of drill to keep you up to scratch, which is hard in this heat. The regiment is very keen on keeping you up to scratch, I can tell you. If cleanliness is next to Godliness, then this regiment is the regiment of God.

Did I tell you I can ride a horse now? It's something seeing the world from that high. No wonder the nobs have big ideas. Did I tell you the MO says I've grown two inches in six months? Says it shouldn't be possible, but I have. I'll be able to look our Tollie in the nose when I get home! Write and tell me what is happening there. Even little things. It is good to get letters. Or it is 'bad' if you don't get a letter on mail day, when the other lads do.

Love Davey

PS Do you see anything of Jonty Clelland? Is he enjoying that college of his? I am writing him a letter with this one for his mam to pass on.

Joan whistled. 'Ridin' a horse. Can yeh believe it. And growing like that.' She laughed. 'Two inches on me and I'd reach the sky. Ouch!' She put her hand in the small of her back.

'What's wrong, Joan?'

'Nowt much. Reckon I'm carrying . . .'

'A baby? What . . . How . . . Who?'

Joan shuffled her feet, frowning. 'A young'n . . . in the way you do . . . and I an't tellin' who.'

'You'll have to come off the farm.'

'No fears. I'll tek it down there till it's weaned then me ma and our Vivian'll watch it. I need to work. They know that.'

It was exactly as Joan said. She had the baby, a great healthy boy, on the Saturday morning and she was back in the barns and the fields on Monday. The baby stayed with her at the farm until it was two months old. After that Susanah would hear his energetic cries over the yard wall as she went about her chores.

Joan's baby was a source of humorous disbelief on the part of the people in Gibsley. She had never looked pregnant, for her layers of clothing and her powerful stride. and the fact that people tended not to think of her as female had prevented the sharp eyes from seeing the usual signs. There were clucks and chucks over the morality of it and much speculation about the identity of the father, who it was commonly held, must be both blind and daft.

Jonty called in on Susanah in his Easter vacation, but Caradoc was keeping her busy with the clocks and she had little time, she said, to sit around. He consoled himself with several visits to the cottage on the hill, where he was supposed to be teaching Isabella the Greek language. The lessons did happen; she was a quick and interested pupil. And she insisted on paying for her lessons in a way which made his steps turn eagerly every second day of his vacation. They played teacher and pupil with great restraint for the first hour and then delightfully reversed their roles for the second and sometimes the third.

'Isabella, I want to spend a night with you. Why can't I stay for a night?' he said one afternoon.

She stroked his face, trailing her fingers down from his chin to the hollow at the base of his throat. 'You have such soft skin for a man. No, dearest boy. The time for that is all gone. I like my nights and my days for myself now. Twenty years ago, maybe.'

'Come to Durham next year,' he pleaded. 'There are hotels.'

'And will you wear a big hat and a moustache as disguise? They'd expel you from that college of yours in a minute.'

'Come! Come! Just once and I'll never, never ask you again.'

'Never, never?'

'Never.'

So it happened. Just once. Jonty faked a letter from his father to say that his aunt in Scotland was ill and they must travel to see her. After much sniffing and clucking and serious talk, it was permitted.

He was wearing a heavy top coat and his cap pulled over his eyes when he met her at the station. He took her small case from her. She laughed up at him. 'What? Where's the moustache? And no cloak?'

She told the cabdriver to go to the Three Tuns Hotel. 'I wired,' she said briefly as they settled down. 'Mrs Jones and her son Mr Jones. Adjoining rooms.' She chuckled.

'It's nearly next door to the college!' He started to panic, his excitement at seeing her draining away.

He kept his eyes on the register as he signed in, avoiding the keen eye of the clerk. 'My son is not well,' confided Isabella. 'Would it be possible to have supper in our rooms?'

As they made their steady way up the stairs a group of men burst through the door leading from the dining room and jetted a gust of cigar smoke out into the already stuffy hallway. Jonty froze on the landing as he recognised two men flanking a tall, heavy well-dressed man. They were wearing clerical collars and one of them was Dr Stowell his own tutor. He pulled Isabella into a doorway and thrust her behind him, then stood like a statue as Dr Stowell's gaze flowed over him. He waited until they were out of the great front door, then bolted upstairs followed by a mildly protesting Isabella.

'What, are you frightened of Lord Chase? Would he know you?'

'Lord Chase?' The man who held Gibsley in his hands. The author of John George's present misery. And he hadn't recognised him. 'No. No. The smaller one with the clerical collar. That's Dr Stowell, my college tutor.'

She chuckled. 'Well I don't know which would've been worse, Chase seeing me or the venerable doctor seeing you!'

She waited while the maid drew the curtains and the waiter set a little table by the big fire in her room. She smiled her thanks and gave him sixpence, then locked the door behind him. Then she knocked on Jonty's door and entered. She found him at the window, staring across the twinkling lights of the city in the general direction of the college.

She put her arms round his waist and laid her face on his back. 'Come on, naughty boy! Don't brood. The dice are thrown.'

He put his lips on hers, waiting for the burn which always came, but this time it didn't. She tapped his face. 'Come back to me! Back to this planet, will you! Now your supper's out. We'll eat in our night clothes. Much more comfortable! Five minutes!' she said briskly.

She was already sitting at the table when he entered. Her hair was loose, floating down to her elbows as she sat. She was wearing something very high-necked, like a Chinaman's garb, green with gold corded embroidery. He stood feeling foolish in his nightshirt, dead in every part of his body.

'Come here, little one.'

He knelt by her chair. She leaned over him, her large firm breasts hard against his cheek, her unique and special smell in his nostrils, her tongue in his ear, as she tugged at his nightshirt till it came over his head. His senses reacted to her, making the very hairs on his skin stand up.

She stroked his shoulder. 'That's better. Now stand up.' she said gently. 'Now the drawers.' She laughed, then. 'I do like to see you standing up all present and correct.'

He wanted to thrust in towards her as he stood, towards her mouth, towards her neck.

She pushed him gently away. 'Now, supper! This lovely beef is getting cold.'

He groaned, 'Bel, how can you!'

'I'll show you later. Now, eat!'

'So what about . . . the fair sex?' said David Wynne, throwing a tennis ball against the bark of the tree under which they were sitting. 'You never mention them, Clelland. Not a word passes your lips.'

It was the last night before the summer recess, and quite warm. They were listening to the thwack of a cricket ball as the first years played in friendly competition against the second. Jonty was thinking about home and wishing he was there.

'That's a silly question,' said Bill Leeson. 'Stop acting the fool, Wynne.'

David flicked the ball off Bill's head so it rebounded from the tree into his hand again. 'Now, don't be pompous, Bill. What about you? Don't tell me you've never had a sweetheart. Some fair Darlington lass, some bewimpled Quakeress?'

'I say shut up, you clown!' Bill Leeson was red with anger.

'No kisses yet? Survived a whole twenty years on the chaste mother's or sister's smack?'

Jonty caught the ball in mid air. 'How about Cumbria? No pretty lasses over there?'

'Waiting, hanging on at the station ready for my arrival!' David Wynne caught his friend's sceptical eye. 'Well, no, if you really want to know. Shoved away to school when I was seven, then to this monastery. Where's the chance?'

'But you're interested?'

'Yeah.' Wynne's eye scanned over to the lounging figure sprawled on the summer grass. 'Not like this lot of lilies who fawn over each other and are apprenticing to be crusty old bachelor teachers.'

'Everything has its place, everything has its time,' said Bill Leeson primly. 'Self-control is a virtue . . .'

David leapt on him then and they started to wrestle, rolling down the slope as they fought. Jonty left them to it for a few minutes before jumping in to part them.

As Bill stood brushing down his trousers, he cocked an eye at Jonty. 'What about you then? On some things you really do keep yourself to yourself.'

Jonty just shrugged, embarrassed. Beavering away at St Barnabas' Teaching College, he could see that his thoughts fell far below the level of purity of the majority of the men, whose preferred style was based on purity in thought and action and a predilection for the company of men. Yet perversely, he was satisfied, even secretly superior about his own less than pure state. Knowledge of Isabella, however carnal, had opened a door for him into himself. And this knowledge made his friends' protestations of purity seem so child-like. He knew that they had noticed that he, opinionated as he was on every other subject, was so silent on this.

After they'd had dinner they were sitting in Bill's study, eating bread purloined from the kitchen block. David was reading an old newspaper he had picked up outside his tutor's study. 'Hey! D'you see this? "Lord Roberts puts forward his demand for conscription."'

'Won't get anywhere,' said Jonty briefly. 'Liberals won't have any of it. If there were conscription there's sure to be a war. Like a dagger on its way down. They know that. They all know it.'

'Well, the French have conscription. The Germans do. The dagger's already on its way,' said David. 'Only a matter of time for us.'

'Would you go?' said Jonty.

'Me?' said David. 'You'd have to, wouldn't you? Anyway when the blast of war blows in my ears I'll be there volunteering. Death or glory, I say.'

'How about you, Bill?'

Bill Leeson bit into his bread. 'No, I wouldn't.'

'They'd shoot you. Prison, at least. Bread and water.'

'I couldn't. It's against God's law. I couldn't kill a man. I couldn't contribute to a system that supported killing a man.'

David laughed. 'You'll not be so certain when they're pushing mouldy bread through the bars at you.'

Bill smiled his sweet smile. 'We'll have to see about that, I suppose.'

The next morning, Jonty was making his way with Bill out of the college, laden down with cases.

'Mr Clelland?' It was his tutor, Dr Stowell. 'Do you have a minute? In my study, please.'

Dr Stowell led the way into his narrow tidy room, then stood before him, not asking him to sit down. 'I was wondering, do you have a brother, Mr Clelland?'

'No, Dr Stowell. But I have a sister. She's across in Penrith, runs this little school with her friend. It's quite successful, in fact . . .' His babble was stopped by a hand held up as if to fend off an attack.

'I do not wish to know about sisters, Mr Clelland. I have no interest in sisters. You have no brother?'

'No, Dr Stowell.' He waited.

'It is just that I glimpsed a fellow in a local . . . building, a week or so ago and he put me in mind of you.' He paused. 'When I returned to check the book I realised it couldn't have been you because it seemed that weekend you were in . . . Scotland, I believe.'

'That's right, Dr Stowell.'

'I just thought I should mention it to you, before we went down for the term. To have a – er – *doppelgänger* wandering around may bring trouble on your head.'

'Thank you, Dr Stowell.'

'It can bring troubles on a man, troubles not so easily solved as that problem with your accent which we tackled so successfully in your first year. Think of it. Education at this level is a privilege not to be set aside lightly.'

'Yes, Dr Stowell.'

The tutor turned coldly to stare out of his window. 'That will be all, Mr Clelland.'

Jonty was still furious when he caught up with Bill Leeson on the long walk up to the railway station. 'Arrogant pig! Supercilious sow. Bliddy rotten old codger.' His home accent came happily back on to his tongue.

Bill pulled him round to face him. 'What is it, Clelland?'

Jonty looked at his friend. 'There was one of your lot. Quaker feller, Fox. He would bow his head to no man. Got me in trouble when I was little,

169

standing up to an arrogant clergyman. Six of the best. Couldn't write for a week. Then there's me in there with Stowell, twice the age now, an "yes-sir-ing" and "no-sir-ing" like some pusillanimous little pip-squeak. This place robs you of your balls – oh, sorry, Bill.'

'What on earth did he say?' Bill's eyes were wide, staring into his.

He sighed. 'I can't tell you, Bill. It'd make no sense to you.'

He saw Bill on to his train, then watched his own train puff and wheeze into the station. He wondered if she would be there at the cottage. He would drop his things at the house and go straight across to see her. She had been on his mind every day and every night since the two endless days and nights in the Three Tuns Hotel, she acting the concerned mother, he the sickly son. Round arcs of flesh, the lily of the valley scent, the delicate adventuring of men and women.

Chapter Twenty-Six

John George was in the backyard when Jonty arrived home. He was sitting on a low stool chopping sticks. Jonty was shocked at the change in his father. He looked thinner and frailer than ever, his face very drawn.

'Now Dad.' Jonty squeezed past him and dumped his case in the kitchen doorway.

'Now, son.' The chopping paused and John George looked up at him, narrowing his eyes slightly at the sun. 'Are you well?'

'I'm fine. Where's Mother?'

'Off to a wedding. Seems Betty Stapleton marries that Cornish footballer feller today. Len's brother.'

Jonty whistled. 'Mervin? They're just children.'

'Old enough. Bea says there's a baby on the way.'

'How is Ma?'

'Fizzing around as ever. I think she's stopped sleeping altogether to fit it all in.' There was a fondness and no irony in his voice.

'And how are you?'

'Well enough.' John George measured his axe against another block of wood. 'Letter inside for you. On the mantelpiece. Came a few weeks ago, but I thought you'd be here for the summer so there was no point in sending it.' His axe came down and splintered the wood. 'From India.'

Jonty raced in and tore open Davey's letter, devouring the bright descriptions of the heat, the strange setting and the bizarre activities of the army in that steaming alien climate. He sat back smiling at the thought of sturdy, matter-of-fact Davey Laydon Jones as the soldier of Empire. Then he rooted in his case for paper to reply to it before he had taken his coat off.

Dear Davey,

I've just picked up your letter a month after it arrived here, having come home on my summer vacation, so I might be a bit out of date. It sounds very exotic where you are. I don't envy all that drill and 'bull', nor the weapons that you carry, but I do envy the chance to see a world so far from ours. I don't know about India but I always wanted to see Africa, as my ma always spun me a tale that that's where my ancestors came from. I used to dream of it when I was little.

It's good to be home again, in a house. As you know I'm at St Barnabas' College in Durham, with Corella's help and my parents

171

scraping the bottom of their savings barrel. Oxford would have been impossible but we are just about managing this.

It's been a hard but exhilarating term. The levels of study are not too challenging, but the arguments and discussions, which follow them, run hot and fast. There are people of every kind here. The largest number, it's true, are church people. But there is a good sprinkling of chapel types, even some who run towards the agnostic. Morning and evening chapel (compulsory) with its high-church feel, took some standing at first, I can tell you. But I tell myself that that is the price of being at college at all. And I've learned that church people aren't all hypocrites and bigots like we used to be told. I suppose they learn the same about us.

My closest comrades in college are called David Wynne, whose own father is a vicar, and Bill Leeson, who is a Quaker and whose father is a shopkeeper in Darlington. Bill's the simplest and most truly good person I have ever met. David's the funniest and most given to tricks and games. You would think him pretty childish, probably not like him at all. We are an unlikely trio. Nevertheless all our free time is spent together.

I've been thinking about you and the killing you have to think about when you train, even if the real thing hasn't happened yet. I'm more convinced than ever that, despite the smell of war emanating from the newspapers and from the casual chatter we hear around, that war-killing for national pride or striving for capital advantage – all this is against logic, against social justice and against the word of God. The only people who fully embrace this position are the Quakers, but I don't think I am a Quaker. I know this will rage against your present position, Davey, which I respect. But I thought you might like my view. (Do they read these letters? If so, this one will not get through.)

As you ask, I've seen a little of your Susanah from time to time, but it is difficult being away like this. I saw her a minute or two during my Easter holiday, but she was busy working for your father. My ma keeps a good eye out for her and your aunt seems to have taken her properly under her wing. Apparently Betty Stapleton is marrying of all people Mervin Sargant. Being out of touch I thought it was Len she was set for. Did you know about it? I see from the paper that your Tollie is still winning goals for Gibsley. Mervin, of course, is doing even better – he's playing for Stockton now and they seem to be winning everything in front of them. Susanah will miss Betty as they are such great friends. Everyone praises Mervin and he is in the way of being a local hero though much changed from the lad we knew. A loss to us now that the Labour party is getting off the starting stumps.

I enclose my college address, and would like you to write to me there. It is not everyone who gets a letter from India!

Cordial good wishes,
Jonty Clelland

Jonty sealed the letter and, still with his coat on, made a pot of tea. He took a mug out to his father and told him he was just off to post this reply to Davey's letter. 'And I might stop by and see one or two folks,' he added.

'Right son.' John George nodded, measuring his axe against another block of wood.

Jonty let himself into the cottage with his key and set about making a good fire for her return. He smiled to himself. She would enjoy the surprise.

But it was Susanah who was surprised to see the light blazing, the open door and the fire flaring away in the little hearth and Jonty Clelland sitting on a chair by the fire, his head sunk over a book.

The book tipped to the floor as he jumped to his feet, his brown face glowing in the heat. He saw the spreading splodges of rain on the skirt of her dress, a shining thing the bleached colour of late violets. He raised his eyes to the ironic gaze of Isabella who was following behind. 'Your door was open,' he stuttered, 'so I thought it would be all right if I . . . I have the kettle boiling here.'

Susanah stood like an icicle. Jonty's certainty of manner, his at-home ease was a puzzle. Isabella gurgled with laughter, unpinned her hat and hung it unceremoniously on a peg. 'How kind of you, Jonty. That wet can perish your bones even in the summer.'

Susanah turned to go and was grabbed for her pains.

'Don't go, dear girl.' Isabella grasped her shoulders and plonked her unceremoniously into the chair which still counterfeited Jonty's shape. 'Just take off that jacket and get dried out, won't you? Yes Jonty, you can make us some tea. Just the thing to help us recover from the festivities.'

Isabella stood by the fire and Susanah followed her example in putting her hands towards it. They warmed themselves in silence as Jonty busied himself around the room in an entirely familiar fashion.

Finally Isabella spoke. 'Jonty's been such a help, Susanah. How I would have done without him, I don't know. He has been such a miss these months, away at college. And I've lost my Greek lessons. Did I tell you he very kindly undertook to teach me a bit of Greek? Just the rudiments, the first steps. It really helps me with my books.'

They followed her gaze to what she called her 'painting corner', by the window. Here, books were propped open on stands, pictures pinned up on to the curtain and a stretch of wall. These all portrayed some element of Greek myth, expressed in carvings and sometimes whole buildings. Her own work depicted the tales of the gods and the architecture of Ancient Greece, recreated as though she were painting some contemporary scene. The detail was immaculate and quite cool, but she used bright washes of translucent paint to make the whole thing glow. Her work was selling quite well. Sometimes she would send a great package of pictures away from Priorton station. Sometimes she would set off herself, with her strappy satchel and vanish to London for a week. She always had money now, money which among other things, by private arrangement with Bea, was keeping Jonty at college.

'It helps me with my books,' she repeated, 'reading them in the original.'

173

Susanah nodded at her and looked up at Jonty who was handing her a bright yellow cup and saucer, the cup shaped like a cornet.

He had changed since Easter, when he had called briefly at the house and she had seen him at chapel. He looked different. His face was thin, and he must have grown two inches. Perhaps it was being away from home, not out in the sun like Davey, that made you grow. His eyes, looking down at her, still had that pale glow that she remembered. But his smile was easier, less watchful. She relaxed.

'Now, Susanah? How are things with you?'

'Things're fine. Did you know about Davey?'

'In the army? Yes, he told me. At the back end of the summer.'

'Told you? Oh, yes, I remember.'

Jonty laughed into her scowling face. 'A bit unlikely, isn't it? Me?'

'I suppose not. He always did talk to you.'

Isabella chuckled. 'I suppose it had to be something harder than the pit. Davey has Caradoc's perversity . . .'

'He's doing all right at present, is he?'

Susanah looked at him sharply. 'I've had a couple of letters. Seems like he's all right. Gone off to India now. He'll be pleased of the fresh air, however hot it is. Always hated the pit.'

'Yes I know. I just had a letter myself. I always knew he loathed it.'

'Did you, now?' Susanah felt her resentment rising.

Jonty took a cup of tea across to Isabella, who was sitting on the sofa. He sat on a chair by the table. 'You both look very smart. What festivities were these?'

'Betty was married today. To Mervin Sargant,' said Susanah.

'Mervin? Oh yes, my father said. What about Len? They seemed to be . . .'

'Well she changed her mind. People do.' Susanah was trying not to hurry her tea. She made herself drink very slowly. When she had finished, she stood up and turned to the door to take her coat from the peg. 'I have to go. I have work to do. A watch and a clock to finish for tomorrow.'

Isabella stood up. 'Jonty, why not walk down to the village with Susanah?' She smiled up at him. 'This girl works so hard. They beat a way to her door from Priorton and even further.'

He reached for his hat. 'Yes, yes. I'll do that.'

'No!' Susanah almost shouted it. The others blinked. 'You two can get on with your lesson. I'll be back down there in no time.' Her new lilac dress swished as she whirled through the door.

Jonty relaxed, dropping into the vacated chair. Now he could concentrate on Bel, sharp and pretty as ever in her usual pale green. 'So, how are you, Bel?'

'Me? I'm very well. The painting's going fine. But I don't know why they buy it, all this false borrowed stuff.'

'Don't say that. They are good. Really!'

'Do you think so?' She picked up a silk scarf and draped it in front of the work in progress, then started to gather the cups and saucers. She looked

174

at him over the yellow stack. 'Do you know, dear boy, all that celebration stuff has left me really tired.'

He leapt to his feet. 'Yes, yes. I must go. They expect me at home. I haven't seen my mother yet.'

She smiled a faint smile. 'Yes. Give Bea my regards, it's weeks since we had one of our chats. She is so refreshing to talk to.'

She kept the table between them as he left and he had to leave for home without so much as a kiss on the cheek.

When Susanah arrived home the house was quiet. The boys were out and the closed middle door told her that Caradoc had retired to bed. He had left the clock and the watch ready for her with the tools, on their velvet cloth on the kitchen table. It was comforting to turn up the lamp and settle down to work which required such concentration that she could think of nothing else.

Two hours later the task done, she rolled up the velvet and put away the tools. Then she reached in a drawer and brought her pen and ink, the paper and an envelope. She smiled to herself, thinking of him out there marching in the heat.

Dear Davey,

Thank you for your letters. They came very quickly on each other, so I thought I'd settle down and write a really good one back, as you seem so far away. It is good to hear that you are flourishing in the sun. Growing two inches is a good sign. I had read in the newspaper that some people get sick over there from the heat. It must be bringing out the best in you.

We have been full of Betty's wedding here. Can you believe that two Saturdays ago we were actually standing inside Lewison's, on the carpeted dais at the far end of the shop? So there I was, standing on the dais, wearing this dress of pale violet sheered cotton. (You did say you wanted details.) Betty was standing beside me pulling the line of the dress hither and thither. She was looking brilliantly Irish herself in the dress she'd just got with money that Mr Stapleton had given her. Green stripes, that was. It sported a rather nicely cut peplum, which hid her growing front very well!

Our Aunt Isabella was sitting on the chair leaning forward, using her umbrella for balance. The really snotty saleswoman was beside her, her eyes glittering like a kestrel's watching for mice. She has a powered face and strangles her words much worse than Miss Antrobus.

Aunt Isabella had said I wasn't to worry about the price. She'd got mad because Da wouldn't pay for a new dress. She stomped round the little front room of her cottage like a little fat puppy in a cage. She's furious too because he hasn't made one step to see her since she arrived.

The dress was lovely. Aunt Isabella said 'We will have this one as well, my dear.' You should have heard the tone, Davey! The saleswoman went red and became very greasy.

I do most of the clockmaking work now. Da has had to show me how to do the more complicated things and the finishing, as his hands are getting clumsy for some reason and he loses his temper with even the simplest job. A sad change, this. He was gentle when he worked with the clocks, not like his other self.

So Betty and I bought our dresses together, hers being paid for by Mr Stapleton, mine by Aunt Bel. I had more pleasure from the dress just because she bought it. Any dress squeezed out of Da would have grudge in every fold.

Afterwards Isabella steered us into Roxby's Photographers and we had our photographs taken before going to Bell's Café for tea. I have ordered a copy of the photograph as I thought you might like it. Mervin and Betty seemed pleased to be getting married, even though this wedding was to be in a bit of a hurry to get it in before the baby's arrival. It's funny how people forget these hurried weddings, once everything is made regular. Even so, Da won't have either of them near our house. Miss A has done a lot of stirring. There were only a few of us in the chapel. Mr Stapleton gave Betty away. He looked very smart in his newly pressed suit. Len Sargant was best man, pretty good of him seeing as Mervin stole Betty away from him. Mrs Stapleton had a new hat. I was the bridesmaid. Isabella was there. Betty insisted on it. She kept on looking around very curiously, as you know she's not one for the chapel.

Back at the Stapletons', there was too much kissing for my fancy. In my view both Mr Stapleton and Mervin made a meal of it. The way that Mervin kissed both my cheek and my neck, you would never think he had just married Betty. She just looked on. There is no harm in her.

We drank blackberry cordial (which you will guess reminded me of Ma and Jenny), and ate fruit cake. Freddy pulled out his squeeze-box and played a few Irish ballads where we all joined in the choruses. Soon, though, Betty and Mervin were keen to be off to their little house and we all left.

I walked right back with Isabella to her cottage. We were glad of her umbrella as it started to rain and I took no persuading to come in for tea. I actually met your friend Jonty Clelland there, as you ask. He seems very grand now. Full of college swank. I wouldn't depend on a letter from him. But you will always get one from your sister.

Susanah Laydon Jones

PS I hope you like my drawing of Aunt Bel with her umbrella. I also enclose the newspaper cutting about Joan Kenton getting fined for clocking a man over the head with a spade as she said he was in her garden to steal her leeks. Apparently she had lain in wait. He said he was just passing and no one else was there. She's a hearty girl. Did I tell you she had a baby? Ten day wonder in the village. She didn't lose a day's work and her mother and Viv are minding the baby between them. She is always interested in any news from you. Love S.

Susanah licked the flap and sealed the letter. As she put it on the mantelpiece ready to post, she smiled at the thought of Davey opening it all those miles away in some dusty barracks and reading her words, written at this table, in this house.

Chapter Twenty-Seven

At home, Susanah's working day seemed to have no end. Caradoc, Lew and Tollie came in and out of the house at different times, requiring different levels of attention and succour. The tides of washing, drying and ironing, cleaning and cooking rolled in again and again. She tried to keep her mother's customs and practice, so that the house was warm and shining, the food good. On top of all this, at the far end of her day there would be the piles of clocks and watches lurking in their box, waiting for her fixing hand.

Miss Antrobus stayed away a week after Susanah had shuffled her out of the house and never came back with the solid day-to-day assurance she had assumed straight after Ceiri's death. Then, one day, she called, with Caradoc's encouragement, carrying cakes and homemade sweets for the boys in a way which made it impossible for Susanah to shut the door on her. After that she started to come again, unbidden, to sit in the chair which had been Ceiri's. One Tuesday in October she came in, muttering about the difficulties of the rain. Susanah looked up from her ironing without speaking as the large woman arranged herself and her spreading skirts with care, then spoke in her strangled tones. 'A cup of tea would not come amiss, Susanah.'

Susanah put the iron on the fireshelf and spooned dry tea into the waiting teapot. She picked up the kettle, her mind rehearsing the pouring of boiling water on to fat knees. But she decided against it as the water would make the stench of violets which always clouded the woman's presence even worse. Instead, she scalded the tea and poured out a cup.

Miss Antrobus held the cup up to the light which was filtering through the rain-scored window. 'Mm, I always did say it takes very close attention to get china really clean.'

Susanah picked up the iron and spat on it, focussing on the bead of spit as it exploded back into the air. Then, working away, she watched it transform the crinkled cotton of Tollie's Sunday shirt to miraculous smoothness. She thought determinedly about the extra problems which rain brought, when you were forced to dry inside; the fabrics crinkled and you missed the smell of fresh air blooming back at you from the smoothing material.

This particular evening, Caradoc's shift meant he was home, so Miss Antrobus stayed on to sit with him. She read aloud from the Old Testament, then from a book of John Wesley's sermons which were her own particular favourite. He sat silent, his hands folded in his lap, his broad shoulders now slightly hunched.

179

Susanah sat at the table in Caradoc's old place, with his lamp beside her, his roll of black velvet spread out before her. Her current work was a woman's silver fobwatch, brought down from Priorton by a man who dealt in fish. He had arrived in a trap, his clothes were tailored, his hands soft, but he had had around him the faint smell of herring.

If she could force her head to rub out the presence of Miss Antrobus, these were Susanah's more peaceful times. She lost herself in the intricacy of the task and delighted in the elaborate mechanisms, celebrating inwardly when a thing which had been broken started to tick away again. Sometimes her mind wandered back to Caradoc as she realised that he too must have had this same feeling, of pattern, completion and fit. A feeling that must be lost to him now he had stopped touching the clocks altogether.

The sound of Tollie clattering down the yard after his late shift brought its usual relief. The woman would have to go, as Tollie would strip off without compunction to wash whether she were there or not, and she made a great play of her modesty.

'Well, I'll go now.'

'Susanah, you walk Miss Antrobus to her house.'

She folded her lip and looked at her father. 'I have the finishing on this watch to do and Tollie's dinner to get.'

Tollie grinned down at the woman, his white teeth gleaming in his black face. 'What say I walk Miss Antrobus home, Da?'

The woman turned. 'Caradoc!'

Caradoc pulled himself to his feet, got his cap and followed her pigeon figure out of the house. That night he left her at the door, grunting his refusal of a little warm and a glass of madeira.

Tollie stood in the doorway pulling off his shirt and trousers. 'She's after a ring on her finger, old Ma Antrobus, ain't she?'

'If she gets it, I'm off. I'm away.'

'You? Where'd you go? What'd you do?'

'There's places. And I'd mend watches.'

After gulping his dinner, Tollie sat beside Susanah doing the apprentice tasks which she had once done. He did this purely to help; it was a real sacrifice for him to sit still for any length of time.

Lew never helped. He was usually out till late. He kept his distance from Caradoc in the house, knowing he carried with him the smoky sour smell of the Steam Mill.

Two days later he came in early, in a truculent mood, having drunk too much and lost the bit of his wage which Caradoc allowed him at pitch and toss in the yard behind the pub.

Susanah had been working at the table, trying to finish the job on the fobwatch and ignoring the clack of Miss Antrobus's voice. Her head had dropped and dropped until she was cheek down, fast asleep. Suddenly Lew pulled her head back roughly by the hair. 'What's this, then?' he demanded. 'Going to sleep on the job?'

The two by the fire looked across.

Miss Antrobus clicked her teeth in disapproval. Caradoc looked up under his brows. 'Get that stuff put away, girl. You should start no job you won't finish,' he growled.

Susanah shook her head to clear it and looked across at them. She took a breath. 'What is it you think I am? A horse? A pit pony that you can work till it folds its knees in the dark?'

'That's enough!' bristled the woman. 'Honour thy father!'

Perhaps it was the jerking out of sleep. Perhaps this time she would have finally spoken out anyway. 'The work I do in this house, Miss Antrobus . . . the cooking and cleaning, the washing of clothes and the cleaning of boots, the taking care of Tollie and Lew, and my father who I should honour, the mending clocks for which I get neither money nor credit . . .' She was losing her breath now, but continued to talk through her coughs. 'I do all this, Miss Antrobus. It is my mother I honour. Only her. Even now when she is dead and in the earth. And if you can do better, Miss Antrobus, just stop making cow eyes at my father and sitting there being waited on and get off your bottom to do a bit of work yourself.'

Caradoc moaned and moved towards Susanah, both hands raised in fists. Lew whistled through his teeth and casually moved into Caradoc's way, absorbing the lashing from his father as though it were nothing.

Blinking back her tears, Susanah ran out of the door, scooping her coat from its peg. She stopped outside the Stapletons' house before she remembered that Betty was no longer there; she was tucked up with Mervin in a neat little house in Stockton twenty long miles away. Then she pulled her coat to herself and walked on.

She kept on, going out of the village and up the hill and down the narrow pathway to the cottage. Isabella was at the door in a second, dressed in a flowing robe with some kind of silk tie around her loose hair.

She pulled Susanah into the little front room and sat her down beside the bright fire till she got her breath back, rubbing her hands and asking no questions. Even so, Susanah felt answers being pulled from her.

'I told the . . . I was tired, you see, asleep on the table . . . They were reading their Bible . . . Then they started on at me . . . Da . . .'

'He hit you?'

'No, not this time. Lew got in the way. This time, I ran.' Susanah put her head back on the plump cushion and closed her eyes. She could hear the clicking of Isabella's slippers and the shirring of her robe as she busied herself around the house. Finally she felt her fingers being wrapped round a cup. She opened her eyes to see a steaming cup of cocoa.

'There. It says in the paper it "Does You Good".'

'I never had it before.'

Isabella sat opposite, watching her drink the cocoa to the last drop.

'I'd best get back,' said Susanah.

Isabella removed the cup from the girl's thin hands. 'You'll not go back there. No. You'll stay here. That man'll kill you one way or another. Just like Ceiri.'

Her head sagged. Her eyes felt sore. 'Tollie . . .' she said. 'Lew . . .'

'Those great boys can look out for themselves till we sort it out. In the meantime, you need some rest before you pass out altogether.' She gave Susanah a silky nightdress. 'No. Take everything off. Right to the skin.'

Susanah felt uncomfortable. Normally, she kept on at least one layer of underclothes. She turned her back to obey.

Her aunt looked on thoughtfully. 'There's not a picking on you,' she said. 'All skin and bone.'

Susanah slipped between the linen sheets which had come from Dolman Castle under a green silk eiderdown which had come from Corwyn Manor. The eiderdown was fat, like the goose the young Isabella had plucked to fill it twenty years before.

Isabella turned off the lamp and prepared for bed in the firelight. She slipped in behind Susanah and put her arm across her body. 'Like I said, dear girl, you're just skin and bone. First thing, we'll have to fatten you up a bit. Then we'll decide what to do.'

'Aunt Bel?'

'Now then?'

'Was my da always like this?'

'Caradoc? That crocodile? No. He was a sweet lad. Shall I tell you which one he was like?'

'Who? Lew?'

'No. Your Davey. Reminded me straight away. Gentle. A vessel for suffering. Perverse. And a bit of Tollie. He'd that bravado.'

'So what happened . . .?'

But the cocoa, on top of the hard day, did its job. She was drifting away in the warm circle of Bel's arm, soon dreaming of her young mother sitting by the fire crocheting away at the counterpane which was to be hers when she left home.

The next morning, Tollie and Lew brought her the boxes and bags which held the tools and the clocks and watches as yet unmended. Standing there, her brothers dwarfed the little front room, reducing it to a doll's house.

Tollie grinned at her. 'I told our Lew you'd be here.'

'Caradoc said you'd need the stuff to finish the jobs,' said Lew.

'Did he?'

'Really squashed when you didn't come back.'

'Last time it was Jenny who ran,' put in Tollie.

Isabella saw her niece flinch. 'Will you boys sit down?'

'No, we'll get off now, Aunt Bel.'

'I don't know whether I'll . . .' began Susanah.

'She'll be staying with me,' said Bel firmly.

'My things . . .'

'He's not back from work till four. The door's open,' said Lew.

Susanah saw them to the narrow front door.

'Oh,' said Lew. 'Coming past the Stapletons'. Mervin was there, looking like a man off. Quite a flurry inside. The bairn's due, is it?'

Before he'd finished Susanah was already putting on her coat.

By the time she arrived, Mervin was sitting on the wall, his bright face unusually strained.

'How is she?'

'Came across from Stockton yesterday. Been on since one o'clock this morning.' He shook his head.

'Can I go in?'

'You'll have to fight your way through all the others.'

Freddy was sitting at the kitchen table playing cards with his sons. Betty's mother was sitting by the fire, her body sagging with exhaustion. She looked up at Susanah. 'She's taking too long,' she said.

'Can I go up?'

Mrs Stapleton shrugged. 'Mrs Richards and Mrs Slee are up there. Says she's taking too long. They sent me away.'

Susanah went up the stairs two at a time. The women, one tall and thin, the other short and fat, looked at her sourly. 'No place for you,' said the shorter woman, Mrs Richards.

She pushed past them. Betty smiled at her weakly, her face strained and old. 'They say I'm a very naughty girl, S'anah. Too lazy. Not working hard enough.' There was a thread of a giggle. 'Always my Da's daughter.'

Susanah pulled up a stool, ignoring the grumbles of the women. She caught hold of Betty's hand which grasped back in desperation. 'You're not naughty. You're a good, good girl.' She pushed the wet hair back on the brow. 'And a bonny one. I'm not saying your hair couldn't do with a good wash, mind.'

A weak smile. 'You used to wash it.'

'Didn't I just?'

'Cold water. Ugh!' The hand and the body were relaxing.

Susanah could see again the back of the Woman's dress, and the triangle of sopping sweat that stained it from shoulder to hem. She could see her stooping and lifting up Auntie Peg's ragdoll body and dumping her in a corner, muttering, 'No use, no use . . .' Then Mama started her moaning again and the Woman's gaze wandered round the room, her grey eye lighting on her, Susanah, in the corner. 'Right, sweetheart! Do you want to do something really special for your mama?' she'd said.

Susanah turned to the women hovering near the window. 'In Wales I saw my mother have my sister. The woman there sat her on a chair, had her kind of squatting . . .'

The women exchanged glances. 'Mrs Morgan, who I learned from, she did it sometimes,' said Mrs Slee uncertainly.

'Dr Bacon'll go mad if he finds . . .'

'He's not here,' said Susanah. 'Go on. Go on!'

Mrs Slee shrugged. 'Nowt to lose, I suppose. We're gonna lose them both as it is. Here . . .' Very firmly she pulled Susanah away from the bed and pushed her into a stool by the door. 'Let's get at her.'

It could have been Ceiri, squatting there. The shudders travelling in a continuous rhythm, the figures either side. One woman kneeling with her arm around Betty, the other down below. The twitches and half groans from Betty, the satisfied crooning of Mrs Slee. She stared hard into Betty's face and could see her mother's face, with its sticky halo of hair. The eyes wide open, but not seeing outwards, only inside, inside her own body. Finally Betty expelled a high-pitched cry, as controlled as a whistle, followed by a long sigh.

'Hey! Tek notice, tek notice!' A rough hand was shaking her shoulder. 'Get hold of this little 'n. We've got trouble here.' The baby, white-haired and hastily-wrapped, was thrust into her arms. He opened a blind blue eye and started bawling.

It was more than half an hour before Susanah could put the child into Betty's arms. Her mind was full now of Jenny. Jenny into her mother's arms. Jenny back in her mother's arms under the earth. There were tears in her eyes.

Her friend's pale face had been washed, her black Irish hair combed back. She smiled a ghostly smile. 'Not so naughty then, S'anah?'

'He's a fine boy. A lovely boy. White-haired like his dad.'

The head turned on the pillow. 'Mervin? Can I see Mervin?'

Back at the cottage, Susanah found Bel painting in her window space with Bea Clelland hunched behind her, watching her every movement.

Bel wiped her brush. 'How is she, your friend?'

'The baby's all right. Betty's a bit poorly, I think.'

'Well, I might have missed a lot, but that? No, thank you!' said Bel firmly.

'It's no picnic,' agreed Bea. 'It always makes me laugh when they tell you that you forget it.' She watched closely as Susanah removed her coat and mittens. 'I was telling your auntie that our Jonty has the promise of a job at the school when he qualifies.'

'You'll like having him home again. He seems to have been away a long time.'

'Well, I don't know. I'd rather he'd gone to London or Paris or somewhere. But it looks as though George'll never get work now, so we need him here, just for a while, to save a bit of money to get on our feet again. Then he can go further afield. He should do that.'

Susanah thought about Jonty; for the first time in years she allowed her mind to see the afternoon on the riverbank and the kingfishers. Here, out of Ceiri's house, she could think it. She thought in sequence of all the times he had approached her since, only to be pushed away. She smiled into Bea's broad face. 'It'll be nice to see him back. He once offered me some art books, but I didn't have time. But perhaps now . . .' She saw the two older women exchange a smile and noticed a resemblance between them. Unlikely sisters.

The rest of the day went quickly. She sat at Isabella's kitchen table and finished the job on the silver watch while her aunt worked away at the window space on yet another picture of the Parthenon.

They had cleared the table and set it for supper when Mervin walked through the door, the bundled baby in his arms.

'Here.' Her arms were out and the baby was in them. 'She said you were to have him. Not her ma. You. She said you had to have the baby. It's yours.' His eyes were red with crying and his hands were icy cold. There was no need to ask what it was all about.

Chapter Twenty-Eight

Mervin went back to Stockton the next day and stayed away for three months. They read of his matches and the goals he scored in the newspaper and every Friday Susanah received a ten shilling note in the post. There was no note or letter from him. The baby was placid, feeding from the bottle with great appetite and sleeping long hours between feeds. Isabella was fascinated by him, touching the silvery hair with an almost timid hand.

At first Susanah took the baby almost daily to the Stapleton house to see Freddy and his wife, but they took little interest in their grandson. The loss of their daughter seemed to have shrunk them, made them seem very old. Betty's mother spent much of the day in tears by the fire and Freddy started missing chapel and going back into the pubs.

Susanah went to see John George Clelland. The door was open and she found him in the kitchen staring into the fire. 'It's about Freddy Stapleton. He's back drinking, he's that upset over Betty.'

'I'd heard. A bad loss, a daughter.'

'Can you help him? You helped him before.'

'Before?'

'When I was a little girl you saved him that time. I was there.'

He smiled and stroked his chin. 'So you were!'

He remembered the sharp little face, the bright wide-open eyes, the gaze which combined fear and fascination. Then he felt inside just a ghost of the power he had felt that day, striding back from Priorton, virtually carrying Freddy Stapleton on his back, so sure that here was one to be saved! He nodded at the earnest face of the young woman in front of him. 'I did, didn't I? I saved him for a while. Perhaps we're all saved just for a while, then our while is over.' His gaze went back to the fire.

'Mr Clelland!' she said urgently. 'Try! You will try!'

He nodded. 'Well, perhaps I will. I can get myself round there. Talk a bit. I don't know about savin' him. Don't do a lot of that nowadays.' He didn't do much of anything nowadays. He felt so tired, so uncertain about things. He stood up stiffly and walked down the yard with the girl. As he clicked the gate behind her he smiled into her worried face. 'Don't you worry, I'll go. But I need to wait till Bea gets in. She's at a women's meeting. Then we'll take a walk over to see them.'

There were marks of tears in Bea's face when she came in. Concerned, he stood up and put an arm around her. 'Crying, Bea? Not like you!'

'Anger, JG. Sheer blind anger. They read a letter out from Miss Marsden. You remember the big lass, the one who laughed so much? She's been very ill. They put her in prison for breaking windows and she went on hunger strike. So . . . they force-fed her. Disgusting, horrible things.' The tears were welling up in her eyes again. 'Oh, what's the use!'

He put another arm around her and hugged her. 'It's all useful, pet. All useful. Now! We have to go across to Freddy's. He's back in the mire since their girl went. We'll be some use there.'

Bea's tears dried and she smiled up at him, delighted that, even for a moment, some of his old strength seemed to have returned. 'Right, JG,' she nodded. 'I'm with you.'

As the weeks unfolded Caradoc sent Tollie up to the cottage with clock work for Susanah. She did the work with an eagerness which surprised even herself. It had something to do with keeping up a contact with Caradoc even though she rarely saw him and he never spoke to her. His customers paid him for the work and so at first she saw little of the money her skill was earning. Then people started to bring individual items directly to the cottage and those who did would pay her directly. For the first time in her life she had her own money. It was a treat to pay Isabella for her keep and to buy herself pretty clothes which as she'd written to Davey, did not have grudge in every fold.

When she had heard nothing from Mervin for six weeks, she took the baby to Roxby's and had his photo taken. She wrote on the back of it, 'This little baby has no name and needs his Dad to give him one.' Then she posted it to the football club, asking them to forward it.

Mervin arrived the following Sunday afternoon, a bag of oranges in his hand. He looked pinched and much older than his years.

She took him by the hand and led him across to the drawer she had rigged up as a cot. 'Here he is. He's good as gold. Go on, let him grab your finger.'

The tiny hand folded round Mervin's finger and he smiled a faint shadow of his former cocky grin. 'Strong grip. 'D make a goalie all right.'

'So what will you call him?'

'I told you. He's yours. B – She said he was yours.'

'But he's yours as well. That's what the ten shilling notes are about, isn't it?'

'Aye. But you name him. You have the mindin' of 'm.'

She looked at the baby, hardly daring to think of him as hers. 'Can I call him Davey?' she ventured. 'I miss our Davey so much, and Fred for Betty's dad . . .'

'Aye. Why not?'

'That's it then. Look, why don't you take him round and show him to your Len? Then maybe to Freddy's.'

'Nah. Canna carry a bairn in the street.' He laughed. 'You come. You bring 'm.'

So the baby was christened David Frederick and Mervin started to come every Sunday to see him and Susanah.

* * *

One spring day they were walking by the river under the viaduct when Mervin stopped to watch a train steam its way across the top. 'Remember the day I tripped over you in Southgate?' he asked. 'Then met you and Betty down here?'

'Yes, that's when you . . .'

'Me and Betty started our courting. She was a jolly lass, Bet. We had some fun. Always good for a joke, no bother. I don't half miss her.'

'You will, Mervin. Me, too.'

They walked on. Then he stopped her. 'Why not you and me get married, Susanah?'

'What?' She gaped at him.

'Betty'd want it. Proper set-up for the bairn.'

Young Davey started to cry and she jiggled him up and down to soothe him and was pleased when the hiccuping and wailing subsided into a gurgle. She loved the baby in the same way as she had loved Jenny: completely, protectively and with a sense of ownership. It was right that Betty had entrusted her with him, it felt like a forgiveness for her failure all those years before. And now, what Mervin was asking her, seemed part of it.

He was staring hard at her. She looked up at him. 'I wouldn't move to Stockton. I have to stay here.'

'That's all right. I'll come back across here. The football'll get me a job one way or another.'

'Right, then,' she said simply.

'Right.'

The day before Susanah's wedding she knocked on the door of the house in Selby Street. Caradoc scraped it open, saw her and turned round and walked back into the house, neither telling her to come in nor shutting the door in her face. In the kitchen, he stood with his back to the tidy fire.

'I'll be married to Mervin Sargant on Saturday, Father. There'll be tea at the Stapletons afterwards.'

'That footballer?' His voice was gruffer than ever. 'A useless thing, that. Taking some woman's offspring and her man on.'

'Betty wasn't some woman. She was my friend.'

'Hadn't a brain in her head.'

'She was my friend. Always kind and good.'

'Drunkard's daughter.' Spit came out with the words.

She took a breath. 'Like to like. The only thing my own father could do when he drove my mother out of her own life was get drunk. So as I say, like to like. She was my friend.' She didn't have time to dodge his blow, which caught her eyebone. She flinched but did not cry. She put her hand on her cheek. 'Then don't come to my wedding, Da. I'm sorry that you won't come.' She paused at the door. 'Oh, no need to send any more watches work to the cottage. I have my hands full with my own work now. And the baby.'

She closed the door very carefully behind her, stilling the trembling sneck with her forefinger.

Tollie was giving young Davey galloping rides up and down the back lane when she arrived back at the cottage. He whistled at the sight of her eye. 'That'll be a shiner tomorrow, S'anah. Did he do it?'

She nodded. 'He was calling Betty, so I called him.'

He handed over the giggling struggling figure of the little boy, his face grim. 'That's it. He needs stopping, that one.'

'Leave him, Tollie. He'll set off after you as well.'

He shook his head silently and strode off down the hill towards Gibsley.

His father was sitting staring into the fire when he burst through the door. 'What do you want giving our S'anah a black eye, Da?'

'None of your business.'

'It is my business. I'm telling you, Da, next time you feel like belting somebody just make it me, make it somebody your own bliddy size, not some little lass that comes up to your elbow. You can stop that with my sister. Or else.'

Caradoc rose out of his seat and faced Tollie, his hands knuckled up into huge fists. He had to look upwards: his youngest son was now taller than he was. Slowly his fists uncurled and he lifted his shoulders in a massive shrug. 'I shouldn't have done it. Any of it.' He bent at his knees and subsided into the chair, his gaze straying back to the fire, with his son looming helplessly above him.

That evening Susanah faked up a veil with tea-dyed lace to cover her black eye and the next day she married Mervin at Priorton Registry Office in a mustard woollen suit she'd bought herself. Tollie and Mr Stapleton were witnesses at Priorton registry office and Susanah could feel Betty's approving presence all around her. It felt like a kind of atonement.

By no coincidence, Isabella was away in London that week selling pictures and buying supplies and a new wardrobe of clothes. Jonty was in London, on Easter vacation again in his last year at college, helping her with all these enterprises. Their arrangement was to meet at the little hotel where she always stayed, the Lantern Hotel in Somer Street. They had rooms linked by a common sitting-room and allowed the fiction to emerge that they were aunt and nephew as they strolled around the museum and galleries, the bookshops and cafés. These arrangements had become regular in the last year as there were no opportunities to meet in Gibsley now that Susanah and young Davey were welcome fixtures in Isabella's household and Mervin was a frequent visitor.

Jonty shook his head with disbelief when Isabella told him of the marriage. 'Mervin? She's marrying him? She can't.'

'She can. In fact, she is. Three o'clock today.' Isabella turned her fob-watch over on her capacious bosom. 'See. Half-past three now.'

'Why? She can't love him.'

'You're right. No question of that. He's not my cup of tea and she does deserve someone special. It's a waste, in my view. I'm only glad to be here not there; she knows I'm not keen on it. Not keen at all. It's for young Davey. No. For Betty.'

'She can't. She can't do it.' His tone was almost petulant.

'Now don't sulk, dear boy. You missed your chance there!'

'Chance!' He groaned. 'I've tried there, as you put it, since we were small children and only once did I get near her. Then it all went wrong and you'd think I was a leper. She's no time for me.'

Isabella sighed. 'Seems things keep working against you, one way or another. Never mind, dear boy, you will just have to console yourself with a culture-laden time with your Auntie Bel and forget about what is happening up there in County Durham. Why don't we go to see this man at the Foster Street Galley, then on to Harrods and buy for a midnight feast. Should we have it in your room tonight? Yes. Your room, I think.'

Mrs Stapleton had offered to keep young Davey down in the village for a few days so the cottage was empty when Mervin and Susanah returned from the late high tea at the Stapleton house.

Susanah fiddled with her bag, watching Mervin's pale open face as he fumbled with the lamp and brought the light up. He had paid her a brief but intense courtship since she had agreed to the wedding. He'd told her stories about football and the men at his foundry and brought her bunches of wildflowers. On the Friday before the wedding they had gone to the seaside on the train with young Davey and sat on the sand making sandpies and watching the sea. This was the first time for Susanah as well as for young Davey and she was as amazed as the child at the ever-deceiving rush of water, coming and leaving, coming and leaving.

Standing always between them was the message from Betty that she was to have the baby. And there was no way she could take the baby without taking the father. When Susanah had agreed that yes, they could marry, it had had all the neatness of a door clicking shut. Now they could both relax. There was no mention, no word of love between them. On Susanah's part it would have been a lie; on Mervin's part it would have been a betrayal of Betty who had flirted her way into his heart on market day all those years before.

But their marriage was now a fact and they stood in the little sitting-room staring at each other. Susanah turned quickly, then rooted in one of Isabella's cupboards and pulled out two glasses and a tall earthenware bottle. 'I have some blackcurrant cordial. My mother used to make it.' She smiled too widely, too brightly. 'She used to distil some of it down to alcohol, but I don't think this is that sort.'

She poured it into the glasses and held one out to him. The light from the lamp gleamed on its rim. 'Good luck to us,' she said.

'Good luck to us,' he repeated and drank his off. He put the glass down, leaned over and took off the mustard hat with the tea-dyed veil and put a gentle finger on the bruise on her eye. 'Get yerself upstairs, flower. I'll be there in a minute.'

It took just a minute to hang up her suit, undress and slither into one of Bel's silk nighties. It only seemed another minute before the door clicked and he was in the room naked. In all of her eighteen years she had lived in close quarters with men but had never seen a man naked. She kept her eyes on his face, away from other parts of his body.

He sat on the bed alongside her and leaned over to kiss her mouth. Her body revolted but she left her lips there. He pressed harder. Seemed angry. She couldn't breathe and turned her head away.

'Dinna worry,' he said. 'Dinnet worry. It'll be all right.'

Then the sheets were back and he was on top of her, rasping his way into her, forcing a groan from her lips. 'Dinnet worry,' he repeated, his face hard and strange. 'Dinnet worry.' He was gasping himself now. 'It'll be all right.'

Her whole being was suffused with panic. She couldn't stand this. It was not possible to do it. There was no space to put that thing in. She felt as if she was breaking and she could see her mother again, head back, face to one side, and that pressing her father did on her. That awful pressing. This awful pressing.

'Stop it,' she was shouting out loud. 'Stop it!'

'It's all right. It's done now.' He rolled off and lay beside her and closed his eyes. She could feel the sticky ooze between her legs and felt sick. She wriggled off the bed and went to Isabella's little washroom and sponged herself down. The water made the bruises sting and she could feel herself breaking inside.

She put on a fresh nightdress and went back and lay, eyes wide open, on the bed, wondering what on God's earth she had done.

A voice came from beside her. 'Dinnet worry. It gets better.'

It didn't.

But their daytime lives worked out well. Mervin was a hard worker, a good friend and a merry father to young Davey. Each night, however, she dreaded the point when he might or might not make his approach. They never discussed it, but eventually Mervin approached her less and less and their daytime selves defined their marriage. Then, once in every month or so, Mervin would come in from one of his long walks and she could smell the desire on him. She could console herself then that if it happened tonight she would have a few weeks' respite.

She stayed at Isabella's cottage and made no attempt to go to the colliery house that went with Mervin's new job at White Pool, and his new place on the Priorton team, which was now working its way up the league.

Despite the difficulties she felt a quiet delight when she found she was pregnant, keeping it to herself until she was five months into it. Mervin, when she told him, was delighted too, picking her up and swinging her around. 'Now, lass, now, lass,' he said, almost in relief, 'we'll be really bound together!'

'We're bound together anyway, you daft ha'porth!' she answered, laughing at him.

He put her down and looked at her soberly. 'I know it's not all, well, like you'd want. Don't think I don't.'

He looked so much like a great puzzled bear that she had to reach up and kiss him on the cheek saying, 'Get away with you, you big soft lad.'

Despite the blinding hot summer weather of 1909 (the papers said it was the hottest since 1868) she carried the baby very easily, feeling glossy and fit right through the pregnancy. It was an easy birth, with Susanah insisting on doing it the way the Woman had shown her. And the pain did not compare with the pain on the first night of her marriage. Nothing could.

Anna was as demanding and noisy as Davey had been placid, showing herself to be a busy hussy from the first. She fed little and often. Feeding her was an unexpectedly sensual pleasure for Susanah, the hard-gummed tugs sending thrills through her that she had never felt before.

Mervin didn't approach her for more than a year during that time. He went out more, sometimes with Lew to pubs and other hostelries, coming home befuddled now and then. He had less to do with Len than ever. His life consisted of work and football and the public house. But his football was falling off and there was talk of replacing him on the Priorton team. She knew he'd never played the same since he'd returned home to be with her and young Davey. But, she told herself, that had been his choice to make.

At work he got into bad feeling too because he voted against the strike called by the miners, now a national federation, in the spring. He generated arguments in the pit and was increasingly restless and sulky at home. One day he came in with a black eye. Susanah looked over the baby's head at her husband as he stood swaying there. 'Looks like you've been in the wars,' she said drily. 'Who've you been fighting now?'

'Our Len. Callin' us a backslider. Callin' us a boss's man. I telt him, like. Labour government? Dinnet make me laugh. Then, wham! I'm down. Then I get on to him about this pacifism. How does that fix with beatin' up yer brother? Wham! Down again! Me! I'm the pacifist, not him. I'd not hit me own brother. But then I telt him, I'm joinin' the army! I telt him!'

'What?' shrieked Susanah.

He waved his hand about. 'Dinnet worry, flower. Your man winnet leave yer! The territorials. Part-time army! Feller told us about it.'

She went on stroking the baby's back, wondering if she was pleased or sorry to hear this.

So when the strike was finally over, Mervin joined the territorials and played football for the army, spending week-ends and sometimes weeks away on special leave from the pit. Susanah enjoyed those quiet times with Isabella and Davey and the new baby in the cottage. She had more work than she could handle with the clocks and watches and Isabella paid a girl from Gibsley three shillings a week to come and clean and watch the babies so that she and Susanah could get on with their work.

The territorials seemed to give Mervin a new lease of life. He seemed more like his old self, relishing all the hard army training. Mervin did not need any compulsion to defend his country. Like Davey, he loved the comradeship of the men. Like Davey, he loved the work above ground, out in the open under the sky.

In the end Susanah did not regret her marriage. Mervin was a merry and frequently absent partner; both features she relished. And she appreciated the fact that his lovemaking was perfunctory and pared to the essentials in time and frequency. Once she had recovered from the shock of the strange violence of the act she was grateful for his politeness and brevity. Despite her vague detachment from him, she grew to like him and felt upset on the special days when the army kept him away: the days when Anna started to walk and talk and when Davey started school. On those days she was hungry for his wholehearted affection and enthusiasm.

Then whispers of a real war began to echo more and more loudly in the papers and in the street. Hearing them, her heart lurched with the thought that one day he'd be marching away down Selby Street into real action, not some adventurous play-acting on a County Durham beach.

PART THREE

1914–1918

Chapter Twenty-Nine

'Mister Clelland, just look at Davey Sargant. He's fell off the coke tip and bashed his nose on the yard.'

Jonty looked from the sly, falsely earnest face of Jacob Smith, grandson to Jade, to the blond thatch and the white face of Davey Sargant: a smeary amalgam of mucus, blood and tears. He sighed. 'You've been in the wars, young man, I think.'

The six-year-old hung his head.

'Take him to the porch, Jacob, and wipe his face. Here.' He pulled out his own handkerchief which was none too clean, and handed it to the young guardian. He watched the larger and smaller backs receding, noting suddenly the finer quality of the infant's clothing.

'Stop!'

The figures scraped to a stop, the faces swivelled round, pictures of guilt.

'Did you say this boy's name was Sargant?'

'Yes.'

'And where does he live?'

'Right out of Gibsley, sir. Up the hill into the wood.'

'That's a long way for a little lad to come.'

'He gets met, sir. Every night, one of them meets him. His ma, or he has this old auntie who wears this hat with a feather. She comes.'

'Thank you, Jacob. Get him cleaned up.'

'Yes, sir.'

Jonty frowned as he continued his yard patrol. He had been in the Gibsley school only three weeks and only knew his own class. His mother had written to him with the news that Mr Robertson had died and that Miss Carmedy would put in a word for Jonty if he wanted the job. His mother's plea was about more than taking up Mr Robertson's job. She was at her wit's end with JG who was morose and surly and quite unlike his old self. He had had to give up his job in an exciting forward-looking school in Gateshead to come home.

He heard the whining creak of the gate and turned round to see the tides of children were parting around the black-crow figure of the vicar who inclined his head to acknowledge the touched forelocks.

'Ha! Mr Clelland! Just the person.' The vicar was panting. He grew fatter and more red-faced with each year which passed.

'Good morning, Mr Stonham,' said Jonty, civility outstripping his dislike for the man. He kept on walking round the yard and the vicar had to sustain a panting pace beside him.

'I have had reports, Mr Clelland,' he puffed.

'Reports?'

'Members of the parish council have brought up the subject of your approach to your task.'

'My task?'

'Your approach. Your teaching of, for instance, history and geography.'

'My approach?'

'They say your approach rather veers towards a less than creditable view of England and the British Empire in world affairs.'

'They say?'

'Some parishioners have – er – deputed Mr Smith to express their concerns.'

'Jade Smith? Ah. I see.' Jade Smith had left the chapel and joined Mr Stonham's flock when he had finally left the pit and succumbed fully to the embrace of commerce. 'I have Mr Smith's youngest boy in my class. He is unintelligent and without concentration.'

'Unintelligent? Mr Clelland! His grandfather is a tradesman and a leading member of this community and this parish. According to Mr Smith, you keep his grandson back regularly as punishment and he is needed in the shops. The unfortunate death of his wife has left him much pressed.'

'I teach sons of miners who are twice as quick. That shopkeeper's son is lazy. Sometimes secretly a liar and a cheat. He needs sitting on to make him work at all.'

'The cane, Mr Clelland! The cane!' The vicar turned his bulk and obliged them both to come to a stop. '"He that chasteneth one amendeth the many!" A useful maxim in your profession.'

'Staying back each night to work can be very chastening, I assure you.'

'Pain, Mr Clelland! Pain! Short and sharp. Much better economics.'

'So he can go and stand behind one of his grandfather's counters? Wallowing in his ignorance? I don't believe in your pain, vicar. I don't believe in it. And my classroom works well enough without it. My results are good. The inspector commended my work.'

'Inspector is as inspector does. There are objections, Mr Clelland. Disloyalty. Radical texts.'

'I teach only knowledge which is accepted in educated society.'

'Tolstoy? Children of this class need facts, Mr Clelland. Facts. The teacher is the vessel, the conduit for the transmission of these facts. But you! The way all this . . . knowledge, this . . .' he paused '. . . stuff pours out of you, it is more than likely to breed traitors and anarchists in our midst.'

Jonty smiled his satisfaction. 'My aim is to make them thinking people, vicar. I come myself from this very same . . . class . . . from these very people. I want to make them think. Be critical of the world in which they live. So that they can take it in their hands, mould it to a shape . . .'

'Critical? Critical? Mould? All you will do is breed discontent which will upturn all which we hold dear.'

'Now, vicar, it's not revolution that I preach. Just self-respect and a clear eye.'

'I regret, Mr Clelland, that I ever allowed myself to be persuaded to endorse your college application. I regret very much that you are not down there now, toiling in a mine with your father, doing something more fruitful than poisoning the minds of our young.'

'My father, Mr Stonham, is down no mine. He can't find work because of some of your tradesmen friends who suspect a thinking mind and a man of principle. I've got to say that your "regret" is your privilege, Mr Stonham. Now, if you'll excuse me, there is a fight in the corner there over which I have to arbitrate.'

'The headmaster. I will be reporting my deep dissatisfaction . . .'

But the young back was impudently turned.

As he clashed the door of his classroom behind him, images of his father swam into Jonty's head. John George seemed to have shrunk now. He would sit quietly, troubling no one, insubstantial in the corner, his books barely read, an unused pencil clasped in his fingers. Bea, fatter now and more breathless, still bustled around with her usual energy about the business of her women's group and the Labour party. But it was with Jonty, not John George, that she shared her disappointment that the party had lost members in the 1910 election, with Jonty that she attended meetings to help sustain its local growth. Jonty watched his father with concern. It was as though, as he grew larger in the house, with school and his other preoccupations, his father seemed to shrink further and further into the corner.

That day, for the first time ever, Jonty was out of school at the sound of the final bell. He walked amongst the children, who tumbled along, emanating the explosive noise, shrieks and sounds of the recently liberated. The blond-haired Sargant child was racing before him, to be swept up finally into the arms of a soldier, brown-faced and handsome in his khaki.

It was a minute before Jonty recognised the boy's collector. 'Davey! I would scarcely have recognised you . . .'

Davey Laydon Jones smiled broadly over the tufted blond head before he swung the boy up on to his shoulders. He reached out to shake Jonty's hand in a sinewy grip. 'Well, look at this. Quite the schoolteacher now, Jonty, ain't we? How about a turn-up like this! Here's you stuck here back in Gibsley and me just back from India. One time I'd'a thought it'd be the other way round. Me planted fathoms deep in this here earth and you wandering its surface far away.'

Jonty brushed the chalk from his sleeve. 'On leave? Will you go back there?'

'No. We've done our stint in India. Back here for training. Then sorting the Kaiser.'

'Soon?'

'Before the summer's out, is my guess. So how's things, Jonty? Your Ma and Da still stirring folks up?'

'Well it's mostly my mother now. My father's just about fading away. He just can't take the fact that he can't work. Doesn't preach, doesn't speak. Nothing. My mother still does the rounds, but worries about him and gets down herself. That's why I'm here. I've been working up at Gateshead three years now, but got special leave to come here because of them. My mother's not too well an'all. They need me here in more ways than one. Or I would have been wandering the surface of the earth. Like you say, Africa was my fancy!'

'Mebbe I'd've stayed here myself, Jonty, ... if I'd been in schoolteachering.'

'Anyway I might not last much longer here at that. I've just had an earaching from Mr Thomas – he's headmaster here now – about what he called preaching sedition. I've had my warning. The vicar's been on at him. Apparently the children must be able to chant the benefits of the British Empire or I'm out.'

'You don't think there are benefits, like?'

'What d'you think? You've been in India for years doing it now, haven't you?'

'Me? Sometimes I think it all makes sense out there. Me being an agent of peace and order and all that. But then I've seen things, aye, and done things that'd make your hair curl. Well, curl more, seeing as it's like a corkscrew already. Times like that I just think it's about orders; makes life interesting, like, with a bit of drama on the side. And your mates. I've had some good mates. And lost them, too. Good soldiers. They say pitmen make good soldiers. Not surprising, everything's ... anything's better than the pit.'

'You like it all?'

'Well, I like the colour. Things're so bright and light, spite of the dirt. And I like the heat that gets to some of the lads. They don't like it. But I like that heat; it goes right through to your bones. The thing I specially like, even now, is the thought of me out there under the sun rather than here under this sod working in that heat and the smell of my own piss.' He reddened. 'Sorry. Soldier's talk.'

Jonty grinned. 'And pitman's talk? Where d'you think I've lived all my life, Davey?' He touched the boot of the child whose leg hung over Davey's shoulder. 'This one was named for you, then?'

'Yes. Susanah wanted it and Mervin didn't mind. She has one of her own now, as well as this'n. And she's expecting again. Seems to be blossoming with it. Sturdy.'

Soft April rain started to plop down and they turned and walked together the way they had walked as boys, coming home from school.

'Working in Gateshead, I've missed a lot that's happened here.' Jonty thought of Isabella. The cottage had been out of bounds to him since the day of Betty's wedding. Through the years they had met away from Gibsley, little scraps of time in the school holidays, spent at holiday resorts: Keswick, Edinburgh, Buxton, Bath, London. Once it was Paris. Islands of sensuality in his bleak schoolmaster's life. He coughed. 'I've only been back in

Gibsley three weeks, Davey. You lose touch. My mother says your Susanah's flourishing.'

'Yeah. She manages pretty well. Strong as an ox now. I could hardly believe it when I saw her. Making a good living with the watches. Mervin, though, he's never there. Always away. One of those playsoldiers. Territorials. Never at work. Always off training to save the country from the rape of the Kaiser. It's more her and Aunt Bel, than her and him, that runs that house.'

'Do you think he'll really do it? The Kaiser?'

'Declare war? They say he's sure to. On a downward run now.'

They walked along in silence, the twittering voices of children far behind. He tried again. 'I can't say I see much of Susanah now.'

'Funny lass, our Susanah. She never could abide you. Myself, I thought you two should get on. Same types. But no, she had to pick fault. That's women, like!'

'And your father?' Jonty's face was red.

'That old bugger? Pardon me again. Stewing away on his own. Antrobus has gone off his scent now, is chasing after Jade Smith now his wife's given up the ghost. Lew's off living with the Stapletons, to the pub when he likes. Our Tollie stays with the Sargants, sleeps in Mervin's bed alongside your mate Len.'

At the end of Selby Street, Davey lifted his nephew over his head and placed him gently on the ground. The child cringed behind the khaki legs in the looming presence of the big boys' teacher.

'Is this a long leave, Davey?'

'Another three days here. Then back to Wrexham to do a training stint.'

'And they say a war's on course.'

'Sabres rattling, Jonty. Nothing so sure.'

'Could you bear it? Taking lives? Killing.'

'Done that already. And not to defend my own land.'

Jonty scowled. 'How can you stand it?' he repeated.

'At that second, it's not hard. There's the pressure of the minute. Almost too easy. But afterwards it's bad. You sense it, the life draining away.' Davey watched as his nephew started to kick against the wall, dislodging a slice of sandstone from the corner. 'There'll be conscription, nowt so sure. Will you go?'

'No. My mind's made up. A few of us are firm. No matter what happens.'

'A few of you?'

'Lads from the meeting. Len Sargant, in particular. Still haven't persuaded your Tollie.'

'All right if you did. Don't want two of us in it.'

'Would you hate us?'

'Who? Me hate you, like?'

'No. Would soldiers hate us? Lads in your regiment?'

'Well, there's not a lot of fancy in the regiment even for conscripts, to be honest. Forced soldiers with no discipline. No nous. Still, most of 'm would see you as a coward if you plead conscience. Even dub you a traitor.

Probably tar and feather you.' He laughed grimly.

'Would you?'

'Me? Not me, marrer. I joined the army to get out of the pit and away from me father. The lesser of two evils. A coward from the pit makes a very willing soldier.'

Jonty wanted to hug him. He wanted to feel the rough soldier cloth against his arms, to engulf the kindness he felt sweeping towards him. Instead he smiled faintly. 'You're a good man, Davey.'

'Should ask my lads in the regiment. Being a sergeant I've gotta be hard on'm. So they think I've got two horns and a tail. I'd think being "good" is more about giving lads like young Davey here a chance so they don't have to stew down the pit. More in a schoolteacher's hand, I'd say. And "good" might be refusing to put on the khaki, just to keep the buggers on top warm in their beds.' He laughed. 'I'll mebbe feel different about it this time next year. I'll mebbe want to tar and feather you meself by then.'

Jonty grasped Davey's hand, putting his other hand over it. 'It's good to see you, Davey. Good to see you.'

'You too, marrer.' Davey bent down and lifted the restless child again on his shoulders. 'Better be back to your mam, young'n. She'll have me hide. Proper drill master now, our Susanah.'

Jonty watched him set off up the path, then called to him. 'Davey? Give your sister and aunt my regards. Tell them I'm asking after them.'

He acknowledged Davey's brisk sketch of a military salute and turned for home. Walking along, he could hear the child's shrieks and the deep chuckles of the soldier uncle recede up the hill. In the house he knew he would be greeted by an imperfectly made stew, two worn but eager faces and a digest of the day's national and international news from the paper. Thursdays were always the same.

August that year was hot and Jonty was sweating as he strolled the streets of London with Isabella on his arm. The pair of them were treated to interested looks. Isabella had filled out even more through the years and had become more clearly a member of his mother's generation. But her taste for bright colours and floating impedimenta around her person was undimmed. The effect of this beside the soberly dressed garb of the young teacher was incongruous. The most casual of passers-by would not label them mother and son and the clerk in the hotel treated them with a mocking politeness. Jonty felt like punching him on the nose but could not create the opportunity to do so.

Over lunch, sitting beside the dusty window of the hotel dining-room, Jonty broached the question of the meeting. 'It's in Trafalgar Square. Keir Hardie's speaking. And Ben Tillet. The marchers are reaching there at four o'clock.'

'They'll be talking against the war, no doubt.'

'Sure to be!'

She sighed. 'But we can't let the Germans have Belgium just like that, can we? Then France? Have you seen what they say'll happen?'

'War and killing can't be the answer. Two wrongs don't make a right.'

She looked at him, pulling her lips back against her teeth, her cheeks creasing into a fine network of wrinkles. 'I don't think it's for me, Jonty, this meeting. I'll stay here, sort some sketches out, perhaps have a little rest.' Their lovemaking, gentle and short-lived now, was only a small part of their intimacy, and it made her tired. 'But you go. You must go. I can see that.'

He was pleased to be on the streets and on his own. People were milling around in the heat, with an infectious, aimless energy. He stepped off the pavement, bringing a taxi to a screeching halt.

The taxi driver put his head out of the window and growled at him. 'Yer want to watch it, mate, yer'll rob the Kaiser of a body afore it bleedin' gets there.' Then he yanked at the gear lever and set off again at breakneck speed. The violence of the movement dislodged the piles of newspapers heaped on the back seat and hurtled them to the floor.

Union Jacks and pictures of the King were everywhere: in shop windows, on walls, carried in sweaty hands. Groups were holding large flags high as they moved in ragged formation towards the square. The peace marchers carried red flags as they arrived, to be greeted with jeers and whistles and catcalls. A stone dusted the crimson silk of one of them and was caught in it like a finger. Someone started to sing the national anthem and the red banner carriers sang 'The Red Flag'.

Jonty found a space with his back to a lamppost. He could hardly hear the speeches for the cacophony of shouts and jeers and was pounced on when he tried to clap his applause at a point being made.

'Agree with that bleedin' rubbish, do yer? What have you got, a fuckin' German uncle or sommat?' The man had a large head and sunken cheeks where his teeth were missing. He wore a scarf round his neck instead of a tie and his large round eyes blinked threateningly at Jonty.

'He's got a point,' said Jonty determinedly. 'It's not right to kill just for territory. Like he says, it's not worth the life of a single grenadier.'

'Bloody traitors, that's all you lot are. Bloody traitors and cowards.'

Now the man was pushing him back into the lamppost. He turned away, only to be met by a punch on the cheek from the other side delivered by a taller man in a neat suit. 'The chap's right. Your sort can't call yourselves Englishmen.'

He was on the floor now, the taller man on top of him, flailing away at his face. Then someone else pulled this man off and started to fight with him. The shorter man was exchanging blows with yet another man. There were fights all over the square now and the speeches were entirely drowned. Jonty pulled himself up against the lamppost and looked around at the heaving square, noting with relief the figures of policemen now moving among the crowd.

As he walked back to the hotel, the bruises on his cheeks stung with the salty tears that were trickling down them. Jonty told himself that this was because the last blow had been to his nose and that always made your eyes water.

The clerk looked blandly at him as he handed his key. 'Been in the wars, sir? Would you like that attended to?'

'No, I'm quite all right, thank you.'

'Seen the papers, sir? Teatime editions say war's certain now. Say there's been fighting in Trafalgar Square. I suppose that's where . . . Well, sir, I'm pleased you gave them Bolsheviks what for. They shame their country, that lot.'

Jonty held his gaze for a moment without speaking. 'My aunt, is she . . . ?'

'She went out for a little walk and bought a paper but she's back in now, sir.'

She was very sleepy when he walked into the bedroom.

The curtains were drawn so the light was dim and she didn't notice his bruises. 'Was it all right, dear? I was thinking tomorrow we might go to Madame Tussaud's. Do you know they have a special exhibition?'

She pushed a paper towards him. Alongside the headlines about the Belgian crisis and the fights caused by the peacemarchers in Trafalgar Square was an advertisement. Tears blinded his eyes again as he read it.

THE EUROPEAN CRISIS
Lifelike portrait models of
THEIR MAJESTIES KING GEORGE AND QUEEN MARY
H.I.M. THE EMPEROR OF AUSTRIA
H.M. KING PETER OF SERBIA
and other
REIGNING SOVEREIGNS OF EUROPE
NAVAL AND MILITARY TABLEAUX
Delightful music.
Refreshments at popular prices.

Her hand drew him down beside her on the bed. The paper fluttered from his fingers. 'What's this, Jonty? Tears? It'll be a show, Jonty. Only a show.'

'A show,' he muttered, 'only a show! How many hundreds, how many thousands to die and they make a show of it! With delightful music and refreshments! Only a show!'

She pulled him towards her and kissed him gently. Suddenly he was returning her kiss with a vengeful ardour which made his bruised face burn again and raised her from the bed in eager response.

Chapter Thirty

'Have ye ever seen 'owt like that?' Davey Laydon Jones shaded his eyes against the brassy August sky of northern France and peered at the bucketing objects which buzzed around, then dropped and seemed to be coming straight for them.

'Airplanes,' said Sergeant Lily Carson standing at his elbow. 'Ain't yer never seen one before? Blimey, ain't yer seen nothing? All yer've ever seen is bloody County Durham pit heaps and the bawdy houses of Bengal.'

Lily – so nicknamed because of his white skin which offended the leathery brown of the old India hands around him – had been astounded when Davey told him he had never been to London, Lily's home city.

'Never?'

'Never. That is, the railway stations aside.'

'Can't see how you can call yourself British, then.'

'Nearly died twice under the flag out there. Twice. That's how.'

The planes were getting larger and more solid as they bucketed and hiccuped on to the lumpy field. Davey peered closer to see one of the pilots as he jumped out of his open cockpit and pulled off his helmet and goggles, his hair springing around his head like a black halo. Davey thought of Jonty Clelland with his fuzzy black hair. He could have been a pilot, Jonty, with his brains, his schooling.

'By, I'd give sommat to do that, get up there,' he breathed.

'What?' squeaked Lily. 'Ye're bloody crazy. Not natural, up there. No contact with the ground.'

'Think of it, Lily. Up there, like some bloody bird!'

Lily turned and set off down the road, shouting over his shoulder, 'Well, mate, if yer can get yer head out of the clouds, how about seein' if we can squeeze a drop o' beer and who knows maybe sommat else out of these very grateful Frenchmen?'

They had been cheered all the way: on the boat as it made its way up the Seine to Rouen, on the train up to Amiens, through the streets of Amiens to their billet. They had both lost their cap badges to the urgent pleas of young Frenchwomen and had been put on a charge. As Lily said, it all made you feel like a hero even if you weren't.

Now, to their regret, they were stuck in Amiens, seeing to the troops who were shoaling past them on their way to the Front, making sure they were fed and watered, kitted out and reassured as they set upon their great adventure.

The day after they saw the planes, they were on duty at the station, supervising their lads who were doling out tea and stew to a crowd of youngsters in ill-fitting uniforms. As always, Davey watched them for a familiar face. Somehow he was always watching now for Tollie.

Davey's arm was nudged. 'Which regiment would they be, sergeant?' The voice was clear and reedy, clipped in officer fashion.

He looked up to see the young pilot with the black hair. 'Dunno, sir. If I did I wouldn't tell yer. War secrets.'

'Well done, sergeant. I wondered if the Durhams had gone through, though. My brother's with them.'

'Durhams, is it? Well, I've been watchin' for some mesel', 'cause of me own brothers mebbe being with 'm.' He had scanned the faces, looking for Tollie, knowing it would only be a matter of time before he was there. No Lew. Too much for himself. And there was Mervin, in it already as part of the Sunday army that came in for so much stick from the regulars at the moment.

The boy laughed. 'Thought I could hear it in your voice. So what're you doing here with all these Welsh?'

'Mostly Brummies, never mind Welsh. An' I'm here 'cos I'm a proper soldier. Not like some of these bliddy johnny-come-latelys what's gonna save us from the Kaiser.'

The boy proffered a silver cigarette case and Davey took two, handing one over to Lily who was lounging silently beside them. 'So, how come your brother's with the Durhams?'

'Home regiment. Grandfather a retired colonel. Chase. They still live up there, he and Grandma. Wendon Hall. You would . . .'

'I've heard of them.'

'I'm Tony. Tony Chase.' The hand was out and it was taken. The grasp was thin and strong.

Davey was taken aback at the friendliness. Officers in his own regiment, some of them good enough sorts, would never have risked the familiarity. 'I'm Davey Landon Jones. And this is Sergeant Lily Carson.' He paused. 'I saw the planes comin' in. Must be sommat, up there in the clouds.'

'Absolutely. It's really something. But more than that, think how useful we'll be. Darting up the line to see just where Fritz is lying. Mapping terrain . . .'

'Droppin' a few bombs,' put in Davey.

The boy laughed. 'Not as easy as you'd think, but I'd hope so. And knocking out a few of Fritz's own planes.'

'Bliddy marvellous,' said Davey longingly.

Tony Chase threw down his cigarette and screwed it beneath the heel of his heavy boot. 'Tell you what, sergeant. We'll strike a bargain. You get a ride on a plane and in return you can watch for my brother and give him my . . . regards. Can't miss him. Hair like mine, name of Chase. He'll be bossing people around. Always was a bully, Clive.'

'A ride . . .' said Davey.

'Be at the field at half-past three tomorrow morning. My mechanic's been tinkering with the steering. Need to test it.' He turned and was off, a slightly rocking confident gait.

'I'll be there!' Davey shouted after him.

'You must be bloody crazy,' said Lily. 'You won't need Fritz to top yer. You'll come tumblin' down from the skies from that fuckin' machine.'

The sky was bright and clear, suffused with white early morning light. Tony Chase, peering under the carriage, saw Davey's immaculately polished boots first. 'Sergeant! Decided to come, then?'

'A promise made is a promise kept. I dinna see your brother yesterday but you can be sure if I do I'll pass on your message. Like I say, I'm watching for the Durhams myself.'

'Here. Take off your cap and put this on.' He offered a tight leather cap. 'And these.' Davey pulled on the goggles and looked around. The steel-rimmed orbs made the farmer's hut on the edge of the field and the cluster of houses beyond shrink to the size and texture of a picture on a wall.

He climbed into the plane and waited while the boy set the propeller and climbed in in front of him. Then he was being pulled forward, the wind tugging at his hair, roaring in his ears. The boy was shouting something back at him but he couldn't hear the words. Then they were bucketing to a lift, off the ground then back down again. The engine roared again and he felt right down to his boots the lurching, heartstopping fear he had last felt as a small boy as the cage sank down, down into the lift shaft into the darkness of the earth. Now, though, here he was racing up into the sky and finally settling on a cushion of air. The wind was whipping his face, cutting lines down his cheek.

The boy signalled with his hand and Davey peered down below. The river that flowed through Amiens was laid down there like a snake, crawling across the countryside in the bright morning.

'See!' The words came screaming, floating back towards him. 'The river Somme!'

Susanah would like this. She would like to see a snaky river laid out like a piece of stitching on a cloth. There'd be no telling her, though. No way he could write it without getting into trouble. That would have to keep for when he was home again.

Suddenly he was flung to one side as the boy tipped the wings of the airplane and turned right. Now they were crossing countryside, wide fields of ripened corn, some half cut; the green of clover and the staining red of beetroot. Clusters of farm buildings were masked here and there by lazy curls of the smoke of early morning fires. Villages huddled round church towers, grander residences with squared gardens stood at a distance. A man trudging along in the dim morning light, a scythe hooked over his back, stopped to stare upwards at them as they buzzed past.

Davey leaned over the side. Now he could see the muddle of tents and wagons along the road that showed the army's path. Flying even lower, they could see signs of bivouacs alongside the road, even in the fields, as the massive army on the move rested where it could.

Then the plane wriggled and lifted at the crackle of gunfire from a wary sentry.

'Think's we're Fritz!' yelled Tony, laughing.

Davey closed his eyes in sheer pleasure for a moment, then opened them wide, ignoring the wind that raged into them, to peer over the side so that he wouldn't miss a thing.

When he got back to the billet there was a letter and a parcel from Susanah. Inside the cardboard box was a blue-striped cloth fastened with a crocheted cord. It was stained with red.

'Why, you bugger.' He held it up. The smell of blackberries hit the air. The berries, bruised by the sudden movement, started to drip and the stain to spread.

'Somebody die?' said Lily.

'Blackberries. Me sister sent them. From the hedges just back of the pit where I used to work.'

Lily leaned over and looked at the letter. 'Sister? She writes more like a schoolteacher.'

'Go away. You're just a big idiot.' Davey turned his shoulder and concentrated on the letter.

'Turn up for the books,' said Lily, later that day, throwing himself on to a greasy mattress in the billet, a school that they had taken over from the French in no clean order.

Davey looked up from his boots, which he was rubbing and polishing with a careful hand. 'What book's that?'

'Them planes set off. You know those fly machines you was so taken with? Setting off down the lines to win the war for us and one of them comes down, splat, there on the field. Pilot and mechanic killed without Fritz puttin' a finger on 'm.'

Davey stood up. 'D'they say who?'

'Nah. But we'll know right enough. According to the captain, we're to be the honour guard at the funeral.'

Davey was there to hear Tony Chase's name spoken by the chaplain before he presented arms and lifted his rifle to fire a shot in honour of the young pilot.

The bullets snapped and cracked into the French air. Davey shivered.

Lily looked through the ranks towards the coffins and the open graves. 'Poor buggers,' he muttered.

'Not the last,' said Davey. 'Not the last by a long chalk, in this bliddy war.'

'What I want is to stop buggering about up here. When'll they let us get at 'm, doin' the job we've gotta do? Instead of sticking here playin' nursemaid. It'll be over by Christmas, they say, and we won't've had a look-in.'

'Over by Christmas? Bliddy fat chance,' said Davey.

That night, with his back to the room, he wrote a letter in his long looping script, using an army issue pencil and paper rifled from a cupboard in the storeroom of the school.

Dear Lady Chase,

You will have heard now of the tragic death of your grandson. I wanted to send condolences for your great loss. We only met for a little time, the day before he died. But we talked of County Durham, our common home. I was struck by what a wonderful lad he was. He was a brave and cheerful lad and a great flyer. His vision of the way that flying would change the war and beat the Kaiser was good to listen to. It is because of him and men like him that we will win this just fight against bad. He asked me to watch for his brother Clive as he comes through this place. I will do that and tell him too what a brave lad he had for a brother. I have brothers of my own that will be coming this way.

> Yours faithfully,
> David Laydon Jones

Virginia Chase looked up from the letter, her face bathed yet again in tears. 'Another one! I must have had a dozen letters, Isabella, from people like this, who just knew him a little . . .' She peered closer at the letter. 'The name. Isn't it your name . . . ?'

'He's my nephew,' said Isabella. 'A good boy. Regular army. He was with his regiment in India. Now straight across there.'

'And his brothers?'

'The youngest one's just volunteered. Out on the coast. Hartlepool, I think. And the brother-in-law's a territorial, still somewhere round the country, not in France yet.'

'All those boys!' The flood of tears was welling up again.

'Now, now!' said Isabella gently, 'Mop up, Virginia, dear. How can I draw you with puffy eyes? And don't you look so distinguished in black. Not many folks can wear black with such style, can they?'

Chapter Thirty-One

The birth of Ceiri, Susanah's youngest daughter, had been as easy as Anna's, Susanah amusing Isabella with her fierce battle with the midwife to do it her own way, squatting during the process.

Relishing the delicate weight of a new baby in her childless arms, her aunt commented. 'That was quite a performance, doing it again like some native woman.'

'It was how Jenny came; I saw it when I was little. It was that or both of them to die. And that's how young Davey finally came from Betty, otherwise he would have been with her in the coffin.' She paused. 'When I was little I thought it was some kind of magic. Woman's magic. I thought for years that the woman that got Ceiri to do it was a witch.'

Isabella smiled. 'Some magic in it for you, anyway. You look fine.'

'I feel fine.'

'And what about that little girl who looked like a skeleton when I arrived? Your cough's all but gone now and you've rounded up.'

'Maybe it's you who are the witch.'

Susanah was up the day after the birth sitting at the table working at her watches. The day after that she was doing her normal share of the housework in Isabella's little house.

Mervin was away at the Front when she had Ceiri; he'd been at camp with the territorials in 1914. He'd also been away when war was declared; he'd entered the war from the first day, when she had her final fight with Caradoc when he challenged her with stealing his clockmender's customers.

She wrote to Mervin afterwards. 'You would have laughed, Mervin. He had the poker in his hand. There was slaver at the corner of his mouth. I took up the kettle of hot water from the fire and offered him a hot bath if he dreamed of using it.'

Many months later she received Mervin's reply.

    ... Glad that you at last gave your dad what-for, Smiler. Funny that you should be the one that gave it him. I heard that your Tollie had a go. Long overdue. I don't forget the black eye he gave you for our wedding ... Things here are much the same. I walked two miles in the mud up the line to see your Davey. They said he was there with some support lot. Not there. What a bloody waste of effort! A long walk, all for nothing. There is a bit of a stew on here because there was an infantryman – a corporal – who was found out to be a woman. Could you believe that? It's a time for seeing strange things. Well, Smiler, not much else here to talk about, so hope this finds you as it leaves me. In the pink.

PS Next day. Good news, for me anyway. They're welding units together because of losing men and who should turn up in the mud last night but Tollie? Seems a long time since we were scoring goals side by side. Maybe now we can score goals against Fritz and help bring this show to a close. Toll sends his love. M.

That was a long letter from Mervin: only the second she'd had, although she did receive a card now and then with some cheery and insouciant message scrawled on the back. She still sent him and Davey long and frequent letters, read by Isabella before they were posted.

'You can really tell a tale, my girl,' said her aunt.

'Sometimes I think I tell the tales for myself, rather than them. Sometimes it brings them into the room with me. Just the writing. Another kind of magic.' She paused. 'I suppose you can tell them too. Tales. All those letters you wrote to Caradoc.'

'You said he didn't read them. Not one.'

'I still have them. That's how I got your address to write to you in Bath that first time.'

'Yes. I remember.'

'My mother treasured them. Kept them in the press with her other treasures.' She paused. 'Her other secrets.'

'You didn't read them?'

'Just the address. I didn't think it right . . .'

'Where are they?'

'In one of the boxes Tollie brought from Selby Street.' Isabella was staring at her. 'I'll get'm for you, if you like.'

She rummaged around and finally found them, still tied with their crocheted cord. Isabella turned the letters over, then, using a knife, she opened them all one by one. She pushed them into Susanah's lap. 'You read them,' she said.

Susanah shook her head. 'You tell me,' she said. 'I want to know about them – my mother and father. I've always wondered about them. I'd get glimpses of 'm, how they really were, but . . .'

'About Caradoc and me? Oh, it's his story to tell.'

'But he'll never say. He'll talk about nothing. You tell me.'

Isabella smoothed her green skirt down with a plump hand. 'Well, our Caradoc, he was quiet, very serious as a boy. A big brother to me, like your Davey with you. The man – I won't call him our father – had us tucked away out of the village, there with our mother. He would visit in the day, quite regular. Those times he was there we'd be put out into the garden, on the grass, Caradoc minding me. I remember clearly his playing cat's cradle with me, making rabbit shadows on the wall as the sun went down.

One day the weather was bad. It got colder and colder, darker and darker, and I cried. I remember crying. Caradoc battered at the locked door to be let in. Then the man was suddenly at the door in his sleeves and bare legs. He got hold of Caradoc and threw him against one wall, then picked him up and threw him against another. Caradoc lay there, his mouth whimpering, but his eyes ablaze. My mother was pulling at the man's elbow but she was slapped for her pains, first one way then the other. He pulled her back into the house and I climbed up on the water butt and peered through the window, worried that he would hurt her more. Then I remember feeling relieved because he was kissing her, seemed to be loving her. Years later, when I was thinking about it, that image came back to me; this time I saw that her hands were slack to her sides, loose. Neither keeping him off nor bringing him close. Then he was right into her, pressing on to her.'

'I know,' said Susanah quietly. 'I've seen it happen.'

'Seen it? Don't be silly. I was only four, perhaps five.'

'I saw it, only it was Da with Ma.'

Isabella drew a breath. 'Poor Caradoc . . .'

Susanah shot her a look. 'Poor Caradoc?'

'He loathed the man. Loathed him. Then to become . . .'

'What about you and Caradoc?'

'Well, I grew. He did, too. But he had no schooling. He was made to help on the farm from when he was six. Then to help the blacksmith later. He went to the pit at ten. Seemed to want it, but still he smiled less and all his brightness faded. I was at school, in the village. Me, I was clever and a favourite with the teacher. Ceiri was his daughter, see? I loved her; she was fragile, like a little harebell. Me, I was a big yellow dandelion beside her. Caradoc watched her from his dark corner from when she was nine. Then when she would be fifteen and he eighteen, he walked out with her. That was the only time I saw Caradoc as he could have been, without this trouble. A few months. A year, at the most.'

'What about you?'

'They kept me at home till I was fourteen. The man gave me lots of attention. Smiles and strokes and ribbons for my hair. Other things.' She paused. 'One day he brought another man and they leaned over the gate watching me as though I was invisible, commenting on my qualities as though I were some prize sow. There was some joke at which they laughed heartily, about "growing your own". Caradoc was in the corner carving wood. He did some nice bits of carving.'

'The spoon. I told you about it. She called it her love song.'

'So it was. Well, Caradoc threw down the spoon and leapt at the man. They beat him. My goodness, did they beat him. One held, the other landed blows. When they had finished, the man turned to me. "Now, Isabella," he says, quite sweetly. "Time you were out into the world to earn your living. The wife of Mr Richards here has need of a nice strong girl. He knows that you're a dab hand at sewing and that you read and write."

'They laughed with each other as they went off. I had this dread, then, that there'd be more than sewing, more than reading and writing . . . Then Ceiri arrived and nearly fainted at the sight of Caradoc. We bathed his cuts and greased his bruises. That night, before we went to bed, he looked at me through his fat eye and told me that if I went off with Mr Richards the next day I was no longer his sister. We all knew that I had to. But he kept saying that if I did that he would not know me. And he's been true to his word. But that was not fair. He knew I had no choice.'

The fire crackled, spat and settled again.

'I think he loved her. I know that now.'

'He did love her. In the middle of all this he sparked with love for that little thing.'

'What about a bracelet? She used to talk about a bracelet. A gold bracelet. But I never saw it, Bel. How could there have been a gold bracelet. How could Da afford gold?'

Isabella frowned; the fine white skin was ageing a little now and the frown was set in fine lines that had not been there a year before. 'No, dear girl. I know nothing about a bracelet. Ask him. That is something you will need to ask him about.'

'He hasn't spoken to me for ages, Bel you know that. Since before the war.'

'It's time you spoke to him,' insisted Isabella. 'He needs it. You can ask him about the bracelet. He is the one to tell you.'

Now for Isabella the image of the truculent sour old man had gone, replacing it with her memories of the younger Caradoc, earnest and oppressed by events outside his power. It was as though in talking to Susanah the letters were finally delivered properly to her brother, and the shame and hurt she had felt from his lack of response had somehow been bled away, leaving room at last for pity.

Jonty waited until all the children had gone before he left his classroom. His footsteps echoed as he made his way out of the boys' department through the central hall. His ear was caught by a rustle in one of the classrooms. He pushed the door open.

'Miss Carmedy? I thought everyone had gone.'

She was perched high at her pedestal desk. She looked at him over her dull black-rimmed spectacles. 'No, Mr Clelland, I have not yet finished my work.'

He leaned against the door jamb. 'You know I'm going today?'

'Yes, Mr Thomas informed us all, after assembly.'

'Did they applaud?'

'There was a mutter of approval.'

'Did you agree with that?'

She stood up, towering above him on her rostrum, and looked him carefully in the eyes. 'I think the school is short of teachers since Mr Robertson died and Mr Gosport . . . joined the war effort. The boys are being only barely taught. They're running wild.'

'But . . .'

'Listening carefully, I do see some moral force behind the arguments of the objectors. But now every time I see you here my heart turns a little. The papers, the talk, these affect me, too. I can only think that the war must end, the enemy must be defeated. How can this happen if every man who can doesn't play his part?'

'But there's slaughter! Thousands are dying in filthy slime to achieve the yards which may be lost the next day. There's deaths from frostbite and gangrene, from illness and exposure. And we're never told the truth. What good's that serve?'

She looked at him speculatively. 'Your intelligence seems very good.'

'There are people who are joining us now who have been there. Had a sickener.'

She looked down at the paper she was marking and said nothing.

He hesitated, then turned and left.

A crowd of boys clustered round the high gates, big lads whom, this week, he had taught quadratic equations and to whom he had read the poetry of Milton. Their lips were out, their heads down and their caps pulled over their brows.

They crowded into him. 'Here's the bliddy teacher that winnet fight for 'is country.'

'Winnet fight, canna fight! Winnet fight, canna fight!'

The tallest, Will Stott, whom he had battled with for four years, put a hand on his shoulder and pushed him. 'What about them lads there, Mr Clelland, fightin' in the trenches? Dyin'. My own brother and me cousin, dead as planks. Fightin' bliddy Huns while fuckin' cowards . . .'

Another boy took it up, pushing him back towards Stott. 'He can read the papers, can't he? Schoolteacher, in' he?'

'Mind you,' said Stott. 'Nee stomach for that, either. Feared o' givin' the stick. Never give the stick. Known for it. Here, Wally, let's show 'm about the stick!'

But suddenly they were falling back and Miss Carmedy was in their midst poking them hard with her umbrella, her voice squeaking out, 'Get off, get off you ruffians. Get off home I tell you! You're a disgrace!'

They stood off sullenly.

'He's a traitor, Miss. A coward,' protested one.

'I'd say, William Stott, that it's cowards that set about in a herd to attack a lone man.' She looked from one young, sullen face to another. She wrinkled her nose at the sweat of excitement in the air. 'The Germans behave with more honour than this.' There was slight movement towards her then but her bright-eyed glare made them falter and finally move away, muttering.

She leaned down to help Jonty up from the ground. 'Does your pacifism extend to not defending yourself at all? Even against thugs like that?'

He dusted himself down. 'I'd like to think I had that courage, Miss Carmedy. To be honest I was scared stiff. They're probably right. I am a coward.'

She looked at his face and his bruised hands. 'It was a bad beating.'

213

'It's not the first time and it won't be the last, getting beaten for this particular reason.'

She smiled slightly. 'Well, Mr Clelland you may not have my approval, but in many ways I respect, even admire you.'

He grinned painfully, 'Thank you, Miss Carmedy. You've made my day!'

The ebb and flow of young men around Jonty Clelland was generating strong and often violent response now in Gibsley. Forbidden the use of the chapel room for their meetings, they met in each others' houses, hammering out their ideas, the surrounding pressure fusing them into a coherent shape. A fierce commitment began to emerge in a pure streak from the jumble of religion and socialism which characterised the meetings. Len Sargant was now well to the fore, gradually equalling Jonty in his forcefulness, keen to preach his ideas further afield.

Every member of the group was beaten in the street; some were castigated as Bolsheviks and heretics in their own homes, by mothers and fathers, brothers and sisters. They were accused of being traitors from some pulpits. Windows in their houses were smashed by unknown hands. Those still working at the pit were taunted into fights and boycotted by their former workmates.

Mr Stonham was smug now that he'd dismissed the young teacher who so irritated him. Jonty decided not to appeal against it, as Len Sargant urged him to do. Instead he found a job clerking at the vegetable warehouse near the station in Priorton. The job was ill-paid and he was dependent on the whim of the owner, Mr Henry Newcombe: an angel when sober, a vindictive demon when drunk, which state he achieved every Thursday when the public houses in Priorton were open all day for the market. On Thursday afternoon, Jonty made sure he was out of the warehouse collecting accounts.

The first time the windows of the house were broken, John George had an attack of nerves and Bea put him to bed. He stayed in the bedroom for days on end, moving only from the bed to a chair beside the window, not wanting to wash and eating very little, only wishing for Bea beside him. He responded to his son's anxious queries in monosyllables. Freddy Stapleton, who came to mend the windows each time they were broken, would sometimes go up and sit with him, saying nothing, just offering his company. For Freddy had time now to do this. He was drinking again, with the gleeful encouragement of Lew Laydon Jones, and had lost his job.

Davey Laydon Jones and his friend Lily found sacks to cover themselves with as they plodded along in the rain. It was hard to make out the difference between the sky, the land and their own feet. Many of the communication trenches were flooded and they had to wade across them: one man vanished altogether into the water and they pulled him out, coughing and spluttering, by his pack.

They were numb with cold and groggy when they reached the trench they were relieving. What little decent shelter there was was taken by their officers, but Davey and Lily found a space with two stone corners and a makeshift roof of pilfered duckboard, which was angled to reduce the boom and unlikely fireworks of the shelling.

The rain stopped just before dawn and the air warmed a little as they settled down to wait for their next orders from the new officer sent in to replace Captain Fitt, who had been killed on their last sortie, dying in no-man's-land as they watched, pinned down for two days.

Lily laughed as Davey got out his letter paper and his stubby pencil. 'God knows what yer'll do when that bleedin' pencil runs out, mate!'

Davey threw him a punch but carried on.

. . . Well, here I am, Susanah. Up nearer the Fritz, ready to sort him out yet again. It's wet and cold here. Very wet and very cold. Reminds me of those early shifts in winter at White Pool. Snow and ice above ground, working on your elbows in ten inches of water underground. You'll know how much I'll like that. The blackies were lovely, more alcohol than fruit by the time they got here. I shared them with my mate Lily, who much appreciated them. Did I tell you we call him Lily because he was so white when he joined us, and us brown as nuts from India? Well, we're all white now. Or grey in some cases. In any case, not so many of the old hands left. We have this new captain assigned from another regiment, having lost our old one. His name's Chase and he belongs to that family at Wendon Hall. I met his brother early in the war, at Amiens. He seemed a good lad. I don't know about this one. We'll have to see.

Your loving brother,
Davey Laydon Jones.

PS Lily sends regards although he hasn't met you.

Susanah smoothed out the paper, her fingers covering the blackened smudge marks of the pencil. She heard the rattle of the fireback next door and went in to see Joan, letter in hand. Bea Clelland was there, filling the only comfortable chair.

Susanah stood and read the letter to them.

'See! I telt yer!' said Joan. 'They're buildin' it up. Gettin' into position.'

'They're pouring them in, pouring them in,' said Bea, frowning. 'The country's goin' mad. The towns and the countryside is emptying of men.'

'Some fellers still here,' said Joan mischievously, knocking Bea on the shoulder. 'I hear your Jonty and Len Sargant'd've been preaching against the war in Priorton market place. Getting beaten up for their pains.'

Susanah looked thoughtfully at the two women, firm if odd friends now. 'Folks like them're not successful enough for me. I've three of them there in the mud now.'

'Nearly lost Tollie here in England, didn't yer?' asserted Joan.

Tollie's first posting had been to Hartlepool to help to guard the coast. Two men close to him had been killed by shells from a German warship.

'Probably safer in France!' said Joan reassuringly.

Susanah didn't know whether to hug her or kick her.

'If you ask me, your Jonty's got the right idea,' she said to Bea.

'Better not say that in the Front Street,' muttered Joan. 'They'll scrag yer!'

Chapter Thirty-Two

The fire was on smoulder and the room was dark. Susanah ran her finger along the table. There was no dust in which to make a mark. The kitchen was bereft of every ornament; she wondered where he had put Ceiri's bits and pieces. The fire flared, catching her eye. She poked away at it until the flames went back to heat the coal, the core.

She sat at the table and looked around. More than ornaments and little pictures, the room was missing its clocks. The ticks and chimes, the angry whirring and the mis-timed strikes, the velvet roll and the minute tools: all had been transferred now to the crowded sitting-room of Isabella's house.

'Mama! Here's a man,' Anna piped up, broad nose pressed to the window. Susanah turned the baby around her knee and took a breath. She heard the familiar shuffling and hanging noises in the lobby and the pantry. Then he came in, carrying bread and cheese and a pot of jam on the bread-board like an offering. He was half naked, his pit clothes stripped off. His skin was grey, with no bloom, his whipcord muscles showing now through its dead surface.

He looked first at her, then at the child in the window, then at Ceiri who lay in her lap.

He frowned. 'You've two children?'

'I've three. Including Betty's Davey. He's seven now.'

'They say he's back on the drink, Stapleton,' he said.

'He comes to see young Davey every Sunday. Takes him for a walk down the garden.'

Caradoc pushed the kettle into the coal and busied himself at the table with the bread. He left the slice, doorstep thick, on the board and stood up. 'What for are you here? Years have gone.' He still, she remembered, had the intonation of the Welsh.

'You know Davey's at the front? And Tollie's there now, as well as Mervin. Him and Mervin are together now at least. I've the letters here . . .' She reached into her bag, then met his hard gaze. '. . . I can read them to you.'

'I need no letters.'

She sat the baby on the rug and stood to face him. 'You do. You should hear.'

'No.'

She pulled a letter out of her bag and he stood unprotesting as she read.

Dear Susanah,

Thank you for all your letters. The lads in the regiment are all jealous of me getting them. Sometimes I lend them to the lads that get down, you know, miserable. The life just comes off the page. I recognised your handwriting on letters I used to get from Tollie. Now he's with Mervin they'll look out for each other. Good out here to have a mate. They were always good mates, weren't they? This show is a different kettle of fish to India. I can only think now about how hot it was there, and how cold it is here. Much colder, much more like home. You know what I will think of that.

We're in good heart, though some of the lads are a bit sore-footed from having to walk such distances. You can tell the difference between the old regimental hands and the new lads, but they're all learning now. Your Mervin'll be shaping up, just like the lads in our regiment. All that play-soldiering must be paying off now. There's some good ones among them, though I don't say it to their faces. Spirits are up and every time we have a crack at Fritz seems like another step nearer home.

There was a bit of a buzz up here on St David's Day. We were back in reserve and there was quite a party, us all eating a leek to celebrate. Do you know where the cook cooked the stew? In one of those religious shrines they have by the road here. Smashed to pieces now, of course. Some of the Frenchies made a play about it, crossing themselves and that. Remember that time you got into trouble with Da for crossing yourself in the privy?

Susanah, there is this idea that's been buzzing up in my head all last night. Driving me crazy. It goes like this. Travelling home from India before, then back down the length of England and then coming across here watching all the comings and goings, all the performance – well it all seems to me like some great dance. Us here moving forward in some great rhythm, then moving back as though called by a drum. You there, Susanah, doing your usual rounds back in Gibsley. Here we are, in our different spaces, in our different companies, making our predictable moves. It seems to me that the whole country's moving just now in some great dance where life and death have distinct parts. (Can you remember those country dancers in Priorton market place on Whit Monday? The ones with the masks?) All we've done up to now is shadow action. My part now is to make my best moves, keep my head down and be there for the final round. I know it's mad, but it has been buzzing in my head all night, and telling you should get it out and let me sleep.

This show here's taking longer than we thought but we'll get there in the end. More than India, this place makes me think of the dangers for us all. It puts other things into different shape. It makes me feel regret for earlier things. I was too easy made bitter and driven away. Our father is in my head a lot and I'm wondering how he is managing. I know more and more how much he'll be missing our mother.

Somehow now, I'm missing her more than ever, as I feel the danger of losing not just her but all of you. Never mind, we are in good heart here and happy to be doing our bit.

Give young Davey a chuck under the chin from his namesake. Give the baby a kiss. The other one must be with you now. I hope it is another girl. You don't want a boy to have to face all this another time. And tell Aunt Bel I am asking after her.

Your loving brother D.

Caradoc turned away from her and looked at Anna, who was sitting under the window peering at him through the spread fingers of one hand. She was waiting for a reaction; this peeping game usually worked on strangers. His shoulders came back and he turned to Susanah.

'What're they called, your children?'

'Well, that cheeky one is Anna. Aunt Bel's idea. She was half of me so she could have half my name. The way she goes on, though, she's more like Aunt Bel. And this one . . .' She bent to pick up the baby from the mat. 'And this one, she's called Ceiri. After the best woman in the world.' She watched him over the baby's downy head, but his face did not change. 'Well, anyway, I just came to tell you about Davey. And about Tollie joining up with Mervin at last. He had a right battle with his friends over it. Came to blows with his mate Len Sargant over it, since Len turned pacifist.'

'Pacifist!' snorted Caradoc. 'Fellers won't work with him down the pit. And there's fights. Anything to stop work. I see that schoolteacher lad of John George Clelland's lost his job, preaching pacifism. Vicar'd have none of it, they're saying.'

Susanah reddened at this but breathed more easily at his conversational tone. 'Well, I dreaded the day when Tollie went. Soon there'll be none left.'

'Your brother Lew'll be left. He'll wriggle out of that one like he wriggles out of everything. Not pacifist, just bone idle.'

She laughed. 'So he will.' She put her hand out for Anna. 'We have to go now, Da. Davey'll be out of school now, and we'll walk back up the hill with him. I'm glad you've heard our Davey's letter.'

Caradoc nodded, sitting back at the table. As he spread the jam to the corners of the thick slice she could see her mother's action, just the same, as she'd spread jam for Jenny all those years ago. He started to cut cheese to go with his bread. 'Is it crowded you are in that little place?'

She looked around. 'It's not so crowded.'

'There's two bedrooms here going to waste. Front room does me.' He bit into his sandwich.

'You want us to come?'

'Would I say?' he growled.

She could smell the scent of blackberries drifting up from the jam. She paused and took two deep breaths. 'We could come. Aunt Bel's been so good, but it is her space. And there's her own work.' She paused again. 'If we did come, then Bel would have to be welcome here. Properly welcome.'

219

As he looked at her she realised his hair had become thinner, softer. It did not shoot out from his head and chin as though to grasp the world of its own will.

'I have no objection to that,' he said.

'I see the Jones girl, no, Sargant it is now, is back with her father.' Bea Clelland closed her book and looked over at her son.

Jonty stopped pacing. 'They differed . . .'

'Must have made up their quarrel. Isabella'll be on her own now. She'll miss the company after . . . It must be five years the girl's been there.' Bea poured a mug of tea from the pot still warming on the hearth. 'It's on your mind, isn't it? Your tribunal?'

He laughed shortly. 'My tribunal? Nothing to worry about there. No point in worrying about a foregone conclusion. I'll end up in prison this time. Watch me.'

'Wouldn't it be easier to . . .'

'Easier? Ma, I never thought I'd see the day . . .'

'People die in prison, Jonty.'

'They're dying in tens of thousands at the front. Only their price for dying is sending some other soul on the same journey. I can no more pay that price Ma, than when I started all this and I didn't register.'

She was at the door which opened on to the stairs. 'I'll take this up for him. He'll be ready to settle now.' She paused. 'His cough was worse today. I'm sure of it.'

'The sooner you get across to Penrith the better. The clean air'll help him. And our Corella'll buck you up. You need some decent company.'

She smiled. 'Your company's always been enough for me. Your company and your energy.'

'Well, once the tribunal's over, I'll be away too. So go. I tell you what. I'll buy your train tickets in the morning. Get you off before . . . before all this happens.'

She sighed. 'Do that then. Yes. Better for your father . . . Are you coming up now?'

'No. It's a fine night. I think I'll get some air. A good walk'll get rid of all my wrinkles.'

Isabella, in her green silk wrap, opened the door wider when she saw who it was. 'Well who is this stranger?' she said, smiling. 'What brings you here?'

He sat down in the larger chair with remembered ease. 'I needed to see a friend.'

He had not been close to her since that week in London at the beginning of the war. She stood before him, plumper and less smoothly finished than he recalled. The eyes, though, still sparked with amusement and secret knowledge. 'Is there trouble, Jonty?'

'I have my appeal in two weeks' time. The Monday. My second tribunal. I'll end up in prison. Worse maybe.'

'You want sympathy? For what you asked for?'

He smiled at the familiar unsentimental tone. 'Not sympathy, Bel. Just company.'

Then her arms were round him. His face embedded in flesh and silk, his brain swimming with the combination of musky body scent and lily of the valley. He kissed the flesh, then, standing up, kissed the mouth and the eyes; the knot inside him loosened and his body hardened in anticipation of the coming pleasure. They did not wait for the bed, but made love there on the rug in the firelight, which bloomed on to Isabella's skin, conferring a youthful glow. At some points she was above him, rearing back, eyes half-closed but still observing the pleasure she endowed. At some points he was above her, obeying her demands for a gentle and insistent rhythm. When she finally permitted him to come, the world broke inside him and resolved itself into very simple pieces. She cried out, then smiled in simple delight.

They rested a while and then she shivered and sat up, pulling on the discarded wrap. She smiled down at him. 'You were always a good apprentice. Your young women must be very . . . satisfied.'

He pulled on his shirt. 'There are no young women. Just that time with you.'

'No one? Not even a kiss? What a waste.'

He pulled up his braces, snapping them against his shirt. 'Once. A long time ago. Only one apart from you I've even wanted to.'

'Who? Who's that?'

'Gone now. She's not around any more.' He put a finger on her lips as they shaped up for another question. 'Thank you for being such a friend. Is there no eager friend around for you?'

She laughed. 'My life has been so full of eager friends, dear boy. In these last years I have had a little family here, and they have absorbed my passion. I haven't missed . . . all this. You knew I had Susanah here, and her family?'

He reddened. 'Of course.'

She peered up at him from her place on the rug. 'I always thought you liked Susanah . . .'

He pulled her to her feet. 'Yes. Well enough. She was always an . . . interesting girl.'

'Well, you believe me. There's a lot of her that no one has ever plumbed. Certainly no man.'

'But she's married.'

'Married? A mother to his orphaned boy and relations to the limits of necessity. That's all. She's not touched, not in any real sense.'

He shook his head. 'You're a wicked woman talking like that to a man about to be locked away.'

She chuckled. 'Something to keep your mind on during the long cold nights.'

She saw him to the door. 'Give Bea my love. Tell her to come and see me. The house is so empty now.'

'She's kept busy with my father. His health's gone right down again now.

221

They're off to visit Corella in the Lake District on Friday.' He pulled out his watch. 'That's tomorrow. The time has flown.'

They stood looking at each other, neither wanting to be the one to turn away first. Finally Jonty spoke. 'Thank you for being the very best of friends.'

She chucked him under the chin. 'Go away, now. I don't know how you manage to bring out the girl in an old woman like me, but you do. I hope that the week after next and what follows is bearable.'

'It will be, now. I know it will.'

She stood in the doorway and listened to his whistle as he made his way down the narrow path towards the road.

Chapter Thirty-Three

Jonty had been ashamed at his feelings of relief when Corella wrote to suggest that their parents move to the safety and the clearer air of the Lake District. This, she suggested tactfully, might help their father's breathing, give him new life.

It had taken weeks to persuade Bea that she wasn't deserting him. But finally, on the Friday morning before his appeal, he put his parents on to the train at Priorton with their boxes and bags.

Bea held him close. 'Wouldn't it be better to do what they say, son? Wouldn't it be easier?'

He kissed her broad cheek, sad to see her early boldness falter, her strong certainties fail. 'Seems hard, right enough, Ma. But no matter how hard, it's better. It's better than killing, Ma. Being in prison's better than the pits, better than listening to friend Stonham, or for that matter the Reverend Simmons, uttering blasphemies to young children.'

She smiled then with some of her old sparkle. 'Preaching again, Jonty! All you lack is a pulpit.' She kissed his cheek before climbing up to sit beside John George, who seemed little moved by the commotion around him. Jonty watched the train as it steamed out of the station, pulled on his cap, and walked through the ornate gates with a jaunty step.

Jonty's boots echoed as he walked with an almost military swing across the wooden floor of the hall, to stand in front of the long table.

He looked along the faces in the line. Two of them he knew. Jade Smith, sitting in a heavy black suit, his gingerish hair slicked to one side, was placing his finger on a sheet of paper on the table before him as though it were one of his shop audit lists. Beside him was Mr Carmedy, trim in a dark suit, his face closed, showing no recognition. The central chair was taken by a stranger, a small man with a round face and a bright sharp look. This must be the famous Jet Gower, one of Len Sargant's early heroes, a national figure in the miners' union, a leading Liberal and a magistrate. At the end of the table, sitting bolt upright, buttons gleaming, was an army major, his stick before him on the table. He had thick hair and moustache, unusually close cut, and the faded yellow skin which had once been brown. Jonty thought of Davey Laydon Jones and wondered if he had known this man in India. No, that couldn't be. Different regiments.

The familiar questioning started and he fell into a semi-daze, sometimes

223

hardly knowing what was being said: the questions seemed to swim backwards and forwards of their won volition. He heard his own voice like that of a stranger, speaking with unwarranted pomposity.

'I must . . . I must refuse the military oath. One must judge for oneself, not blindly follow orders. I take responsibility for my own conscience, to do things consistent with my desire to serve God and my fellow men.'

'Fine words to cover cowardice,' began Jade Smith. He faltered into silence at a gesture from Jet Gower, whose eyes bored into the square young face in front of him. 'You don't *desire* to serve your country in the way you are asked?'

'I serve my country . . . I can best serve my country in its desire for a just and lasting peace by holding out the hand of fellowship to my comrades from another land.

There would be peace, and a lasting one, if all the working men refused to fight, to be instruments of others' unscrupulous ambition.'

'Disgraceful!' Mr Stonham finally exploded.

The major moved his stick one inch to the left. 'That statement can only be interpreted as disloyal.'There was a pause. The clock on the wall was ticking very loudly.

'There is this matter of conscience,' said Mr Carmedy. 'Is it true that you are no longer a member of the chapel of Gibsley?'

'It is true that I withdrew from the chapel. But this is not because there's no religious impetus in my conscience. I withdrew because I could no longer sit in a chapel which has taken on the justification of war as a religious crusade. I now attend the Primitives chapel. They don't pursue war with such non-Christian vigour. I've also discussed my views with friends who are Quakers and find that their position on conscience absolutely fits mine.'

'Are you then a Quaker?' asked Mr Stonham.

He looked his old enemy full in the eyes. 'I've not yet taken that step.'

'It's true, is it not, that you have been dismissed from your position as schoolteacher?'

'As you know only too well.'

'For teaching seditious views . . .'

'Not fit to have children in his charge,' interrupted Jade Smith.

'I taught truth, evidence and rationality as I saw it.'

Jet Gower sighed, then pushed his papers together. 'Well, gentlemen, do you think we've heard enough?'

Two minutes later Jonty was leaning against the doorjamb in the room outside the hall; he closed his eyes tight to stop his head swimming. When he opened them, his glance rested on the next person waiting.

'Why if it isn't the schoolteacher.' Lew Laydon Jones was leaning back, pushing his spindly chair on to two legs. 'What's the verdict, then?'

'Bad.'

'Oh. Sorry about that, bonny lad. Me, I'm on your side. You should get yourself a decent job and keep your nose clean. No need for us all to jump under the guns.'

'You seem confident enough. But you're still sitting there.'

'Matter of form, old lad. Can't do without me at the pit. Just going through the motions here, according to my mate Mr Carmedy.'

Jonty straightened his back and brushed the flat of his hands down his jacket. 'The rest of your family? How're they?'

'Our Susanah hears from the lads now and then. Tollie's away now and that's really upset her. She gets on with things. House runs like clockwork and then there's her clock work.' He laughed. 'That's good. Clock work? I fancy being back in there myself but the old bugger won't hear of it. So I sneak in when he's at work and catch up on a bit of grub and gossip. She's usually good for half a crown.' He stood up straight and reached to shake Jonty's hand. 'Well I never thought I'd really see the day we'd be on the same side, mate. But here's good luck to you, and see you survive it all just to show'm. Don't let the buggers get you down.'

Jonty stood up straighter and smiled into the handsome, hard face. Then the door opened and out peered Mr Carmedy's disapproving face. 'Mr Laydon Jones! Get yourself in here!'

Chapter Thirty-Four

For some time, Tollie Laydon Jones had hovered on the edge of Jonty's group. He had listened to their arguments and defended them from beatings. And he had always stood by his friend Len Sargant, whose house he had shared when banished from Selby Street by Caradoc.

But, with the catapult reality of the war, with Davey and Mervin already away, and some Gibsley men already dead, Tollie too felt the need to take sides. Many men from Gibsley and Priorton, not all of them young, had volunteered eagerly in the first months of the war. Most streets and most families had such headstrong heroes, Mervin Sargant amongst them. Tollie waited for conscription and watched Jonty and the others go through the slow rigmarole of refusal. But when he was called up he was willing enough to go.

Late on his last night at home, he went to see Len, who stood in his doorway, blond hair glinting in the moonlight. He put out a hand. 'I'm off tomorrow, kidder. Shake hands for no hard feelings.'

'No hard feelings!'

They shook hands with fervour, then stood restlessly looking up and down the street. Suddenly Tollie grinned. 'Seems a long time since me and your Mervin were up mornings, kicking about on the green? Moon-down, sun-up, and practising long shots. I'll think about that when I'm out there.'

'They play football out there. Scratch games, like, they would be.'

'Well, that's summat to look forward to.'

'They play behind the lines.'

'Can't believe that.' Tollie shook his head.

'True, I tell you! They played a game between the Germans and the English. First Christmas.'

Tollie did play football in the army with some success. He did play behind the lines, within the echoing sound of guns. He played the day before his death, which came about when he and Mervin were killed by British fire falling short of its target. The letter which came to Susanah talked about both Mervin and Tollie in intimate terms, mentioning their gaiety and staunch comradeship. It assured her that their death in action had been quick, that they would have felt no pain.

Susanah felt as if she had been widowed twice over.

'Cigarette, sergeant?'

Davey took the cigarette from Captain Chase, lit and drew on it grate-fully. It was cold, but not raining. A windless, starless night.

Four men squeezed past them on the narrow corner and trudged wearily on.

'Any luck, mate?' called Davey.

'Nearly there,' said the last man, a Welshman called Richard Evans. 'C'n hear Fritz mutterin' in that heathen tongue just feet away. But there was a fall and we lost Corporal Simon, see? So we've stopped diggin' for tonight.'

'All these miners in this bliddy battalion!' grunted Davey. 'They come away from the dark, the dirt and the stink back home. And what are you doin' here? Grubbin' around in the dirt, the dark and the stink. Gettin' killed in much the same way, drowned in the earth. Like back home.'

'It's not like that, really, sergeant, is it? If those lads can get under Fritz before he gets under us and get their charges set, it could save hundreds of lives.'

'Have you ever been down a mine, then, captain?'

'No. To my shame.' The tone belled out, fresh and young.

'Yer missed nowt, I can tell yer.'

The rustling busy routine of digging and clearing, was going on all around them: the movement of dead and dying being retrieved from the mud under cover of darkness; the digging and mining parties repairing the ravages of the day. The characteristic sound was the sloshing and sucking of mud against boot, against body, against the hard metal of weaponry. Davey was used to this routine now, as used as he had been as a child to the routines of washday and baking day, the Sunday routines with the inevitability of chapel and his father's dour presence.

'Look at that!' Captain Chase indicated with his cigarette.

Davey pulled up his head. In the distance they could see the long silver sausage balloon used to protect the big British guns. Fizzing around it, always too close, was a German plane. On his second approach the pilot managed to set fire to the balloon, making a bright white light flare up high into the still darkness, the flames licking red and white around the struc-ture.

As they watched, the observers jumped from the balloon and their parachutes bloomed in the darkness. Davey breathed out.

'Oh, no!' whispered Captain Chase as a fluttering scrap of flaming mate-rial drifted gently down and settled on the second parachute, which flared up merrily in its own turn. The observer plummeted to the ground, fast and deadly as an arrow.

'That's him done for,' said Davey. 'Clever piece of flying, like. That Hun flier.'

'My brother was a flier.'

'I know. I met him once.'

'What?' Chase gaped at him, astonished.

'In Amiens. Right at the beginning of this show. We were stuck down there at first, seeing the lads through. He gave me a ride in his machine, the day before . . .'

228

Clive Chase threw down his cigarette and it fizzled in the water. Lily, lounging a yard away, kept his eye on it for later retrieval.

'You went for a ride?'

'Yeah. Early one morning. Right the way up to here where we are now. Right along the Somme. Looked down on this land. You should'a seen it! Fields of corn. Villages. Churches. Green. Green and gold everywhere. I remember him saying, shouting. "See there! The river Somme!"'

Their eyes were drawn to the east where they could see the stumps of Ypres shimmering in the haze. Davey coughed. 'He told me to look out for you. Look out for my brother Clive, he said. Give him my best.'

The mutter and mundane grizzling in the trench seemed for a moment stilled. Clive Chase folded his lips. 'Did he say anything else, sergeant?'

'Aye. He said you were a bossy bugger! Beggin' your pardon, sir.'

There was a chuckle from Lily and the muttering and shuffling in the trench began again.

The captain smiled slightly. 'Well, sergeant, that reminds me why I came down here. I need assistance on a . . . sortie. I thought you, being an old hand, and Private Carson here . . .' He gestured towards Lily. Lily had been reduced to the ranks during their last period in reserve for a little misdemeanour over drink.

'I ain't no old hand, sir,' he growled.

'Yes, well, Private Carson, this lot makes old hands of all of us.' He stood up and put his chin high to give him a clear view. 'See the church?'

'We've been watching it all day.'

Some of the dead and the near-dead, now being painstakingly retrieved from no-man's-land, had been mown down by machine-gunfire spitting out from the ragged stunted finger which was all that was left of a church tower.

'I want to get there, take him out, and blow the tower. I'm told it has to be volunteers.'

'When?'

'Now.'

Davey stood up straight and grinned. 'Right!'

He liked this, when the sheer squalid routine of war in the trench was broken and you got a chance to go out and make an individual mark, to know the face of the man you killed, to break his gun and know at least that your own death wouldn't come from that direction.

He pulled Lily to his feet. 'Howway then, marrer. Let's get across there and show him what we're made of.'

'Good man!' said Chase. 'Good man!'

The letter which Susanah received about Davey was couched in the same terms as those she had had for Mervin and Tollie, talking about bravery and comradeship, honour, and a death which was mercifully short.

The last words rang hollowly through her head like a clapper resonating a cast iron bell. She knew for certain that it had taken a long time for Davey to die, having herself lain awake two full nights about that time and spent the day between shivering in a chair, images swimming before her eyes, half asleep even when she was awake. Her muttering had frightened the children who were finally taken off to the cottage by Isabella, leaving Caradoc sitting upright by the fire, listening to the strange muttering which was coming from upstairs.

'This must have been a church, Davey,' she'd muttered to herself, to him. 'See the deep walls and there . . . where the arch begins before it's broken off? Dark? Yes, it's dark, pet. But there, beside your hand on the floor, can you move your fingers, scrape off that mud? It's glass. Fragments of glass, blue, red and amber. Close your eyes, Davey. Close them now. Can you see the light shining through, the sunlight coming through the coloured glass? Think of the red. Cold? Yes, pet, I feel the cold, too. I know the mud's cold and the water's freezing. But think of that red glass, Davey. Think of the red. Think of the amber. What was it you said about India, the colours there? The bright light. The warmth. Hold on to that Davey. Hold on, pet. They'll come soon, your friends. Think of the red, think of the amber . . . Here. Here they are. Take care of him. He's my brother.'

Four days after the letter arrived Lew stormed into Isabella's little cottage and, sprawling back so far in a chair that it was creaking on two legs, glowered at her. He did not speak but filled the whole space with his presence. Isabella stared at him then picked up little Ceiri. Young Davey and Anna looked up uneasily from the floor where they were playing.

'It's so bad about Davey, Lew. I'm so sorry. I hardly knew him. But in some ways he's . . . he was . . . so like his father.' She paused. Lew glowered at her. 'And this, after Mervin and Tollie. Oh, that boy was always so full of life, Tollie!'

The seat crashed to the floor and Lew leapt up, his face crunching into a scowl. Ceiri whimpered and Anna and young Davey moved to stand behind her chair. 'That's what I mean. A total bloody waste, this war. Any war!'

'How's Susanah, Lew? How is she?' She had had the children for three days now and she was exhausted herself.

'She used to go funny as a young'n you know, our Susanah, get these dreams. Once I found her in the privy, kneeling in some sort o' trance. Not so much now. But she knew our Davey was dead the day it happened! Swears he was left there two days before he finally went.'

'How is she, Lew?'

He lifted up the chair and set it quite gently in its place. 'She's better. Downstairs now and sorting round. Fire's on, dinner's in the oven. Says I'm to take the young'ns back and she'll be up to see you tomorrow.'

'I'll come down with you. I want to see Susanah, and Caradoc too. All this must be hitting him hard.' She sighed. 'Not that he'd show it.'

Ministers like Jack Simmons, clerics like the Reverend Stonham saw the war as a righteous conflict, a battle with the Antichrist. It was called God's war from some pulpits. Jack Simmons in his pulpit seemed to Susanah the very image of a recruiting officer, his face reddening, his neck bulging, his eyes popping from his narrow face, his voice resonating through his nose and cheekbones as he advocated God's crusade against the Kaiser.

There was a rumour in Gibsley that Simmons' rhetoric had recruited Joan Kenton for the army. She had walked out of the chapel one Sunday night and straight to York to sign on. She left behind two illegitimate children in the care of their uncle Vivian who was now chief delivery man at the Co-op, his weak chest preventing his call-up.

The rumour was widely scorned; there were mutterings in the shops and in the chapel vestry that Joan had just dumped her children and gone off. Not a normal mother at all. The Lord knew where those poor children had come from, who the father was. In the public houses the rumour about her joining up was seen in the end as all Vivian's fancy. He had never known his arse from his elbow, after all had he?

After enduring a good deal of mockery and the occasional clod thrown by contemptuous children pleased at a target, Vivian kept his own counsel.

One day, though, he did turn up on Susanah's doorstep and stood there refusing to come in.

'What do you want, Viv?'

'I want yer to look at these.' He thrust three cards into her hands. She looked at the pictures first, so familiar that when she turned them over she half expected to see one of Mervin's light-hearted messages. They were addressed to Mrs V. Kent, covered with cheery messages for the children and signed 'Love from John'. Then a letter was thrust into her hands. This was the letter from the officer telling Mrs Kent that her husband had been a brave and forthright comrade, and had not suffered, etc.

Susanah put the papers back into his hands and grasped his arm. 'I'm sorry Viv, I'm very, very sorry.' And she cried as she had not managed to cry for Mervin or Tollie or even Davey, tears falling down her cheeks and into the neck of her dress.

He watched her quietly, his face entirely closed. 'Called herself John, see? She was a good lass, strong and true.'

Susanah nodded her head and her weeping slowed.

He loosened his hands from hers. 'Thanks for thy tears. No need to say 'owt. They wouldn't believe it round here anyways. Could you do one thing? Could you write to Mrs Clelland? Joan liked her. She was a canny woman.'

In time, Susanah drifted back to the chapel; just being in the building had been some help during the memorial service for Davey, Tollie and Mervin. Each Sunday night she would sit beside Isabella, who always had Ceiri on her knee. Young Davey and Anna sat at the other side, beside Caradoc whose bearded head moved slightly to the rhythms of the words he was hearing. He seemed to have shrunk a little in recent months; he was getting used, with difficulty, to the new and guarded peace with his sister. He sat there, big and heavy, eyes glittering, the very image of the Old Testament prophets whom Jonty Clelland used to cite before the war, when he preached against rulers and established religion.

But Susanah ignored the prayers and sermons and kept her heart and

231

mind on the light as it filtered through the clear polished glass, changing with every mood of day and season.

Chapter Thirty-Five

Some months after Davey's death, Susanah received two letters. One was from Lady Chase. The other was from his friend Lily.

> . . . I think I know you, as your Davey talked about you and let me read your letters, me getting none of my own. He was killed in a brave action which saved the lives of other men, including me. We were on the same sortie. The young officer was killed and me injured and Davey more so. We had some shelter in the ruins of an old church, but Davey made me crawl back, him giving covering fire over my head. It was two days before they could get to him. We thought he would make it but he didn't. Myself, I was shipped back home and am writing this from hospital in London, by the offices of a nurse, as my arm is shot up. Davey pushed me off to safety and said to write to you. I can only say he was the finest comrade and the greatest of men. He said I was to tell you about him having a ride in an airplane, right at the beginning of the war. He said to tell you how he could see the land below him laid out like a carpet, fresh and unspoilt. That was what he said. Fresh and unspoilt. He said you would like to hear about that, as you nagged him to hear about everything, even the pit. And he couldn't tell you about it in letters as the censors would spot it and he'd be on a charge. As I say, he was a fine man. The finest.
>
> Yours, John Carson, but Davey would tell you they called me Lily.

In response to Lady Chase's letter Susanah sent young Davey with a note to Joe Castle, who, as well as doing funerals, had a trap for hire. Joe was there on time, his trap gleaming, and Beatrice, his horse, in good fettle.

'Wendon Hall, is it?' He helped her in, placing her basket carefully beside her before he clambered back up.

'Yes.'

He chuckled. 'I get to take a few folks up there, one way or another. But never from Selby Street nor anywhere down Gibsley. You'll be going on business? They say you're best on clocks around here now. Like yer da was.'

'I'm not going on business.'

He let a few more minutes go by, muttering endearments to Jessie, who tossed her mane and went her own way whatever he said.

He tried again. 'It's just, like, funny, you going there.'

She laughed. 'I'll tell you what, Mr Castle. I'm off up to Wendon Hall to have tea with Lady Chase.'

'Bliddy hell! Pardon, missis.' After that he concentrated on Jessie, at a loss for more useful questions.

The butler, a tall man with a dirty neck, showed her loftily into a sitting room crowded with tables and cloths, ornaments and pictures. Looking closer, she recognised Isabella's work in a set of pictures above the draped piano, inevitably inspired by Greek antiquities.

Lady Chase whirled in in a cloud of black wool and lace, followed by a heavy maid pushing a large wheeled trolley. She strode over and shook hands heartily and settled Susanah on to a small sofa and shooed the maid out.

'There!' she beamed. 'We can take care of ourselves, Mrs Sargant, can't we?' Susanah sat there dumbly while a china cup was thrust into one hand and a china plate with the smallest of cakes on it, in another. Finally Lady Chase settled back into the sofa opposite Susanah, clutching a cup.

Susanah sought for something to say. 'My Auntie Bel sends her regards.'

'Yes. My dear Isabella. I see too little of her. There's no doubt that when I see her I feel better afterwards.'

Susanah grinned. 'I feel the same myself.'

Lady Chase leaned forward and peered short-sightedly at her. 'There's a resemblance, but I wouldn't really say you were like her.'

Susanah pulled back in her chair. 'She says I'm like my grandmother, her mother.' She paused. 'It was kind of you to invite me.'

'Ah, yes. Your aunt says you're a skilled clockmaker.'

'No. Clockmender. I've not had the training nor the opportunity to make clocks.'

'There are many clocks in the Hall. I was saying to Lord Chase they need attention.'

Susanah looked around. There were four clocks in this room alone: two grandfather clocks, a mantel clock and a curious apparatus which hung on the wall. 'I see.'

'I wondered if you would like to take care of them. On a regular basis.'

Susanah frowned into her cup. 'Why?'

'Why? Well, your aunt told me of your skill. I trust her.'

'Why tea? Why not get your housekeeper to see me? Or that butler feller.'

Lady Chase glared at Susanah, then relaxed. 'Direct! Direct! Just like Isabella.' She hesitated. 'The tea isn't about the clocks. That was just an afterthought.' She poured herself some more tea, then sat back heavily on the couch. 'Your brother David . . .'

'Davey? What about him?'

'He sent me a letter.' She pulled two letters out of her heavy black skirt. 'He saw my grandson, the day before he died. And was kind enough to write to me.'

Susanah read the letter, heat staining her pale cheeks, then smiled as she handed it back. 'He always wrote a good letter, Davey. And he was a kind lad. Did you know he died over there too?'

234

'I do.' Lady Chase fluttered the other letter in the air but did not hand it over to Susanah. 'My other grandson was killed in action and Lord Chase pursued some enquiries as to the precise details of his death. It seems that David Laydon Jones . . . your brother Davey . . . was there, when it happened. He was killed alongside him.'

'Oh dear. I'm sorry. Two grandsons!'

'Last of our name, I fear. Your family too, it seems suffered great loss. Your brothers, your husband! Such losses for everyone.' She sighed. 'I only hope it's worth it.'

'I have my doubts,' said Susanah grimly.

'You do? It's a brave person who says it nowadays.' She paused. 'Isabella told me that you . . . had a kind of vision of your brother. That you saw it happen.'

'Mebbe a dream. Not sure what it was.'

'I wondered . . . Clive . . .' She looked across at the young woman, neat in a dark green dress with a white crocheted collar. 'You didn't see . . .?'

Susanah met her gaze. It would have been easy and kind to say yes, to weave a heroic story. She shook her head. 'Just Davey. We were very close, you see. Always very close.'

The other woman sighed. 'I can't say I was close to the boys. I loved them, yes. But not very close. They were always at school or abroad with that mother of theirs, looking down her nose . . .'

She tucked the letters back in her pocket. 'But it seems our families are bound together without knowing it. Those boys knew each other, however briefly. So' – her voice sharpened up – 'just to bless that contact in a strange land I would like you to do the clocks. And I'd like to give you the cottage where Isabella lives. She won't take it and now there's no one to leave it to. It's mine, a gift when I first married.' She paused. 'No loss to this great estate.'

'What?' Susanah put down her cup. 'The cottage?'

'Isabella said you'd be prickly. But she said I had to say it was for their friendship. Between the boys. For Davey.'

Joe Castle had his nose up against Jessie's mane and was busy telling her secrets when Susanah came down the steps.

'Business done, hinney?' he said, clambering up.

'I told you,' said Susanah, 'it wasn't business! Now you can take me to Priorton. I've got some shopping to do and I might as well use you while I've got you!'

Joe nodded, enjoying being bossed around by this headstrong young woman. She certainly had a spark about her.

Back, home Susannah heaved the baskets on to the table and started to lift out the vegetables and the bags of flour. She turned her head to listen to the house, missing the rustles and mutterings which betrayed the presence of children in its far corners.

An hour later shouts and squeals in the back yard heralded young Davey, who burst into the kitchen, followed by Anna, then Isabella, with Ceiri clinging to her aunt's back like a little monkey, dislodging the green feather cap in the process.

'Where's Caradoc?' asked Susanah. 'I left them with him.'

'I can't say. He called at the cottage and asked to leave them with me. I was to bring them back about now. Some business to do in Priorton, he said.'

'I was there. I didn't see him.'

'Perhaps his business wasn't in the market.' She cocked a knowing eye at Susanah. 'Did it go well, up at the Hall?'

'You knew.'

'Of course I knew.'

'A bit strange, inviting me up like that.'

'She is a bit strange. Else how would she have anything to do with me? Doesn't really fit with them. Doesn't really fit with us. So anyway. Are you my landlady?'

'Well, yes, I suppose I am.' Susanah laughed. 'So you'd better mind your P's and Q's, or I'll send the bailiff round.' She was taking off coats and putting them on pegs, taking off boots and putting them in a row by the wall and lifting children into another row on the wooden settle. 'Sit down there and get your breath back. You too, Bel.'

'No. I'll get straight back. I've some letters to finish. I've been writing to Bea Clelland for days now and can't somehow find the will to finish it. It'll be as heavy as the Book of Kings by the time it gets to the Post Office.'

'How is she, Mrs Clelland?'

'In her element, it seems. Sounds as though she's running that little school herself now, with Corella and her friend Bessie away proving their worth in France.' Isabella's tone was dry.

'She always was clever, Mrs Clelland. I wrote to her about Joan. I told you. She'll make a grand teacher.' Susanah thought about Miss Carmedy.

'Yes, well, Bea needed something to do after John George died. Her letters were full of dying then. And passion. Indecent in a married couple. Thought I'd seen a bit of it in my wandering. But nothing to touch those two.'

'Passion?'

'Yes, you know. The loving with every part of you, your brain, your heart, even your body. Or perhaps you don't. Anyway they were that way right up till he died. No wonder she misses him.'

Susanah went to the pantry and took her time returning with toffee apples bought from a gipsy in the market. She put on into each eager hand as it reached out from the settle. 'I did wonder what had happened to Jonty Clelland . . .'

Isabella smiled, watching her thoughtfully. 'Bea said in her letter that he's out of prison now. Working away, somewhere further north.' She paused. 'Anyway, I must go. I always hang on too long here.'

'You should live here.'

'No, dear girl. There may be a time for that, the bridges now being built between Caradoc and me. But not yet . . .'

The children were in bed and the night was dark when Caradoc finally returned. His gaunt frame filled the doorway. She looked up at him from the table where she was working.

'Long business,' she said.

He grunted and rooted in his greatcoat pocket, then produced a small newspaper parcel which he opened out on to the table, pushing her velvet roll to one side. She moved the lamp closer to see more clearly. Half hidden inside the hard-edged cracks and folds two small circlets of gold glinted against the dense walls of newsprint: bracelets made of gold twisted like fine cord. The open ends were finished with a small knob in the shape of a bird's head.

'I made one for the littl'n. Like her grandma. Then there had to be one for the sister. Thought I'd forgotten how, but it came back in a crack, once I was there in that workshop with that feller Perlman. His tools're good.' Then he put his hand in his waistcoat pocket and brought out a golden coin which he rolled between his finger and thumb. 'I thought the little lad'd do with a sovereign.'

Susanah took a breath. 'Ma . . . Ceiri . . . she talked about a bracelet. When she was . . . upset, she looked for one, all over the place.'

The chair creaked as he sat down. 'I made her one, your mother. Then once when I pressed her too hard she threw it at me.' He sighed then shook his head, the soft silver fronds catching glints of firelight. 'I sold it the next day. Vengeance is mine, as the Book says. Was mine.'

She stood up. 'Shall I go to get the littl'ns? So they can see?'

He shook his head again. 'No. They'll all still be there in the morning, bracelets, bairns and all.'

She watched him uncertainly. 'Ma would have been pleased,' she offered. Then she offered more: 'She'll be pleased. Where she is.'

'And where might that be?' he said sullenly. 'Anyway, what could make up for all that?' He turned away.

When Anna and Ceiri discovered their bracelets the following morning, they plagued Susanah to wear them for their Sunday walk. Susanah looked at Caradoc.

'They should wear 'm,' he said slowly. 'Seeing it's Sunday.'

Then young Davey insisted on taking his sovereign with him and Susanah had to sew it inside a handkerchief which in turn was sewn inside his jacket pocket.

Susanah kept the Sabbath in her own way now, only occasionally attending chapel. The only work she avoided on Sunday was working on the clocks and the watches. Most Sundays she read and baked in the long mornings; sometimes she even drew, conscious that Caradoc looked with close interest at the small studies she produced. On the finer afternoons, she would take the children down by the river, under the viaduct. They would sit there watching the trains and she would tell them tales of Betty and Jenny, Tollie and Davey when they were all very young.

The Sunday the girls first wore their bracelets, she sat on the grassy plain under the viaduct watching the children as they played. Ceiri, the baby whom Mervin and Davey had never seen, was scrambling around beside her. Like a harebell, she thought, tender and bowing to the hard wind. One to watch and care for. Then there was young Davey, a serious nine-year-old waiting patiently for a fish to catch on his home-made line. This sturdy bright-haired dandelion would survive placidly in any soil. Anna was sitting at the water's edge, poking a stick into the water and calling the fish to her. She was the hedge rose, open-faced and very pretty, always charming the passers-by.

Susanah's gaze wandered past them towards the bridge, where she could see a figure standing there. Broad boned but thin, the man had a scarecrow look. The thick black hair, receding to show a bony brow, was now springing grey at the edges. Even at this distance she could see that his skin was almost too brown for these parts.

She knew he would make his way down to her. No teacher's suit today. No preacher's gear. Older clothes: clothes a workman would wear.

He towered over her for a moment, shutting out the sun, then came alongside to sit on an outjutting stone, his face turned half away from her. 'Bel said you'd be up here. You come up here most fine Sundays, she said.'

He had been away for nearly a year. A stretch in prison, then sent up to help some Northumberland farmer, according to Vivian Kenton, gossiping over the yard wall this morning. No jobs in schools for pacifist teachers.

She spread out her skirt and pulled Ceiri over to sit on it, alongside the outline of her legs.

'Sometimes I go to chapel,' she said.

'I thought you had given up chapel.' The schoolteacher's voice, deeper now, no longer grated on her ears.

She moved her shoulders. 'I go sometimes. I go because I like the building. The stone and the glass with the light coming through. I try hard enough to take no notice of this war-preaching, the way they make good out of bad, that stuff about the war. Now that Mervin and our Davey and Tollie are whirled away down some plughole filled with blood. I try to ignore it all, but I do get fed up with them . . . and going on about people who don't want it . . .'

'Traitors and Bolsheviks like me and Len Sargant?' He leaned over and pulled the baby's pinny down, stroking the cloth as though it were fur. 'They say you're back with your father.'

She stayed quiet, looking over the water to the far bank where a goat was pulling against his tether on a high ledge. She could feel the presence of this man like a warm weight against her side.

He pressed on. 'I'd have thought that you'd have been all for it. For the war, that is. With your man having devoted his life to it. And Tollie and Davey. He was a good man, Davey. I liked him, always. A fine man.'

She took a breath, then she looked him in the eye. 'Do you remember the summer camp, Jonty? The kingfisher? In the woods? A lot was spoiled on that day. Really spoiled. But I've been thinking about that camp lately. All that talk, all that argument. You still called yourself a preacher, then. Or at least they called you one.'

238

He frowned down at his fingers, pulling at the bony knuckles.

'Do you remember all that talk, Jonty? It was suffrage, then. Women being fit to vote. Equal under God, fit to think, all that. Your Corella at full belt was something to see.' She wiped the baby's nose with the corner of her apron. 'Bel was saying Corella's at the front?'

'Well, it seems she's just 'ticed my mother to take her place teaching, so that she can go nursing close behind the front. Wants to work near the sound of the guns. Her version of making good out of bad, I suppose.'

'She would get into the thick of it, wouldn't she?'

'You listened, then, down at Livesay? And you didn't forget the kingfisher? And all the talk? You listened to the talk, Susanah? As well as drawing your pictures.' He shook his head slowly. 'But you said nothing. Nothing at all. Always on the edge . . .'

She laughed. 'Not a word in edgeways, you mean. You with words streaming from you like stars on a chain. Your Corella and Bessie Jones, no less bright. There was no use me putting my words in there. And there was no connection between you and me. And them. But I did listen. There was sense for me in the words. It makes more sense of this war than what Jack Simmons says in his pulpit. It makes more sense.'

Ceiri started to whimper, so Susanah pulled her back on to her knee, stroking her hair down the side of her face. A bee was buzzing somewhere; a creak of birdsong stirred the water on the river.

'So you still have some faith?' He said it abruptly.

That was the funny thing about him. They called him a Bolshevik and an Antichrist yet the words he delivered were still loaded like those of the preacher he was, before the Circuit dismissed him when he began to preach against the war: his manner was direct and full of challenge, like that of the teacher he was before the Reverend Stonham made sure he was sacked from the school.

She sighed. 'I don't know. I say my prayers, and kneeling down too. I read gospel stories to the children. I miss all the singing we used to do. But then Jack Simmons once said to Betty and me it was sinful to love singing so. Like lust, he said. Too much passion.' She laughed.

He pulled a stalk of grass and started to suck its juice. 'I'm thinking of joining the Society of Friends. Do you know of them? They are unequivocal against the war.'

'Must you . . .? D'you always need to join something? Anything?'

He looked hard at her, then stood up, wiping one hand carefully against the other. 'I think I do, Susanah. I think I do.'

She looked at the thin fingers, blue veins bulging on brown calloused hands. The nails were dirty. She set Ceiri on her feet and called to Anna to play with her. She watched the baby totter towards her sister, then looked up at the man beside her. 'How are you feeling now, Jonty? Yourself?'

'Good enough. I had pneumonia that left me with a cough but it's nearly gone. I'm working as a gardener, the other side of the Tyne. Fresh air in plenteous amounts.' His tone was crisp and sharp.

'Sit down. Sit down here beside me.' She stroked the grass with her palm,

239

then watched as he obediently took the space recently vacated by Ceiri. 'They say you . . They say they have a bad time in there. Prison.'

'Everyone has a bad time in prison. The people there anyway, they have a bad time. And us? We're traitors, scum, they say. So we deserve a bad time.' He paused. 'You know about Len? Mervin's brother?'

She tipped her head up towards him, screwing her eyes against the sun. Thinking about Len, she could see Mervin on those mornings when he called for Tollie. The once-a-month flash of his white hair. Then, with the ball spinning and balancing on one hand, one knee, his broad forehead. 'Yes. He was Mervin's brother. Course I knew him. A good man. Our Tollie was fond of him. Worked together in the pit . . . It was in the paper. They took him off after a tribunal. To prison in the South somewhere.'

'He's dead. They killed him.'

'He can't be.' She put her hand on his arm, feeling the tense muscles underneath. 'He can't be dead.'

'He's dead. The man handcuffed to him says they pushed the lad about. Beat him. Knocked his head off the wall . . .'

Then suddenly she was remembering Caradoc pushing her once, against the cold hard stone of the scullery wall. She was wriggling to get out, her eye already stinging from the first clout. Then he was close to her, prickling, pushing against her as he started to bang her head against the wall, swinging her by her long loosened hair. Then her mother was between them, forcing him off with a broomshank. Ceiri's slight body had shaken with the effort as she'd thrust herself between them in total silence.

'It was the day he got in there,' Jonty was saying, his mouth trembling. 'He had been in no time.'

Her hands were on both of his. 'They should enquire . . .'

He smiled: a cold grimace. 'There'll be no enquiry. Or any enquiry they set up'll be a parcel of lies. A travesty.'

His eyes were glittering, the tears wetting the broad planes of his face. It was very easy for her to draw him close, put her face against his and kiss his salty cheeks, just as she would if young Davey had come with a sore knee or a scratched hand. Jonty took his hands from hers and put them on her shoulders to pull her even closer. The moment he returned her kiss, his tears stopped. He felt wholesome and human again. The cold he had felt for more than a year now was chased from his body by the fire racing right down to his heels. He laughed and slipped on his back, collapsing into the grass. Then she was above him, kissing his face and stroking his hair, joining in the laughter.

'Mammy, can we play?' Anna's voice piped up above them.

They looked up at three small faces, three pairs of eyes. Susanah felt Jonty flinch, but she opened her arms and the three children were enveloped between them both, a thresh of arms and legs, faces and feet. Jonty relaxed a little and let them crawl over him while he held on to her like a dying man. He was used to children, but never so close, never the warm and springing flesh of such tiny children.

'So who have we here?' He spoke to overcome his own embarrassment.

'This is young Davey.'

'We've met I think. In the school.'

'Davey is a very lucky boy. Aren't you, Davey?'

'Yes.'

'Why?'

''Cause he has two mammies,' Anna interrupted before her brother had a chance to answer. 'One up there in the sky called Betty. And one down here called Susanah.'

'And this cheeky little thing is called Anna. She's more her Aunt Bel's girl than mine. They make quite a pair.'

Anna gave him a melting glance and a sweet smile.

'And that little flower sitting on your foot is Ceiri. Named for her grandma and like her in spirit.'

'Fine family,' said Jonty.

'New dancers,' said Susanah.

'Dancers?'

'Our Davey once wrote that all of this, what we do and what we are brought to do, it is all like some great heaving dance. Well, in our set there's three dropped out. That's Davey, Tollie and Mervin. So here's three new dancers to take their place. But one short now, if we count Len.'

Jonty struggled to his feet, finally disentangling himself from Anna. He was trying to smile down at her.

'What's wrong?' she said, not deceived.

'I came in search of you specially,' he said. 'To tell you about Len. His body's home. Funeral early Wednesday evening. An old colleague of mine from Newcastle will officiate. Friend Simmons is unwilling. There'll be so few people there for the lad. His brothers were against him. Wouldn't even work with him in the pit. So he was sacked in the end and wouldn't take the khaki. And all this started.'

'It's a shame,' she said.

'I wondered if you'd come. To the funeral. For Len. And for Mervin and Davey, for Tollie and all the others.'

Chapter Thirty-Six

Funerals in Gibsley had been big events ever since the village was just four streets fanning out beside the first pit. They would be marked, like festivals, by large gatherings and substantial amounts of food. There would be intense talk and the occasional uneasy spurt of laughter among survivors. Whole streets attended; for a leading person it seemed as though the whole village came. For a miner killed in the pit they would carry the Lodge banner. The sight of this, fluttering behind the coffin draped in black, served as an assurance of respect and support. The day they buried Robert Smith, the first Gibsley man to be killed in action in France, the colliery band was there, as was the banner, escorted by an enormous crowd. Jack Simmons had been on form that day, intoning his litany of virtuous sacrifice, sure salvation and the battle made sacred by God's approval.

The bodies of Mervin and Tollie had never been found; they never had a funeral proper, only their names read out in a larger memorial service. All that remained of them were objects, little bits and pieces left behind when they went forward: a set of dominoes and a pack of greasy playing cards which brought the smell of war into Susanah's kitchen; her letters; her drawing book which Mervin had taken without her knowing. The messenger who delivered the bits and pieces had said it was a pity about the burnt edges of the pictures. Such fine work. She said as far as she could see that the damage had not been done in France; it had been burnt in the fire when she was a child. These things were delivered to the house in Selby Street in a battered brown parcel. The messenger was an officer, a man several years younger than Susanah. He spoke his well-rehearsed words about character, bravery, and courage. And how the end had been quick; how they had not suffered.

But with Len at least Susanah had a funeral to go to. At Isabella's suggestion, she took Anna with her. 'Take Anna, lovely. She's such a bright one. She'll keep you cheerful and remind you about the living.'

Susanah shook her head. 'You're a queer 'n, Bel.'

Her aunt's face, much fatter now, dimpled. 'Aren't I just?'

Susanah always liked to have Isabella in this house where Ceiri had lived and where Caradoc now presided like some large grey ghost. She brought life and humour into the house with her.

Lew often called when Caradoc was out. He would bring a rabbit he had caught in the woods, or a joint of meat won in a card game. He sold these to Susanah and often 'borrowed' money. He would sit in Caradoc's chair beside her blazing fire, rambling on about the past, indulging his self-deceiving vision about a happy childhood. He was obsessive about money, telling her again how their mother had taken money from the old man, bought liquor when she had run out of her own cordial. He would talk, too, about the money Caradoc was making now, with his toolmaking on top of his pay from the pit. How this allowed him to act as banker for his neighbours when they were on hard times. This in turn added to the money in the pot. In Lew's opinion, that pot must be pretty big now.

Now, on her way out of the house to the funeral with Anna, Susanah met Caradoc at the gate. He looked from her in her Sunday best across to Anna standing beside her. 'Where is it you're going?'

'See, Granda! I got my bangle on.' A small fat wrist was thrust towards him. The gold glittered.

'We're going to Len Sargant's funeral. There'll be no one there. They've all turned their back on him. He'll have no mourners.'

Caradoc still stood before her, barring her way.

'Len's dead,' she went on. 'The others are all against him. There'll be so few there. And I promised Jonty Clelland I'd go.'

Caradoc straightened up, his lips pulled back into some kind of smile. 'Wait on. I'll come with you.'

When they finally set away they were stopped again by a shout from behind.

'Hey, missis!' It was Joan Kenton's son, a heavy boy. He had two tightly arranged posies of forget-me-nots, one in each hand. He gave one to Susanah and the other to the delighted Anna. 'Me Uncle Viv sent these. One for the lad that was killed, the other for thee mother and thee sister.'

Gathered at the Sargants' house were Jonty, James Armstrong, a faithful member of Jonty's group, Corella and her friend Bessie. These two friends were both thinner and much older and growing more like each other in their face and their style of dress. Mr Sargant, Caradoc's old workmate, was there, but the big blond Cornishmen that made up the rest of this handsome family were missing, working their shift as though it were a normal day.

The plain wooden box was carried by Jonty and James Armstrong, Mr Sargant and Caradoc. Susanah wondered what would have happened if Caradoc had not been there. Probably Corella would have helped. She was tall enough.

The men carried Len on their shoulders from his house in Middle Street to the chapel. Susanah and her daughter walked one step behind the stiff figure of Len's father. She had tried to take his arm, but he had twisted away, avoiding her gaze.

Neighbours clustered in their doorways to watch the procession and a knot of old men gathered on the corner.

Out of the general hum of disapproval an occasional voice would howl out. 'A disgrace!'

'Traitors, the lot of yer!'

'Hanging's too good!'

At one point Susanah had to pull her daughter's face into her skirt, to save her from a clod of earth which spat its dirt on to the cobbles. Others made their mark on the coffin.

In the chapel the minister from Newcastle who led the short service talked about paying the final price for conscience and the courage it took to be a peacemaker. As Susanah looked past Jonty's head at the neat golden figure hanging to the right of the pulpit, the tears came and she started to shake. Then Caradoc's hand came down on her shoulder and the shuddering stopped.

Later, they made their way steadily through the crowd of people at the cemetery gates, ignoring the muttering and low-throated growling which was emerging from rigid mouths. As the box with its posy of forget-me-nots was lowered into the ground, bricks skimmed off its surface, spreading fine red dust into the air. Susanah lifted her head and blinked, the clearer to see the crowd gathered beside the high iron gates of swagged steel and iron flowers. How many times had she seen the same faces in chapel, transfixed in praise? Those same faces she had seen at the market and in the shops, friendly and full of normal concern. Now they resembled the gargoyles that leered threateningly from the high gutters of St Andrew's.

She looked on further. At the back of the crowd, standing at ease, his hands in his pockets, stood her brother Lew.

She could feel them all around her. Jonty, Corella and her friend Bessie, singing in their chapel-trained voices so full of tune. Then Tollie's voice came to her ears, then Mervin's, then Davey's. New words. Different from that camp at Livesay, those words were about keeping the red flag flying. Caradoc, standing like a rock, was silent. Behind him a waving sea of faces, all familiar, all strange. Red dust danced in the bright slants of evening sunlight. Then there was a black place, a crumpled figure awkwardly propped up against a mud wall. The eyes pulled open and through the dust she could see Tollie, with his bright young smile. It's all the same, she thought, he is no more nor less dead than his golden-haired friend here who has just been spat upon by his own.

Enduring the watchful silence, she walked across with Anna to the headstone by the wall to place the second posy. 'Ceiri and Jenny,' it read. 'One Again. Resting.'

The crowd had welded itself into a wall again as they came to the cemetery gate. Susanah found herself between Caradoc and Jonty. The human wall parted reluctantly before them, but the shouts and mutters continued right to the door of the house in Selby Street. Here Jonty turned to Caradoc and shook his hand.

'A fine gesture, Mr Laydon Jones. My father would have appreciated it.'

Caradoc looked coolly at the younger man. 'There is a beast in all of us, man. It teks a war like this to make it show. It doesn't take a schoolmaster to make us see we have to push against it, those of us who've finally seen it ourselves.'

Jonty's face hardened and Susanah protested, 'Da!'

Caradoc's shoulders came up in a shrug. 'Nothing against you, lad. I'm not against what you've done.' He turned to Susanah. 'Will there be tea in the pot for the schoolteacher?'

Susanah relaxed and turned to lead the way into the house.

Young Davey leapt up as she came in. 'Auntie Bel's broke her foot!' he said in some delight.

Isabella looked up from her place on the settle where she was lying with little Ceiri asleep on her lap. She smiled apologetically. 'We were playing hopscotch.'

'Hopscotch!' said Jonty, grinning.

'She was winning!' said Davey.

'Then I turned my ankle.'

'Let's see.' Susanah moved towards the foot, which was covered with a clean teatowel.

'Don't touch it. I'll just have to rest.' She looked from Susanah to Jonty. 'I can't see how I'll make it back to the cottage.'

'Stay here.' They all looked with surprise at Caradoc. 'You can't get around with a bad ankle. You'll need to stay here.'

Isabella smiled at her brother, not worrying about the grave face that still betrayed no feeling. 'Yes, yes. You're right, Caradoc. I'll do that.' She turned to Susanah. 'Before you take off your things, perhaps you could go and get some nightclothes for me. And things for tomorrow. You know the kind of thing. Caradoc and I . . .' She turned to her brother. '. . . Caradoc and I can hold the fort here.'

'Can I come?' asked Davey.

'You stay alongside me,' said Caradoc. 'You can help me with this shovel I'm hammering. Mebbe Mr Clelland'll help our Susanah carry the stuff. Be sure to get plenty. She'll be staying a time.'

Isabella smiled her appreciation. 'Yes. Why not go with Susanah, Jonty? There might be quite a few things. And the house needs locking up. It's so out of the way.' She looked him hard in the eye. 'And take your time, won't you? You've had a difficult day. Enjoy a bit of fresh air up there.'

He nodded. 'Certainly.'

Susanah looked from one to the other, saying nothing.

'Well, off you go,' said Isabella, settling back on her cushions. She smiled at them. 'As I say, take your time. We'll hold the fort.'

The two of them walked in silence along the back street with two feet of space between them. As they turned the corner, Jonty took her arm and pulled it through his. She glanced around the deserted street and left her hand on his arm. She could feel the heat of his flesh and the muscles under his skin. She looked straight ahead as they made their way up towards the edge of the village. All she could think of and feel was him. She knew, too, how conscious he was of her.

In the cottage, he stoked up the fire, then turned to her. 'Why don't you sit down? Bel did say we were to take our time.'

She looked around. 'You always look quite at home here.'

'Bel was – has always been – a good friend to me. Just as she's been for you. Go on. Sit down.'

She sat on the little padded chair by the fire. He sat on the rug, his back to the chair opposite. 'I'm glad Len had at least something of a funeral,' he said.

'More than Mervin. Or Tollie. Who had none. Or our Davey who's lying out there in some war grave,' she said softly. 'Your Newcastle friend spoke well.'

'He's had a few stones thrown at him for speaking like that in his time. All over the place.'

'What he said was right. He at least did the lad some justice.' She paused. 'I was thinking our Tollie would have been there, if . . .'

'Yes, he would. Davey, too. Nothing so sure. What about Mervin?'

She smiled. 'Well, he started with those ideas. But they faded. But he wouldn't have thrown stones.'

Jonty poked the fire again and shuffled forward until he was sitting cross-legged in front of her. 'Do you know the first time I saw you?'

'No.'

'The first day you were in Gibsley. Caradoc was way ahead like some Moses and you were a little kid with a smutty nose, trailing your Tollie behind you.'

She shook her head and smiled down at him, waiting.

'And the time I saw you washing Betty's hair. When my dad had decided to "save" Freddy. I was mad when he thought you were Freddy's daughter. I remember being mad.'

'I like Freddy. Do you know he comes every Saturday for young Davey? Loves him.'

He kneeled up and put his hands on the arms of the chair. 'Then by the river, watching the kingfishers, I knew about us two then, what it meant.'

She nodded and took his hand where it lay on the arm of the chair. He lifted his other hand and stroked her face, first on one side then the other, as though he were memorising it. He turned her hand over in his, kissing it on the back, then the palm. 'Rough little hand.'

'It's the soda. Makes 'm red. Invites the chapping.' She turned his hand over. 'What about you? Here's you with dirt in your nails. Some teacher.'

His hand gripped hers, hard. 'I'll be that again. You'll see. This war'll never go through a fifth Christmas. Then we'll all be back. They'll need us. You just watch. Everything'll be different. Schools, work, people, life. It'll never be the same.' He paused and took a breath. 'I'll ask you now, or it will all run away from us again, into other people's lives. We've got to be together, Susanah. Married.'

She smiled, the flames of the fire reflected in her shining cheeks. 'Our turn to be partners?' she sighed. 'No, I don't think so.'

He sat back on his heels. 'Why?'

'There's that side to marriage . . . With Mervin, I hated it. I couldn't. I can't . . .'

He frowned. 'You feel nothing?'

'Yes, I feel something.'

'Here?' He touched her briefly, just on her waist.

She did not answer him.

'Can I show you something? It might make it . . . right.'

She looked at him carefully, then nodded slowly.

'You need to trust me. Nothing will hurt. None of it. I promise.'

As she nodded again, he took her feet into his lap and took off first one shoe, then the other. He started to run his hands over her stockinged feet from calf to toe in long strokes. She wriggled, trying not to laugh and not knowing what to do. She closed her eyes to avoid his gaze and began to relax as she concentrated on his moving hand. Then she felt him at her hair, unpinning it. She moved her head.

'Stay still.' Picking up thick sections of hair he started to brush it over the back of his hand to get rid of the wind-driven tangles. Then he was making long strokes from her brow right to the very ends of her hair. Her mother had liked to do that when she was little, when there was time.

Then his hands were on her neck and cheeks, then down to her shoulders. She was taking long deep breaths. His hands came from behind for the buttons of her blouse and her bodice. She put her hands over them as he undid them and helped him to lift them over her head. Then the strokes were from her waist to her throat flowing lightly over the contours. Her face was aching, her lips burning.

Then he was in front of her again, following his hand track over her breasts into her lap and down her legs back to her feet. He unfastened her skirt and her chemise and brought them to her feet. Reaching behind him he produced a silky wrap smelling of lily of the valley which he placed in her lap. He looked up at her with eyes so brilliant that they had lost all colour. Then he sat back on the chair opposite.

'Now you do the same for me,' he said.

She pulled on the robe, tying the tasselled sash at the waist.

Then she was there before him, timid at first, then bolder, laughing at the sparking power of his curly hair which stood out in a halo after its brushing. She was surprised at the softness of his skin, how smooth it was to the touch. Finally, before him again, she stroked her hand down from his throat over his chest to his thighs, her hands not touching the rising bulge between.

'Oh.' It was half a groan. He was sweating. 'Now, my dear girl, nothing happens. Nothing. Unless it is you who wants it. Now. Can we lie together?'

'Here?'

'Here.'

She reached up to pull him towards her and they tumbled awkwardly to the floor. He stayed above her and she raised herself to kiss him, to unloosen the ache that was building up inside her. Then they were locked together, touching and testing each other, relishing this first real flavour. Thrusting and plunging one to the other with equal fervour, they laughed when their mouths were free to do so. Three times she lost herself in some weird land of heat and fire; three times before his body suddenly started to burn. He spurted into her, his whole frame rippling. Then he was finally still.

Holding him to her in comfort for the loss, she watched the patterns of firelight on the ceiling and waited for the magical ripples of tension to recede from her flesh, her bones. She could hear the ticking of Isabella's dainty French clock. A coal fell with a crash in the fire.

At last he lay back, his eyes closed, his hand pulling and stroking a strand of hair down on to her breast. She breathed in the heat of him, the yeasty scent of their joining together.

'So lovely,' he said. 'I knew it. You are so lovely.'

'It's all new. New to me. I thought . . .' Her voice faded. Caradoc's father and mother, Caradoc pressing on her mother. Mervin with his mercifully quick despatch. '. . . It was different.'

'We are different. Everything will be different. We two, we can be together now. It's about time you joined me, instead of standing there on the edge. My partner. Isn't that what you should be?'

'Mmm,' she said sleepily. 'Can I ask a question?'

'Anything.'

'Can we do all that again?'